TOTAL CREATIVE CONTROL

JOANNA CHAMBERS

SALLY MALCOLM

Total Creative Control

Cover art: Natasha Snow

Published by Joanna Chambers

ISBN: 978-1-914305-01-6

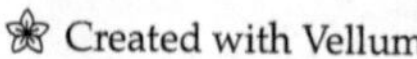

Total Creative Control

Sunshine PA, meet Grumpy Boss...

When fanfic writer Aaron Page landed a temp job with the creator of hit TV show, *Leeches,* it was only meant to last a week. Three years later, Aaron's still there...

It could be because he loves the creative challenge. It could be because he's a huge *Leeches* fanboy. It's definitely *not* because of Lewis Hunter, his extremely demanding, staggeringly rude...and breathtakingly gorgeous boss.

Is it?

Lewis Hunter grew up the hard way and fought for everything he's got. His priority is the show, and personal relationships come a distant second. Besides, who needs romance when you have a steady stream of hot men hopping in and out of your bed?

His only meaningful relationship is with Aaron, his chief confidante and indispensable assistant. And no matter how appealing he finds Aaron's cute boy-next-door charms, Lewis would never risk their professional partnership just to scratch an itch.

But when Lewis finds himself trapped at a hilariously awful corporate retreat, Aaron is his only friend and ally. As the professional lines between them begin to blur, their simmering attraction starts to sizzle.

... And they're both about to get *burned.*

PROLOGUE

Lewis

Reclined Pigeon Productions, Shepherd's Bush, London

It was only ten-thirty in the morning, but Lewis Hunter, Creative Director at Reclined Pigeon Productions, was already having a bad day.

The latest episode of *Leeches,* his cult hit show, had dropped last night, and he'd strolled into the office in a pretty good mood—until he'd passed Chris's desk.

Chris—who until two hours ago had been the latest temp PA assigned to work for Lewis—had informed him, with ill-concealed glee, that there was a Twitter storm raging over last night's episode. He had offered his phone to Lewis to read the thread, and Lewis, who usually paid no attention to social media, had been enraged by the stupid comments. He'd sent an immediate, profanity-laced response to the first comment and was working on a second when Chris had become hysterical, and they'd got into a tussle over his phone.

Well, how was Lewis supposed to know the response would go out in Chris's name? It wasn't as though it was his *real* name. Who the fuck cared what @teamcocopops was saying?

After that, things went downhill quickly.

Chris stormed out, dramatically announcing that this was *"the last straw"*. There had been quite a few other straws apparently, including ones that had featured in feedback from all the other ex-temps. Like Lewis's short fuse, inability to work technology, and frequent requests for overtime assistance.

All of which meant Lewis was forced to phone Sophie, again, and ask her to call the agency. Again. Which had prompted a visit from the head of HR, who had subjected him to a long and boring lecture. Again.

After sitting through that, Lewis had started trying to set up his own Twitter account, only to be thwarted by technology. Which was where he found himself now, his irritation growing exponentially as the little fucking circle spun around and around uselessly in the centre of his screen. And hell, he needed to be on an important call at eleven.

Shoving his chair back, he got to his feet, stalked to the door, and flung it open. Chris was long gone, but Jason, Toni's PA who sat at the neighbouring desk, looked up from his computer screen.

"Jason," Lewis clipped out. "I need your help."

"Okay," Jason said warily, pushing his glasses up his nose. "Is it urgent? I'm busy pulling together the cost figures for Toni's production meeting."

"Very urgent, " Lewis replied. "I need to respond to some comments on Twitter immediately, but it's not letting me set up an account."

Jason's gaze shifted away. "Right," he said slowly. "So you're, uh, still working on that then?"

"Goddamn right I am. Have you read the comments? Fucking defamatory bullshit!"

"Maybe you should let Legal deal with it?" Jason suggested tentatively.

"Fuck that," Lewis snapped. "Legal never do anything. Last time I reported something to them—"

"Ah, there you are, Lewis," a new voice said, a faint note of warning in the overly cheerful tone.

Lewis turned to see Sophie, the office manager, approaching.

"Sophie, perfect timing," he said quickly. "My computer's fucked—I need a new one. Like, right fucking now."

"Yes, well, before we talk about that, let me—"

"Soph, I really need this sorted *now. My—"*

"Lewis," she interrupted, raising her brows and giving him a significant look. "I've got your *new temp* here?" Somehow, she managed to keep her smile in place, though it was morphing into more of a grimace. "Why don't we go into your office so I can introduce you?"

Lewis glanced at the young man standing behind her before returning his gaze to Sophie. "Fine, but after that, I need to get this situation sorted out—I've been trying to set up a Twitter account—"

"Hmm. So I heard. Are you sure that's a good idea?"

Lewis bristled. "Why wouldn't it be?"

Sophie held up her hands. "Well, you know what happened last time…" She trailed off meaningfully.

"This is a point of principle," he insisted. "You wouldn't believe what these dicks are saying."

Sophie and Jason exchanged a glance that made Lewis narrow his eyes suspiciously.

"Have you noticed any, um, IT issues, Jason?" Sophie asked.

"IT issues?" Jason said, frowning. Then his expression cleared with sudden understanding and he added, "Now you mention it, I think the"—pause—"Wi-fi might be playing up again?"

"Really?" Sophie turned back to Lewis with a placid smile. "Well, that could certainly be a problem if you're trying to set up a social media account. Why don't you have a chat with Aaron while I get IT on the case?"

She stood aside then, beckoning to the young man behind her to step forward. He was an inch or so shorter than Lewis and slim, with light brown hair and the sort of pretty face young girls idolised. Lewis could see him in a boy band, crooning forgettable ballads.

He looked too young to be a PA to a senior director, never mind someone as irascible and difficult to please as Lewis.

And… wait was he…?

Oh yes, *definitely* gay. Lewis had magnificent gaydar, and he didn't miss the way the young man's gaze swept over him in a quick but thorough onceover that was most certainly carnal. In fairness, he managed to mask his interest quickly, though his eyes still shone as he approached Lewis, albeit with a different kind of admiration.

"Hello," he said nervously. "I'm Aaron Page, the new temp. I just about passed out when the agency told me I was coming here!" He offered a smile, then bit his lip, as though to keep it in check.

Lewis raised his brows, watching curiously, and with some amusement, as Aaron's face pinkened. "And why would that be?"

"Well, I'm a bit of a fan." Aaron laughed softly, self-consciously. "As in, a huge one. Huge fan, I mean. Oh my God, last night—" He closed his eyes briefly, then opened them again, saying sincerely, "It was amazing. The reveal about Merrick was just—It just blew me away. My best friend Janvi too."

"Yeah?" Lewis said, reluctantly pleased. "And you didn't mind the cliff-hanger?"

"*Mind* it?" Aaron echoed. "God, no, I *loved* it. This whole storyline with Faolán tracking Merrick down is just awesome.

And Faolán's relationship with Skye is"—he broke off, blushing—"Oh God, I'm babbling aren't I? Sorry."

Lewis smiled at that. After all, who didn't like it when people admired their babies? And *Leeches* was definitely his baby. "It's cool," he said. "I'm interested to hear what you think. Faolán's a pretty new character, so it's good to hear he's had an impact."

"So much," Aaron gushed. "He's such a great character. Janvi's convinced you're going to kill him off—please don't! I really want him to stay." He paused, then added, "You know what they say—*Don't bury your gays.*"

Lewis struggled to maintain a neutral expression. Aaron would be disappointed to learn that Faolán was indeed being lined up for a dramatic exit after the season three cliff-hanger. Poor Faolán was destined to be blown to smithereens when the Family's HQ exploded, though that wouldn't be revealed until the opening of the next season, which they were currently working on. Still, Lewis was glad that Aaron was enjoying Faolán for now. The emotional payoff would be all the better that way.

His pleasure in Aaron's reaction withered, though, when he recalled the Twitter storm and the comments he'd read this morning. He found himself saying, drily, "Apparently, not everyone liked last night's episode as much as you and your friend. There's a bunch of twats online who've been moaning about it all morning."

Aaron rolled his eyes at that. "Were they? Let me guess—the Jägerbombers? And they hated the shippy scene with Amy?"

The what scene?

Lewis eyed Aaron for a moment, then he turned on his heel, saying, "Come on into my office so we can sit down while we talk."

Aaron obediently followed him inside, closing the door carefully behind him.

As Lewis rounded his desk, he gestured at the chair opposite. "Take a pew."

"Um, thanks," Aaron said. Lifting off his messenger bag, he sat down on the edge of the chair, the bag on his knee.

"So," Lewis said. "Tell me about the scene that these Jägerbombers fixated on."

"Well, er, I suspect it's the scene in the bar where Skye takes Amy's hand? And she says, *'I didn't think you'd feel so warm?'* and he just looks at her."

Lewis stared at him, and Aaron shrugged. "The Jägerbombers hate that stuff. They're all about Skye's relationship with the Family. Especially his brother. Wow, they *really* loved 'Family Ties'. You know the one in season two when the Family kidnaps Skye, and his brother has to—?" He stopped, blushing. "Sorry. Of course you know it. You bloody wrote it."

"I did," Lewis said, then added cautiously, "And they… the Jägerbombers liked that one?"

"Are you kidding? They adored it."

He frowned. "I thought they hated the show."

"What? No! They're huge fans. I mean, don't get me wrong. Some of them are arseholes about it. But they wouldn't be talking about *Leeches* if they didn't love it." He smiled. "You only need to worry when they stop giving a shit."

Lewis blinked, thinking back on the comments he'd read this morning. "That… actually sort of makes sense."

"You should see how much fanfic that group has produced, just based on that one episode," Aaron added eagerly. "It's probably the single biggest—"

"I never read fanfic," Lewis interrupted flatly. "It's practically piracy, not to mention being derivative rubbish."

Aaron's eyes widened at that. He opened his mouth as though to say something, then closed it again, perhaps thinking better of it.

For a moment, neither of them spoke. Then the door opened, and Sophie poked her head around the gap. "Me again. We do seem to be having a Wi-fi issue right now, though it's just affecting this floor, which is super weird..." She made a face.

Lewis waved his hand. "It's okay. I don't need to set up that Twitter account anymore."

For a moment, Sophie looked taken aback. She blinked. "It's—you don't?"

"No. Though, obviously, I will need to use my computer at some point, so maybe you could try and hurry IT along on getting this fixed?"

"I—that is—yes. Yes, absolutely." She gave Lewis a blinding smile, then turned her gaze to Aaron. "I'll pop back to check on you in a little while. In the meantime, I'll leave login details for your PC on the desk outside and my direct line number, okay?"

"Uh, great, thanks," Aaron said, watching her go.

The door clicked softly behind her.

"So, I assume you have all the relevant PA skills?" Lewis said.

Aaron turned back to face him. "Of course," he said. "I've been doing this sort of temping for quite a while. On and off, while studying. I'm pretty good at fitting into new environments."

"Good," Lewis said. "That's good. And you obviously know a lot about *Leeches*."

Aaron grinned. He had a great smile, boyish and charming.

Undeniably, he was a very attractive guy.

Lewis frowned at that unbidden thought and said abruptly, "Do you mind if I ask you something personal?"

"Of course not," Aaron said, still smiling. "Fire away."

Lewis cleared his throat. "Are you gay?"

Aaron blinked.

"I mean, you can tell me to fuck off, if you like," Lewis went on quickly. "I'm pretty sure HR would have my balls for asking you, but I do have pretty good gaydar, and it *is* relevant."

"Relevant to what?" Aaron said faintly. "What does my being gay have to do with this—With anything?"

"So you *are* gay," Lewis said. He nodded to himself, considering that, then added, curiously, "Do you find me attractive?"

Aaron gaped at him. "Oh my God," he said. "Are you one of those blokes who think all gay men are panting after every straight guy they meet? Because I can tell you—"

Lewis waved his hand, cutting Aaron off. "Don't be ridiculous. I'm gay myself. No, I was asking because—"

"You're gay?"

"Yes," Lewis said, dragging the word out, amused by Aaron's expression.

"So, wait, why were you asking me if…?" He trailed off, seeming baffled.

"It's best to be clear from the outset about these things. Especially if you decide to stay on."

"*What* things?" Aaron blinked. "Wait, stay on? I only just got here. I was told this posting was just for this week."

Lewis leaned back in his chair. "I've been trying to find a good PA for a while."

"Well, I'm only temping for the summer. I've got something permanent lined up for September."

Lewis frowned, then wondered why he was frowning. "Wouldn't this be kind of a dream job for someone like you? Being such a big fan of the show and all?"

"I suppose so, if my career plan was to be a PA," Aaron said, shrugging. "But I'm starting as a teacher at a secondary school in Dorking in September."

Lewis raised his brows. "How old *are* you?"

Aaron looked faintly offended. "Twenty-four, why?"

Lewis shrugged. "With a face like that, they'll eat you alive. What subject?"

"History," Aaron said tightly. "It's a good job. Very stable."

"Stable," Lewis said. "Right."

"Besides," Aaron went on, glaring now, "I only just got here. I haven't even done anything yet. I might be the worst PA you've ever had. From what I'm told, none of the recent ones have lasted more than a few days."

"True." Lewis laughed then, liking Aaron's show of spirit and the way his grey eyes sparked with annoyance. "But the thing is"—he smiled ruefully—"you love the show. I've never had a PA who loved the show before."

Aaron's annoyance visibly melted away. He smiled again, a little tentatively, his eyes warming.

Lewis, sensing his advantage like a shark scenting blood in the water, said quickly, "Okay, history boy. How about this? We'll see how this week goes, and if you're half-decent, we can maybe talk about you staying on till September."

Aaron looked uncertain, but there was a definite glimmer of excitement in his eyes too. "I guess I could stay till September," he said slowly, then smiled, raising one brow. "*If* you decide I'm half-decent."

Lewis grinned back. "Okay then." He leaned forward, setting his elbows on the desk. "So, I have a couple of important rules for people who work for me."

"Yeah?" Aaron said. "Fire away."

"Obviously, we're working on a popular show here, and you'll have access to a lot of confidential material."

Aaron nodded, understanding. "I already signed a confidentiality agreement when I went through my forms with Sophie."

"That's good," Lewis said, "but I always mention it myself because a lot of people seem to forget all about it between signing the agreement and arriving at their desk. Bottom line:

you don't talk about anything you see at work outside the office—and that includes online."

"Understood," Aaron said seriously.

God, he was cute, Lewis thought helplessly, before determinedly shoving that unhelpful thought aside.

"The second rule is related," he continued. "I expect total honesty. I need you to be up-front with me about anything that could affect your conduct at work."

"Got it," Aaron said. "Anything else?"

There *was* something else, a final rule that Lewis always tacked on to the end of this speech. It was a rule that had been given to him by his first boss and one that he believed in wholeheartedly, after seeing what havoc could be wrought when it was broken. But for some reason, on this occasion, Lewis found himself hesitating.

Until a little voice at the back of his mind whispered, *Don't let yourself be tempted.*

"Just one last thing."

Aaron was smiling, waiting.

Lewis cleared his throat. "I'm not saying this to be a dick, but since we'll be working together, I just want to be clear... I don't get involved with colleagues. Ever."

Aaron looked gobsmacked.

Lewis held up a hand. "I realise that sounds pretty fucking vain, and I'm honestly not assuming you *actually* want to jump my bones, but I think it's best to be clear about this sort of thing from the start."

Aaron blinked. "Well, you've certainly been clear," he said faintly. "Message received and very much understood."

"Good stuff," Lewis said, wondering why he suddenly felt so flat.

Shaking that thought off, he clapped his hands together. "Right then, there's lots to be done today, so let's make a start, shall we?" He grinned. "I'm ready to see what you can do, history boy."

FAOLÁN'S REPRIEVE

<u>LEECHES SEASON FOUR, EPISODE 1: "The Lotus Eaters" by Lewis Hunter</u>

CUT TO: INT. CELLAR - CONTINUOUS

Faolán is still slumped against the wall in his chains—dirty, exhausted, and delirious.

Suddenly, the door bursts open, and a guard comes flying into the cell with enough force that he crashes against the same wall Faolán is chained against.

Faolán stares at the guard's unconscious body, eyes wide. His gaze tracks from the guard to the door and the tall, shadowed figure standing there in a long coat.

The figure steps into the light. It's Skye. He stalks to Faolán's side, dropping to his knees beside him.

SKYE

(struggling to hide his shock)
Jesus, Faolán, are you okay? I thought…

Faolán
(Blinks, then looks at the unconscious guard)
I'm much better now.

Skye yanks the bolts holding the chains out of the wall, then breaks off most of the chain, leaving Faolán with the cuffs and a short length of chain.

SKYE
Come on, we're getting out of here.

Faolán holds up his chained wrists.

Faolán
What about these?

SKYE
No time for that now. We need to move. Amy's rigged everything up - this place is going to blow in (he checks his watch) eleven minutes.

He reaches down and hauls Faolán to his feet by the front of his jacket.

SKYE (cont.)
Stay close to me. We've got to get back through the vaults - are you up to that?

Faolán nods, but as Skye turns to the door, Faolán grabs his wrist.

Faolán

Skye, wait. I'm sorry I didn't listen to you. I was stupid. (Beat)
Thanks for coming back for me. I didn't think you would - I thought that was it for me.

SKYE

(His expression softens)
Me too, reporter boy. (briskly) Now get your arse moving. If we don't get to the surface in the next ten minutes, we're toast.

CHAPTER ONE

Aaron

Three years later

"Wait," Aaron said, sitting forward excitedly. "Wait, I've got it. Skye turns to Faolán and says, 'The difference is, if it had been you in there, I'd have ripped his bloody head off.' And then we end on that. No need for those last two lines at all."

He was sitting cross-legged on the floor of Lewis's office, pages spread out around him, the wall behind him filled with post-it notes. An organised kind of chaos that only he and Lewis fully understood. On the far side of the room, Lewis was pacing in front of the window. Or had been. He'd stopped when Aaron started speaking and now stood stock still, a slow smile curling one corner of his mouth.

"Yes," Lewis said, moving back to his desk and dropping into his chair, reaching for his laptop to make the change. "Yes, that's it. Perfect. Fuck, I wish we'd thought of that an hour ago."

Aaron glanced at the clock on the wall—it was getting on

for nine—and reached for another slice of pizza. "It would have saved some time," he agreed, taking a bite. "But we got there. We just had to work through it."

Sitting back in his chair, Lewis folded his hands behind his head and eyed his laptop screen with satisfaction. As always, Aaron's gaze arrowed in on the point where his shirt stretched over his broad, toned chest and the buttons pulled slightly, revealing a sliver of tanned skin beneath.

Guiltily, he looked away.

Despite his best efforts, he couldn't master his adolescent obsession with his boss's body, not even after three long years of working for him. He couldn't even call it a crush, not really. When it came to the kind of relationship Aaron wanted, Lewis was a non-starter. Definitely not boyfriend material. No, it was lust, pure and simple. A physical response that had nothing whatsoever to do with Aaron's heart and everything to do with his unruly dick.

And it was embarrassing as hell. Though thankfully Lewis seemed to be oblivious.

"Yup, I think we've got it," Lewis announced, nodding to himself. "That's looking good. We can leave it there for tonight."

"Really?" Aaron looked at him in surprise; these sessions usually went on much later. In fact, he'd been kind of counting on that tonight.

"Yeah," Lewis said, "you should head home. We can work on the final scene tomorrow."

"I don't mind staying." He nudged the pizza box towards Lewis. "There's still some left."

But Lewis put both hands on his desk and stood up. "I appreciate the offer, but actually I have to go. I'm meeting my brother for drinks in—" He looked at his watch, grimaced. "Shit, in ten minutes."

Ignoring the spike of disappointment, Aaron reached for his phone. "I'll get you an Uber, then."

"Thanks." Lewis snapped shut his laptop and reached for his bag. "We're meeting at the Bat and Belfry." He hesitated, then added, "You're welcome to join us, if you like."

"No, I should get back," Aaron said because that's what he always said. Because that's what Lewis expected him to say. Since day one, there'd been a tacit understanding between them that they didn't socialise outside work. They'd never explicitly acknowledged it, but it was there all the same, an invisible but nonetheless clear boundary. Aaron flashed a smile he didn't really feel. "Say hi to Owen for me."

He liked Lewis's brother. Owen dropped past the office occasionally. He was a less... intense version of Lewis. Lewis but with a few more social graces.

"I will." Lewis glanced around the office at the detritus of papers and post-it notes. "Fuck, the cleaners…"

"I'll tidy up," Aaron said, climbing to his feet. "You get going. Your ride will be here in"—he checked his phone—"three minutes."

"You're a diamond," Lewis said as he came out from behind his desk.

Aaron lifted an eyebrow as he opened the office door and said flatly, "See me sparkle."

Amused, Lewis snorted, but he stopped on the threshold, so close that Aaron's dick pulsed with painful awareness, a familiar, helpless reaction to Lewis's six-foot-two of lean muscle, his thick black hair—ruffled now from running his hands through it all evening—and his intense blue eyes.

"Seriously," Lewis said, "you *are* a fucking diamond, Aaron. This was a massive help. You've got a great ear for character voices."

"Yeah?" Coming from Lewis, that was high praise. He felt his cheeks heat. "Thanks."

Lewis studied him, still standing just that little bit too close. "You know what it is? There's no bullshit in your writing. You don't write lines to make yourself sound clever. You write them to make the characters sound authentic."

"Isn't that the point?"

"It is, but a lot of writers don't get that." He gestured to the pages they'd been working on that evening, piled in haphazard heaps on the floor, and made a face. "Ryan's always shoving his own words into the characters' mouths, and it shows."

Ryan was a freelancer who'd pitched several ideas to Lewis over the years, and a couple had been picked up in the latest season—mostly because it was five episodes longer than usual and, as hardworking as Lewis was, even he couldn't write every single script himself. Mind you, given the amount of time they'd just spent tearing Ryan's draft apart and putting it back together again, Aaron had to wonder at how much time it had really saved.

Out loud, he said, "He does have quite a…distinctive authorial voice."

"Yeah, well," Lewis said darkly, "I don't want to hear his fucking authorial voice. I want to hear Skye and Faolán." He met Aaron's gaze. "That's what you're so good at."

And that right there, that praise, was what kept Aaron in Lewis's orbit. Even when others said it was time for him to break free and take his career onwards, he found himself looping back around Lewis's star.

"You should go," he said abruptly, disconcerted by that thought. "I'll see you in the morning."

Lewis frowned slightly, but gave a curt nod, wished him a good night, and headed out.

When the wheezy clanking of the lift had faded, Aaron found himself acutely aware of the lonely silence in the office. The hum of the lights and printers, the quiet tick-ticking of a settling building. Outside, it was already dark. Even though summer was still lingering by day, the early September evenings were drawing in with a reminder that autumn was on its way, that liminal season of new pencils and new beginnings.

Not that Aaron was beginning anything new. Quite the opposite in fact.

Shaking off a sudden restlessness, he gathered up the pages they'd been working on. Then he snapped a few photos of the post-it notes on the wall to use when writing up their plan the next day, before pulling them all off and piling everything on his desk ready to deal with in the morning. Briefly, he considered making a start on it then, but no. That was being cowardly.

As awkward as it would be, he should just go home and face up to the possibility that Colin might still be there, clearing out his stuff. It was the least he could do after ending their two-year relationship.

So he turned off the lights, grabbed his jacket, and headed downstairs, past the empty reception desk and through the glass doors onto the street.

It was a short tube ride from Shepherd's Bush to his maisonette in North Acton, and the time went by too quickly. Despite his good intentions, he found himself dawdling on the walk from the station to his home, a craven part of him secretly hoping that Colin might have already finished his packing-up and left.

No such luck. Colin's red Seat Ibiza was parked outside the maisonette, boot open and half full. Their front door stood open. Aaron dithered, briefly tempted to phone Janvi and see whether she was free for a pint, until Colin came clumping down the stairs lugging a heavy suitcase.

He stopped in the doorway when he saw Aaron, his handsome face tightening, lips thinning. "I thought you were working late."

Aaron shrugged. "Got away earlier than expected." He glanced at the car boot. "Uh, need a hand or…?"

"I can manage." Colin stomped down the short path to the

pavement, suitcase banging against his leg, gym-honed muscles straining beneath his t-shirt.

Aaron stepped back to let him pass.

Objectively, Colin was a good-looking man. Tall and fit, with a handsome face and thinning blond hair that he kept buzzed very short. But to Aaron's shame, it had been a long time since he'd found himself attracted to Colin. A long time since he'd found himself attracted to anyone but Lewis.

Worse than that, recently, when he and Colin were in bed, his mind had started painting images of Lewis. When Colin touched him, it was Lewis's broad hands on his body. When Colin fucked him, it was Lewis driving him towards orgasm.

Sometimes, it was only thoughts of Lewis that pushed him over the edge.

Which was… disturbing. And a big part of why Aaron had ended things with Colin. How could he have done anything else? Colin deserved a boyfriend who wasn't lusting after his boss like a hormone-addled teenager. He deserved a boyfriend who wanted him, body and soul. And that wasn't Aaron.

Sighing, he left Colin to wrestle his suitcase into the car and trudged upstairs into the maisonette. The small, open-plan kitchen-living room looked rather bare, with the exception of two cardboard boxes on the counter stuffed with Colin's—and, frankly, a number of Aaron's—possessions: the lamp from Colin's side of the bed, three of the six Emma Bridgewater mugs Aaron's mum had given them last Christmas, Colin's muddy football boots, and a half-finished packet of chocolate digestives.

Ordinary things, dull things. Their life in all its spectacular tedium.

Aaron knew he should feel more. More bereft. More regretful. More *something*. If Skye was leaving Faolán, Faolán's heart would be breaking, or cramping, or feeling like it was being crushed in a steel fist.

But Aaron's heart just… wasn't.

What the hell was wrong with him?

"Are you just going to stand there in the way?" Colin groused, coming into the flat behind him.

"Sorry, I was just…"

"Thinking?" Colin said acidly. "Yeah, what a surprise."

"Christ, thinking isn't allowed now?" He immediately felt guilty for snapping. *He* was the one who'd ended it, not Colin. *He* was the one apparently incapable of a normal healthy relationship. The least he could do was be generous about their parting. Grimacing, he ran a hand through his hair. "Sorry, I didn't mean—" Christ, he was tired. "Long day."

"They're always long days, Aaron."

Another of Colin's peeves, one they'd discussed *ad nauseam*. Aaron let it go. He took himself around the breakfast bar and into the living area, perching on the edge of the sofa as he watched Colin bang about in the kitchen cupboards.

"I'm taking the juicer," Colin announced after a while. "I know it was a joint purchase, but you don't use it, and I need my—"

"It's fine. Take it."

To avoid the sight of Colin systematically dismantling their shared life, Aaron turned his gaze to the Blu-Ray copies of *Leeches* he kept in pride of place on the shelf below his TV. In turn, that led his thoughts back to the evening's work with Lewis. Season seven was going to be fantastic given the way Lewis was developing the bromance between Faolán and Skye. Well, Lewis called it bromance; Aaron called it romance. Which is exactly how all the Skylán shippers would see it. He couldn't wait for the episodes to air. The fic potential of that last line of dialogue Lewis had agreed to tonight was—

"You're doing it again," Colin said, yanking open the door of the cupboard where the juicer lived—on the top shelf where Aaron couldn't reach it, but Colin could.

Aaron half suspected Colin kept the thing up there for that very reason.

"Doing what?" he said wearily, though he knew what was coming.

"Zoning out," Colin fumed as he dragged out the juicer. "You can't stop thinking about Skye bloody Jäger for five minutes, can you?"

Aaron considered pointing out that he'd mostly been thinking about Lewis, but that would only open another can of worms. One he couldn't afford to unleash. He sighed heavily. "Don't be stupid."

Colin turned back, dumping the juicer down on the worktop. "Oh, *I'm* being stupid?" He levelled a finger, pointing into the living room where a life-size cut-out of Skye Jäger brooded in the corner. "The only stupid thing I did was get involved with a bloke who's so obsessed with a dumb TV show he has no time for an actual relationship."

"That's not true—"

Colin laughed. It wasn't a nice sound. "You work for the man who writes the show, and when I say work, I mean you're at his beck and call twelve hours a day, even at weekends—"

"For which I get generously paid."

Ignoring that, Colin bulldozed on. "And when you *are* at home, you spend all your time writing weird porn about—"

"It's not porn!" Aaron howled—this was an old, old argument. "It's fucking fanfic, Colin. Loads of people write it."

Colin scoffed. "No, Aaron, they don't. Not normal people."

Normal people? Christ.

Aaron opened his mouth to start on all the reasons why Colin was wrong—why fanfic was not only wildly popular but creatively important—but really, what was the point? They'd been over this a million times. They were never going to agree. So in the end he just shrugged and said, "I enjoy it. I never understood what your problem was with it."

Cramming the juicer into the least-full box, Colin said, "My problem isn't the writing, Aaron—it's Skye Jäger. It's that you're in love with a fucking *fictional character*. It's that you write all that romantic shit about Skye and Faolán because in your head, *you are* Faolán." He gave a derisive snort. "No surprise you dumped me. I can't compete with that. Nobody can."

"Bollocks," Aaron snapped, suddenly angry. Okay, so maybe he was a bit in love with Skye and Faolán's *relationship*, but that was totally different. That was just fandom fun, just entertainment. It wasn't bloody real. "*Leeches* had nothing to do with why I—With why things didn't work out between us."

"Didn't it?"

"No, it didn't."

Colin snorted. "You need to face up to facts, Aaron, or you're going to end up alone, stuck in your shitty job as a secretary—"

"I'm a Personal Assistant!"

"You trained to be a teacher."

"Yeah, and that was my parents' idea. I never actually *wanted* to be a teacher," Aaron said, for about the fiftieth time. "It was doing this job that helped me realise that."

Colin looked unimpressed. He hefted one of the boxes into his arms. "Whatever, Aaron. My advice? Do yourself a favour and get a life. Otherwise, you'll still be here in five years' time, doing your crappy job, writing your weirdo porn, and wondering where the hell the last decade went."

And with that, Colin flung open the door and stalked out.

Had Aaron been writing the scene, it would have ended there: fade to black, next chapter. Unfortunately, real life was less tidy, and Colin had to come back five minutes later for the second box.

By then, Aaron had his laptop out and had taken refuge in his latest story. He pretended not to hear the clink of Colin's key on the countertop or the door closing on his bitter, "Have a nice life, Aaron."

CHAPTER TWO

LEWIS

Owen was leaning against the bar with a mostly drunk pint in front of him when Lewis walked into the Bat and Belfry. He paused in the doorway, watching his brother contentedly sip his beer. Being Owen, he wasn't scrolling on his mobile phone, and there was no hint of impatience or irritation on his face, despite Lewis being late. He looked, as usual, very Zen. But then, he was the complete opposite of Lewis in temperament.

In other ways they were quite similar. For one thing, they were both tall and broad. Lewis had an inch on Owen in height, but Owen had more muscle. The kind of muscle you got from working physically hard every day for a couple of decades, as opposed to the kind Lewis had, which you got from running and going to the gym. They were both dark-haired too—Lewis's hair was black, while Owen's was dark brown—and both blue-eyed, though Owen's eyes were a lighter, less intense hue than Lewis's, like faded denim. And they were warm when he smiled. Kind.

When Owen introduced Lewis to people, he always said,

"Lewis got the beauty and *the brains in our family"* which irritated Lewis no end, not least because it wasn't true. Though he suspected Owen thought it was, and that always made him feel sad. Sad and irritated together.

Even if it had been true, Owen definitely had the family monopoly on the things that were more important than beauty and brains. Like guts. Like *grit*. It had been Owen who'd held everything together after their mum died, when Lewis was fourteen and Owen seventeen. Owen who'd managed to convince everyone that their Aunt Veronica was living with them for those precarious few months till he turned eighteen, when it was, in reality, just the two of them. Owen who'd left school and got a job on a construction site, labouring for cash.

In fact, he'd spent the next six years labouring—as well as doing other, less legitimate stuff on the side—to keep a roof over their heads and the bills mostly paid. And while he'd been grafting, Lewis had done his GCSEs and A levels. And had started writing obsessively, desperately trying to land a position as a runner in a TV production company—which he'd eventually done, talking himself into the role with the help of a CV that was packed with lies.

Looking back, he cringed to remember how much he'd taken his brother for granted.

Just then, Owen spotted Lewis. He grinned and lifted a hand in a greeting, then pointed at his beer and raised his brows. Lewis nodded and began making his way through the crowded pub, easing his way round groups of rowdy drinkers. By the time he reached Owen, the barman was already pulling their pints.

"Sorry I'm late," Lewis said, allowing his brother to pull him into a quick half-hug.

"It's okay," Owen said affably, patting his shoulder before easing back. "Did you get held up at work?"

"Yeah, I stayed late to finish some rewrites and lost track of the time."

The barman set two pints of Fullers down in front of them, and Lewis went to pull out his wallet.

"I'll get it," Owen said, pushing his arm down, and Lewis bit back the automatic protest. Owen could be funny about paying for stuff. Lewis assumed it was a pride thing, that Owen felt weird about his younger brother having so much more money than he did. There had been a time when it used to really get to Lewis. He'd got his first decent salary when he'd started working on a daytime soap—back then, Owen had been struggling to pay the bills, but he'd steadfastly refused any help from Lewis. They'd argued about it a lot. It wasn't so bad now, that Owen was doing well for himself. His landscaping business had taken off a few years ago, and he had a crew of guys working with him. He'd even bought his own place a few years ago, a bright, sunny, ground-floor flat in Beckenham with its very own pocket-sized garden. It was amazing how much Owen had done with such a tiny space. His garden had an astonishing array of plants, of all different shapes, sizes, and colours, a narrow path that looped around the perimeter, a mini-greenhouse, and even a small pond where Lewis had spotted some froglets in the spring. There were tons of flowers too, from spring right through to autumn, a rhubarb patch, and a hidden bed of dwarf strawberries.

Lewis, who couldn't even keep a single potted plant alive for more than a few months, was endlessly astonished by Owen's ability to coax so much life and beauty from what had been little more than a sad little patch of weedy lawn when he'd first moved in.

Once Owen had tucked his wallet away, he lifted his pint and grinned at Lewis. "Cheers."

"Cheers," Lewis echoed, lifting his own glass, and they both drank deeply.

"So, did you get your rewrites finished?" Owen asked, when they'd set their glasses down.

"Not quite, but we can finish them tomorrow."

"We?"

"Me and Aaron," Lewis clarified. "He says *hi* by the way."

Owen smiled. "I hope you pay him overtime for all these extra hours he does."

"He's well paid," Lewis said defensively, even as he felt a pang of guilt. The HR director had spoken to him last week about how many extra hours Aaron did.

"We're concerned that you might be putting pressure on him without realising it..."

Lewis frowned, remembering that. But then he thought of Aaron earlier this evening, his eyes sparkling with excitement as he outlined his breakthrough idea. His eagerness to keep working, even after Lewis had announced it was time to call it a day.

"Do you think I take advantage of him?" he said now, looking at his brother.

Owen regarded him for a long, silent moment. In typical Owen style he didn't answer the question directly. "I don't remember any of your other assistants staying late at the office to work with you quite so often—and when they did stay, you always used to moan about how useless they were. What's different about Aaron?"

Lewis frowned, not liking the curiosity in his brother's gaze, but he tried to answer honestly. "He's not actually doing the same job as my old assistants. I mean, he does do all the PA stuff, yes, but he also works on the script side with me, so it's different."

"Does he?" Owen seemed surprised.

"Well, yeah," Lewis said, frowning. Didn't Owen know this already? Hadn't Lewis mentioned it loads of times before? "You know he was a massive fan of the show before he came to work for RPP, right?"

Owen nodded, sipping his beer.

"Well, because of that, he has this huge fount of knowledge about it—honestly, when it comes to tiny details, he remembers more stuff than I do—so that's really helpful with story lining and edits. And besides that, he's got a great ear for dialogue and a ton of natural writing talent." Lewis realised he was smiling like an idiot and quickly scowled. He shot Owen a sidelong glance and muttered, "I'm sure I must have mentioned all this before."

Owen gave him an odd look. "Not really. I mean, I knew he was a fan and that the two of you talked about the show a lot. And yeah, you've mentioned working late with him plenty of times, but I didn't think he was actually working on scripts with you. I kind of assumed he was—I don't know, typing and stuff?"

Lewis snorted. "What, taking dictation? Um—that's not really what PAs do. Not this century anyway."

"How am I supposed to know?" Owen asked, holding up his hands in a defensive gesture. "I'm a getting-my-hands-dirty kind of guy, not a soft office worker like you."

"Oh, fuck off," Lewis said without heat. "And no, Aaron doesn't spend his time *typing* for me. His job as my PA is to work side by side with me, making sure I'm where I need to be, that I know what I'm doing and that I have everything I need."

"And on the script side of things?"

Lewis considered that. "It kind of… evolved over time."

"Yeah? How?"

Lewis frowned, thinking back. "It probably started with him making little comments about the show. Insightful stuff. Smart, you know? And then, after a while, I started asking his opinion on bits and pieces, and then sharing script drafts with him, and asking for his suggestions." He shrugged. "It grew from there."

"But officially, he's still your PA."

And there was that pesky pang of guilt again. "Well, yeah, that's his job title," Lewis said, "but everyone knows what he does, and he's not on a standard PA salary anymore. I make sure he gets paid properly for his work."

"Hmm." Owen was wearing his neutral expression. The one he used when he didn't approve of something Lewis was doing but wasn't going to come out and say as much.

"What?" Lewis said irritably.

Owen met his gaze impassively. "What do you mean, '*what*'?"

"What was that look for?"

"There was no look."

"Oh, there was a look," Lewis said, narrowing his eyes. "If you've got a point, just fucking make it."

"I don't have a point. I suppose I'm just wondering…"

"Wondering what?"

"Well, you spend a lot of time with Aaron, and you obviously have a lot in common."

"So?"

"So… has anything ever happened between you?" Owen's expression was mildly interested. "He's a very attractive guy."

Weirdly, the thing that irritated Lewis most was the last part—the knowledge that Owen had noticed how attractive Aaron was. Which was really fucking idiotic because yes, Aaron was *obviously* attractive, and Owen was bi, and with his slim, tight build, Aaron was very much Owen's type.

"Absolutely not," Lewis bit out. "And nothing ever will happen between us. Aaron is a colleague. Sex is definitely not on the table."

"No?" Owen said, raising one sceptical brow. "Because a lot of people meet their life partners at work, you know."

"I'm his *boss*," Lewis said repressively. "Besides, I can easily find partners outside of work, thank you very much."

Owen looked thoughtful. "Speaking of which, what does

Mason think of all the evenings you spend at work with Aaron?"

"Mason?" Lewis said stupidly. For a moment, he was genuinely bewildered by the question.

"Yes, *Mason,*" Owen said. "You know—your boyfriend?"

Lewis blinked at that. "Boyfriend," he echoed, frowning. "Erm, no. We were seeing one another for a bit, but it's pretty much over. And for the record, we were never boyfriends."

"Pretty much over?" Owen's brows arched in disbelief.

Lewis shrugged. He didn't do relationships—more like flings with fuzzy endings. Most guys took the hint when he stopped answering their calls.

"Okay, more like *actually* over," he amended. "For a couple of weeks now."

Owen studied him for several long moments, till Lewis felt himself doing that guilty squirming thing that made him feel about twelve. How did Owen still manage to do that to him?

Eventually, Owen said, "That's funny because I saw him on Monday, and he definitely thinks you're still together."

Lewis stared at him, aghast. "Does he?" *Damn.* Looked like Mason was one of those guys he needed to be blunter with. "Wait, where did *you* see Mason?"

Mason was a model. It was difficult to imagine where he and Owen could possibly have run into one another.

"I was up at a house in Wimbledon to talk about a job. Massive grounds. Guy's a photographer. Mason was arriving when I was on my way out." He frowned at the memory.

"So what did he say about me?"

Owen blinked. "Hmm?"

"Mason. What did he say that made you think he believes we're still together?"

"Oh, right. We said hello, the guy asked how we knew each other, and Mason said, *'He's my boyfriend's brother'* so…" Owen shrugged.

Yeah. Maybe Mason did have the wrong end of the stick.

"I'll talk to him," Lewis said, taking a swallow of his beer to mask his discomfort.

"Do that," Owen said. "But be nice, okay?"

Lewis glared at him. "What's that supposed to mean?"

Owen sighed. "For someone who makes his living crafting words, you're sometimes very tactless."

Lewis shook his head, though not in denial. "I just hate bullshit, you know that."

"Yes, I know, but—" Owen broke off.

"But what?"

"Some people are just more sensitive than others. Your Aaron might be able to deal with your grumpy moods and rude comments, but—"

"He's not *my Aaron,* for fuck's sake. And as for Mason, he's a big boy. He can cope with a little rejection, I'm sure."

Owen eyed him doubtfully for a moment; then he shrugged. "Fine," he said, turning away to lift his now-empty glass and wiggle it at the barman, who nodded in acknowledgement.

Lewis sank the rest of his pint while the barman finished up with another customer. When he wandered back over to them, Owen ordered two more pints of Fullers and a couple of bags of salt-and-vinegar crisps.

"Can I ask you something?" Owen said, once the fresh beers and snacks had arrived.

Lewis opened a bag of crisps and stuffed a handful in his mouth. "Go ahead," he said through a mouthful of crumbs.

"Ugh," Owen said, eyeing him in disgust. "So, you know how you just said that Aaron's not *your* Aaron?"

"Yup."

Owen met his gaze squarely. "How would you feel about me asking him out?"

"What?" Lewis stared at his brother in angry disbelief.

How could Owen imagine for a second that that would be acceptable?

"Like I said earlier," Owen went on, as though Lewis hadn't spoken, "he's a very attractive guy, and if there's definitely never going to be anything between—"

"Fucking *no way*!" Lewis snapped. "Jesus, Owen!"

And then Owen—the fucking bastard—burst out laughing.

"Oh my God," he said between gasps. "Lewis, your *face*!"

"Fuck off," Lewis grumbled, horribly aware of the sudden heat in his cheeks. "Of course I don't want you shagging my assistant. He's the best PA I've ever had. I don't want you chasing him off." Then he scowled harder and added, "Besides, he's already got a boyfriend."

"Sure," Owen said, eyes sparkling with amusement. "It's because he's your assistant. Got it—aaand since you're such a possessive dick, I won't even bother asking about Mason." And then he was off again, chuckling at his own lame joke. Which really was lame, because Lewis couldn't care less if Owen shagged Mason six ways from Sunday. Aaron, however, was an entirely different kettle of fish.

"It's not jealousy," he muttered. "I'm just not risking losing my assistant because you fancy getting your end away."

Owen clapped one big hand on Lewis's shoulder. "Whatever you say, little bro," he said and lifted his glass again. "Whatever you say."

CHAPTER THREE

Aaron

Mid-September brought an unseasonal heatwave that had Aaron melting on his morning commute, crammed nose-to-armpit on the Central Line. Not that he really cared, too absorbed in reading the thirty-six comments that had been posted overnight on the latest chapter of his fic.

Each one fizzed in his soul like little golden bath bombs of joy. It never got old, that thrill of knowing that someone—some random stranger—had read his words and been moved enough to respond. Even after a decade of writing fanfiction, feedback still left him buzzing with gratitude.

OMG I LOVED THIS SO HARD. It read exactly like an episode.

Such sweet, tortuous pining! Poor Faolán. I just can't!

I stayed up way too late reading this and will pay for it tomorrow, but I don't care because your stories are just SO GOOD. You've got the character voices spot on, and your writing is really beautiful. Amazing work. Thanks for sharing it with us.

Had he been able to, Aaron would have given every commenter an enormous hug. Instead, he would spend a couple of hours that night responding to every comment, trying to convey how much they meant to him.

Feeling hyped, he piled off the train along with everyone else at Shepherd's Bush and marched through the station, then up and out into the warm September morning. Winding through the commuting crowd, he made his way to Grinder, his favourite ironically named coffee shop, and picked up two bacon rolls along with Lewis's current favourite froufrou nonsense drink—a mint hot chocolate with whipped cream and sprinkles—and a black Americano for himself.

It was a short walk from there to the offices of RPP, which were located in an unprepossessing building on Charecroft Way, tucked behind the busy Uxbridge Road. Waving his pass over the sensor pad outside the office, Aaron pushed through the revolving door into the reception. "Morning, Dymek," he called, lifting his hand to wave. "How was the match last night?"

"Terrible. Chelsea play very bad." Dymek shook his head from behind the security desk. "Their goalie has butter for fingers."

Aaron gave him a thumbs up. "Butterfingers. Excellent use of the idiom."

"Yes." Dymek grinned as he held out a stack of post. "Mr. Hunter is already upstairs. He is wanting his breakfast, I think. Very grumpy." He glared at Aaron to illustrate the point.

Aaron grabbed the post, juggling it with the bacon rolls, and nudged open the door to the stairwell with his hip. "Should have bought his own, then, shouldn't he?" He rolled his eyes with exaggerated exasperation. "But thanks for the heads up. I'll brace myself."

Given how slow and unreliable the lift was, Aaron took the stairs most mornings. Besides, climbing four floors was good exercise, and he didn't need Colin to tell him that he spent far too many hours hunched over a laptop—for both work and leisure. The thing was it was difficult to find time for the gym when you could be using those precious hours to write the next chapter, and it was impossible to—

His thoughts derailed at the sight of Jason Tsang waiting for him at their office door, his black hair coiffed to sleek perfection but his face grim behind the bright red frames of his designer glasses. Jason, the senior PA in their department, was assistant to Lewis's boss, Toni Beckford, Head of Drama. Toni didn't do mornings, and so Jason rarely came in before nine. That he was here now was a Bad Sign.

"It's going to be a day," Jason warned, taking the bacon rolls from Aaron's hands and walking with him down the corridor to the pod of desks they shared at the far end. "Lewis has been in since seven."

"And you're in too."

Jason grimaced, depositing the bacon rolls onto Aaron's desk on the way to his own workstation. "Charlie called late last night. He moved the *Leeches* pitch forward to this weekend because he's flying back to the States next Monday. He wants to see Toni *and* Lewis. Together."

Charlie Alexander was a senior executive at Telopix Entertainment. Telopix had been in discussions with RPP about a US version of *Leeches* for a while and Charlie, who had a reputation in the business for dropping projects over 'creative differences', would be making the final decision on whether to green light the project.

"Uh-oh." Aaron set down the post and the cardboard carrier holding their drinks, glancing toward Lewis's closed office door. From within, he could hear Lewis talking irritably.

"Tell me it's not at Safehaven." Safehaven was Charlie's country pile, and his favourite place to host meetings.

"It's at Safehaven."

"Crap. Lewis hates it there."

"And doesn't he make sure we all know it?" Jason made a face.

"Come on," Aaron said. "It's not his fault it makes him feel uncomfortable. Charlie's bullshit brings him out in hives."

Jason snorted. "So he has to walk around in a big mood, making *us* all feel like crap too?"

Aaron felt a swell of irritation. "That's not fair. He doesn't mean to—"

"Aaron. Just don't." Jason held up a hand to stop him.

"Don't what?"

"Defend him! The man's a selfish prick, and you know it."

"Not true. He's—"

As if magically summoned, Lewis's door flew open, and he stormed out. There wasn't actual smoke coming out of his ears, but not far off. "Finally," he growled, glaring at Aaron. "Where've you been?"

"At home, in bed. Sleeping. Then on the tube. Ten minutes in Grinder—the coffee shop, not the app. Why, where've you been?"

Lewis blinked, his irritation successfully punctured. He scrubbed a hand through his hair, leaving it dishevelled and sexy. *Sexier*, damn it. "I expected you earlier."

"And I expected to win the lottery. Life's full of disappointments." He picked up one of the bacon rolls and the hot chocolate, which was already oozing cream and sprinkles, and set them on the corner of his desk for Lewis, who immediately brightened.

"I hear you're going to Safehaven this weekend?" Aaron said, as Lewis pulled the bacon roll out of its bag and took a bite.

He grimaced. "There's no brown sauce."

"Yes, there is," Aaron replied placidly, watching as Lewis opened the roll, lifted the bacon, and finally grunted agreement.

"They should spread the sauce to the edge of the roll," he said after a moment, his tone grudging.

"I'll be sure to pass on your valuable feedback." Aaron shucked off his jacket and hung it over the back of his chair, taking a seat and pulling his laptop out of his bag. "Good job we drafted the *Leeches:* USA pitch last week," he said. "It's in good shape, but I imagine you want to do another polish before Charlie sees it?" He glanced up and found Lewis watching him, nodding as he chewed his breakfast. "Jase, are they still meeting at ten, or can we move it earlier?"

"Toni's coming in for eight-thirty," Jason said, sliding in behind his own desk. "She's...not ecstatic. But she's panicking about the budget—Charlie wants to go through it." He sighed. "I'm still trying to make it readable. Bloody Excel."

Luckily, budgets were Toni's department because if anyone ever asked Aaron to create a pivot table, he'd probably throw his computer out the window. Lewis might do the same. Neither of them was good with figures. Putting a narrative around the figures, though?

Well, Lewis Hunter was a genius when it came to storytelling of any sort. Even now, after working for the man for three years, Aaron was still in awe of his talent. He'd read every *Leeches* script Lewis had ever written and still referred to them constantly as a guide to economy and elegance in storytelling. Aaron's own fannish scribblings paled by comparison.

In fairness, most things paled by comparison with Lewis Hunter.

Everything about him was bigger and bolder than life, from his brooding good looks to his shocking bluntness, uncompromising South London accent, and enormous creative talent. Even now, in the process of shoving the second half of a bacon roll into his mouth, Lewis was the most compelling thing in the room.

Quite the opposite of Aaron, who'd been unremarkable his whole life: unremarkable school career, unremarkable history degree, unremarkable working life. The only place where he'd ever stood out, where he'd ever shone, was in the secret world of *Leeches* fanfiction. A hidden, precious space that Aaron couldn't live without.

A place that nobody at work could ever discover.

While he waited for Outlook to boot up, he said, "Lewis, I'll put in a half-hour catch-up for us after your meeting with Toni, so we can go through everything you'll need for the weekend. I think we have our ducks in a row—most of them, anyway—so no need to panic."

"I'm not panicking."

Aaron raised an eyebrow. "All right then."

"I'm not panicking," Lewis repeated. "I'm just pissed off that Charlie fucking Alexander thinks we all dance to his bloody tune. The *Leeches* pitch has been in the diary for months. Who the fuck does he think he is, pulling it forward by three weeks?"

"I assume he thinks he's Head of Global TV at Telopix Entertainment."

Lewis glowered. "He's a wanker."

"That too." With Outlook finally open, Aaron started calling up calendars and shuffling meetings. "Was there anything else you needed me for this morning?"

"Yes, I need you in the story lining meeting with Ryan. Did you read his pitch for episode ten?"

"Of course." Reading about *Leeches* storylines wasn't exactly work. "I thought it was okay. I did love the idea of using the Highgate Vampire myth." Something he'd actually used himself in *Bleeding Hearts and Dry Bones,* one of his first *Leeches* fics.

"Yes!" Lewis levelled a finger at him. "That's the best part."

Aaron couldn't help preening, even if Lewis would never know why. "I wasn't sure about Skye essentially using Faolán as bait, though," he admitted. "It feels out of character."

Which was putting it mildly. Of course, if Aaron was writing it, Skye would rip the throat out of the Highgate Vamp before letting him within ten feet of his beloved Faolán.

"That whole idea is bollocks," Lewis agreed, taking a slurp of his hot chocolate. It left him with a whipped cream moustache, which he licked off. "Skye values Faolán way too much to risk him like that."

Aaron glanced at him in surprise, then bent his head to hide the smile that curved his mouth, because those were words that would warm the heart of any Skylán shipper. Trying to temper his fannish enthusiasm back to something resembling professionalism, he said, "You would write it better."

"Yeah?" Lewis smiled, with a slow, almost-flirtatious grin that lit his blue eyes and set Aaron's pulse spiking. "Maybe I will."

"Maybe you should."

For a moment, they just smiled at each other. Then Jason cleared his throat and said, "Do me a favour, Aaron, and get the budget up on the big screen in Lewis's office?"

The weird moment of connection popped like a balloon.

Aaron took a gulp of coffee and slipped out from behind his desk. "No problem. I'll do it now, before Lewis takes out everyone's Wi-Fi."

Jason snorted from behind his screen.

"Hey," Lewis objected as Aaron squeezed past him into his office. "That was one time."

Aaron gave a strained laugh as his arm brushed Lewis's chest, stupidly aware of the heat radiating from Lewis's body and the fresh scent of his Neroli Sun aftershave.

His face heated, goosebumps rising along his arms.

Almost more dangerous than the risk of accidentally exposing his fanfiction habit was the risk of accidentally exposing his ridiculous lust for Lewis, a lust that had his brain melting at the slightest contact. Christ, it was mortifying.

Aaron crossed to Lewis's desk and reached for his laptop.

Jason was right. It was definitely going to be a day.

CHAPTER FOUR

Aaron

By nine-thirty, Lewis and Toni were still locked in Lewis's office arguing about their pitch to Telopix. Through the narrow strip of window in the door, Aaron glimpsed Lewis from time to time. Sometimes lounging back in his chair, sometimes pacing, sometimes with his fingers tugging at his hair in frustration. Once, Lewis popped his head around the door and bellowed, "Aaron! The fucking laptop's buggered."

In fact, he'd somehow managed to dislodge the HDMI cable connecting it to the projector. God knew how because Aaron had screwed that bastard in himself. Hard. But Lewis was a magnet for technical gremlins. They followed him around like Jägerbombers on a mission.

He'd only just sat down at his desk again when reception rang. Fumbling his headset back on, he accepted the call. "Yep. Aaron Page."

"Aaron," came Dymek's voice. "One of Mr. Hunter's 'friends' is here."

That was a euphemism for one of Lewis's many ex-boyfriends. Aaron sighed. "Tell him Mr. Hunter isn't in."

"I did. But it's you he wants to speak to, not Mr. Hunter."

"*Me?* Why? Who is it?"

Dymek sighed. "How do I know? Pretty boy. They all look the same."

"You could try asking his name."

"You ask his name. He is in the lift."

"What?" he squeaked. "You sent him *up*?"

The noise that came down the line was the vocal equivalent of a Slavic shrug, and then the phone went dead. Aaron stared at it, then set it down. "I think Dymek is done dealing with Lewis's exes."

"As you should be," Jason said, without looking up. "That is *not* part of your job."

"My job is to make Lewis's life easier."

"His working life, not his love life."

Aaron huffed out a sigh. "When they show up here, it *is* his working life."

Jason did look up then. "You know, Toni would never expect you to do this for her. Not in a million years. She'd treat you with respect, nurture your professional development..."

"And yet, I'm still not applying for the *Bow Street* job."

"I don't get it," Jason said, shaking his head. "Getting to spend six months working with Toni developing the pilot for a new show? It's a fantastic opportunity. I thought you'd jump at the chance."

"In case you haven't noticed," Aaron said, gesturing at his full desk, "I already have a job. A great job."

"Come on, Lewis could spare you for a few months."

Aaron gave him a speaking look. "You think so?"

"There *are* other PAs, Aaron. Admittedly, not ones who'd fetch Lewis a bacon butty every morning. But he'd survive." Jason tipped his head, frowning. "You're really good at the script development stuff. Don't you want to move into that kind of role?"

Aaron shrugged, glancing along the corridor towards the lifts. "I haven't really thought about it," he lied.

Jason gaped. "You haven't *thought* about it? What about Lewis? Hasn't he suggested it? I'm not interested in script development but Toni's always looking for ways to develop me in my role. I'd have thought he'd want—"

"He's a little busy for that," Aaron said, standing up to greet the man who'd just appeared around the corner of the corridor. Tall, slender, and beautiful, he walked with the sullen grace of a catwalk model—all sharp hips and pouty lips—which, of course, was exactly what he was.

"Mason," Aaron said. "Nice to see you again."

Mason Nash was—or rather, had been—Lewis's latest. They'd been together over a month, which, for Lewis, counted as a long-term relationship. Aaron had quite liked Mason, who could be funny and was surprisingly sweet underneath his spoiled ways. Aaron believed he'd been genuinely hurt when Lewis dumped him.

"Is he in?" Mason said, glancing anxiously at Lewis's office door.

"He's in a meeting." Aaron came around from behind his desk in an attempt to usher him back the way he'd come. "Sorry, mate, but this isn't a great time. Lots on today."

Mason ignored Aaron's not-so-subtle hint and dropped into the visitors' chair like a Victorian maiden collapsing onto a fainting couch, long legs sprawling. "You're my last hope, Aaron. Say you'll help me?"

"Er...." Warily, Aaron perched on the edge of his desk. "Help you how?"

"You have to intercede."

"Intercede? With Lewis, you mean?"

Mason leaned forward, hands pressed together like a prayer or a namaste. There were elegant grey circles beneath his startling green eyes that gave him the look of a suffering poet. Aaron felt oddly sorry for him. Well, as sorry as any normal man could feel for an impossibly beautiful and pampered male model with an ego the size of Chiswick. "I really need to speak to him."

"Mason—"

"Please? I just need to know why he ended it. He just.... One moment we were shagging like randy tomcats, and the next… Boom. Dumped."

Aaron grimaced, trying not to dwell on the tomcat image. "Look, I'm sorry, but that's kind of what he does."

"But *why*? I mean…" He gestured to himself and added without so much as a blush, "I doubt he got a better offer."

Jason made an odd sort of noise behind his laptop, half cough and half snort. "Sorry," he said, clearing his throat. "Allergies."

Mason narrowed his eyes in Jason's direction for a few moments before letting his gaze slide back to Aaron. "I've tried to talk to him, but he's been avoiding me ever since he dumped me last week. And now he's blocked my bloody phone. I just want to understand why. I deserve that, don't I?"

"You do. He's been an absolute shit," Aaron said soothingly. "But I don't see what I can do—"

"Talk to him for me. Make him see me. Or at least take my calls."

"I can't *make* him take your calls, Mason."

"Why not?"

"Because…" He gave a helpless shrug. "He won't listen to me."

"Are you joking?" Mason slumped back in the chair. "You're the only one he *ever* listens to."

Aaron laughed at that idea, a rueful huff. "Maybe about which end of the charger goes into his phone. Not personal stuff. We're not—We don't have that kind of relationship."

Not that they weren't friendly, because they were. They bantered easily, thanks to a shared sense of humour and a ton of inside jokes, but they were both careful to steer around anything too intimate.

Mason regarded Aaron sceptically, saying nothing. After a long look, he turned his head to gaze out of the window and sighed. "God, this is fucking humiliating."

Aaron winced because, yeah, it must be. Lewis had this effect on people. He drew them in, magnetised them. *Enthralled them,* he thought. *Beguiled them*. And then dropped them like a stone when something—someone—new caught his eye.

"If it's any consolation," Aaron said gently, "it's not you. He does this to everyone. He's just...a bit of a bastard, sometimes. I don't think he actually realises it though. Like, he doesn't *mean* to be a shit."

Mason blew out a long breath. "I know I'm probably better off without him..."

On cue, Lewis's muffled voice rose in anger from his office.

"Of course you are," Aaron said, glancing warily at the door. "Definitely. One hundred percent better off without him."

"It's just…" Mason sighed again. "He's so *much.* And when he's gone, well, he leaves quite a gap."

Aaron could imagine that. If he was honest, it was one of the reasons he wasn't interested in the script development role. He just couldn't imagine not working with Lewis every day. Not having that fizzing, dangerous energy in his life. It would feel like dousing the sun.

He'd miss it, even when the sun was threatening to combust.

Through the strip of glass in the door, he could see Lewis on his feet now, gesticulating, his voice getting louder and louder. Combustion was imminent.

"Tell you what, Mason, why don't I buy you a coffee and a

cake? I'm due a break, and you look like you could use some comfort food."

Mason smiled, amused. "Aaron, you smoothie. Are you making a move?"

"What?" Aaron blinked, taken aback. Hurriedly, he said, "No, of course not."

"Are you sure?" Mason ran his eyes over him, which was mortifying. As if Aaron would ever imagine that a man like Mason would look twice at him. "You know, I always thought you were quite—"

"Then Charlie Alexander can fuck the fuck off!" Lewis's muffled voice rose behind the door.

Aaron stood up. "Okay. Mason, you need to leave now."

"But—"

It was already too late, though. The office door banged open, and Lewis stormed out. "I'm not turning *Leeches* into fucking *Twilight*! Not for Charlie Alexander, not for Telopix. Not even for you, Toni! It's my show. *My* creation. And I won't fucking cheapen it for anyone." With that, he turned on his heel, ready to stalk off. "I'm going for a fucking walk!"

Aaron held his breath, hoping Lewis would ignore them completely. If he could just get rid of Mason without Lewis noticing...

Unfortunately, Mason had other plans. "Hello, Lew," he said, rising smoothly to his feet. "Bad day?"

Crap. Crappity-crap, crap, crap.

Lewis stopped dead, a rabbit-in-headlights. "Mason?" He threw a furious glance at Aaron. "What the hell is *he* doing here?"

"I came to—"

"He came to see me," Aaron chipped in brightly. "And he was just leaving. Thanks for stopping by, Mason. Great to catch up. I know you're in a rush."

Lewis scowled. "Why would he come to see *you*?"

"Er—"

Mason's gaze darted between them. Then he quickly stepped closer to Aaron and draped a proprietary arm around his shoulders. "Not that it's any of your business," he told Lewis, "but we were just arranging a date."

Lewis's eyebrows drew sharply together. "A *date*?"

Oh, good grief. Aaron tried to pull away. "That's not—"

"What's wrong, Lew?" Mason carried on, completely ignoring Aaron's attempts to free himself. "You're not jealous, are you?"

Lewis's expression darkened. *Glowering*, Aaron's thesaurus brain supplied. *Glaring. Scowling*. "Fuck's sake, Mason. Let him go."

"Oh my God," Mason crowed, delighted. "You *are* jealous."

Frankly, Aaron thought that was extremely unlikely. Lewis never looked back with regret at the men he'd loved and left—or rather, fucked and left. In the three years Aaron had known him, he'd never once seen Lewis jealous. Some people, specifically, Jason, thought that meant Lewis was a heartless bastard. And Aaron might have agreed had he not seen Lewis's heart bleed out on the pages of his scripts. Especially when he wrote the bromance between Skye and Faolán, even if he wouldn't acknowledge that was what he was doing. In his scripts, he revealed a sensitive and romantic soul. One Aaron would have staked his life on finding beneath all Lewis's bluster.

Unfortunately, it was buried deep. Very deep. Too deep to ever uncover, realistically.

"Let me make myself clear, Mason," Lewis said in a dangerously soft voice. "I don't care who you're fucking, but keep your hands off my PA. I don't want him distracted. Besides, Aaron already has a boyfriend—a bloody awful one, as it happens—but he certainly doesn't need another."

With that, Lewis turned on his heel and stalked off down the corridor.

Into the ringing silence that followed, Aaron said, "Well, that was fun. Thanks for popping in, Mason. Always a pleasure."

Mason's gaze was still fixed on the direction of Lewis's departing figure, his eyes narrowed. "He *was* jealous," he muttered. "I bloody saw it." Then he looked over at Aaron, tipping his head speculatively. "So did you want to get that—?"

"Aaron!" Lewis barked from further down the corridor. "With me. Now."

Aaron gave Mason an apologetic shrug. "If I were you," he said, "I'd go out and get laid tonight. Wash that man right out of your hair. You can *definitely* do better."

Mason didn't reply, but Aaron felt his eyes on his back as he speed-walked all the way down the corridor, at the end of which Lewis waited, his expression disgruntled.

"Kitchen?" Aaron asked lightly. "Or do you want to walk and talk?"

"Kitchen."

It was empty, thank God.

Aaron made a beeline for the kettle and flipped it on. "Tea?"

Lewis shook his head and wandered over to the window, staring out.

Aaron watched him, frowning. Unfortunately for Mason, he was dead wrong about Lewis being jealous, but clearly *something* was going on. Even by his own low standards, Lewis had been shockingly rude. Now, his profile was thoughtful, absorbed, as he gazed out across the street, his broad shoulders bunched and tense, fingers curled into fists.

Bristling, Aaron thought. *Prickly*. For some reason, Lewis always triggered a desire in Aaron to paint him in words.

"Before you say anything, I know," Lewis muttered, without turning around. "I was fucking rude. I'll fucking apologise, okay?"

"To whom? Mason? Me? Toni? That's quite the hat trick you scored in, oh, about two minutes."

Silence.

Aaron got a mug out of the cupboard and dropped a tea bag into it, occupying his hands with the mindless task. "What happened in the meeting?"

A rise and fall of those broad shoulders as Lewis sighed, scrubbing one hand through his hair, clenching it there for a moment. "Charlie Alexander wants me to 'sex up' *Leeches* for the American remake. He thinks the British version is 'too dark'."

Aaron winced. "Ouch."

"He wants a fucking love triangle."

Rather disloyally, Aaron's heart jumped with excitement. Because *Oh my God, yes please!* "Oh?" he said mildly. "Between Skye, Amy and...Faolán?"

Please, please, please!

"I won't do it. I don't care if we don't sell it to Telopix."

"Fans *do* love the Skye/Faolán bromance," Aaron reminded him lightly, reaching into the fridge for the milk. "I mean, a lot of fans ship them. Maybe you could just...amp up their attraction?" *Please do that.* A canon romance between Skye and Faolán would be *amazing*, even if it was only in the US remake. "I actually think it would be really popular."

Lewis turned from the window, the sunlight catching his dark hair, his eyes almost the same cool blue as the sky behind him. "Yeah, but Charlie Alexander wants to make Faolán straight. The love triangle would have Amy, not Skye, at the apex."

"*What*?" Aaron fumbled the milk, almost dropping it. "You're joking."

"Nope."

"But that's bollocks. Sorry, but—Jesus Christ, they can't do that. That's outrageous!"

Lewis smiled, a quiet, rueful expression that relaxed his

face, softening him. He huffed out a grim laugh. "I knew you'd say that."

"But—Faolán's *gay*. That's a key element of his character. It's what makes his relationship with Skye so intense. It's what fans love about their dynamic."

Lewis lifted his hands, palms out. "Preaching to the choir. That's exactly what I told Toni."

"But surely she doesn't agree with Charlie?"

He let out a blustery sigh, shoved his hands into his pockets, and perched on the windowsill, watching Aaron.

"No, but she'd say this deal would be good for RPP, and a massive break for me personally. And she'd be right."

"But..." The idea of remaking *Leeches* with Faolán as a straight character hurt in a way Aaron struggled to articulate. It felt personal, like an attack on him, on everything the show meant to him. On his very identity. "They can't make you do it," he said, embarrassed by the emotion in his voice. "Can they?"

"No, they can't," Lewis said. "*Leeches* is my show."

But this deal could launch Lewis's career in the US, taking it to a whole new level.

The truth hung, unspoken, between them.

"Okay, look," Aaron said, crossing the kitchen to close some of the distance between them. "Why does Faolán have to be straight for there to be a love triangle? For God's sake, it's the twenty-first century. Half the fandom already thinks Skye and Faolán are shagging."

"Most viewers don't." Lewis stayed where he was, leaning against the windowsill. "Charlie says women—who are our key audience demographic—would be more invested in the storyline if Amy was at the centre. *And* he thinks the US audience is more conservative than the British and European ones, that they wouldn't accept a central same-sex relationship."

"Bollocks. There are loads of US shows that have same-sex

relationships, especially on streaming services." He folded his arms. "Maybe it's Charlie who's conservative?"

"Ha!" Lewis pushed away from the windowsill. "Wouldn't that be fucking ironic?"

Aaron gave a huff of laughter. "Just a little." Charlie was always banging on about being a champion of diversity. It was one his favourite topics to brag about on his awful YouTube channel. "Bloody hell," Aaron sighed. "This sucks."

"Yeah."

"What are you going to do?"

"I don't know. But Charlie wants to 'thought drench' it this weekend, whatever the fuck that means." He tunnelled his fingers into his hair, and Aaron watched, transfixed by the flex of muscles in his tanned forearms, by the silky fall of hair through his fingers. It was embarrassing how attractive Aaron found him, but, Christ, Lewis was a beautiful man. He and Mason had been dazzling together.

"Thanks for sense-checking me," Lewis said after a while, dropping his arms and looking up. "I always value your perspective."

"Any time."

Their gazes locked for a moment. Then Lewis turned away, heading over to the counter where the kettle was boiling. "You, ah, you're not really going on a date with Mason, are you?"

"Of course not." Christ, it was ridiculous to even consider the idea. "He was just trying to make you jealous. I doubt I'm actually his type."

Lewis flicked him a look. "Why not?"

"Hmm, maybe because he's a model? And I'm…" His face heated. "Anyway, he's not *my* type, either."

"Good." He poured water into the mug. "And, of course, you have Colin the Caterpillar."

"That's not—Please don't call him that."

"Why not? I think there's a striking resemblance. It's the nose."

"We're talking about Mason, not Colin," Aaron said evasively.

"If you're not going out with him, what more is there to talk about?"

"Maybe the fact that he doesn't seem to have accepted that you and he are finished? He wants to know 'why'."

Lewis scowled and rubbed his shoulder. "Why can't people just move the fuck on? First, Mason won't take my bloody obvious hints, and then, when I tell him in words of one syllable that it's over, he won't accept that either. What does he want now?"

Aaron considered that. Carefully, he ventured, "Mason's quite young, you know, and a bit spoiled. I think this is the first time in his life he's been the dumpee rather than the dumper, and he honestly doesn't understand why things ended between you."

Lewis sent him a sharp look. And well he might. This was straying into forbidden territory. For all the time they spent in each other's pockets, for all Lewis's teasing rudeness about Colin, and all their shared jokes, there were some things that they never spoke about—things they had silently agreed fell outside the boundaries of their close but carefully managed working relationship. Personal feelings were definitely one of those things.

At the very least, Aaron was getting uncomfortably close to that boundary.

After a pause, Lewis said, "What's to understand?" He turned to face Aaron, leaning his hip against the counter, displaying that fine, broad chest that constantly battled the confines of his shirt. Shrugging, he said, "We fucked a lot. And then we stopped. It was fun while it lasted, but… it was just sex."

Aaron kept his eyes fixed on Lewis's face, avoiding the

tantalising glimpse of tanned skin at the open collar of his shirt. "Yeah, well, not everyone sees sex that way. Mason clearly doesn't. So you need to explain it to him. He won't like it, but at least then he might understand and stop pestering you."

"Ugh." Lewis sighed in surrender. "Fine. I'll try to call him tonight. I thought we were both adults though, not angsty fucking teenagers who have to fucking *talk* about everything."

"Talking is actually the adult thing to do," Aaron said, smiling despite himself. After a pause he added lightly, "So is apologising." But he knew Lewis was practically allergic to the word *Sorry*. He'd far rather buy someone an expensive gift than make a simple apology to them. Especially if he didn't actually mean it. Lewis would say it was because he hated bullshit, but it was more than that. He hated dishonesty.

Lewis glared at Aaron but said nothing.

Aaron lifted an eyebrow. "And on that note, shall I put in ten minutes with Toni, so you can say sorry for yelling at her like that? Or shall I just go straight to HR and ask them to book you in for another *Appropriate Behaviour in the Workplace* session?"

"Bloody hell." Lewis turned back to the tea, fishing out the teabag and adding milk. "All right, stop nagging. I'll go and see Toni now."

"Good. Take her a coffee. And some cake."

"Where the hell am I going to find cake?"

"Grinder is two minutes away." Aaron snagged the tea before Lewis could add sugar, keeping it for himself. "She'd love a latte and a slice of Double Choc Fudge cake."

Lewis glowered at him. "You know, sometimes I wonder whether you know who the boss is around here."

"Oh," Aaron said, sipping his tea. "I know."

CHAPTER FIVE

Lewis

Lewis went straight to Toni's office when he got back from Grinder.

She looked at him over the top of her tortoiseshell cat's-eye glasses, her dark eyes cool. "Do you need something?"

"No," he replied shortly. "Just delivering this." He set down the brown paper bag on her desk.

She looked inside and drew out the carefully wrapped slice of cake. "Ooooh!" she said, rubbing her hands together. "Double Choc Fudge cake! Thank Aaron for me."

"I bloody bought it. You can thank me," Lewis complained, sinking into the chair in front of her desk.

She raised her eyebrows at him, and he sighed.

"Fine. Don't thank me. It's an apology." He scrubbed his hands over his face.

"Hmm." Her tone was sceptical. "I could argue with you about that, but it's a reasonable proxy for an apology, so I'll take it. Have you calmed down now?"

"Nope," he said, popping the 'p' extravagantly.

"You're going to have to before we go to Safehaven."

Lewis groaned. "Please don't call it that."

"Why not? That's its name"

"*Safehaven.*" Lewis rolled his eyes. "It was called Belchpark Manor when Charlie bought it, you know."

Toni laughed. "Was it? I didn't know that. I knew he changed the name. He told me he called it Safehaven because he wanted it to be a 'safe space where his guests could be their authentic selves'."

Lewis shook his head. "Safe's the last thing I feel in that hellhole."

Toni chuckled and swigged her coffee. "I know. He spouts all that shit and then turns around and tells us we need to make Faolán straight."

Lewis sighed. "Remind me why we're doing a US version."

"Because the money is amazing," she said. "And it's going get you known Stateside. That's the main reason you agreed, isn't it?"

Lewis gave a grunt of assent. Since he'd first started work in the industry, breaking into the US had been his dream, and this deal with Telopix could be his foot in the door.

"And it *will* be awesome," Toni continued. "They'll throw resources at this we could only dream of. Besides, Charlie's promised you'll get creative control—he swears you'll get final script approval on every episode."

"Come on, Toni. We're talking about Charlie Alexander here. By the time the contracts arrive, final approval will have been watered down to 'being consulted,' but the funding will already be in place, and the locations will be sorted and the actors cast, so we'll decide to go ahead anyway, and fucking Charlie will get *exactly* what he wants, just like he always does, because Telopix's money's too good to turn down."

Toni opened her mouth to respond, but then closed it again. They both knew what he said was probably true.

Charlie Alexander might act like an affable hipster, but the truth was, he was a great white shark in fucking tie-dye.

"Look, I get it," Lewis said wearily. "The money will be great—and it will be an amazing opportunity for me personally—but there are some things I *really* don't want to compromise on." He rubbed at the perennial sore spot between his neck and his right shoulder where the nerve pinched. He needed a decent massage.

"Okay," Toni said seriously, leaning back in her chair. "Let's talk about what you don't want to compromise on. Obviously, I get why you don't want to change Faolán's sexuality, and we can absolutely address that. For example, we could make him bi instead of straight."

"Toni…"

She held up her hand, acknowledging his protest. "*Or* we introduce another central gay character that can carry those storylines. But my question is whether your issue with the request goes deeper."

"Deeper than Charlie's plan to erase Faolán's fucking sexuality?"

"Deeper than a question of representation. You've always said that Skye's straight. That there's no canon UST between him and Faolán. From that point of view, Faolán's sexuality doesn't actually impact the story."

"I've always seen Skye as straight," Lewis conceded. "I never planned to get Faolán and Skye together romantically, but their relationship—their friendship—is still key to both characters."

In fact, when Claire, their development executive, had brought up the possibility of developing the 'bromance' a couple of years ago, he'd been adamant he'd never consider it. He'd given her a twenty-minute lecture on why the will-they-won't-they between Amy and Skye was a key pillar in the story structure and that making Skye and Faolán more than friends would undermine the integrity of that.

Even then, though, he'd been secretly aware that matters were not quite so clear-cut as they'd been when the show began. Over the last few years, he'd found Skye and Faolán's friendship increasingly compelling, to the point that, now, the idea of Faolán's attention switching from Skye to Amy felt utterly out of character. Wrong. Amy was like Faolán's *sister*, for God's sake.

"All right. So, it's not changing Faolán's sexuality *per se* that's the problem?" Toni suggested, once again displaying her witchy ability to read his mind. "It's the idea of his storyline being less focused on his relationship with Skye and more focused on his relationship with Amy."

He eyed her. "Go on."

She canted her head to the side. "How do you see Faolán's character?"

Lewis leaned back in his chair and thought. "I didn't intend him to become a major character when I introduced him," he said at last. "He wasn't even meant to last the season."

"Season three," Toni mused. "Yes, he was supposed to die after the cliff-hanger finale, wasn't he? When I saw that he'd survived the massacre in the early season four scripts, I thought, *Ah!*"

"Don't bury your gays," Lewis said softly. He was silent then for a few long moments. "The Skye and Faolán scenes just *worked*. Maybe it was partly the actors, but from early on, it felt like Faolán *got* Skye in a way no one else did, not even Amy. There's something about that relationship that's just special." He frowned, thinking. "Maybe it's that Faolán's the only one who ever criticises Skye, you know? Skye's so cocky that everyone thinks he's immune to disapproval, but..." He trailed off, then added honestly, "Maybe it's that I feel protective of that relationship dynamic. I don't want some clunky romance plotline taking Faolán's focus away from that."

"I get it," Toni said, smiling. "You don't want Skye to lose his only real friend. The only person who is unequivocally loyal to him."

Lewis blinked at her. Goddamned *witch*. How did she see stuff like that so easily?

"Can I just give you another perspective on this?" she said. "Just something to mull over."

Instinctively, he wanted to say no, but he didn't really have a choice. And he had to admit, Toni was good at stuff like this. "Okay."

"So, I know it's galling to have major changes imposed on your story, especially on important characters and their relationships, but one big issue we know we're going to have is that the US version will need a bunch of extra episodes. Charlie wants to keep the basic story structure and plotlines, but he's going to need more characters—and more drama between them—to fill those extra hours. From a totally practical perspective, a Skye-Amy-Faolán love triangle is a great solution for that."

"I didn't dispute that—"

"I know," Toni said, holding a hand up to silence him. "And another thing we both know is that, once you start outlining this, you can absolutely make this sing. Whether that's by working your magic to protect the stuff about the Skye-Faolán dynamic that's important to you, or whether that's by introducing a new character—who may be gay—to replicate that dynamic and letting Faolán develop in a different direction. Either way, I know one thing for sure: once you start, all you're going to care about is making the show as awesome as it can possibly be."

Lewis felt suddenly, stupidly emotional. A tightness seized his throat. He shrugged again. "Probably," he conceded gracelessly.

"So listen," Toni said, "my advice is this. Just let your mind turn all this stuff over for the next couple of days, and I'll do the same. And then, when we go to Safehaven or

Belchy Park or whatever it's called, we can have another brainstorm and see where we get to. Does that sound okay?"

He groaned. She'd outplayed him again. Planted a seed in his brain knowing full well he'd have no way of stopping it germinating and growing out of control between now and leaving for Safehaven.

And yeah, she was probably right about everything else too. While he still hated the idea, his reaction to Charlie's plan had been a bit knee-jerk, born of being told, too many times, that the audience—for which, read investors—weren't ready to see a romantic relationship between two male main characters on screen. Looking at it pragmatically, though, Faolán *was* just a character. A figment of Lewis's imagination. It wasn't even as if the same actor would be playing him in the US version—Charlie wanted a completely new American cast.

Not that Aaron would see it that way.

No, Aaron would fight this all the way, but then Aaron was an idealist—though not in a pie-in-the-sky way. He was fucking phenomenal at coming up with solutions when the script team boxed themselves into a corner.

"We could do with Aaron at Safehaven," he said idly. "He's fantastic at brainstorming."

Toni brightened. "You're right. Let's take him with us."

"No!" Lewis said, horrified. "I mean—that is, I didn't mean he should *actually come*."

Toni frowned. "Why not? It'll be good for him—and for you. I've taken Jason before. And like you say, Aaron's invaluable on script development. He knows the characters better than anyone. Plus, he can run interference between you and Charlie. You know how irritated you become, and Aaron's great at noticing when you're getting annoyed and stepping in without making it obvious."

Lewis blinked, faintly galled that she'd noticed that.

"So what's the problem?" Toni pressed.

Lewis chewed his lip. He couldn't think of one

goddamned thing he could say to excuse his reluctance. The truth was that taking Aaron on work trips was just one of those things that he made a point of never doing —like going for drinks after work or following Aaron on social media. It was all part of the buffer zone Lewis kept in place between them, a sort of intangible area of personal space that, by silent mutual consent, they did not breach.

Toni was frowning now. "You know, you can't keep holding him back forever. He's got a lot of potential."

"I know that!" Lewis said, stung. "I would never hold him back."

"But you don't exactly nurture his development, do you?"

"Of course I do."

Toni raised a single brow. "Then why isn't he trying for the script development role on *Bow Street*?"

"Because he doesn't want it," Lewis blurted, but his chest felt tight. "He's happy where he is."

"Are you sure? I'd have thought a historical would be right up his street. Maybe if I had a word with him—"

"Absolutely not." Lewis glared at her. "Stop trying to poach him."

Toni studied him over the rims of her glasses. "You can't keep him forever, Lewis. I'm not the only one who sees his potential."

He could, Lewis thought savagely, and he would. But he didn't say that to Toni. He just pointed at her, narrowed his eyes and hissed, "Hands. Off."

She chuckled. "All right. On condition you bring him to Safehaven."

Lewis scowled at her. "Fine," he gritted out.

But it wasn't fine. The prospect of spending a weekend with Aaron outside of the office was almost as alarming as the prospect of Toni poaching Aaron from under his nose.

Both left him feeling unsettled and out-of-sorts.

He brooded on that as he walked back down the corridor

to his own office. And then, for some reason, he found himself thinking about that moment when Mason had plastered himself to Aaron's side and the weird fury that had stirred in Lewis's gut at the sight. A fury that had absolutely nothing to do with Mason and everything to do with Aaron.

Lewis shook his head, frustrated at himself. It was Mason's fucking fault, pawing at Aaron like that. He'd made Lewis look at Aaron in that way that Lewis tried so very hard to avoid—as a man. A desirable man. Someone *Lewis* desired.

The trouble was, there was just something so very *appealing* about Aaron. Not in the glossy, impossibly beautiful Mason sort of way, but in a way all his own. While Mason spent a fortune on his sexy 'just got out of bed' hair, Aaron achieved the same result by simply never having time for a proper haircut. And while Mason enhanced the beauty of his green eyes by having his eyebrows threaded and his eyelashes dyed, Aaron's eyes needed no artificial assistance—they were bright and warm and mischievous in a way no one else's were. When Aaron looked at him, Lewis felt more *seen* than by anyone else. He felt like Aaron noticed everything about him. No, more than that, he felt like Aaron was *interested* in everything about him. As if he found Lewis endlessly fascinating. Probably everyone felt like that around Aaron, but even so, it made Lewis feel good. As did Aaron's kindness, because yes, Aaron wasn't just hot, he was a lovely, kind guy. A people person. Naturally generous. And those were qualities that were always attractive, even to a misanthrope like Lewis.

But attractive or not, Lewis couldn't allow himself to dwell on Aaron's charms.

For all the obvious reasons.

"Er, do you need something?"

Lewis blinked, only then realising that at some point he must have started walking again because he was now standing right in front of Aaron's desk.

Aaron watched him, fingers paused mid-type, eyebrows raised. "Because you're just sort of … lurking."

Feeling stupidly flustered, Lewis said, "I was *thinking*." He waved his hand airily, to convey that it was a writerly thing. "But now that you ask—"

"I don't have time to fetch you lunch," Aaron said, going back to work. "Not if you want these script notes before the meeting. Also, Dot's waiting in your office. She needs a word."

Lewis groaned. Dot Thomas was head of finance and a constant thorn in Lewis's side, always wanting to go over budgets and spreadsheets that made Lewis's head ache. "What does she want now?"

Aaron shrugged without looking away from his screen. "She didn't say."

Lewis felt a small stab of annoyance over Aaron not looking at him. He frowned.

After a moment, he said, "You'll be pleased to know I don't need you to fetch my lunch. Look." He held up his own bag from Grinder, only belatedly realising that he should probably have brought Aaron something back too. He'd been rude to him as well this morning, hadn't he? Crap. He never thought of these things until it was too late or until Aaron pointed them out.

Not that Aaron seemed particularly bothered. "Great," he said, glancing up briefly before returning his gaze to his computer screen.

Lewis remembered then that there was something he needed to mention to Aaron. Awkwardly, he cleared his throat. "Actually, I… need to ask you something."

"Oh yes?" Aaron said, his fingers drumming out words even as his eyes scanned his handwritten notes.

Lewis cleared his throat, his gut already twisting unpleasantly. "I was wondering—that is, Toni and I were wondering

—whether you could come with us to Charlie Alexander's place this weekend?"

Aaron's fingers stilled on his keyboard. Slowly, he looked up, and their eyes met. Then he blinked. "You want me to… come to Safehaven? With you?"

"And Toni," Lewis said quickly. "She'll be there, too. Actually, it was her suggestion." Something in Aaron's grey eyes went flat at that comment, and Lewis found himself adding stupidly, "Though we both want you there, of course. To brainstorm with us." He paused, then said roughly, "So, are you up for it?"

Aaron was still staring at him. And so was Jason, whose head had popped up above his screen like a fucking meerkat as soon as Lewis started talking.

"It'll be work, so I'll sort out overtime pay if you can make it," Lewis added. That comment was mainly for Jason's benefit, to avoid any misunderstandings as to why he was asking Aaron along. Not to mention the fact that Jason was a bit of a self-appointed shop steward at RPP.

Aaron was quiet for a few moments. Then he said, "Actually, I do sort of have plans this weekend."

Lewis should have felt relieved, but… he didn't.

Not at all.

Perhaps it was because he'd just assumed Aaron would agree to come—he usually fell in with Lewis's requests without complaint.

Suddenly, all Lewis could think about were the reasons that it would be good to have Aaron there. He'd back Lewis up when Toni wanted to give way to Charlie's demands, and he'd come up with smart workarounds for any problems they encountered. But most of all, he'd understand how Lewis felt when he was at Safehaven. Because Lewis *loathed* it there. Every time he went, he ended up surrounded by a bunch of posh arseholes swanning about with their half-chewed silver spoons hanging out their mouths.

A pulse of angry irritation swept through him, fuelled by the mortifying self-knowledge that he just… didn't want to face it alone again. Toni was fine, but she fitted in with them. She might not be in Charlie Alexander's league, but she'd gone to the right sort of school and had her Oxbridge degree. She didn't understand the true depths of Lewis's discomfort. Not really.

But Aaron would. If he would just fucking agree to come.

Even as he recognised that his irritation was unreasonable, the words tumbled out of his mouth. "For fuck's sake, can't Colin polish his own football boots for once?"

Aaron's eyes widened, his cheeks pinking. "Actually, Colin—"

"No." Lewis held up a hand to cut him off as his stomach pinched again in that annoying way. "Don't. I have zero interest in your tedious boyfriend's tedious plans. Less than zero. Negative interest."

Unreasonable or not, he hated fucking Colin. At the last two office Christmas parties, he'd been forced to make small talk with the man and had almost fallen asleep. Colin was *the* most boring human on the face of the planet. His only interests were football, cars, and fucking protein shakes. Subjects upon which he could wax lyrical until your ears bled. God only knew what Aaron saw in him. Couldn't be the conversation, so it must be the sex. And that thought only pissed Lewis off more. Frankly, the very concept of Colin pissed him off.

Of course, Jason, the little suck-up, chose that moment to jump in. "Oh, come on," he said. "Colin can be quite a laugh sometimes."

Lewis snorted. "Really? Since when?"

Ignoring him, Aaron said, "Thanks, Jase. But I know Colin was a bit… well, *staid* for the RPP crowd."

Jason's eyebrows rose. "What do you mean 'was'?"

"Er…" Aaron rubbed awkwardly at the back of his neck,

darting a quick look at Lewis then back at Jason. "Colin and I kind of split up. He moved out a couple of weeks ago."

"No!" Jason slapped a hand over his mouth in horror.

A jolt of something electric shot through Lewis, shocking him right to his marrow. Pleasure, he realised as his lips curled into an irrepressible smile.

No, *triumph.*

Which didn't make a lot of sense until he made the obvious connection that, with Colin out of the way, Aaron would have a lot more time for *him*. Specifically, more time for him this weekend. At Safehaven.

Thank fuck.

"Things hadn't been right for a while," Aaron was telling Jason. "I suppose we just grew apart. It wasn't really anyone's fault..."

"Either way," Lewis said, delving into the lunch bag for his sandwich—it was his favourite: white bread, butter, ham, nothing else—"it's excellent news."

He was about to take a bite when he realised that Aaron was staring at him. And not in a good way. "You know," Aaron said tartly, "most people would say something like, '*I'm really sorry to hear that. Are you okay?*'"

"Would they?" He shrugged. "Well, I'm not sorry to hear it because Colin was a boring prick. And you're obviously okay." He waved the sandwich at Aaron, who appeared as perky and wholesome as always. "I mean, look at you."

Warily, Aaron glanced down at himself, then back at Lewis. "Colin and I were together for almost two years," he said. "We lived together for one of them. That's a long time to be with someone."

"No shit," Lewis said, with feeling. "I can't believe it took you so long to dump him. What a waste of two years."

Beneath his breath, Jason muttered, "Christ on a pogo stick...."

Lewis glared at him, then turned his attention to Aaron.

He wasn't sure what he'd been expecting. An eye roll, perhaps. A sigh, or a tut. Perhaps a swallowed smile and a flicker of amusement. It certainly wasn't the tight look that dimmed the brightness in Aaron's eyes or the way he turned back to his computer and coolly said, "Dot's waiting for you, and she has a meeting at two, so you should probably get in there."

Damn. Had he hurt Aaron's feelings? Frowning, he tried to run over his last few comments in his head, but he was distracted by the unhappy line of Aaron's mouth and his determinedly averted gaze.

And fucking Jason giving him the evil eye.

Aaron tapped away on his keyboard for a moment, and when Lewis didn't leave, he looked up and said tightly, "Was there something else?"

The hint of challenge in his voice made Lewis pause warily. Clearing his throat, he said, "Yes, there was—*is*—something else. We'll need a car tomorrow morning. Buggered if I'm driving up there myself. Send one to my place for half-seven, will you? We have to be at Safehaven by ten, and we'll need time to pick you and Toni up as well."

Aaron held his gaze. "I haven't actually agreed to go yet."

"Yeah, but you will, won't you? I wouldn't have asked if I didn't really need you there, Aaron. Please." Their shared look lingered, becoming uncomfortably intense. Lewis broke it, turning away with a shrug. "After all, you won't have to watch Colin dribble his way around the football pitch on Saturday morning." When Aaron's brows drew together in annoyance, Lewis added in a wheedling tone, "And if you don't come, who'll stop me from drowning Charlie Alexander in one of his awful fucking cocktails?"

Finally, Aaron's lips twitched with a reluctant smile. For several long heartbeats, he seemed to be thinking. Then, at last, he sighed. "Fine. I'll order a car."

Lewis resisted the urge to punch the air in triumph.

"Thank you," he said quietly, but as he turned away from Aaron's desk, his face broke out into an irrepressible smile, the weekend suddenly a far less horrifying prospect than it had been just a few minutes earlier. "Oh, and pack something half-decent to wear," he said over his shoulder. "Charlie will probably have one of his godawful dinner parties on Saturday night."

His buoyant mood sank as soon as he noticed Dot Thomas leaning in his office doorway, one perfectly sculpted eyebrow lifted in a disapproving expression he knew all too well, a sheaf of papers in her hand.

"Lewis," she said, stepping aside and inviting him in with a sweep of her arm. "A word?"

He sighed, took a big bite of his sandwich, and followed her inside.

CHAPTER SIX

Aaron

Since he was giving up his weekend, Aaron felt justified in buggering off at six on the dot that evening. He had plans—his fortnightly meetup with Janvi and their small group of real-life *Leeches* friends—and for once he'd actually like to arrive on time.

Before he left, he poked his head around Lewis's door and found him, feet up on his desk, chewing the end of a red pen as he marked up a script.

"Hey. Anything you need before I go?"

Lewis glanced up. "Hmm?"

"I'm heading out. Do you need anything before I go?" He hoped the fact that he already had his jacket on, messenger bag slung across his body, would be a hint. Not that Lewis was particularly adept at taking hints.

"Oh." Lewis frowned, and those two perfectly symmetrical little creases that Aaron found annoyingly sexy appeared between his dark brows. "I don't think so," he said vaguely. "What time is it?"

"Six. I emailed you the amended notes on Ryan's script

and the updated pitch for *Leeches*: USA. Also, there's a chicken salad sandwich in the fridge, in case you're staying late. I put your name on it, so Ray won't 'accidentally' snag it."

"Great. Thanks." Lewis swung his feet off the desk and sat up, reaching one hand behind him to rub at that niggly bit between his neck and shoulder. Aaron had noticed earlier it was bothering him again.

"I'll sort you out an appointment with Amanda for your neck for Monday."

Lewis's sudden grateful smile made Aaron's stomach turn over—it really wasn't fair that he looked that good smiling *and* frowning.

"Thanks," Lewis said gruffly. After a pause, he added, "Um, listen, I appreciate you giving up your weekend. I really am glad you're coming; it'll be so much easier with you there."

"It's okay. I mean, it's work. It's not like I won't get paid extra, right?"

"Right." Lewis nodded firmly. "Exactly. It's work."

But he looked tired and rumpled, and for some stupid reason, Aaron suddenly wished he could take that last comment back. Which was ridiculous because Lewis had already mentioned overtime pay, and it wasn't as though he would imagine Aaron was going to Safehaven with him just to help him out. He wouldn't even *want* that; their relationship was strictly professional, after all.

Just then, Lewis groaned and rolled his neck. "This fucking shoulder," he muttered irritably.

The movement drew Aaron's attention to his strong throat, his broad shoulders, the tight fit of his shirt across his chest. He was gripped by a sudden, visceral desire to cross the office and put his hands on Lewis's tense shoulders, to feel their powerful contours beneath his palms, and to lean down until his mouth touched the dark scruff on his jaw, his lush lips…

Shit.

Jolting himself out of the daydream, cheeks hot, he croaked, "Well, I'll be off then."

After an awkward pause, where Lewis looked like he might be about to say more, but didn't, Aaron added, "See you tomorrow. Car's booked. It's picking me up first. Should get to yours for seven-thirty. Oh, and don't forget to call Mason tonight."

Lewis grimaced. "Fine. I'll see you tomorrow. Casual dress, by the way. Charlie wants us to be our authentic fucking selves."

"What if my authentic fucking self wants to wear a suit? Or a top hat and tails?"

Lewis grinned, dimples flashing, as sudden and transformative as the sun burning through storm clouds. "You want to wear a top hat and tails," he said, "knock yourself out. I wouldn't mind seeing that."

And Aaron's foolish heart tripped over itself, just like it always did when they skirted those invisible lines they'd drawn in the sand. "Maybe next time," he said. "My top hat's at the dry cleaners."

They said goodnight after that, and Aaron headed out of the office smiling at the exchange. Coaxing a grin out of Lewis always felt like a triumph.

Unfortunately, he found Jason lurking by the lifts, jacket on and waiting for him with a look on his face that suggested he meant business. Aaron smiled, bracing himself, and no sooner had the lift doors shuddered shut behind them than Jason said, "You do *not* have to go to Safehaven. Lewis Hunter does not own your weekends."

Aaron sighed. In truth, weekend working *was* part of his job. Granted, this was the first time it had ever been outside the office, but wherever it was, he'd get paid—well paid—for it. The other truth, one he'd never admit to Jason, or even to Janvi, was that he enjoyed being in Lewis's orbit, enjoyed seeing him in action, and being part of that action. Being needed by someone as vibrant and alive as Lewis Hunter was addictive. It made *him* feel alive, too.

He said, "I honestly don't mind."

"I thought you had plans."

He *did* have plans. But those plans were mostly to finish posting *We Are All Creatures of the Night*, to catch up on replying to the comments on the earlier chapters, and then to start work on the new idea circling his brain: *what if Faolán got a boyfriend?* A normal, human boyfriend. An all-around nice guy who was good for him. What would Skye do then? Admit his feelings? Scare off the boyfriend? Or decide that Faolán was better off without him, better off with a normal life and out of the fight? Of course, Faolán would never be better off without Skye, and the nice-guy boyfriend might turn out to be hired by the Family to—

"Toni wouldn't pressurise you into giving up your time like that." Jason jabbed the ground floor button. "She's a *great* boss. A great mentor. And she thinks you have potential as a script writer."

Aaron shook his head, smiling. *Everyone loves a trier.* "Yeah, you've mentioned that once or twenty times," he said. "Just like I've mentioned I'm happy working for Lewis. Anyway, I've never been to Safehaven. I kind of want to see whether it lives up to the hype. Or, down to it."

Jason wavered. "It *is* an experience," he conceded. "And the food is... memorable." Then, in a softer tone, he said, "Hey, by the way, I'm really sorry about you and Colin. I thought you guys were golden."

Golden? Hardly, although Aaron supposed he'd worked hard to make it appear so. Especially at work, especially in front of Lewis. He said, "Thanks, but it's fine. It was kind of mutual."

"Kind of?"

"Well. I mean, technically, I broke things off, but he wasn't exactly surprised or heartbroken." He shrugged. "You know how it goes. Sometimes, relationships just drift on when they should have ended ages ago."

Jason nodded. "Yeah," he said, although Aaron doubted that he did know. Jason and Liu had been together since uni, had got married last year, and were excitedly expecting their first child.

At their wedding, Colin had taken Aaron's hand during the vows and squeezed hard, giving Aaron a meaningful smile. And Aaron…

Aaron had imagined Skye and Faolán at the altar, wondering what they'd wear, how they'd say their vows. 'Till death do us part' takes on a different meaning when one partner is immortal. Later, he'd framed a 50k-word fic around the wedding, which had ended with Faolán forcing Skye to turn him so that death would never part them. *Death Do Us Part* got a fantastic response and won the Best-Angst category in that year's Skylán fic awards.

"You need to be careful," Jason said. "Or you're going to get stuck."

"Stuck?" He glanced around the lift.

"Doing this. You're what? Twenty-five?"

Aaron grimaced. "Twenty-seven."

"Well, then. Do you want to be a PA your whole life?"

Truly, Aaron didn't know. As much as he enjoyed his job, what he enjoyed most about it was working with Lewis. But in terms of what he produced, the work that mattered most to him, that provided him with the deepest satisfaction, was his writing. And sharing his writing with the *Leeches* fan community. Of course, Jason wouldn't understand that. Most people didn't.

Feebly, he said, "There's more to life than work."

Jason dismissed the cliché with the disdain it deserved.

"You need to ask yourself why you're staying in this job," he said, watching the numbers on the lift as they made their juddery descent. "And whether it's a good enough reason."

Aaron studied him, took in the uncomfortable jut of Jason's jaw, the way he was purposely not making eye contact, and his stomach pinched. Shit, did Jason *know*? Was Aaron's weird obsession with Lewis obvious? He forced an unconvincing laugh. "Are you saying Lewis's charming personality isn't a good enough reason?"

As the doors opened, and they walked out into reception, Jason said, "Loyalty's one thing, Aaron. But if you don't move up now, you might never move at all."

Aaron didn't have anything to say about that because Jason was right. Of course he was bloody right. But the idea of leaving Lewis… Even the thought left him winded, and he was sharply reminded of Mason's plaintive words that morning: *when he's gone, he leaves quite a gap*. Lewis and Mason had only been together for a month. Aaron had been with Lewis for three years.

Once they were outside, they paused, standing a little awkwardly together, and Jason reached over and squeezed Aaron's shoulder. "Just think about it, yeah? It'd be a really good move for you. I'd hate to see you miss your shot."

"I will." He nodded, trying to look sincere. "Thanks, Jase."

With that, they parted. Jason strode towards the bus stop, and Aaron headed for the tube, turning Jason's words over in his mind as he walked.

Part of him knew that he should go for the script development role, that he'd be good at it and would enjoy it. Those late-night sessions with Lewis, doctoring scripts or brainstorming story ideas, was the most fun he had at work, and working on the *Bow Street* pilot would be a fantastic opportunity to use that experience and develop further. But whenever he imagined leaving his job, leaving Lewis and *Leeches*, a larger part of him recoiled. Just thinking about someone else doing his job—someone else benefitting from Lewis's extraordinary creative energy—left him feeling angry and resentful.

Sometimes people told Aaron they thought he was a saint for putting up with Lewis, marvelling at his patience and his ability to tolerate Lewis's moods. They didn't seem to see Lewis's good points. How passionate he was, how talented and creative. How he charged the very particles in the air around him with that creativity, making everything more exciting, more interesting, more energetic… just *more*. Aaron didn't care about Lewis's grumpiness—that was just a surface-level thing anyway, Lewis's way of dealing with anyone or anything that got between him and what he was trying to achieve. Because Lewis was single-minded. Absolutely focused on what he was trying to achieve.

If Aaron and Lewis stopped working together, Aaron would miss that.

He could envisage exactly how it would play out. Once they were in different parts of the building, working on different projects, their interactions would inevitably dwindle to quick hellos as they passed in the corridor or awkward catchups at the Christmas party.

Aaron frowned, not liking the thought. Not liking the way it made his stomach clench and his chest ache. And not wanting to examine why he felt that way. Shoving the thoughts back into their box, he slammed shut the lid and began to walk more quickly.

His spirits rose as he hurried down the steps into the underground, swept along by the great throng of people heading home or out for a night on the town. Now wasn't the time to be agonising over his future. He had a night out with friends to look forward to, and after that a weekend with Lewis Hunter at a multimillionaire's country estate.

All in all, life was pretty bloody good.

Tomorrow could take care of itself.

CHAPTER SEVEN

Lewis

Lewis didn't call Mason that night. He meant to do it, but the thought of the inevitable questions that would follow practically brought him out in hives. Even if he did manage to spit out some kind of acceptable reason, Mason would start trying to analyse what he said, and he'd end up being rude. Instead, he arranged to send an expensive arrangement of flowers with a brief but clear explanation that—considering he was a writer—took him an embarrassingly long time to compose.

"That's the message?" the woman on the phone said when he gave her the order. She sounded disapproving.

"That's it," Lewis confirmed.

She read it back to him. *"I enjoyed our time together, but I don't want to take things any further with you, so we should both move on now. Have a great life. L."* There was an uncomfortable pause, and when the woman spoke again, her voice was distinctly frosty. "Is that correct?"

"Yup."

What more was there to say? Mason wanted to know 'why'? Well, that was the reason. The words were blunt, and certainly not the most elegant he'd ever written, but they were true.

The woman *hmmmd*. It sounded like a judgmental sort of *hmm* to Lewis, and a pulse of embarrassed resentment ran through him. What was the point in sugar-coating it? The message would be the same in the end. Besides, it wasn't his fault Mason was being so difficult to shrug off. Aaron was right about one thing: Lewis needed to be crystal-clear with the guy if he wanted Mason to stop pestering him.

After he had the flower order sorted, he shovelled down a microwaved pasta thing for dinner, then got back to work. By the time he finished his markup on the script, it was midnight, and his shoulder was throbbing. He didn't feel the least bit tired, though, despite having gone into the office early. The Amy-Skye-Faolán triangle was an insidious itch at the back of his mind that wouldn't let him alone. He couldn't stop thinking about it. Or about the looming weekend at Safehaven.

Or the fact that Aaron was going to be there.

He needed to get some sleep, but he felt restless and wired. Even a long, hot shower and a wank didn't help.

A drink was what he needed, he decided, padding through to the kitchen in his underwear. He opened a bottle of wine, grabbed a glass, and took them through to the living room.

Deciding that some music might help distract him, he shuffled through the vinyls in his record box, finally settling on a Dolly Parton album. Carefully taking it out of its sleeve, he set it on the turntable and dropped the needle. The speakers hissed and crackled as the needle passed over years-old scratches, and then the music started.

The album had been his mum's. Owen had let him have all her vinyls. There weren't that many. Dolly, ABBA, Culture Club, Whitney Houston, some old hits collections from the seventies and eighties. Nothing that really went together, just a random selection of stuff that she'd liked or that someone else had thought she might like. She'd definitely liked Dolly. He remembered her playing those ones a lot, and singing along.

Settling on the sofa, he tried to let the music do its thing of chasing his tangled thoughts away, but it wasn't working tonight. His body relaxed, but the itch in his brain wouldn't let up. Toni had been right earlier. Faolán's relationship with Skye *was* important to him. He just couldn't put his finger on why, and it was a thought he couldn't let go of.

He let both sides of the record play out and drank most of the bottle of wine, but eventually, he couldn't resist any longer. He grabbed a spiral notebook off the coffee table and started scribbling notes, a twisting, tumbling stream of consciousness about Skye and Faolán and all the threads that connected them. It was only once he'd begun pouring all of it out onto the page that the tension began to leave him. But even then, he still felt that he was missing something. Something important that he needed to get straight before he started brainstorming with Toni and Aaron tomorrow. Something that would help him explain to Aaron the compromises that needed to be made.

At some point, he realised his eyelids were finally drooping over his hot, gritty eyes, and then, quite suddenly, he was overwhelmed by a dragging wave of tiredness that had him yanking the sofa throw off the back of the couch, pulling it over himself, and finally falling into an exhausted sleep.

~

He woke to the sound of someone hammering on his front door.

Confused, he blinked, then lurched upright, only then realising where he was. "What the—?"

The hammering started again.

"All right!" he yelled. "I'm coming." Stumbling off the sofa, he immediately tripped over the throw tangled around his legs and sent the open bottle of red wine on the floor flying. He didn't think he'd left much in there… but it looked a lot when it was sprayed all over a cream mohair rug.

"*Fuck*!"

More hammering.

Cursing, he tore his gaze away from the horror of the rug and stalked to the front door which he yanked open violently. "What the fuck do you—?" he began, before breaking off and saying stupidly, "Aaron?"

And then it came back to him—Safehaven, the weekend, the car that Aaron had booked.

"Shit, I'm sorry," he said. "I only got to sleep a few hours ago—bad night. Am I late?"

Aaron was staring at him in what appeared to be stunned silence. His mouth was open, but no sound came out, and his grey gaze was fixed on Lewis's chest.

Sudden colour flooded Aaron's cheeks, and unbidden, Lewis's cock stirred, taking interest.

Shit. They hadn't even left London yet, and already lines were being crossed.

"Um, Aaron," he croaked.

Aaron's gaze shot up, his expression guilty, cheeks pink. "What? Sorry—I mean, yes, you're late. The car got here ten minutes ago. I tried your phone, but it must be off. We're supposed to be picking up Toni at eight."

"Shit, I switched my phone off last night," Lewis said, turning around to shield his swelling crotch, in case Aaron's gaze dipped again. "Come in and text Toni while I get dressed and pack a bag."

Aaron sighed, but he followed Lewis inside, already tapping at his phone.

"Yikes," he said when they got into the living room. "What happened in here? Was there a murder?"

"Wine bottle," Lewis muttered. "I kicked the fucking thing over when I jumped up to answer the door. I better quickly clean it—"

Aaron interrupted, tucking his phone into his pocket. "Go and get dressed. I'll sort this out."

Lewis's gut twisted uncomfortably. "You shouldn't have to do that."

"I know," Aaron said. "But honestly, I'd do it for anyone else in this situation, and you don't get special treatment, okay?"

Lewis had strategically positioned himself so that his crotch was out of sight, but it didn't matter. Aaron seemed to be carefully avoiding looking at him now, studying the rug with close attention.

"Okay," Lewis said. "Kitchen's just through there. Do you want—I don't know, salt or something? Isn't that meant to help?"

"That's a myth," Aaron said promptly. "Lots of water's what we need."

"You sound like you know what you're talking about," Lewis replied. "Did you used to have a cleaning job?"

"No, but I've spilt quite a few glasses of red wine in my time," Aaron said, walking past him towards the kitchen. He made a shooing motion at Lewis. "Go and get dressed."

Lewis obeyed, heading off to his bedroom, where he quickly dressed, efficiently packed a weekend bag, and stuck a nice suit in a garment bag in case he needed it—you never knew at Safehaven. Tonight, they might be offered a seven-course tasting menu with a flight of wines, or they might be invited to forage berries for dinner before spending the evening squashed inside Charlie's sweat lodge talking about auras.

Neither was appealing, truth to tell.

When he returned to the living room, he was confronted with the far too provocative sight of Aaron on his hands and knees, his very nice arse in the air as he rubbed energetically at the rug—a rug which now appeared to be soaking wet but amazingly white again.

Aaron looked over his shoulder at Lewis and grinned. "Better?"

Lewis's cock said an enthusiastic *yes* to that, hardening rapidly in his jeans while he swallowed against an inappropriate desire to *growl*. Instead, he held the garment bag over his crotch, cleared his throat, and said, "Um—yes. You were right about the water for sure. One hundred per cent."

Aaron got to his feet, then bent to pick up the cloth and bowl he'd been using. "You should hang it up somewhere to dry off while you're away," he said over his shoulder, heading for the kitchen again.

"On it," Lewis replied, setting down his bags, hoisting up the damp rug and carrying it into the dining room, where he arranged it over the back of three chairs.

Aaron joined him a few moments later with an armful of towels which they laid down to catch the drips, working together seamlessly, no need for words.

"Thanks," Lewis said sincerely when it was done. "What would I do without you?"

"Oh, wither away and die, I expect," Aaron said dryly. "Come on. Let's go and get Toni."

An hour later, Lewis watched as Toni climbed into the Mercedes people carrier Aaron had arranged and settled herself into one of the comfortable seats opposite Lewis. The car was pretty good: spacious with big seats and collapsible tables that could be pulled out so he could easily write without having to balance his laptop on his knees.

"Sorry we're late," Lewis said as the car pulled away from the curb. "Needless to say, it's my fault."

"I don't doubt it," Toni said wryly. "Where's Aaron?"

"He got the driver to drop him off at a coffee shop two minutes down the road that he says does good breakfast stuff. I'm supposed to find out what you want and text him."

Toni smiled happily. "Ooh, lovely! That lad is a treasure. Almond croissant and a latte, please."

Lewis fired off the text.

"It's about two and a half hours to Charlie's place," Toni said. "We should be able to get a decent bit of brainstorming done on the love triangle idea before we get there."

Lewis frowned. "Yeah, about that…"

"What?"

He wrinkled his nose. "Can we not talk about it in front of Aaron just yet?"

Toni looked confused. "What? But that's why he's here, isn't it? Besides, you talk about everything in front of Aaron."

"I know. It's just he's not going to like it and—" He let out a long breath, struggling to articulate the weird sense of disloyalty he felt at entertaining an idea Aaron so vociferously opposed.

"Oh right, I get it," Toni said, her tone sympathetic. "You don't want him to talk you out of it before you've talked yourself in, is that it?"

"Something like that. I just need to turn it over in my own mind a bit more, you know?"

"I get it," Toni said. "Anyway, we've got plenty of other stuff to talk about, especially since I missed the meeting yesterday. How did it go with Ryan?"

Lewis sighed, and Toni's brows went up. "Not well?"

He made a face. "He's a good writer."

"But…"

Lewis opened his mouth to answer, but the car had begun

to slow again, and he realised they'd already reached the coffee shop.

"I'll pop in and see if Aaron needs a hand," Lewis said. "Back in a mo'."

There was a queue of customers waiting at the counter inside, at the head of which stood Aaron, giving his order. He was laughing at something the tattooed barista was saying, and the guy was grinning back. The barista was young, maybe early twenties. Jobbing actor, probably; Lewis could spot them a mile off. He looked like he'd had his teeth recently bleached because they were a bit too white, on the edge of ridiculous really, but he was so hot that he kind of carried it off.

Lewis felt a bolt of irritation.

What was the guy grinning about anyway?

He stomped past the waiting queue, stopping at Aaron's shoulder.

"Hey," he said to Aaron, even as he eyed the barista suspiciously. The guy was wearing a nametag that said, somewhat confusingly, "Tag".

Aaron whirled around. "Oh! It's you," he said. "You made me jump." He tucked his company credit card back in his wallet. Technically, he wasn't eligible for a credit card, but Lewis had insisted he be given one because he needed to pay for stuff for Lewis all the time.

"Of course it's me," Lewis said tightly. "Who else would it be?"

Had Aaron forgotten he existed? The thought made him scowl.

The scowl only seemed to amuse Aaron, so Lewis directed it at Tag instead. Annoyingly, Tag didn't notice. He was too busy scribbling something on a piece of paper which he handed to Aaron. A receipt.

"My number's on the back," Tag said, winking. "I better

get back to serving now. Your order will be at the end of the counter in a couple of minutes, okay?"

Aaron smiled and shook his head in a sort of *Don't you ever give up?* way. "Thanks, and like I said, I'll think about it."

"That's all I ask," Tag said cheerfully as they moved away towards the other side of the shop. "You know where I am."

"Think about what?" Lewis hissed, while Aaron grabbed sachets of sugar, salt, and sauces from the station at the end of the counter.

"What? Oh, he asked me to go for a drink with him."

Lewis frowned. "Do you know him?"

"Not really, just to say hello. He's auditioned a couple of times for RPP projects, and Colin and I used to come in here sometimes."

"So, what, Tag's been hanging around all this time waiting for his chance with you?" Lewis demanded. He was vaguely aware that he sounded outraged on Colin's behalf.

Aaron plainly thought that was as weird as Lewis did. His brow scrunched up in confusion. "I doubt it, but apparently, Colin was in here the other day with—Well, with someone else."

"Hmmm," Lewis said. "Didn't take *him* long."

Aaron shot him an odd look—as well he might. Lewis was coming off like some sort of Victorian maiden aunt.

"It was after the breakup," Aaron said, shrugging. "Besides, it's fine. If Colin has someone else, I'm happy for him. He likes being coupled up."

"And you don't?" Lewis heard himself say the words almost as though it was someone else speaking. What was he thinking asking something so personal? They never talked about stuff like this.

"Um, well," Aaron prevaricated. "I'm not really sure, to be honest. I had my first boyfriend at uni, and that lasted three years, then a break, then Colin. I might need to play the field a bit to find out what it is I like." He gave an oddly breathless little laugh. "I should probably call Tag, shouldn't I? At least that would be a start."

No, Lewis wanted to say. *You shouldn't.*

Instead, he waited until another employee bustled up to the counter with Aaron's order and started setting down paper bags and drinks and offering cutlery and napkins. He waited until Aaron was good and distracted before he leaned in and said quickly, "Can I see that receipt for a sec?"

Aaron, busy confirming that, yes, he would like a drinks tray, unthinkingly pulled the receipt out of his pocket and handed it to Lewis without pausing. Lewis pretended to check it, then crumpled it in his fist.

"Shall I grab the hot drinks?" he asked before Aaron could remember to ask for the receipt back.

Aaron—who was trying to balance two bottles of water, a large freshly squeezed orange juice, a half dozen paper bags containing breakfast sandwiches and pastries, and a tub of yoghurt and granola—smiled gratefully.

"That would be great. Thanks."

"No worries," Lewis said, lifting the tub of yoghurt and granola from its precarious position on top of the pile of paper bags Aaron was carrying and settling it into a gap on the drinks tray. "Let's go."

As they left the coffee shop, he dropped the receipt in the bin.

CHAPTER EIGHT

Aaron

"Jesus!" Aaron exclaimed when they swept round the final bend of the drive and he got his first glimpse of Safehaven. "It's not small, is it?"

He'd expected a pretty English manor house with some nice gardens, but this was something else. The grounds were extensive—they'd passed through the security gate a good half mile back—and the house itself was huge. Huge and very square. Two great square towers on either side of a square entrance, and all of it in red brick with mullioned windows.

It looked surprisingly formal and forbidding, considering how very informal the man standing on the drive waiting to greet them was.

Charlie Alexander wore baggy green harem pants, an orange vest, and a multicoloured Fair Isle cardigan. His feet were bare, and his dirty blond hair was pulled back into a messy bun. He was practically bouncing.

Lewis sighed, and Toni said quietly. "It's just two nights. This too shall pass." Unclipping her seatbelt, she climbed out and stepped forward to greet Charlie with air kisses and a big smile.

Lewis climbed out after her, and Aaron brought up the rear.

Once Charlie had greeted Toni, he stepped forward to grasp Lewis's hand.

"Lewis, glad you could make it," he said in that way the very rich had of sounding both sincere and indifferent. Then he nodded at the Mercedes and added, "But did you have to come in the gas guzzler? There's a train station ten minutes away."

Aaron itched to point out that Charlie had a helipad at the side of the house and had flown in from the US for the weekend. He pressed his lips together to stop any words escaping.

"It's electric," Lewis said. His tone was mild, but Aaron heard the faint note of irritation in it and wondered whether Lewis would be able to keep his temper at bay for the whole weekend. It wasn't his strongest suit, but RPP needed to keep Telopix sweet. In this case, keeping Telopix sweet meant keeping Charlie Alexander sweet: he'd be the one green-lighting the *Leeches*: USA deal. Aaron wasn't sure how close the deal was to completing, but things were definitely heating up, and although neither Lewis nor Toni had given much away on the drive here, it was obvious this weekend was important.

It didn't help that Charlie was an insufferable prick who presented himself as a chilled-out hipster when he was really a complete control freak who always expected to get his own way.

"Andy, isn't it?" Charlie said to Aaron, his head cocked to one side in query.

"Aaron," he corrected shortly.

"Aaron, right. Like the great Sorkin." Charlie grinned at him and slapped his shoulder, and Aaron smiled stiffly.

Charlie was one of those almost-but-not-quite-good-looking men. Everything about him was just a little average. A little *medium*. On the two or three occasions he'd come into the office to see Lewis, he'd always seemed to Aaron to be trying to make up for that somehow, with his overbearing manner and his ridiculously pretentious outfits.

Aaron suspected that deep down Charlie knew he could never hope to measure up to Lewis, who oozed raw talent and driving energy without even trying.

It turned out there really were some things money couldn't buy—and for all his bonhomie, Charlie resented that.

"Is anyone else coming this weekend?" Toni asked.

"Just Mils and Geoff," Charlie replied, turning back to Toni. Mils—or Milly as everyone else called her—was some kind of executive at Telopix, though she didn't seem to have any recognisable role or particular responsibilities. She and Charlie were both from wealthy families—in Milly's case, a titled one—and had attended the same exclusive private boarding school when they were kids. Toni had told him that Milly and Charlie had been romantically involved for a few years. That was supposed to be over now, but they still lived in each other's pockets, with Milly's entertainment lawyer husband, Geoff—or 'poor Geoff' as he was invariably referred to by Toni—appearing mostly baffled by their antics.

Aaron was quite intrigued to finally meet the notorious Milly, and poor Geoff, after everything he'd heard about them.

"That's nice," Toni said brightly, and Aaron had to bite back a smile. Toni despised Milly, though she seemed to not mind Geoff so much. Or at least, she felt sorry for him.

"Yeah," Charlie said. "It'll be enough for the workshop, anyway. We need at least three couples because we'll be working in pairs."

"Oh Jesus," Lewis groaned. "Not a workshop, Charlie, please. For the love of God, it's the weekend."

Charlie hooked his arm over Lewis's shoulders and drew

him towards the entrance. "Don't be like that," he cajoled. "I've done this one before, and it's amazing at centring you and cleansing you of your negative energy. We'll do it tomorrow, before we speak about *Leeches* on Sunday, and I'm telling you, it's going to be a gamechanger. You are going to chill the fuck out, my friend, and open your mind up to new possibilities."

"Only if you put fucking Rohypnol in my tea," Lewis said.

Charlie's brow furrowed in irritation for a moment before he rallied. "Come on," he said, slinging his other arm around Toni. "I'll show you to your rooms." And with that, he led Lewis and Toni through the arched entranceway.

Aaron, left behind, eyed the numerous bags and garment carriers that the driver had unloaded from the car and that everyone else seemed to have forgotten about. Sighing, he hefted his own rucksack on, slung Lewis's bag over his shoulder, got Toni's wheeled case lined up, carefully laid the garment bags over one outstretched arm, and hurried after the others as best he could.

The interior of the house was very beautiful and austere. The big central open hall was floored and panelled with dark honey wood and high above perched a minstrel's gallery. There was scarcely any furniture, just a few wooden benches and chairs scattered around the perimeter of the hall. In the middle of the bare floor, a lone skateboard lay on its side, abandoned.

Aaron spied the others disappearing through an open archway to the left and almost tripped over his own feet hurrying after them.

By the time he caught up, they were already on their way up a huge flight of stairs.

Annoyed, he cleared his throat.

Lewis immediately looked over his shoulder and had the grace to look abashed. "Oh, sorry. Let me help you."

Ignoring Charlie's irritated expression, he descended the stairs to where Aaron stood.

"You should have just left that stuff outside," Charlie said, his tone suggesting Aaron was moronic. "One of the staff would have brought it in."

"Most of us don't assume someone else will come running to pick up after us," Lewis said, mildly, before Aaron could respond. Stepping close, Lewis slid his fingers under the strap of his bag and carefully lifted it over Aaron's head.

Aaron felt suddenly… odd. Lewis was too close, too kind, too overwhelmingly *there*.

That was the thing about being in lust with your boss. You had to be on guard all the time in case you betrayed yourself. You got used to keeping a certain careful distance. You developed strategies to make sure you never breached the unspoken zone of personal space. Aaron was an expert at handing things to Lewis so that they didn't touch. At leaving cups of hot chocolate on the corner of his desk so their fingers were in no danger of accidentally brushing. At always, always keeping a good two feet of space between them.

Which must be why, the very instant Lewis got close, Aaron felt like he was about to hyperventilate. The memory of Lewis opening the door of his flat wearing nothing but his snug Calvin Kleins was suddenly all Aaron could think about. Lewis, sleep-rumpled and bare chested, standing in his front doorway, gazing at Aaron expectantly…

Hell. This weekend was already screwing with the boundaries he'd so carefully put in place around Lewis. And they'd only just arrived.

"Aaron?" Lewis frowned down at him from the step above, brow creased. "Okay?"

"Er, yes… Sorry, just, um—Could you take this, too?" He handed off one of the garment bags, laughing awkwardly. "Guess I need to hit the gym or something."

"God no," Charlie called from where he was waiting for

them at a turn in the stairs above. "Screw the gym. Get a personal trainer. Theo has done wonders for my abs." He slapped his stomach proudly. "Yesterday, I held the plank for a full five minutes. Even took a call from LA on the Bluetooth while I did it. I'll show you later."

"Please don't," Lewis muttered, turning to trudge up the stairs, and Aaron smothered a smile.

As he followed Lewis, Aaron concentrated on slowing his heartbeat and willing the heat to leave his cheeks. Christ, he hoped Lewis hadn't noticed his reaction. After Jason's comments last night, he was afraid his secret attraction might not be as secret as he'd believed. Mortifying didn't begin to cover how he'd feel if Lewis found out when he'd been so clear from the start that their 'mutual attraction' couldn't go anywhere.

At the top of the stairs, Charlie led them through a picture gallery. Again, it was a huge space with golden wood flooring and panelling halfway up the walls. What looked like a badminton net was set up at the far end. But it was the walls that fascinated Aaron. They were covered with paintings, the portraits of dusty old aristocrats interspersed with… Well, Aaron supposed they were art. It was difficult to be sure, and he was no expert. His mum would sniff and say a child could have daubed the bright splashes of clashing paint on the canvases, and secretly, Aaron agreed. If he was honest, they were pretty ugly. He looked around, but couldn't see any handy labels identifying the artist.

"Do you collect art?" he asked Charlie as they walked through the gallery.

Lewis shot him a horrified look, making a slashing gesture across his throat.

Too late.

"Oh!" Charlie beamed as he whirled to face them. "Do you like them? They're my heart paintings. The paintings of my heart." He gestured to one garish splash of orange, green and purple. "It helps me get in touch with my creative heart. Mils taught me the technique. You just pick up the brush, close your eyes, and… paint. Paint your heart. I call this one *Ad Meliora.*"

Lewis scowled. "I call it—"

"Fascinating!" Aaron said, channelling his amusement into a broad smile. "So you paint with your... eyes shut?"

Charlie tapped his chest. "Eyes shut, heart open, Andy. Heart open."

"Amazing," Aaron said, grinning. Charlie would be a great character to use in a fic—he could just imagine what Skye Jäger would have to say about 'heart painting'.

"Self-indulgent bollocks," Lewis muttered under his breath, and Aaron buried a laugh.

Exactly.

"This way!" Charlie said from up front, leading them out of the gallery and into a corridor that had been modernised and looked rather hotel-like, with carpet and several doors leading off on either side.

"Lewis, you're in *Spirit,*" Charlie said, opening the first door. The word 'Spirit' had been painted in an elegant script across the door in a pretty shade of duck-egg blue. "It will soothe your soul, my friend."

Lewis grunted but said nothing as Charlie led them into the room.

It was gorgeous. Decorated in blues and creams, with a large four-poster bed, an en suite bathroom, and an elegant three-piece suite arranged around the pretty leaded windows overlooking Safehaven's grounds.

Which were, objectively, green and beautiful. A formal garden close to the house led on to a wilderness, beyond which rose a wooded hillside. In the distance, Aaron glimpsed the sparkle of the sea, and his heart lifted like it had as a child when he and his family made their annual summer pilgrimage to the seaside. Not far from here, in fact.

"I've Feng-Shuied the shit out of the place," Charlie said happily. "We even dowsed for geopathic stress, so it has great energy. *Spirit* is designed to help your yin chi flow cleanly. It's a really restful space, Lewis. One night here and you'll wake up with your chakras open and ready." He squeezed Lewis's shoulder. "Which I think will help."

"Help what?" Lewis said, with the look of a man about to dive out of the window and bolt.

Charlie rubbed his arm. "Well, *this*," he said. "You're tied up in knots, my friend. I'm not surprised you're so resistant to evolving *Leeches*. Your energy is obviously blocked."

Lewis's jaw clenched, eyes narrowing, his whole body stiffening as he pulled away from Charlie's hand. His touch-paper had been lit; the countdown began.

"Wow, what a view!" Aaron said, abandoning Toni's case and pushing himself between Charlie and Lewis as he headed for the window. "Is that the sea, Charlie?"

"What? Oh yes." Thankfully, Charlie left Lewis and followed Aaron to the window, squinting against the bright sky. "That's Swanage over there. Bit of a tacky tourist trap, I'm afraid."

"We went to Swanage on holiday every year when I was a kid," Aaron said, smiling at the memory. "I loved it."

"Did you?" Charlie gazed at him curiously. "I suppose it must have been nourishing for you to escape the Big Smoke and reconnect with nature. Even in a limited way. Staycations can be quite special."

Escape the Big Smoke? Aaron looked at him, half affronted and half amused. "I grew up in Guildford, so… not really smoky. Or big. And it's not a staycation if you go to the seaside. It's a holiday. Staycations are when you stay at home."

Charlie shook his head. "I don't think so. Staying at home isn't any kind of holiday, is it?"

Behind them, Lewis muttered, "For fuck's sake…"

Toni said, "Am I next door, Charlie? I'll just pop my things inside and—"

"No!" Charlie spun away from the window. "No, darling, I've put you down at the end, in *Heart*. Next door to Milly. She always stays in *Soul*. They're both very female-centred spaces. Come on, let me show you."

He was halfway out the door when Lewis said, "What about Aaron? Where's his room?"

"Oh, upstairs." Charlie waved toward the ceiling. "We have guest rooms for visiting staff. Billy will show him."

There was a silence, deep and profound. Toni's eyebrows rose; Lewis went very still. And Aaron felt his face heat.

Staff?

"Aaron is not 'staff'," Lewis said in a voice Aaron hadn't heard before. Not his usual angry bluster, but cold and controlled. Furious.

Charlie looked confused. "But I thought he was your assistant." Then his eyes widened, and he slapped a hand to his forehead. "Oh God, is he your boyfriend? I wondered why you'd brought him. I'm so sorry. I didn't realise. Of course you can share *Spirit*—"

"Nope," Aaron said quickly, his blush deepening. "Not his boyfriend. And upstairs is fine."

"No it fucking well isn't," Lewis said, chewing his words. "Aaron is my colleague, Charlie. Just like Toni. And just like you. In fact, he's of more use to me than either of you. *That's* why he's here."

For an instant, Charlie looked displeased, his ordinary features turning severe, but the expression was gone in a flash, swiftly masked. "Yes," he said, "yes of course. I admire that philosophy, Lewis. We are *all* colleagues, and *all* our contributions are equally valid and valuable. Thank you for reminding us. It's a good lesson."

"It's not a fucking lesson. It's a fact, and—"

"I'll put him next door to you, in *Body*," Charlie said,

lifting a hand for silence. "It's a great space, although perhaps a little more yang than appropriate for Andy." He laughed. "And Geoff won't mind sleeping in *Mind*. He'll enjoy the irony."

Yin or yang, Aaron didn't give a flying fuck. Mostly he just wanted the floor to open and swallow him whole.

I wondered why you'd brought him.

Ugh. What a dickish thing to say. Even worse was the fact that it got to him, that it left him feeling belittled and out of place. Had that been Charlie's intention? Or had he simply been heedless of how his words would make Aaron feel? Aaron wasn't sure which was worse, but either way, Charlie was a wanker.

Lewis's intervention, though? That had been gratifying, sending little champagne bubbles of warmth fizzing through Aaron. He liked that Lewis had thought about him, that he'd been offended on his behalf. That he'd seemed to care how Aaron felt.

Toni's sharp scrutiny of Lewis as he'd let loose at Charlie was less pleasing. There was a troubled expression in her eyes that made Aaron uneasy. He wondered what she was thinking.

Body turned out to be a room much like Lewis's, only decorated in shades of burgundy and scarlet, with gold accents. Charlie pronounced it a 'sensual space of lavish physicality'.

Aaron thought it looked like a brothel.

Truth was, he'd probably have been happier upstairs with the staff in what was no doubt a small beige room with a mass-produced seascape over its single bed. But after Lewis had made such a fuss, he could hardly object, and so he made all the right approving sounds as Charlie pointed out the rain setting on the shower and the 'raw masculine energy' of the room.

When Charlie left, and Aaron was finally alone, he sank

down on the edge of the bed, exhausted. They'd been in Safehaven for less than an hour, and he already understood why Lewis couldn't stand the place. Neither safe nor a haven, it seemed designed to leave you feeling like a fish out of water. Or perhaps that was just his painfully lower-middle-class sense of inadequacy talking.

But Aaron wasn't the sort to let someone like Charlie Alexander get to him for long. Already he was taking solace from the prospect of including Charlie in his next fic. Maybe he'd let Skye rip his throat out. *I always try to eat organic,* Skye might quip before sinking his fangs in.

Smiling at the thought, Aaron shook off his irritation and set about unpacking before they got to work. Brothel-vibe aside, the room was the most luxurious place he'd ever stayed, and he snapped a couple of selfies to share with Janvi and the others in their WhatsApp group.

He was posing with the gold taps in the bathroom when he suddenly looked up to find Lewis standing in the doorway, his flinty gaze taking in the picture Aaron made, semi-reclined over the sink as he tried to take the photo. *Shit*. When had he come in?

Lewis's gaze flicked down, snagging on something, and that finally prodded Aaron into action. Scrambling upright, he righted himself, realising a moment later that his t-shirt had come untucked. He'd probably been flashing a strip of his pale belly. How attractive.

Blushing, he said irritably, "Don't you have any manners? You could knock, you know." Straightening, he stalked towards the bathroom door, relieved when Lewis turned and walked into the bedroom ahead of him.

"I did knock," Lewis said, sounding unconcerned. "You didn't answer. I wanted to check you were okay after that fucking embarrassing shit with Charlie." He parked himself on the end of Aaron's bed, leaning back on his hands. "What a wanker. He gets worse every time I come here. And what the hell was he wearing? He looked like he'd got dressed in the dark."

Aaron laughed, trying not to think about the fact that Lewis was looking mouth-watering in a gorgeous pair of dark jeans that hugged his long, muscular legs and a soft, fitted flannel shirt with the cuffs rolled up to show off his perfect forearms. For a while, when he'd first started working for Lewis, Aaron had kidded himself that he admired Lewis's style. He'd told himself he wanted to dress like him. But pretty soon he'd admitted that he mostly wanted to *undress* him. And today, with Lewis lounging on the end of a large bed in a room full of 'raw masculine energy', that want became suddenly, inappropriately fierce.

He felt it in the heat prickling beneath his skin, and in the sudden heaviness of his cock.

Shit. This was worse—*way* worse—than having these feelings in the office.

And just as that thought occurred to him, Lewis looked up, running a hand through his hair. Aaron's heart skipped. It literally skipped, like he was a teenager.

Bloody hell, he was screwed.

"That was bollocks, all that crap about you being staff," Lewis said. "You know that's not how I see you, right? You're not my… my maid, for fuck's sake."

"I know." Aaron smiled; he couldn't help it. Sometimes Lewis could look—could *be*—surprisingly vulnerable.

"I know I ask you to run errands and… You really didn't have to clean my rug this morning. Or buy my breakfast, or —" Again with the hand through his hair, leaving it sticking up in spikes that Aaron itched to smooth down. "Fuck, I don't want you to think I'm anything like Charlie fucking Alexander."

"I don't," Aaron said, touched. "You're not. And I don't mind doing those things for you. I *am* your assistant, and I'm happy to assist."

God, the things he'd assist with if he only had the chance…

"But I meant what I said—you *are* more useful to me than anyone else." Lewis held his gaze, eyes bright and clear and devastatingly honest. "Not the fetching and carrying—anyone could do that—I mean with the show. I value your creative input, your opinions. Your judgment." He looked away, seeming uncomfortable now. "I know I can be a moody bastard in the office, but I hope you know that you're… valued."

And that knocked the stuffing right out of Aaron. It took him a moment to catch his breath, so he sounded rather winded when he said, "Good. I mean, thanks. I mean, you're welcome."

Lewis glanced at him, his gorgeous mouth ticking up at one side in a tiny smile. Then he looked away again, gazing out of the window. "Swanage, huh?"

Relieved by the change of subject, his heart still racing, Aaron said, "My grandparents retired there, so we stayed with them for two weeks every August. It was great. I loved it there, tourist trap or not."

"We used to go to Brighton," Lewis said, lost in thought. "Just for the day, on the train. Me and Owen, I mean. We'd eat fish and chips on the beach. It's a really fucking pebbly beach, and the sea was always freezing." He gave a soft huff. "But I loved it anyway. Then we'd mess about in the arcade on the pier and get candy floss and those big sugar dummies. And get home after midnight. It was brilliant."

Aaron was silent, not knowing quite what to say and not wanting to spoil what felt like a fragile moment. Lewis rarely talked about his past or his family. Aaron knew his mum had died when he was pretty young, and that Owen had cared for him in the teeth of opposition from social services. Most of that he'd read in an interview in DigitalSpy, picking up other tiny details from throwaway comments Lewis had made over the years. It wasn't something he mentioned often.

The picture Lewis painted now, of two motherless boys taking a day trip to Brighton together, pierced his heart. It made him ache for the difficult, talented, prickly man sitting before him. One arm twitched, as if trying to reach for him, but Aaron overruled the desire. Instead, he said quietly, "That sounds like a good memory."

"Yeah, it is."

"And *that's* a staycation by the way."

"Right?" Lewis glanced up, their eyes meeting in shared understanding. "Charlie lives in a different world."

"Yeah," Aaron said softly. He turned away and reached into his backpack, pulling out the shirt and waistcoat he'd brought in case he needed something smart for dinner. "And the funny thing is, he has no idea." He went to the wardrobe to hang his clothes up, hoping the creases would drop out. He hadn't had a garment bag at home and hadn't had time to get one. He'd done his best to fold his stuff into his backpack, but everything seemed to be creased to hell, and the room didn't offer anything as prosaic as an iron. Probably because Charlie had 'staff' who did that sort of thing for him. "He doesn't seem to realise how different most people have it."

Lewis sighed. "Yeah, well, none of them do." He got to his feet; Aaron could hear the bed creak as he moved. "Wait until you meet fucking *Mils*. A tenner says she's mentioned Oxford within the first two minutes. She and Charlie went to the same college."

"I'm not taking that bet," Aaron laughed, turning back to face Lewis.

Lewis grinned. "The worst is, she always does it with a dash of Uriah Heep."

"Oh my God, I know the type," Aaron said. He mimicked a posh accent. "God knows why they let me in. I'm such a dolt!"

Lewis snorted, his laughter lighting up his whole face and turning his handsome, often forbidding features into something boyish and, frankly, heart-stopping. Laughing with him, Aaron felt giddy with the pleasure of the moment.

Suddenly, Aaron realised he was staring at Lewis, fixedly. Lewis cleared his throat and shoved his hands in his pockets, his gaze sliding away from Aaron's.

"I'd better get moving," he said. Then he sighed. "Charlie wants to talk at three."

Aaron raised his brows. "I thought the meeting was Sunday. You know, after he's broken our spirits?"

Lewis laughed, but this time he sounded strained. "Yes, the *main* meeting is on Sunday. This is more of a quick chat—Charlie called it a *'pre-meeting'*. What he really means is that he's going to tell me and Toni what he wants to happen, then leave us to chew on that for two days. It's a tactic he always uses."

Aaron made a face. "All right," he said. "Are you going to give me a knock when you're ready to go down?"

Lewis blinked. Then his expression shifted guiltily. "I, um… look, I think Toni and I can probably handle this pre-meeting ourselves."

Aaron's face instantly flooded with heat.

"Oh—oh right, of course," he stammered. "Sorry, I shouldn't have presumed—"

"No, don't be daft," Lewis said quickly. "Ordinarily, I'd definitely want you there. It's just—"

"You don't have to explain," Aaron said quickly. "You're the boss."

Something Aaron would do well to remember this weekend.

"I would, though," Lewis insisted after a moment's pause, his perfect brows stitching together. "I just want this one thing over with as soon as possible, and I figure the fewer of us there are, the easier that might be." He smiled stiffly before adding, "I'll come and see you after the meeting to let you know how it went and what's happening this evening."

And then he was gone, leaving Aaron to his own devices.

Oh well, Aaron thought. *At least I can spend some time on* We Are All Creatures of the Night.

Sighing, he turned away and reached for his laptop bag.

CHAPTER NINE

Lewis

"Okay," Toni said, in her usual calm, friendly way. "We've heard you, Charlie. We know what you want. We'll regroup on Sunday and see at that point where we've all landed on this individually." She smiled easily. "Like you say, it's a process."

Lewis ground his molars together. They were in Charlie's office—sorry, *collaboration space*—and Lewis was determined to let Toni run the show. He wasn't even sitting at the table with her and Charlie. Instead, he stood by the window, his arms crossed, staring out at the smooth surface of the helipad outside and trying to look relaxed.

Trying not to give in to his urge to tell Charlie he was a fucking moron without the slightest understanding of the characters in the show or the dynamics between them.

"Whatever happens, we can make this work," Toni had said before they'd gone in. "You *can make this work, Lewis. You can make these characters do anything."*

He knew, without vanity, that she was right. He was no prima donna, liable to throw a fit over requested changes.

Years of scraping by in shit internships and badly paid runner jobs while writing his first scripts had cured him of any such ideas. He prided himself on his discipline and practicality. His ability to ruthlessly cut and change and mould the shape of the story to meet commercial demands.

When he got started on making the changes, he'd probably even relish the challenge. But… there was something about this particular request that bothered him in ways he couldn't quite understand.

"You happy with that, Lewis?" Charlie asked.

Lewis turned his head to find Charlie watching him. The guy might be channelling relaxed hipster dude, but underneath the trappings he wore so diligently, there was a corporate snake of the first order.

Lewis shrugged. "I need to let it sink in. Kick the tyres mentally."

Charlie nodded and leaned back in his chair. "Yeah, makes sense," he agreed. "Okay then, let's call this a day. For now."

Toni smiled and got to her feet. "Great, so what time's dinner tonight?"

"Didn't Paula send you the itinerary?" Charlie asked, frowning.

"She might have," Toni replied, waving her hand vaguely. "Jason's off today—usually he'd keep me right on stuff like that."

"You know about the workshop, though?" Charlie said, his gaze narrowing.

"Uh, yeah—well, you mentioned it earlier."

"You *don't*, do you?" he said, his tone sharp with irritated disbelief. "Toni, it's an intrinsic part of why we're here this weekend!"

"Oh, sorry," she said, her expression mortified. "I didn't realise it was to do with the show. I thought it was just—"

"It's a touch and movement creativity workshop," he snapped. "And you should have been fasting for it since you woke up this morning. Have you?" He shifted his gaze to Lewis. "Either of you?"

Toni took a deep breath. "Okay, I wasn't aware of that," she said, "but don't worry. All I've had this morning is some tea, and Lewis was running too late for breakfast, so he's fine too. Right, Lewis?"

Lewis blinked, astonished by the smoothness of Toni's lie. "What? Eh, oh, yeah." He bit back a grin, remembering the all-day breakfast panini and chocolate croissant he'd polished off earlier.

Charlie eyed them both suspiciously. After a long, uncomfortable pause, he said, "All right then. Well, since we're fasting, there won't be any dinner served tonight, but there's plenty of drinks in your rooms—water and kombucha in the mini-fridge and a tea tray with pretty much every herbal tea on earth." He chuckled as though what he'd just said was incredibly charming rather than utterly depressing. "Paula will email you your packs for the workshop along with individual links for your meditations."

"Meditations?" Lewis said slowly.

"Yes. Hippolyta—she's running the workshop; she's *incredible*—has recorded a guided meditation for each of us to do this evening. They're completely individual." He pointed finger-guns at Lewis and winked. "I asked her to do your one on opening yourself up to others' ideas. I think you'll find it very beneficial."

A familiar urge to punch Charlie's annoying face surged. Lewis ground his molars again.

"Well, it sounds like we've got quite a bit to do," Toni said quickly, forcing a laugh. "We'd better get back to our rooms, Lewis."

Charlie gave an indulgent chuckle. "By the time you've read the pack, done the meditation, and had some tea, you'll probably be ready to sleep—we're starting at seven sharp tomorrow morning. Hippolyta recommends getting a good night's sleep tonight. These workshops are emotionally *so* draining. You'll be amazed how tired you feel after."

"Seven o'clock," Toni echoed in a hollow voice. She was not a morning person.

Charlie nodded. "And I'm sure you won't mind, Toni, but I've paired you up with Geoff for the workshop."

Toni frowned. "Geoff? But won't he and Milly..."

Charlie shook his head. "I promised Mils that she and I would do this one together—we work so closely, and I feel like some of the energy between us has become a bit *blocked* recently, you know? Besides, you got on well with Geoff last time."

"Um, we had a chat about rugby, but that's not really enough of a foundation for doing, you know, *couples touch therapy*."

Charlie waved a dismissive hand. "It's not *couples* touch therapy."

Toni, who was finally beginning to look frayed, said tightly, "You just said we'd be working in couples."

"Pairs, not couples," Charlie said airily. "Besides, no one will be with a *life*-partner-partner. We'll all be working with a colleague. Lewis will work with Andy."

Toni opened her mouth again, maybe to point out that she and Geoff were not and never had been colleagues, or possibly that Charlie and Milly used to be fuck buddies—or maybe even that Aaron's name wasn't fucking Andy—but in the end she just gave a gusty exhale and said, "Fine, okay."

"That's the spirit," Charlie said, beaming now that he'd got his own way, as usual.

Meanwhile, Lewis's gut had begun to twist at the thought of being paired with Aaron tomorrow. Doing *touch* therapy with Aaron. *Christ.* What did that mean? What the fuck even *was* touch therapy? The thought of touching Aaron made him feel panicky and hot and excited and dismayed, all at once.

Lewis didn't really *do* touching. He had two modes when

it came to touching: fucking hot men in controlled environments and otherwise keeping his distance from everyone. He put up with his brother's occasional hugs, but that was pretty much the sum total of the non-sexual physical affection in his life.

Lewis was not a hugger.

"All right then," Charlie said, standing up and clapping his hands. He began to walk them towards the door. "Like I said, Paula will be emailing out the workshop packs and links to your tailored meditations. We'll be meeting Hippolyta in the Long Gallery tomorrow morning at seven for some intentional movement exercises to get started, so don't be late. Are you excited, guys?"

Lewis grunted.

"So much," Toni said, faintly.

Once the door had closed and they were halfway down the corridor, Lewis muttered, "Nice save on the fasting thing. But even after that huge breakfast, I'm going to be seriously hungry later. Do you have any food?"

"Absolutely," Toni said. "I never come here without a bunch of snacks." She glanced at Lewis. "I'm going to do a quick flick of the workshop pack, watch the meditation on fast forward while I'm in the bath, and then it's jim-jams and Netflix with a Pot noodle and a multipack of Monster Munch."

Lewis groaned. "I might have to come and scavenge off you."

They had reached Toni's room now. She slowed to a halt and opened the door. "I can spare you a Pot Noodle if you get desperate." She winked. "If I'm feeling kind, I might even let you have one of my Curly Wurlys."

"I love you," Lewis said, seriously.

Smiling, she slipped into her room. "I know."

Lewis decided to go and update Aaron on the workshop debacle and dinner—or rather the lack of it—before heading for his own room. Aaron was not going to cope well with the idea of fasting. He was one of those naturally lean guys who could eat whatever they wanted and never put on a pound. It never ceased to amaze Lewis just how much food the guy packed away without it having any discernible effect on his tight, lightly muscled frame. Earlier, when he'd seen Aaron draped over that bathroom sink, his t-shirt riding up to expose a tempting slice of lean belly…

Lewis halted suddenly in the middle of the corridor, scowling. That image belonged in the 'humorous' box—he should be laughing at the memory of Aaron's expression morphing from sultry to horrified as he'd jack-knifed upright from his ridiculous pose. But Lewis wasn't thinking about that. He was remembering how Aaron had looked during those brief, thudding heartbeats of time when Lewis had been standing there, watching him, unnoticed. Watching as Aaron gazed at his phone screen with that half-amused, half-sexy expression, his long body all relaxed and inviting, and that slice of skin, just begging for…

Fuck.

Lewis squeezed his eyes closed and pinched the bridge of his nose.

What the hell was he thinking?

Abruptly, he abandoned the idea of updating Aaron. He was going back to his room for a fucking cold shower. He'd deal with Aaron once he'd calmed down.

Before he was even able to turn on his heel, though, Aaron's door was thrusting open. And suddenly, there he was, all rumpled and wide-eyed and holding up his phone.

"Oh, thank God, it's you!" he said. "I thought I heard someone out here—have you *seen* this?" He pushed the phone at Lewis, and Lewis automatically stepped forward, squinting at the screen.

Did he need reading glasses now? What a mortifying thought.

"What is it?" he asked. Then a thought occurred to him. "Wait, is that from Paula? For the workshop tomorrow? Charlie said something about us all getting a pack and our own link to a—"

"Tailored *fucking* meditation!" Aaron finished for him. "Which is bad enough, but are you aware that we're not even getting *fed* tonight? And then, tomorrow, you and I have to get inside a special white balloon—"

"Wait, *what?* Are we going zorbing or something?"

"Zorbing?" Aaron looked momentarily confused. "Oh, you mean those big plastic ball things you get inside and roll down hills in? No. This is an imaginary balloon." He waved the phone again. "It's all in here. We've got to get in an imaginary balloon and use the healing power of touch to connect with our inherent creativity." His voice was rising hysterically. "I can't do it, Lewis! I won't!"

Lewis stared at him, astonished at the sight of his capable, unflappable assistant in such a state. And then—he really couldn't help himself—he dissolved into laughter. Helpless, overwhelming laughter that bubbled up inside him like a champagne glass filled too quickly, spilling over extravagantly.

It was the look on Aaron's face—so fucking horrified and desperate—and the ridiculousness of it all. And maybe too it was that twisting feeling in his gut that was part dread and part anticipation about what tomorrow would bring. The feeling that the workshop would be okay because Aaron would be there, coupled with the contradictory conviction that pairing up with Aaron for that workshop was a really terrible idea.

Somewhere along the line, Aaron started laughing too, and by the time Lewis had himself under control, they were both wiping their eyes and grinning at one another.

Aaron turned and ambled back into his room, beckoning

Lewis after him. "Come in here—I've got a sort-of plan if you're up for it."

Lewis followed him inside, closing the door behind him and watching as Aaron flung himself onto the enormous, and already quite rumpled, bed, reaching for his open laptop.

"What sort of plan?"

Aaron looked up, his silvery eyes glinting with mischief. "A dinner plan. Do you like fish and chips?"

Lewis's stomach grumbled. "Who doesn't?"

"Swanage is about three miles from here. You get the best fish and chips there. I was just looking at Google maps, and we can walk it in less than an hour."

"Oh my God," Lewis said. He was salivating already. "You're the best assistant in the universe."

Aaron grinned. "I am," he agreed. "Will we be able to break out of here easily enough?"

Lewis shrugged, unbothered at the prospect of being caught. "If we're seen, we'll say we're going out to do some intentional movement in nature."

Aaron's grin widened. "I'd better take that line. You're a terrible liar."

Lewis smiled back. "It wouldn't be a lie," he said. "It's just a fancy way of saying we're going for a walk."

"And what if we're asked if we're planning to eat anything?"

Lewis wrinkled his nose. "You can take that one," he said. "I'm going to get changed before we go if that's okay?"

"Yeah, fine. I want to take a shower anyway." Aaron paused, then added, almost diffidently, "Should we ask Toni?"

Aaron didn't want to, Lewis realised.

And neither did Lewis.

Fuck.

Lewis cleared his throat. "I'll mention it to her," he said

gruffly. "She had plans for Netflix and Pot Noodles though, so I suspect she'll leave us to it."

~

After Lewis had showered and changed, he found himself dithering outside Toni's door, staring at the word *Heart* scrolling across it in dusky pink paint. From inside came the soft sounds of music and slightly off-key singing. Toni would probably already have the bath running. Truth was, had Lewis really intended on dragging her along on this jaunt, he'd have asked her *before* he spent half an hour dithering—again—over which sweater looked best with his black jeans. He tugged at the sleeves of his burgundy cashmere, the one Mason had once told him brought out the blue in his eyes.

Well, he had to ask her to come along. If for no other reason than Aaron would know if he lied about it, and that would send a signal that he couldn't afford to send. Lewis was all too aware of his and Aaron's relative positions, of the power relationship between them. The last thing he wanted was Aaron imagining that Lewis was engineering a situation, especially in light of Charlie's fucking stupid comment about Aaron being Lewis's boyfriend. *Ugh.*

So, he'd leave the decision in the lap of the gods. If Toni fancied fish and chips, so be it.

He rapped on the door.

Abruptly, the music switched off. There were some frantic shuffling and rustling sounds. Then the door cracked open, and Toni's face appeared in the narrow gap.

At least, he assumed it was her face.

She was dressed in a fluffy pink dressing gown with the Telopix logo embroidered on the lapel, her hair wrapped in a matching pink towel, and she peered warily from behind a bright orange face pack. "Oh, it's you." She sagged in relief as the door opened more widely to reveal a rumpled bed and a large packet of Monster Munch poorly hidden beneath the duvet. "I thought it was Charlie, checking up on the fasting."

Lewis raised his eyebrows. "You look…"

"Don't say it," she interrupted. "But if he's not going to feed us, I'm at least making use of the complimentary toiletries." She pointed at her face. "This is going to de-oxidize and re-energize my face using the power of organic goji berries and pomegranate."

"It's doing a passing impression of Donald Trump, too."

She rolled her eyes. "Costs thirty quid, usually. I googled it."

"I'm guessing," he said, very aware of the jumping excitement in his chest, "that you're not up for a three-mile hike to the chippy."

Toni laughed. "You guess right, my friend." Her eyes narrowed behind the orange goop on her face. "You and Aaron escaping for the night?"

It would be ridiculous, and unnecessary to lie. So he said, "Yep. It was his idea."

"He's a gem."

"One I'm keeping."

"Hmm," Toni said.

And Lewis didn't have time for whatever thoughts were brewing behind that ridiculous face pack. "Enjoy your Pot Noodle," he said. "I'll see you tomorrow at seven. God help us."

He headed down the corridor, towards Aaron's room, as Toni's voice drifted after him, "Don't do anything you'll regret in the morning!"

He lifted a hand in acknowledgment but didn't turn around or slow until he heard the click of her closing door. Then he let out a breath and paused for a moment in the middle of the empty corridor.

Nothing's going to happen.

That was a fact because Lewis wasn't going to *let* anything happen. Given his position of authority, it would be inexcusable to allow it. So, that was that. No need for dithering or doubting. They were going to walk into town, get some food, and walk back.

That. Was. It.

Somewhat settled by that conviction, Lewis went to knock on Aaron's door.

Aaron opened it immediately, as if he'd been waiting. Knowing Aaron, he had been. He wasn't one for being late when he could be five minutes early.

Unfortunately, Lewis's certainty about the evening took a bit of a knock at the sight of Aaron's shower-tousled hair, skinny jeans, and slim-fitting pink shirt. Aaron didn't wear his sexuality on his sleeve, but neither did he try to hide it. He was honest about himself in an understated but confident way. Lewis liked that about him.

"Ready?" Aaron said, pulling the door closed behind him.

"Yeah, let's get out of here."

As he locked the door, Aaron said, with admirable nonchalance, "No Toni?"

"Nope. Last seen in a face pack and dressing gown with a giant packet of Monster Munch."

Aaron laughed. "Great!" He turned around with a broad smile. "I mean, great for Toni. Sounds like a relaxing evening."

"I don't think she's one for hiking," Lewis agreed.

They left the house the way they'd arrived, down the grand staircase and through the vast, empty entrance hall with its abandoned skateboard. Neither spoke, and they walked quickly, Lewis casting cautious glances around as he went. But there was no sign of Charlie, thank God.

Finally, they were outside, standing on the broad gravel driveway. It was beautiful, the early evening sunshine still warm and the sky the kind of pure, cloudless blue you only got near the coast. Lewis took a deep breath, filling his lungs, genuinely relieved to be out of the house's oppressive atmosphere.

"Okay," Aaron said, studying his phone. "There's a footpath we can take to save walking on the road the whole way. Looks like we can cut across the grounds and pick it up…" He squinted, lifting a hand to shade his eyes. "...over there, through that gate in the wall."

"After you," Lewis said, with an extravagant sweep of his arm.

Aaron smiled, and off they went.

Safehaven loomed behind them, and Lewis had to actively resist the temptation to glance over his shoulder as they crossed the pristine grass, making a beeline for the tall wooden gate.

"I keep thinking he's going to come running after us," Aaron said with a nervous laugh. "To drag us back."

"He can try. But I've got a couple of inches and at least half a decade on him."

"And I'm a pretty fast runner, when I'm motivated."

Lewis could believe it. Aaron had a runner's build, long and lean and lithe. "You look like a runner," he said. "Where do you run?"

"Where? Er, for the train sometimes?" He flashed a rueful smile. "I know I should make time to exercise. Colin was always telling me."

"You probably have better things to do," Lewis said. Fucking Colin.

On that subject, though, he felt a nagging twinge of guilt. Relief had probably made him…insensitive when Aaron had told him about breaking up with Colin, and the memory of Aaron's tight-lipped expression popped unhappily into his mind. They hadn't spoken about it since, but the idea that his comments had genuinely hurt Aaron made Lewis uncomfortable.

They'd reached the gate by then, and Aaron was fiddling

with the latch, trying to open it. While his back was turned, Lewis said, "I was a bit, um, blunt the other day, when you told me you'd split up with Colin. I hope I didn't hurt your feelings. It's just that—"

"It's fine," Aaron said, rattling the gate. "There was no big drama—it might have been my decision but in all honesty, it was pretty much mutual."

"Well, then he's a bigger idiot than I took him for."

Aaron glanced over his shoulder, the evening sun catching his hair and highlighting little threads of gold amid the brown. "Thanks. I think?"

Lewis huffed a laugh. "What I'm saying is, you can do better." He frowned at the thought, realising he didn't much like it. "Will do better, I guess."

"I guess," Aaron echoed, turning back to the gate. "Crap," he said, giving it another shake, "it's locked. We'll have to go around."

"Back down the drive?" Lewis peered into the distance. "That's got to be at least half a mile."

"Half a mile in the wrong direction."

"Bugger that." Lewis eyed the gate. "I reckon we can climb over it."

Their eyes met in a glittering moment of *hell, yes*! Aaron grinned. "Now it really feels like *The Great Escape*."

"I'll go first," Lewis said and took a running jump, grabbing the top of the gate and hauling himself up and over, then jumping down the other side.

He landed in a meadow, lit golden by the low sun and dancing with wildflowers in all shades of purples, whites, yellows, and reds. Stunning.

Behind him, he heard a thud as Aaron jumped and then scrambled up the gate. But he ended up sitting awkwardly astride it, looking like he was about to castrate himself. "Fuck!" he yelped. "Now what?"

Lewis snorted. "Don't stop there. You can't straddle it."

"I know! But I can't get my other leg—"

"Here." Lewis reached up, grabbed his dangling foot, giving him some support. "I've got you. Now swing your other leg over…that's it."

In an ungainly slither, Aaron made it over the gate, and somehow Lewis found himself supporting him as Aaron lowered himself down. Goosebumps prickled up his arms and the back of his neck at the feel of Aaron's muscles flexing beneath his hands, the hard lines of his ribs, and—*bloody hell*—the shock of warm skin as Lewis's fingers accidentally slid beneath the hem of Aaron's shirt. Lewis sucked in a sharp breath, and the scent of Aaron's apple-scented shampoo filled his head, making him dizzy.

Fuck, but touching him felt good.

And then Aaron was down and turning around, and Lewis wasn't letting go or stepping back. He was awash with a flood of desire, and, had Aaron been any other man, Lewis would have pressed him up against that gate right then, right there, and kissed the living daylights out of him. And more.

But he couldn't. He *couldn't*.

So they just eyed each other until, with a breathy laugh, Aaron tugged down his rumpled shirt and said, "Well, that was elegant. You can tell I was crap at PE." His cheeks flushed adorably pink.

Adorably pink?

Christ, this was why they never left the fucking office.

Manfully, Lewis made himself let go and shuffle back a step. But before he could find any coherent words, Aaron's eyes widened. "Oh!" he said, looking past Lewis. "Wow, this is gorgeous."

Lewis had forgotten the wildflower meadow. Dragging his eyes away from Aaron, he turned around, grateful for the chance to cool the fuck down.

And it *was* gorgeous.

"Listen," Aaron said, softly. "You can hear the bees."

You could. The air was rich with the lazy hum of insects, a couple of crickets chirping, and the sigh of a gentle breeze soughing through the trees. Exactly what you'd imagine if you thought of a rural idyll, genuine natural beauty. It stood in direct contrast to all the affected bullshit on the other side of the locked gate.

Suddenly, a loud gurgle intruded into the quiet.

Aaron slapped a hand over his stomach. "Sorry!" He giggled, an actual fucking giggle. "I'm really hungry."

And he looked so perfect standing there in the meadow with his tawny hair gilded by the sun, silvery eyes laughing, that Lewis felt a helpless upswell of fondness. A confusing feeling with which he was neither familiar nor comfortable.

Swift on its heels came a flare of panic, or maybe excitement, or something between the two, because he was sailing in uncharted waters now, off the edge of the map.

And all he could say was, "Well, then. Lead the way to Swanage."

CHAPTER TEN

Aaron

They approached Swanage from the north, walking into town along Shore Road with its quaint little B&Bs until they reached the seafront. By then it was just gone six, and Aaron was ready to gnaw off his own arm despite the emergency Snickers he'd scoffed before he showered.

The beaches were empty, the tide high, but there were a few people still milling about enjoying the last of the lingering summer. Most of the brightly coloured beach huts lined up along the seafront were closed, but some stood open with sandy people sitting inside or perching on their steps, drying off and enjoying a cuppa or the final ice cream of the day.

Aaron's heart lifted. It was all so familiar, and he was swept away on a wave of nostalgia. He hadn't been here in years, and now he wondered why he'd left it so long. Then he remembered: Colin's idea of a holiday was two weeks toasting himself on a Mediterranean beach. He wouldn't be seen dead in a place like Swanage.

The sun, setting gracefully behind the headland, threw

long shadows over the promenade, but further out to sea, the water glittered in its golden light. And above the soft shushing of the surf on the shore came the clatter of the amusement arcade further along the front, reminding Aaron of Lewis's story about day trips to Brighton.

He glanced over to mention it and was startled to find Lewis already watching him. Their eyes met, then glanced off each other as they both looked away. And Aaron's awareness that they were increasingly off-piste ratcheted up another notch.

"So this was your summer bolthole?" Lewis said.

Aaron laughed at the description. "Well, it's where my grandparents retired," he said, pointing back the way they'd come. "They lived about a twenty-minute walk that way."

"I like it," Lewis pronounced, looking about as they walked. And that was the thing about Lewis. When he said something like that, you knew he meant it. Lewis never idly flattered.

"I loved it as a kid," Aaron said, "so I'll always love it. You know?"

Lewis nodded. "I know exactly."

Aaron risked another glance, wondering what memories Lewis guarded. He wasn't bold enough to ask and didn't really have the right. Despite the unexpected shift in their relationship this weekend, there was no way he dared probe into Lewis's childhood. That was way over the line—too intimate, too dangerous.

And yet…

His skin heated as he remembered the feel of Lewis's hands on him earlier. It had almost been worth making such an embarrassing hash of climbing over the gate to have Lewis help him down. Even now, he could feel the lingering heat of Lewis's hands against the bare skin at his waist, the jolting physical connection like a circuit closing.

The intense look he'd seen in Lewis's eyes before he'd let go.

Predatory, his mind supplied. *Hungry.* For a frantic moment, Aaron had imagined Lewis might kiss him. He'd felt his hands tighten on his waist, and then…

Well, then nothing.

Because of course Lewis wouldn't kiss him. He'd made that very clear from day one. Besides, only a month ago, Lewis had been sleeping with Mason Nash, an actual model. Lewis could get anyone he liked into bed—and frequently did—so why the hell would he be interested in Aaron?

More to the point, why would Aaron be interested in Lewis? The last thing he wanted was to be his boss's latest one-hit wonder. It was stupid—not to mention, risky—to even contemplate it.

"There's a fantastic fish-and-chip restaurant right on the front," Aaron said, to distract himself from his thoughts, "with loads of outdoor seating. It's great, but you do have to fend off the seagulls."

"Fucking seagulls." Lewis chuckled as he spoke. "Once, in Brighton, one of the buggers snatched a pasty right out of Owen's hand. Frightened the life out of us. Then Owen started chasing it down the pier, yelling at it to give his bloody pasty back. He was so fucking outraged! I nearly killed myself laughing."

Aaron grinned at the image. "Did he succeed?"

"Nah, the seagull got it." He was still smiling though, the expression smoothing out the divot between his brows. He caught Aaron looking and glanced away, still smiling.

Within another ten minutes, they were at the restaurant, which perched on the promenade and overlooked the harbour. Aaron grabbed a picnic table just being vacated by a tired-looking family, while Lewis went up to the counter to order for them both, coming back with two bottles of lager and a buzzer so they'd know when to collect their order.

They sat opposite each other at the picnic table, the sea stretching out to Aaron's left and the last of the day's sunshine warming his back. Lewis lifted his beer in salute. "Here's to fasting and meditation."

Aaron knocked his bottle against Lewis's. "May your chakras be always aligned."

Lewis barked a laugh, then tipped back his head to drink. Helplessly, Aaron's gaze was drawn to those mobile, expressive lips wrapped around the slim neck of the bottle, and to the movement of Lewis's throat as he swallowed.

Jesus, he was sexy. All the more so because he didn't even try. He just sat there in his gorgeous sweater with the wind ruffling his hair, looking effortlessly stunning.

Eventually, Lewis lowered the bottle with a satisfied sigh, and Aaron quickly took a gulp of his own beer to hide that he'd been staring. But when he set his bottle back down, he found Lewis's eyes trained on *him*. On his mouth, in fact, before lifting slowly to Aaron's eyes with an expression Aaron might have described as *avid* if he hadn't known better.

He broke their gaze, making a sound painfully like a nervous giggle, which he covered by saying, "We should go paddling, after we've eaten."

"Paddling?"

"Yeah. You can't visit the seaside and not get your feet wet. It's the law."

Lewis raised one beautiful eyebrow. "I've never heard of that law."

"Well, luckily for you, I'm here to keep you on the straight and narrow."

"Ha," Lewis said, smiling. "Is that what you're doing?"

Jesus. Was he *flirting*?

Aaron twisted his bottle on the table, staring at the damp ring it left on the wood. "You know me. Not so much of the straight."

And was *he* flirting back?

Across the table, their eyes met again, Lewis's serious and searching and… Aaron might have said *uncertain* if that hadn't been patently ridiculous. Impossible, in fact. Lewis Hunter was the most certain man Aaron had ever met.

"It would be—" Lewis began, just as the buzzer went off, making them both jump.

Lewis grabbed it and stood up so fast the whole table shook. "I'll go get the food," he said, disappearing with the alacrity of a man saved by the bell, leaving Aaron bemused and wondering what, if anything, had just happened.

Or nearly happened.

Luckily, for the next half hour, they were both too busy eating to worry about anything else, engrossed in delicious battered fish and enormous portions of crispy, fluffy chips smothered in salt and vinegar.

"Bloody hell, these are good," Lewis said when he finally came up for air.

Aaron nodded. "Everything tastes better by the sea."

"But these are *really* good," Lewis said, waving a chip at him. "These are the best fucking chips I've ever eaten." He shoved the chip in his mouth, then sucked the salt from his fingers.

Aaron dropped his eyes back to his own food, trying not to imagine what those lips would feel like on his own.

"Do you play arcade games?" Lewis said then, gesturing to the arcade behind them. "I haven't been to one in years."

"Then we should go. Mum and Dad hardly ever let me in there, so I'm a bit crap. We'd play air hockey sometimes, though."

Lewis grinned. "I *love* air hockey."

And that's how they spent the next hour, whizzing plastic disks across the table at each other, Lewis's competitive streak out in full force and Aaron laughing hard at his ridiculous victory dances. Then they tried a racing game, a stupid dancing game which had them both in stitches, and finally, they wasted twenty minutes on the shove-ha'penny. Without winning a thing. Naturally.

By the time they left the arcade, it was dark. Aaron knew they should probably head back, but he was reluctant to end the evening. He'd had more fun than he'd had in a long time, more fun than he usually found anywhere but deep in his writing. It felt magical, in a way, a little soap bubble of joy he didn't want to pop. Regretfully, he said, "I suppose we should be getting back. It'll be tricky finding our way in the dark."

"But we haven't got our feet wet yet." Lewis reminded him. "Rules are rules, Aaron." His eyes gleamed with the rainbow reflections of the arcade, lips curling into a cajoling smile.

Not that Aaron needed any cajoling.

"I suppose they are," he said, smiling at Lewis, falling into that dark, glittering gaze. Christ, he wanted to kiss him. It felt like every nerve in his body was straining towards Lewis, yearning for his touch.

"Come on." Lewis's hand landed lightly on Aaron's back, lingering tantalisingly as he turned him toward the sea.

Aaron could do nothing but comply.

On the beach, they shed their shoes and socks, rolled up their jeans, and padded over the cold sand to the water's edge.

"Fuck!" Lewis hissed, laughing as their feet hit the water. "It's freezing."

"Of course it is!"

But it felt glorious too. Aaron loved the wash of the waves around his ankles, the sand shifting and sinking beneath his feet, oozing between his toes. He took a deep breath, closed his eyes, and let the sea breeze wash over him, through him, ruffling his hair and clothes and blowing out all the cobwebs. "God, I love it here," he said, tipping his face to the wind. "Everything feels so *alive*."

And it occurred to him then that he hadn't thought about

Skye or Faolán all evening. He wasn't even sure he could imagine them at the beach. Which was odd, because usually he could imagine them anywhere...

After a moment, quietly, Lewis said, "It's been a fantastic evening. I've had…" He blew out a breath. "This was so much better than anything I'd expected to be doing tonight."

Aaron smiled, kept his eyes closed, and for a moment—so brief he wasn't sure it was real—he thought he felt Lewis brush his knuckles against the back of his hand.

But before he could be sure, Lewis yelped, "Wave!" and they both stumbled backwards as the surf splashed up over their ankles, soaking the ends of their rolled-up jeans. Lewis lost his balance as he scrambled up the beach, Aaron grabbed him, and suddenly they were both clinging to each other, laughing.

And then, just as suddenly, they weren't laughing.

They were simply standing there in the moonlight, clutching each other's arms, gazing at each other. Lewis looked dishevelled and windblown, undone in a way that transformed him from idol into someone more real, more tangible, his dark hair blowing across his forehead, and his eyes the deep blue of the twilight sky. He swallowed visibly, lips parting, chest rising and falling. Breathing hard. His fingers tightened on Aaron's arms, drawing him closer.

Heart leaping into his throat, Aaron's gaze locked with Lewis's, his whole body vibrating with tension as they moved slowly closer. *Yes,* he thought wildly. *Yes…*

"Aaron…" Lewis sounded airless. "Fuck." He screwed his eyes shut. "Fuck, we should probably get a cab back."

"A cab?" Aaron blinked, dazed. *Was he suggesting…?*

But, no, Lewis had already dropped Aaron's arms and shoved his hands into his pockets, taking a step back. Scowling down at the sand, at their bare feet, he said, "Early start tomorrow."

Well. That was clear enough.

"Right," Aaron said, his heart still rabbiting. He couldn't seem to catch his breath. "Yeah, right. Good idea. I'll just…" He indicated the promenade above them, suddenly desperate for some distance. "I'll go and google a local cab company."

And with that the evening was over, like fireworks bursting in the night sky and fading to nothing.

CHAPTER ELEVEN

LEWIS

Lewis didn't usually sleep well at Safehaven, but that night—and despite his mind teeming with thoughts of Aaron on the beach and what had very much felt like an almost-kiss—he had fallen into a deep and dreamless sleep.

He was woken by the shimmery notes of his phone alarm, feeling well-rested. Scratching his belly, he yawned and stretched, then got out of bed, padding to the bathroom to take a piss.

On his way back to bed, he spied his laptop, open on the desk, reminding him that he still hadn't so much as glanced at the workshop information pack. He'd better at least give it a quick onceover before he went down.

Sighing, he flicked the laptop on and, while it booted up, investigated the contents of the tea tray glumly. Needless to say, there was no hot chocolate to be found, only the dreaded herbal teas. Grumbling, he went to the mini-fridge instead and selected a goji berry kombucha. It didn't taste too bad, to be fair, though it needed more sugar in his opinion.

Plunking himself back down on the bed, he grabbed the

laptop and opened his email, quickly locating the email from Charlie's assistant.

"The link to your personalised guided mediation is below"—hmmm, no time for that—*"and information on the workshop is attached. Please do read this carefully."*

He glanced at the time. Fuck. It was already 6:47. And he still had to shower.

Quickly, he opened the attachment, groaning when he saw it was sixty-three pages long. The cover featured a woman with blonde dreads who looked a bit like Tilda Swinton. She was in a sort of half-squat with her arms above her head and her eyes closed, her expression slightly anxious. She looked sort of constipated, Lewis thought.

Underneath the photo, it said, *Movement therapy: release toxic emotions; let your creativity thrive.*

Shit.

It was worse than he'd imagined.

Panic flapped like a trapped bird in his chest as he swiftly scrolled through pages that were dense with text and peppered with images of the same, severe-looking woman. *Hippolyta Grant,* the text informed him. *Energetic healing and wellbeing professional.*

The final page was entitled, *What preparation do I need to do for the workshop?*

His gaze dropped to the opening paragraph.

All you need is loose, comfortable clothing…

Oh, thank God!

… and a willingness to open yourself up emotionally to the group.

Shit.

He didn't bother reading any further, tossing the laptop aside and heading for the shower, which he set to cold, for no reason other than that it took his mind off what was coming up. When he finally emerged, teeth chattering, he briskly towelled dry and quickly donned his running gear, since it was that or jeans, and he was definitely more comfortable in running trousers.

Once dressed, he glanced at himself in the mirror and frowned. He just knew this was going to be awful. And whatever it entailed, he was going to have to go through it with Aaron, which was both a relief and a worry. He'd far rather it was Aaron than anyone else—the very thought of touching Charlie Alexander while 'opening up emotionally' had him practically dry-heaving—but after last night, he wasn't sure how he was going to react when he saw Aaron this morning.

What a night it had been.

What a stupidly perfect night.

Lewis groaned aloud and turned away from the mirror.

It had been one of those time out of time things. Just the two of them, him and Aaron, in that little seasidey town, away from everyone they knew, away from the office, as though real life didn't exist. Drinking beer and eating salty chips in the fading warmth of the late summer day. Laughing. Playing air hockey. A thrilling, intoxicating mix of the familiar and the new.

He closed his eyes and saw Aaron on the beach, standing in the freezing cold waves with his head tipped back.

Beautiful.

And then, that moment…

He'd wanted to kiss Aaron so fucking badly. For a moment or two, that want had almost overridden his brain function, a strange and sudden recklessness urging him to *just do it*. He'd seen that Aaron wanted it too; that there was no question of him pushing Lewis away.

Maybe that was what had stopped him. Knowing there would be no going back. Whatever it was, suddenly his heart had been pounding with something that felt a lot like naked fear.

Or maybe it had just been his common sense reasserting itself.

A light knock at his door dragged him out of his thoughts.

"Lewis? Are you ready?"

Toni.

He rubbed his hands briskly over his face, grabbed his phone, and went to the door.

"Morning," he said, taking in Toni's hip yoga outfit without surprise. The woman was always perfectly attired.

"Have you been for a run?" she said, eyebrows drawing together. "You need to change."

"No," Lewis replied flatly, stepping out and closing the door behind him. "This is all I have, since I didn't know I was going to have to do a fucking movement therapy workshop before I came."

Toni chuckled without much humour and stepped towards Aaron's door, which she knocked on.

"Ready, Aaron?" she called.

"Just coming," a muffled voice behind the door said.

A moment later, the door opened, and there stood Aaron in plaid sleep shorts and a plain, fitted navy t-shirt, a pair of sliders on his bare feet.

Toni stared at him, and he rubbed the back of his neck.

"Is this okay?" he asked. "My PJ shorts are the only loose clothing I have with me."

"They're fine," Lewis said shortly. "I've had to wear my running gear, and that's not even loose."

Aaron glanced at him, his gaze going straight to Lewis's tightly clad thighs, then quickly back up to his face. His cheeks pinkened, but he quickly quipped, "So long as you can express your inner pain through the medium of dance in those, you'll be fine."

"Oh God," Toni said faintly. "This is going to be so bad. Did you read the information pack thingy, Aaron?"

Aaron closed his door, and they started off down the corridor together.

"Yeah," Aaron said tightly. "Couldn't help noticing there

was a lot in there about *choice* and *control* and *autonomy*. Which is pretty rich given we've been given no choice about attending."

Lewis halted in the middle of the corridor and grabbed Aaron's arm. "Hey," he said urgently. "You don't have to do this. It's fine to pull out."

Aaron blinked at him. "But we've got to work in pairs. Charlie said—"

"Fuck Charlie!" Lewis snapped. "*I'm* your boss, and I'm telling you—you don't have to do this if you don't want to."

Aaron's light grey gaze searched his face. "Are you going to do it?"

Lewis felt like he had rocks in his stomach, but he shrugged like it was no big deal. "I have to, but you don't."

Aaron nodded. "Well, if you're doing it, I'm doing it," he said simply. For a second, their gazes met and held. Then Aaron started walking again.

"Did you read the part about being prepared to experience *intense emotion*?" Toni said after a few moments. She snorted. "Intense embarrassment, maybe."

Lewis glanced at her sharply. "Have you done this before?"

"Not this one. But when I was down in March, Charlie made us do laughter yoga." She shuddered. "It was awful. Poor Geoff hated it too."

Poor Geoff.

Lewis glanced at Aaron, who met his gaze and bit his lip against amusement.

Weirdly though, Toni's words did make him feel better. At least if this was humiliatingly embarrassing, he wouldn't be the only one feeling it.

When they got to the long gallery, it was to find Charlie and Hippolyta Grant already there, looking oddly like siblings, since they were a similar height and build and had similar colouring, though Hippolyta was fairer, her brows and eyelashes almost invisible. She wore no makeup, which gave her face a naked, stark look.

"Here's the troops," Charlie said cheerfully as they approached. He was wearing what could only be described as a unitard in military green, the top half a tight-fitting, short-sleeved shirt open almost to the navel, the bottom half a pair of shorts that hugged his toned thighs with a canvas belt around his waist.

There was something distressingly 1970s about it.

"Are you guys pumped for this?" Charlie asked. Hippolyta glanced at him, frowning faintly.

"So pumped," Lewis said drily, turning away to look at his phone. He pulled up his email and started scrolling through his messages, though the truth was, he wasn't really seeing them. Unfocussed anxiety gnawed at him.

"I'm excited for us to strip back the layers and start getting honest with each other," Charlie enthused. "Last time I did this, Hippolyta took me to an intensely creative place."

For a moment, no one said anything. Then Toni cleared her throat and said into the awkward silence, "That sounds amazing."

"It *can* be very powerful," Hippolyta said. Her voice was low and husky. "But it can also be quite intense. Did you all read the pack? I sent it to Charlie's PA last week, so you'd all know what we do and to check you're comfortable with it."

Last week? Charlie had organised this *last week*? Why the fuck had he waited till yesterday to spring it on them?

Lewis pretended not to be listening—he could *not* get into this shit with Charlie, or he was going to blow. He stabbed his phone screen unseeingly, opening an attachment he barely registered. *Busy guy here, catching up on my inbox.*

"I read the pack," Aaron said in a cool voice Lewis knew well. It was the voice he used when he wasn't pleased. The one that always made Lewis pause and think, *Okay, maybe this time I fucked up.*

"And?" Hippolyta prompted in her low voice. "How do you feel about doing the workshop?"

To be fair, she sounded like she honestly wanted to know.

"Oh, Andy's up for it, aren't you, mate?" Charlie said with lethal bonhomie.

"I asked Andy, not you," Hippolyta said without tone.

Charlie opened his mouth to speak again, but before he could get a word out, Aaron said, "Actually, it's *Aaron*. And to be honest, I'm not sure how I feel about it."

Charlie made a scoffing noise, but Hippolyta said calmly, "That's fair, and I'm glad you've been honest. If you feel uncomfortable, you can sit it out, or you can give it a try and just raise a hand if it gets too much. Communication is important. And it's absolutely okay to take a time out if you feel you need to."

"I'm sure that won't be necessary," Charlie interjected, adding before anyone could respond, "Oh, it's *Miss Mils*! How are you, my lovely?"

Lewis did glance up from his phone then, to see Milly prowling down the long gallery like a pocket-sized catwalk model, five foot nothing of chiselled cheekbones and pouting lips, dark hair woven into a complicated-looking crown of plaits. Amusingly, she seemed to be wearing a female version of Charlie's outfit. Lewis sucked his lips into his mouth and bit down hard to hold back his grin, determinedly avoiding Aaron's gaze, which he knew would likely set him off.

"Charl-eeeee!" Milly squealed. She did a sort of ungainly baby gazelle run for the last few steps, before throwing herself into his arms.

Milly was undoubtedly one of the dullest people Lewis had ever met. She looked a bit like a Disney princess, all wide eyes, white teeth, and cloudy hair. Her small and dainty frame was, sadly, matched by a small and even more dainty brain.

While Milly practically made out with Charlie, her hapless husband, Geoff, brought up the rear.

In contrast to Milly's Tarzanesque get-up, Geoff wore utilitarian grey joggers and a matching t-shirt.

He was kind of grey all over. Greying brown hair, greyish, pasty complexion from far too much time spent at his desk. He wasn't a terrible-looking guy by any stretch, but he was a workaholic with a slight paunch and a receding hairline. It was easy to see that, next to Geoff, Charlie might look quite glamorous, even if he was a complete dick.

Not for the first time, Lewis wondered why Milly had married Geoff. He supposed that, objectively speaking, the guy might be viewed as quite a catch. He was a highly paid entertainment lawyer, at the top of his game. Supposedly he could pretty much pick and choose his clients.

But ultimately, his biggest assets were his wealth and his power, and on those two fronts, he simply could not compete with Charlie Alexander, whose family were bona fide billionaires. Charlie could buy and sell Geoff twenty times over and would not hesitate to do so if it suited him.

As Geoff watched his wife hanging all over Charlie and giggling her inane little laugh, his unremarkable face was utterly miserable.

Toni took pity on him. "Hi, Geoff," she said, drawing his attention away from them. "It's good to see you again. How have you been?"

Geoff blinked, his expression at first puzzled, then grateful. "Hi! Toni, right? I'm good, thanks. And you?"

"Never better," she replied mildly and launched into the small talk she was so good at. Lewis tuned out of their conversation, uninterested, and, pocketing his phone, moved towards Aaron.

When he reached him, he said, under his breath, "So, you actually read the information pack?"

"Yup," Aaron replied. "I couldn't get to sleep last night."

His gaze on Lewis was suddenly intent. "I gather you didn't?"

Lewis laughed, though it was a hollow sound. "Fuck, no. Bad enough that I have to be here." He tried for an insouciant smile but could tell from Aaron's expression that he'd failed. Aaron's light brown eyebrows furrowed.

He looked—worried?

"It can't be that bad," Lewis said. "No one ever died of embarrassment, right?"

Aaron opened his mouth to say something else, but stopped when Hippolyta clapped loudly and said, "Okay, we're all here now, so we'll make a start very soon."

Everyone fell silent and looked at her. She smiled serenely.

"Before we get going, I want to tell you a little bit about what we'll be doing today. Then we'll have a short break to give you all the opportunity to come and speak privately with me if you have any concerns or questions about the process. And then those of us that want to go ahead will make a start."

"I really don't think you need to—" Charlie began, but he fell silent when she shot him a look. Hippolyta let the silence drag for a few moments, letting it just edge into awkwardness before she returned her gaze to the broader group.

Lewis felt like cheering. He glanced at Aaron, expecting him to be biting back a smile too, but Aaron's brows were still knitted together in that faint frown.

"So," Hippolyta said, "for the next few hours we're going to be focusing on using movement to unlock creativity. We're not aiming to get too heavy or deep, but sometimes, this sort of work can open difficult things up for people, especially anyone who might have any unresolved issues." She let her assessing gaze travel over the group, and Lewis felt a prickle of discomfort travelling up his spine.

"As it happens," she went on, "most people experience some level of emotion during the workshop, so again, if that's something you think you'd be uncomfortable with, please do speak to me. In terms of what we'll actually be doing, I prefer to let that unfold over the course of the workshop, but in very basic terms, you'll be working in the group and with your partner in a variety of movement-related exercises which will help you identify and explore areas where you may feel creatively congested."

She went on in the same vein for a while longer, blabbing on about movement being the *primary human language* and how it could help people having problems accessing their creativity to *address internal obstacles through an alternative form of creative expression.*

Lewis fought the desire to openly scoff. His shoulder twinged, and he rubbed absently at the sore spot. Hippolyta caught his eye and, raising her brows, said, "You may even find it helps you with that sore shoulder you've got."

Before he could respond, she was clapping her hands again. "Okay, so take a few minutes just now. Anyone who has questions, come and see me at the other end of the gallery. Everyone else, get yourselves some water from the drinks area and each pair grab a mat. Spread yourselves out—each pair should be a good couple of metres away from the other pairs. Oh, and we're going to be working barefoot, so take your shoes off."

With that, she strolled off, leaving the rest of them standing there.

Charlie immediately set a proprietary hand on Milly's shoulder and steered her towards the drinks table. Geoff stared after them forlornly.

Toni sighed and walked over to him, saying cheerfully, "I gather you and I are going to be partnered up." Geoff smiled wanly at her.

Which at least proved to Lewis that today *could* be worse. He could be Toni. Stuck with the guy being cuckolded by a billionaire.

Putting Toni and Geoff out of his mind, Lewis took a step towards the pile of rolled-up mats.

"What are you doing?" Aaron asked.

"What does it look like?" Lewis retorted, turning to look at him. "I'm getting a mat. Figured we'd do that first, then grab our drinks."

"But aren't you, you know…?"

Lewis frowned. "Aren't I what?"

Aaron was silent for a moment. Then he blurted, "Aren't you going to speak to Hippolyta?"

Lewis glared at him. "Why would I do that?"

Aaron was quiet for long moments. Then he said, his tone hollow, "So… that's a 'no' then?"

"No! In fact, *fuck no*! Why would I?"

Aaron didn't reply, but his gaze was heavy. At last, he shrugged and looked away, but his expression stayed worried and frowning. Lewis didn't ask him why. He didn't even try to work it out. Instead, he focused on selecting a mat and laying it on the floor, ignoring his pounding heart.

After a moment, Aaron sighed. "I'll grab us some water."

CHAPTER TWELVE

Lewis

When Aaron returned, he was barefoot. He had nice feet, Lewis noticed. High arches.

"Where did you put your sliders?" he asked, accepting the water bottle Aaron proffered.

"Over there." Aaron pointed at a small pile of shoes in the corner.

"I suppose I'd better take mine off too," Lewis said reluctantly. He felt oddly self-conscious about the idea of being barefoot.

"Yeah." Aaron's expression was watchful, wary. Lewis felt his face heat; he had the horrible feeling he was behaving strangely.

Striding over to the corner, he quickly untied his trainers and toed them off, then walked back. He felt weirdly naked, vulnerable even, and when he reached the mat, he didn't look at Aaron, instead grabbing his water and sipping at it till Hippolyta—who no one had gone to speak to—returned to their end of the long gallery.

She halted some distance from the three mats, an upright figure with her pale, severe face, watching them.

For a while she was silent, and everyone—except Charlie —shifted uncomfortably. Then, finally, she said, "Welcome."

Everyone watched her, unsure what to do. She made an extravagant beckoning gesture with both of her arms, a gesture that commanded them all.

"Welcome," she said again, and her voice was all serious and dramatic. Honestly, it just felt so bloody *silly* to Lewis. He glanced at Aaron, who shrugged. They both glanced at Charlie and Milly, who were already walking away from their mat towards Hippolyta. Moments later, Geoff and Toni followed, Geoff doing a rather embarrassing little sideslip to situate himself next to his oblivious wife. Lewis and Aaron brought up the rear. The six of them—choreographed by silent hand signals from Hippolyta—shuffled into a semicircle formation facing her.

"Welcome," she said yet again, in that grave, actorly voice. Lewis barely suppressed a snort.

Hippolyta pressed her hands against her heart hard, closing her eyes. She stayed like that for several moments before opening her eyes and stretching out her arms to Charlie on her left.

"Welcome, Charlie," she said, meeting his gaze.

Charlie nodded gravely and pressed his hands to his own heart as though capturing something there. Lewis wanted to retch.

Then it was Milly's turn.

"Welcome, Milly."

Milly copied Charlie to the letter, though her movements were more graceful, like a dancer.

And oh, fuck, Hippolyta was going to go round them all, wasn't she?

Geoff was next. He looked panicked, his cheeks faintly flushed, but after a moment, he gave his chest a sort of pat without meeting her eyes and quickly dropped his hand. Toni, who could bullshit for England, took it in her stride, smiling easily and insincerely, while crossing her palms briefly over her heart. Somehow, she managed to make it look like no big deal.

Aaron was next—he just nodded curtly.

Hippolyta canted her head to one side, considering him for a few moments in silence. Then she gravely nodded back and turned to Lewis.

Lewis's stomach hurt, and his heart was racing, but when she stretched her arms out to him, he grinned like a lunatic and gave her a fancy bow, with one hand making circles in the air like a storybook cavalier holding his feathered hat.

She… laughed.

Straightening, he blinked. He hadn't expected that somehow.

"That was my welcome to you," Hippolyta was saying now, even as she performed the same gesture again, pressing her hands to her heart and then stretching out her arms, though this time she spread them wide, encompassing everyone. "It was a physical expression of welcome. And each of you, whether you realised it or not, expressed something physically to me in return." Her placid gaze travelled over them. "The language of movement is something we do all know—connect with—in some way, even if we're not conscious of it."

Lewis's gaze flicked to Charlie, who was wearing a smug smile.

Ugh.

"We're going to start with some body awareness exercises," Hippolyta said. She began to pace and stretch, circling her arms. "For the next few minutes, I'd like you all to just move freely, breathing, and exploring the space around you." She moved her head in a circular motion and twisted her shoulders. "Use all of your body but keep the movements simple. Build an awareness of your body in this space."

Charlie was already swaying, eyes closed, arms raised.

Christ, he was punchable.

Milly was moving too, again with that dancer's poise. In fact, she looked like she *was* dancing, with the ease of practised movement. In Lewis's book that was just cheating. If you looked good, you weren't really suffering your way through this.

Slowly, reluctantly, everyone else began shuffling too.

"Explore the space in front of you and behind you," Hippolyta cried, spinning in a circle. "And the space above you!"

Charlie whooped and jumped up, punching the air.

Aaron met Lewis's gaze and rolled his eyes so hard Lewis was surprised they didn't fall out of his head. He smothered a laugh.

"And now the ground," Hippolyta said, dropping dramatically to the floor and beginning to roll around.

Bizarrely, that prompted Geoff to start doing a distressing version of the Caterpillar in what appeared to be a vain attempt to get his wife's attention.

Lewis averted his gaze in pity, grimacing.

For what felt like hours, they did this, swaying and pacing and writhing and rolling while Hippolyta called out random instructions. Eventually, though, she called time on the warmup and sent them off to their mats.

"Now," she said, "with your partners, I want you to explore the space on your mat by creating relationships based on movement. Let's start with different forms of opposition. Begin with time. For the next few minutes, one of you will explore quick movement and the other slow movement. I want you to observe what you prefer—what feels most familiar to you, what best *expresses* you. Remember, we're trying to cultivate self-awareness here."

Lewis wasn't sure how flailing his arms around was supposed to achieve that, but he trudged off after Aaron—who so far had been possibly even more awkward than Lewis—to their mat.

Aaron took one end, sitting cross-legged, and Lewis took the other, facing him. He tried not to focus on Aaron's bare legs or the little mole on the inside of his right knee. *Kissable,* his unhelpful brain supplied.

"I feel like a right idiot," Aaron muttered, circling his wrists unenthusiastically. "This is me exploring slow movement, by the way."

From where he was sitting, Lewis could see Charlie with his legs spread in a V and Milly wedged between them punching her little fists in front of her like a diminutive Rocky Balboa. Charlie, meanwhile, was swaying slowly from side to side, eyes closed like he was tripping. Maybe he was.

On their other side, Geoff was engaged in some aggressive squats, his face turning redder and redder. "Fifty a day," he puffed at Toni, "keeps the doctor away."

Lewis returned his attention to Aaron, shaking one hand vigorously, as if forcing feeling back into numb fingers. It made his sore shoulder twinge, and he grimaced. "I'm about to explore fast movement out the bloody door."

Aaron grinned, ducking his head to hide the smile, making his hair fall over his forehead. Alarmingly cute. "I'm starving," he muttered. "I hope we can eat soon."

Lewis was hungry too, and he didn't like the sensation. It made him feel anxious and out of control, which was odd and added to his general and growing sense of unease. His shoulder ached in sympathy with his growling stomach, and he reached up to rub the sore spot between shoulder and neck.

"Now, I want you to observe your partner," Hippolyta droned from somewhere behind him. "Become aware of their movements and your own. Be aware of your differences and synchronicities. Notice their breathing, and your own. Their body, and your own."

Lewis needed no prompting to be aware of Aaron's body. He was already hyper-aware, especially after last night. He could still feel the warm slide of his hands on Aaron's bare skin in the wildflower meadow. Aaron in his arms on the beach, his silver eyes brimming with laughter, then softening with something else.

Fuck.

He glanced at Aaron, who gave him a weak smile.

"Be aware of the space you're creating around yourselves. Stretch out your arms to feel its edges, to your sides and now above. This is your space, your created space. It's a soap bubble, a trust balloon, temporary and powerful. Within the bubble of acceptance that you have created with your partner, I want you to start exploring ways to communicate with each other without the use of your voice. Observe your partner, observe their movements, observe the pain points in their body."

Staring at Aaron felt simultaneously awkward and the most natural thing in the world. Maybe, Lewis thought, as his gaze ran over Aaron's lightly muscled body, that was because he looked at Aaron all the time. His face, with his smiling grey eyes and expressive mouth, the scattering of freckles over the bridge of his nose, and the single dimple in his left cheek, was as familiar to Lewis as his own. And when their gazes met, the communication was always instant—they'd been talking without words for years, thank you very much, Hippolyta.

Aaron chewed his bottom lip—a familiar gesture—and Lewis felt a sudden heaviness in his cock. Not being a horny seventeen-year-old, he willed it away, but still… The reaction shocked him. Made him wonder whether last night had short-circuited some of his customary defences, leaving him exposed.

"Now turn your gaze inward, to your own body. Do you feel resistance?" Hippolyta's shadow fell over them. "Do you feel pain? Good. Go deeper into it, interrogate the pain. Within your trust bubble, you're safe to explore painful feelings without judgment. You're free to allow your body to speak when your conscious mind cannot."

Aaron's expression turned from awkward to decidedly unhappy. Lewis rolled his dodgy shoulder, wishing he'd had time for that massage yesterday. His shoulder had given him grief for as long as he could remember, and he rubbed at it, an inexplicably anxious thrum resonating in his chest. He felt a little nauseous.

Fuck, he *hated* this bullshit.

"Now I'd like you to touch your partner," Hippolyta said, hoving into view behind Aaron. "Not intrusively, and with their consent." She held out both her hands, then pressed them together. "Let's start with palm to palm. Reach out to your partner. Greet them with your body."

With an eye roll, Aaron lifted one hand palm out, as if stopping traffic. Under Hippolyta's approving gaze, Lewis mirrored the gesture until his palm touched Aaron's. Eyes locked, Lewis felt his breathing speed up, saw Aaron's chest labouring too. And then, Aaron's hand softened, his fingers slowly moving until they were interlaced with Lewis's. And despite his racing pulse, Lewis felt his anxiety ease. He pulled in a deep breath through his nose, trying to disguise how much he needed it.

Aaron's touch was a comfort, he realised.

"Very good," Hippolyta said in her low, breathy voice. "Now, in the safe space between you, express to each other what you see. Where are your partner's resistance points? Where are they holding pain? Place your hand there, guide them to it."

For a long, heavy moment, neither of them moved. Then Aaron lifted his free hand, hesitating before laying it gently over the sore point between Lewis's neck and shoulder. His touch was warm, his fingers strong, and Lewis felt an immediate, intense wash of relief. Helplessly, his eyes fluttered closed as he breathed out a silent sigh. It was an unexpectedly powerful reaction, and he felt a weird upsurge of feeling. Of *gratitude*. He couldn't explain why.

"Allow your partner's touch to open your mind to the resistance within your body," Hippolyta went on. "Explore that resistance. Where has it come from? What is its root? Is there something there you would like to let go?"

No. Lewis tensed. No, he couldn't do that.

Instead, he focused on Aaron's warm fingers, on his thumb moving lightly against Lewis's neck. Soothing. Comforting. Arousing? Yes, he felt the faint stir of desire in his blood, the prickle of goosebumps along his spine, the weight in his cock. But those were familiar sensations. Safe and comfortable in their way. What shook him was the unexpected churn of emotion, of *feeling*, that wouldn't go away. Where the fuck was it coming from? He didn't know.

He sucked in a breath, mortified at the way it shuddered.

Aaron's grip tightened. "Lewis?"

"And remember," Hippolyta said mildly. "You can step out of the bubble at any time. Take some water and fresh air."

"Not necessary over here," Charlie piped up in a breathy voice. "God, Mils, that's *exactly* the spot."

Opening his eyes, Lewis found Aaron watching him, brows stitched into a frown, silently asking, *Okay?*

Lewis nodded, belatedly realising that their hands were still joined and had come to rest on the mat between them. He was holding Aaron's hand. He hadn't held hands like that with anyone since his mother—

A stab of pain, sharper than he'd felt in years, made him pull back. He pushed the pain savagely aside, tugging his hand free of Aaron's grasp.

Aaron's other hand fell away from his shoulder, his wide-eyed gaze concerned.

"All right," Hippolyta said from behind him, "we'll leave it there for now. We're going to come back together as a group to share our first paired experiences. Please, everyone, move out of your trust bubbles and form a circle."

It must be skipping breakfast, Lewis thought. *Low blood sugar or something.* Because he felt weird. Anxious and breathless. The faint nausea from before was back too.

What the fuck was wrong with him?

He tried to shake it off as he stood up and sipped his water, but he was finding it difficult to look at anyone. Except Aaron. And thank God Aaron was sticking to him like glue, following him into the circle and sitting close enough that their knees touched where they sat cross-legged on the floor like kids in school assembly. Shamefully, Lewis realised he needed that contact. Needed the tether of Aaron's presence to keep him from washing away. *Fuck.*

"Who would like to share first?" Hippolyta said, tossing her dreads over one shoulder.

"Me!" Milly's hand shot up.

Hippolyta didn't look surprised. "Thank you, Milly. Please, go ahead..."

"Well, first," Milly gushed, "I want to say how literally *amazing* this has been, Hippolyta. Thank you." She performed a practised namaste. "I mean, I knew it would be enlightening, but honestly, I feel like I've learned more in the last hour than I did in three years at Oxford."

"And what is it you've learned today?" asked Hippolyta. "Can you expand on that?"

"Um, well..." Seeming startled by the question, she glanced at Charlie, who was lounging at her side in a semi-reclined pose like an under-endowed Greek god in a onesie.

"I think we've learned how deeply we're bonded," Charlie

said, squeezing Milly's thigh. "Our bodies are as sympatico as our minds, right, Mils?"

On the other side of the circle, Geoff emitted a distressed huff.

Into the awkward silence that followed, Toni said, "Well, *I've* learned that I need to join a yoga class. I can't believe how stiff I am!"

Hippolyta smiled benignly. "I would advocate a regular yoga practice to anyone." Her gaze turned to Lewis, rested there for a moment, and when he didn't speak, she moved to Aaron. "Do you have any observations to share, Aaron?"

Tersely, he said, "My observation is that a workshop like this isn't for everyone."

"That's certainly true. As I said at the beginning, anyone can step out if they feel it's becoming too intense."

"But intensity is what we need!" Charlie objected, surging upright. "We need it to blast through the blockers and release our creative vision."

"That's interesting, Charles," said Hippolyta. "Are you happy to tell us about a block you've discovered this morning?"

"Well, obviously, *I'm* pretty free-flowing, creatively. But within the group I sense some negative energy. Some parochial thinking."

Lewis's hackles rose. "Some *what*?"

"Nobody's fault." Charlie raised a placating hand. "No blame here. We've all travelled a road to reach this point. We've all faced challenges. And inevitably they've left a mark." He sent a speaking glance Lewis's way.

What the fuck? The nerve in Lewis's shoulder pinched hard, making him wince.

"But we can't let our baggage stop us from forging a new path," Charlie went on. "Even if it's difficult, we must tear off our labels and free ourselves to embrace a new direction."

"Oh, totally," Milly echoed. "We have to reject labels. I

mean, I literally hate the 'Oxbridge' label, you know? It's like, yah, I went to Oxford. So what? It doesn't define me."

Charlie rubbed her thigh again. "You're so much more than that, Mils. So much more."

Hippolyta looked displeased. "That's not...exactly the purpose of this workshop, Charles."

"Nonsense." He bared his shark's smile at her, full of teeth. "The workshop is about whatever we need it to be about. Isn't that what you told me? Personally, I'm finding it incredibly liberating."

"Incredibly," Milly echoed.

Lewis tipped his head to one side, trying to stretch out the sore muscle. The twinge in his neck was getting worse, and so was the nausea. Now there was a smell, familiar and unpleasant… He sniffed the air. What *was* that? Disinfectant? It smelled like a hospital. He tried to shake it off, ignoring the way his heart had started galloping and the sudden outbreak of sweat on his forehead.

"All right." Hippolyta sounded curt. "Let's return to our pairs. I want to explore opposition again. Think about free movement and bound movement, about the ways in which you bind yourself and can free yourself. Take hold of your partner's hand and pull while the other resists. How does that feel?"

Back on their mat, Lewis was vaguely aware of Aaron taking his hand, but he was distracted by the disinfectant smell, and the nausea, and the pain in his shoulder.

Where the fuck was that smell coming from?

He looked around. Milly had Charlie pinned to the mat, both of them laughing and writhing. Lewis ignored them. Toni and Geoff were engaged in a desperate discussion with Hippolyta, who was squatting next to them, and—

Something caught his eye. A stack of chairs, pushed up against the far wall in a neat pile. The kind of chairs you might see at a conference.

Or in a waiting room.

The nerve in his neck twanged so hard he gasped and clutched his shoulder.

And suddenly, he was back there. That night.

Exhausted by fear and grief, gritty-eyed, trying to sleep on the comfortless plastic chair beneath the neon glare of the hospital lights, his head twisted at an awkward angle. But the pain in his neck was nothing to the pain in his breaking heart.

You can come in now, boys, the doctor said gently. *It's time to say goodbye to Mum.*

Lewis sucked in a breath, horrified by the wet, shuddery sound he made, helpless to stop the unrelenting wave of memory that swept up and over him, drowning him.

He screwed his eyes shut. His lashes felt wet.

Fuck. Fucking hell.

The memories wouldn't stop. He couldn't stop them.

Owen looking at him. *Come on, Lewis. Let's go in now.*

Someone grasped his shoulder, right over the pain point, squeezing hard. Strong fingers, warm and sure.

"It's okay," Aaron said softly. "Lewis, look at me."

CHAPTER THIRTEEN

Aaron

"Lewis, look at me." Kneeling in front of him, Aaron tightened his grip on Lewis's shoulder. "Open your eyes."

Hippolyta took a step towards them, concerned, but Aaron shook his head. The last thing Lewis needed was a fuss. Shit, he'd been afraid something like this might happen ever since he'd read the welcome pack with all its talk about delving into past pain. What the fuck had Charlie been thinking?

After a moment, Lewis opened his eyes. But he wasn't all there. Aaron could see part of him was absent, caught up in whatever had put that look on his face.

"Lewis, tell me five things you can see," Aaron said gently, still gripping Lewis's tense shoulder, feeling the minute tremors running through him.

"What?" Lewis said hoarsely.

"Tell me five things you can see right now."

Lewis blinked, but eventually said, "You. I can see you."

"What else?"

"Um. The mat. The floor."

"That's three."

"The window," Lewis said, his gaze growing more focused. More present. "The trees outside the window."

"Good." Aaron gave him an encouraging smile. "Now four things you can hear."

Lewis shook his head, impatient, but said, "Birds outside. Your voice. A plane overhead…" His eyes lifted to Aaron's. "Charlie, dry-humping Milly."

That was more like it. Aaron's smile broadened, and he relaxed a little. "And three things you can touch?"

"You," Lewis said immediately and squeezed Aaron's fingers. "You."

"That's only one."

Lewis opened his mouth to speak, closed it again. His expression was raw, torn open in a way Aaron had never seen before and didn't want to see again. "Sorry," he said in a rough voice. "I was…" He trailed off, shaking his head.

"Want to get some fresh air?"

"I'm fine."

"You don't look—"

Lewis shrugged Aaron's hand from his shoulder. "I said I'm fine."

That was bollocks, but Lewis had a mulish look on his face now which was at least reassuringly familiar. Aaron didn't argue, glancing past Lewis to where Hippolyta was crouching next to Geoff and Toni, encouraging them to perform something that looked like *Row, Row, Row Your Boat*.

Sensing his look, Hippolyta glanced up. She was perceptive, he'd give her that much. Rising limberly to her feet, she said, "And now we'll take a pause to reflect on what we've learned so far. I'd like you to step outside into the open air and move consciously within that external space. Be aware of what we've discussed—speed, direction, power of movement. Consider which you like best, which expresses you most deeply. Meditate on what that means."

Charlie was on his feet immediately, prancing down the gallery like a wanker, with Milly skipping along in his wake. "Speed! Precision!" he was calling out. "Quick as a fox!"

Geoff made a sort of halting half gallop in the same direction, then gave up with a heavy sigh, shoulders slumping.

"Shall we get a coffee?" Toni suggested, kindly.

Geoff brightened, then threw an uncertain look at Hippolyta. "I think we're still meant to be fasting…"

"That is entirely your choice," Hippolyta said, frowning slightly. "I hope that was made clear."

"Er…" Geoff scratched his jaw.

Toni took his arm. "Come on, Geoff, let's find a coffee and a croissant. I'm *dying* to hear more about your trip to Machu Picchu."

And it wasn't until she threw a concerned look over her shoulder at Lewis, slowly climbing to his feet, that Aaron realised she'd noticed his meltdown. Well, no surprise there; they'd been friends for years, and Toni was nothing if not observant.

Lewis didn't look at any of them, though. He just crossed the floor, grabbed his trainers and, without pausing to put them on, stalked down the gallery on his own. Aaron was about to follow when Hippolyta touched his arm. "Wait," she said.

Once Geoff and Toni were out of earshot, Hippolyta said, "That was very intense for Lewis."

"Yes."

"I'm glad you were there for him. I can see that you have a very intimate relationship, that he trusts you deeply. It was beautiful to watch your connection."

Aaron laughed, but not in amusement. "We're not—I'm just his PA."

She looked doubtful. "However you define your relationship, Aaron, you are clearly not 'just' anything to Lewis. The body doesn't lie. I saw how he responded to your presence today." Frowning, she added, "But I gather he didn't prepare fully for the workshop?"

"Given that Charlie only sprung it on us yesterday afternoon, no, he didn't."

Her lips thinned in annoyance. "I'm very sorry to hear that. It's not what I expected or asked for." She tipped her head in the direction Lewis had taken. "You should be with him now; he'll need your support. I believe he touched on something very profound this morning."

Aaron only nodded, having no intention of saying anything about Lewis. Not that Aaron knew what had been going on inside his head, but his distress had been visceral. And painful to witness. Surprisingly so for Aaron. He'd never seen Lewis vulnerable like that, visibly upset, his usual arrogant façade all crumbled away. Aaron still felt shaken by it, his stomach hollow.

"Please tell him that if he chooses to continue with the workshop, we'll be focusing only on healing relaxation for the rest of our time together. I'm not prepared to continue with the more intense work given the group's"—she paused, then added tightly—"lack of appropriate time to prepare."

Aaron nodded, reluctantly appreciating her obvious concern about Lewis. There was no doubt that the workshop had opened up something profoundly upsetting for him, but it wasn't her fault Lewis had been pressganged into attending. That was on Charlie fucking Alexander.

After thanking her, Aaron headed out in search of Lewis. He finally found him sitting on a bench in the formal gardens at the back of the house.

Despite everything, he looked as spectacular as ever in his leave-nothing-to-the-imagination running gear, his thick, dark hair mussed from running his hands through it. Aaron halted a few yards away, and for several long moments, he just stood there, staring. Lewis really was a beautifully made man, but right now, he was all alone in his misery, sitting with his forearms resting on his knees, his broad shoulders hunched in angry defeat as he stared moodily at the ground between his feet.

He looked utterly miserable, and Aaron's heart couldn't stand it.

Trotting down the three steps into the sunken garden, Aaron made his way over to the bench, crunching across the gravel in his sliders.

"If you want to be left alone," he said gently, drawing to a halt near the bench, "I'll go."

Lewis didn't look up. "I feel like a fucking idiot," he said, directing the words at the ground, his expression hidden by the fall of his tousled dark hair. "I don't even know what the fuck happened."

"I spoke to Hippolyta," Aaron said, perching gingerly on the other end of the bench. "She was pissed off that Charlie sprang this on us at the last minute. We're just doing relaxation for the rest of the workshop if—"

"I'm not going back in there."

"Fair enough. I don't blame you."

Lewis blew out a gusty breath and sat up, pushing back his hair with one hand. "But if I don't, Charlie will never let it go."

"Fuck Charlie."

"No thanks."

Aaron huffed a soft laugh, and Lewis almost smiled, a faint glimmer of amusement in his gaze. "Thanks for… for whatever it was you did in there."

"No problem. It used to help when my sister had anxiety attacks."

Lewis glanced at him. He hadn't managed to rebuild his façade yet, and his expression was still raw and open. It hurt to look at him.

"I didn't know you had a sister."

"No," Aaron agreed, smiling. "Believe it or not, there are a few things you don't know about me." Some of which he could never know.

Lewis regarded him steadily. Then he said, "So, Hippolyta said just relaxation after this?"

"*Healing* relaxation."

Lewis looked away, over the ordered grounds towards the wilderness beyond. "I don't want Charlie to think this rattled me."

"Rattled you?" Aaron frowned. "Wait. You don't think he did this on purpose, do you?"

Lewis shook his head wearily. "Nah. Charlie's all about Charlie—he's too self-absorbed to be that Machiavellian. But he does love seeing people unsettled, and he'll definitely take advantage of it if he thinks he'll get some leverage over me." He glanced at Aaron, his mouth twisting in a wry smile. "Basically, he's just a common or garden corporate bastard in hemp sandals."

Aaron nodded. "I bet Geoff would agree with that assessment."

"Poor bastard." Taking a deep breath, Lewis pushed to his feet. "Fuck it, I have to finish this bloody workshop."

The sun was behind him, and Aaron had to squint to see his face. "You really don't, you know. You could just go back to your room and rest."

Frankly, that sounded like a great idea to Aaron. After his sleepless night, a nap was exactly what he needed.

But Lewis shook his head. "And let him win? No fucking way." Then, to Aaron's astonishment, he held out his hand, his expression uncharacteristically uncertain. "Come with me?"

Maybe it was all the touching they'd done in the workshop, but it didn't feel strange to take Lewis's hand and allow himself to be pulled to his feet. Nor did it feel strange to be close enough to feel the heat of Lewis's body beating against his own as he met the man's bruised, unguarded gaze.

And maybe it was also why, when Lewis went to drop his hand and step back, Aaron found himself tightening his grip, just for a moment, and saying, "Of course I will. I'll always be there if you need me."

Lewis stared at him for a moment, his bright, blue eyes searching Aaron's face, as though verifying his sincerity. Then he nodded and whispered, "Thanks."

Aaron let go of his hand, and they turned and began walking back to the house.

When they arrived, it was to find the others were all in the Long Gallery.

Hippolyta and Charlie were standing off to one side. Hippolyta was talking in a low voice while Charlie listened, but his expression was mutinous, lips pressed into a hard line.

Milly was chattering inanely to Toni, who wore a polite expression, while Geoff stood beside them, hanging on his wife's every word.

Toni glanced Aaron and Lewis's way as they approached. She met Aaron's gaze, signalling subtle concern. Aaron gave her a slight nod and hoped she took it as reassurance.

As they drew closer, Toni said, "Hey there. If you're hungry, there's muffins and Danish pastries on the table. Tea and coffee too. Hippolyta organised it." In a lower voice she added, "I don't think we actually *had* to fast last night."

"Oh, but it *was* recommended!" Milly piped up, earnestly. "Charlie said so, and I for one feel *amazing*. So light and, you know, *unburdened*?"

"Yeah, well, you fast all the time," Geoff said. "You're always on some faddy diet or other." He smiled at her, but it was a tight sort of smile.

She narrowed her eyes at him. "No, I'm not," she said, a note of venom in her tone that was completely at odds with that cutesy thing she had going on the rest of the time. "And you know I literally hate the way you police my eating."

"Maybe if you ate enough to—"

But he got no further. Charlie was stalking towards them, his whole body exuding irritation, while a calm Hippolyta brought up the rear.

"Okay, guys," Charlie said. "We're going to bring the workshop to an end a bit early." He sent Lewis a quick, accusing look then, added tightly, "Apparently, some of us are more blocked than others and are finding the process rather challenging."

Hippolyta interjected calmly, "It may have been easier if everyone had been given time to prepare correctly and knew what we would be doing today." She smiled around the group. "I'd be more than happy to come back and run the full workshop again another time, or see any of you privately if you would like. But for today, I think we'll just close out with some simple movement exercises."

Aaron felt a sharp stab of relief. He glanced at Lewis and was glad to see that, while he still looked tense, he definitely seemed less hunted.

The final thirty minutes were relatively bearable. Hippolyta led them through a not-too-embarrassing sequence of movements, then repeated her 'welcome' schtick with a 'thank you' twist, addressing each of them in turn. Finally, they had to make a circle, hold hands, and each make a positive affirmation to the group. Charlie offered up, "I have the courage and confidence to do incredible things". Milly went with, "Every day, I am closer to becoming the best version of myself", Geoff with "I deserve to be loved", and Toni with "I am in charge of my life".

When it was Aaron's turn, he said, rather vaguely, "I am capable of more than I think"—which was cheating, as it was one of the examples Hippolyta had given them before they began. To her credit, Hippolyta didn't so much as blink at the blatant plagiarism.

At last, it was Lewis's turn.

Quietly, firmly, he said, "I am in control."

Charlie's eyes narrowed.

And then, finally, *thankfully*, it was over.

"Okay, dinner's at seven tonight," Charlie said, as they dropped hands and the circle drifted apart. "But I want all of you in the lounge from five for drinks, okay? Be on time and *no* excuses." He gave an insincere smile. "In the meantime, enjoy Safehaven. Have a swim, use the gym—one of the staff can sort you out with a bike or a Segway if you like. Just make the most of the place. I've got a few calls to take this afternoon, so I'll leave you all to it." He glanced at Milly and pouted, adding, "I know, I'm a fucking workaholic. Forgive me?"

"Of course!" she replied. "And I'll do better than that. I'll literally come and help you!"

Geoff's face darkened.

"You will?" Charlie said. "Oh my God, Mils, you're the fucking *best*."

As though he didn't have at least five flunkies to offload work on if he wanted to. *Jesus*.

Toni—never one for heroics—was already sidling away from the looming domestic-drama, and when Aaron glanced at Lewis, he saw that he was doing the same.

"Okay then, see you all at dinner," Lewis said, raising a hand in farewell and heading for the door.

"Yeah, cool, cool," Charlie said. "We'll make up for last night's fast tonight, yeah?"

"Yeah," Lewis said over his shoulder, without pausing. "Sounds good."

Aaron hurried after him.

They left the Long Gallery, exiting into the big, echoey hallway. As they crossed the floor, heading for the stairs, a figure rose from one of the wooden benches.

Hippolyta.

She looked at Lewis. "I was hoping to speak with you," she said.

Lewis came to an abrupt halt. Discomfort radiated out of him. Politely, he said, "I thought the workshop was done?"

"It is," Hippolyta said simply. She smiled. "I just wanted to offer you a couple of reflections. If you're willing to listen."

Lewis stared at her for several painfully long moments. Then he sighed. "Okay, fine." He turned to Aaron. "I'll see you later, okay?"

It was an obvious dismissal, and it bought Aaron up short.

Stupid to feel rejected, but he did. After last night, and then the weird intensity of the workshop, he'd thought... Well, what *had* he thought? That they were friends, now?

Don't be an idiot, Aaron Page.

Wrangling his expression into what he hoped was an indifferent smile, he said, "Yeah. Later," and walked away.

CHAPTER FOURTEEN

Lewis

Lewis stared after Aaron, frowning. He'd seemed… had he been *annoyed*?

"Aaron mentioned he's your PA."

Lewis turned back to Hippolyta, who was gazing at him in her disconcertingly direct way.

"Yup," he confirmed, popping the 'p'. It was a pretty juvenile way of letting her know he didn't really want to talk to her. She didn't look offended, though. In fact, she looked faintly amused, and somehow that was worse.

"Look," he said tightly. "I think I'm done with the whole workshop thing for one day."

She nodded. "I understand. Neither of us was expecting what happened to you today."

"Um, not sure what you think happened, but—"

"Please," she said gently, settling her hand on his forearm. "Don't pretend. We both know you experienced something intense. For what it's worth, I'm sorry. If I'd known—"

"No offence," he interjected. "But maybe you should go peddle this to someone who wants to hear it? Charlie seems to lap it all up. As does that pea brained woman he's been panting after all morning."

Hippolyta met his gaze. "I'm not peddling anything, Lewis. I just wanted to check you were all right."

"Yeah? Well, I'm fine. Fucking dandy, actually."

"Are you sure about that? It seemed to me you were experiencing an intense memory flashback. Has that ever happened to you before?"

"I don't know," he said irritably, before honesty compelled him to add, "Maybe. A long time ago. I'm fine now." He rubbed at his shoulder. "I just need some painkillers."

Hippolyta's gaze moved over his face. At last, she nodded. "Okay. I just wanted to let you know that I was very clear with Charles that today's group were to be given information about what the workshop would entail well in advance. I'm sorry that didn't happen. I'll make sure it doesn't happen with anyone else in future."

Lewis sighed. "It's fine. The truth is it wouldn't have made any difference. I'd still have had to do it."

She frowned. "Why?"

Lewis laughed without humour. "Because Charlie always gets what he wants."

"No, he doesn't," she said firmly. "You *can* say no to him, you know."

"You think?"

"I know. He wanted me to keep going with the workshop as planned, but I refused."

"Didn't he threaten not to pay you?"

"Of course. He threw quite the tantrum." She laughed. "I'm not getting a penny, apparently."

"*What?*" Weirdly, he found himself feeling affronted on her behalf. "That's outrageous!"

She shrugged. "I'm chalking it up to experience."

Lewis shook his head. "I'm sorry."

"Don't be. Just"—she fished in her pocket and pulled out

a piece of paper—"take this. In case you have another of those episodes and decide you want to speak to someone about it."

He opened it up. She'd written, *"Grace Collins, Chartered Psychologist / CBT therapist"* and scribbled a number and email below.

"Grace is very good," she said simply.

He folded the paper back up and slid it into his pocket. "Thanks."

For a moment, they stood in silence. Then Hippolyta said, "Aaron was very protective of you today. You're lucky to have a friend like that."

"I know."

She eyed him as though she wasn't sure he really did know. But at last she nodded and stepped back. "Stay safe, Lewis. It was interesting to meet you."

"You too," he said.

As he watched her go, he wondered what she'd tell Skye Jäger about *his* issues and knew she'd be cropping up in one of his scripts soon enough.

As soon as he got back to his room, he fell on the bed, exhausted, and before he knew it, he was sleeping. When he woke, it was half-past two, and he was ravenous.

He decided to go and beg Toni for some snacks. On the way past Aaron's room, he knocked, figuring Aaron might be peckish too. As he waited for an answer, his stomach knotted up with nerves, and he realised he was worried about what he'd see on Aaron's face after all the drama of the morning.

But there was no answer, even when he knocked a second time. Aaron must have gone somewhere.

Feeling oddly flat, he traipsed along to Toni's room and rapped at her door.

"Oh, it's you," she said when she opened it. "Let me guess. You're after one of my Curly Wurlys."

"If you gave me a Curly Wurly, I'd love you forever. Even longer for a Pot Noodle."

She rolled her eyes but opened the door wide to let him in while she rummaged through her case. She emerged with not only a Pot Noodle—sweet & sour flavour; his favourite—but a grab bag of beef Hula-hoops.

He salivated.

"Don't say I'm not good to you," she said as she handed them over.

"You've made an old man very happy."

"*Old*?" she said, raising her brows. "I've got ten years on you, you young whippersnapper. Now, make sure you give me a knock before you go down for drinks. I don't want to face that lot alone."

"Ugh, me either," Lewis said, making a face. "Hey, do you know where Aaron went?"

"He said something about going for a walk, but that was ages ago. Is he not in his room?"

Lewis shook his head.

"*Hmm.*" Toni looked thoughtful. After a moment, she said, "What about you? What have you been doing all afternoon?"

"Sleeping. I was done in. You?"

"I spent a good hour trying to shake off poor Geoff—he was bending my ear about that bloody awful wife of his. She and Charlie deserve one another. Then I escaped up here and caught up on my emails."

"At least you've been productive," Lewis said, as he headed for the door. "Once I've scoffed this lot, I might do the same for a bit before we have to go down. Fucking drinks at *five*?"

Toni sighed. "Yeah, it's going to be a long night."

"I might have to get smashed to get through it," Lewis warned her.

She sighed. "I'd be grateful if you'd refrain. You're even more impossible to rein in when you're drunk."

"There's only one thing for it, then."

"And what's that?"

"Join in. If you're drunk too, you won't care."

She sighed. "I don't have a good feeling about this."

Neither did Lewis, but what choice did either of them have? Unlike Hippolyta, they couldn't walk away from Charlie and chalk it up to experience. Not if they wanted *Leeches*: USA to happen.

So Lewis would be there for drinks at fucking five, no matter how on edge he still felt, and no matter how much he'd have preferred a repeat of last night, eating fish and chips on the beach with Aaron.

~

After inhaling the snacks Toni had given him, Lewis managed to power through a good hour and a half of productive work before taking a shower and dressing for dinner in a fitted black shirt and trousers.

At five minutes to five, he left his room and knocked on Aaron's door.

Aaron answered quickly, as though he'd been waiting. His eyelashes flicked down as he gave Lewis a quick onceover, and Lewis did the same, taking in Aaron's white grandad shirt, tweed waistcoat, and jeans. The sleeves of his shirt were rolled up to his elbows, a chunky watch on his left wrist. Lewis's gaze got stuck there for a moment before he managed to wrench it back to Aaron's face, only to find the other man watching him half-curiously, half-warily.

"Hi," Aaron said huskily.

"Hi," Lewis returned. His mouth felt weirdly dry. "Did you have a good afternoon?"

Aaron shrugged. "It was okay. I went for a long walk. You?"

"Slept and got some work done."

"And—" Aaron paused, adding carefully, "Are you—? That is, is everything okay?"

Lewis felt his cheeks warm. "Of course. Everything's fine."

"Right," Aaron said, too quickly. "Good."

Lewis cleared his throat. "We should go and get Toni. For someone who claims to be so chilled out, Charlie's incredibly anal about everyone being on time."

Aaron gave a chuckle that sounded forced. "He does like to run the show."

They headed down the corridor, not looking at one another, and Lewis hated the weird awkwardness between them. After the morning's events, it was inevitable, he supposed, but why should that be? Why was it that, when something so intensely, unexpectedly intimate happened between two people, it seemed almost to blast them further apart? To make it even harder to be close to them?

Or maybe that was just Lewis.

Mason had told him several times that he had intimacy issues—and Mason wasn't the only one who'd expressed that view over the years—but Lewis had always shrugged such comments off. It was only now, walking beside Aaron, that it struck him that that it might be an actual problem because the idea that this could affect his relationship with Aaron permanently was fucking unbearable. There weren't many people in this world that Lewis gave much of a shit about. The sad truth was, most people he could take or leave. But somehow, Aaron was one of the very few who had slipped under his invisible barriers, and now the thought of losing their easy intimacy was unendurable.

He had to get things back on the right footing again. Reestablish their fragile boss-PA-sort-of-friends-but-not-quite dynamic.

Toni's door opened before they even reached it. She wore a purple, halter-neck, maxi dress that was simultaneously casual and glamorous. She'd ditched the glasses for contacts and wore huge gold hoops in her ears.

Aaron gave a low wolf whistle, and she winked at him.

"Sexy lady," Aaron said, grinning.

"You look quite dapper yourself."

"*Dapper?*" he protested, laughing. "You make me sound about seventy."

Toni laughed. "I can't call *you* sexy—even though you are. You're twenty years younger than me. You'll think I'm after you!"

"I'm here too, you know!" Lewis grumbled, stupidly irritated by this mutual admiration society that he appeared to exclude him.

"Yeah, well, you can shut up," Toni replied.

"*What?* Why?" he demanded, outraged at this unfairness.

"Because you look like a fucking supermodel, and you know it," she threw at him. "So no compliments for you."

Aaron laughed, and Lewis turned to gape at him. "*Et tu, Brute?*"

"Well, you *are* disgustingly pretty," Aaron said, and just for a moment, alongside the amusement in his silvery gaze, there was pure, heated admiration.

Lewis's gut twisted, and he couldn't think how to respond to that, but it didn't matter because Aaron was already turning away and heading for the main stairs with Toni, and all Lewis could do was follow them, trying to pay attention to their light-hearted conversation.

When they entered the lounge a minute later, the others were there already, Charlie standing behind an honest-to-God fully stocked bar, while Milly and Geoff lounged at opposite ends of a huge sectional sofa that looked like it could sit about ten people. They were both sipping cocktails already, Geoff's a long tea-coloured drink and Milly's a rose-pink confection, with a layer of white foam on top.

"Welcome, welcome!" Charlie greeted them. "Let me make you all a drink. Do you trust me to choose for you?"

There was a brief silence as all three of them obviously thought *"No"* before they all muttered unenthusiastic affirmatives.

Charlie beamed, either oblivious to the undercurrents or actively enjoying them. He loaded up a cocktail shaker with ice and began pouring a lethal number of shots into it.

"I love your dress," Toni said to Milly in her easy way, smiling as she settled herself on the sectional. Milly began babbling about dress designers, and Lewis tuned out, grateful for Toni's ability to talk to anyone about anything. It was a skill he singularly lacked.

Aaron glanced at him and murmured, "I suppose we should sit down too. We'd better head for the other end, I suppose."

Lewis unenthusiastically eyed Geoff, who was giving off vibes of angry misery, but he nodded.

Aaron sat first, and Lewis settled down beside him, only realising once he'd sunk into the plush cushions just how close he was to Aaron. Their arms brushed, and he could feel the heat of the man's body beside him. Like they were a couple.

Fuck. But it would look bad if he moved now. Deliberate. Pointed.

Charlie was doing his bartending, energetically mixing, shaking, and pouring.

"Do you think he's going to roofie us?" Aaron muttered, and Lewis laughed, though in truth it wasn't something he'd confidently bet against.

A few minutes later, Charlie emerged from behind the bar with a tray of drinks. He presented a lilac-hued drink to

Toni, saying, "Purple Sunset seemed apt for you tonight, darling."

Toni laughed, then sipped it. "Wow, that's delicious!"

Charlie smiled smugly. Next, he handed a thick tumbler to Lewis. It had a huge ice cube and was filled nearly to the brim with scarlet booze.

"Jäger Negroni," Charlie drawled. Lewis raised his eyebrows, then took a gulp. It was, at least, satisfyingly alcoholic.

Aaron's offering was a much more froufrou affair, a sunny yellow drink presented in a classic coupe glass complete with a prissy little pink umbrella weighed down with red glacé cherries.

Charlie smiled thinly at Aaron. "Sidekick," he said succinctly, before turning away to reach for the last drink on the tray, a blood-orange concoction in a classic Nick-and-Nora glass. Rather than sit on the sectional, he settled himself on the floor in some kind of seated yoga pose.

"What have you got, Charlie?" Toni asked. She'd already necked half of her Purple Sunset.

Charlie smiled his smug smile again. "It's a Commander-in-chief."

Aaron pressed his lower leg against Lewis's, and when Lewis glanced at him, he had his lips pressed tightly together against his obvious desire to laugh.

Oh Christ, but Lewis really shouldn't have looked because now his lips were twitching too. He made himself look away and took a gulp of his drink, but even as he did so, he pressed back against Aaron's leg in answer, and then—he wasn't even sure why he did it—he just left his leg there.

He couldn't even pretend it was to soothe himself, or to stay calm, because that was definitely not the effect this contact with Aaron was having on him. Quite the opposite. His heart was racing, and his cock was pulsing and hardening.

"Earth to Lewis?" Charlie said pointedly, and he blinked hard, realising he'd completely zoned out while Charlie had been talking to him.

"Sorry," he muttered. "I was miles away."

"Yes, I did notice," Charlie said repressively. "You really should work on being present in the moment, Lewis. It's absolutely vital if you're going to give of your best. Not to mention being respectful of others around you."

In other words, *fucking pay attention, minion.*

Lewis ground his molars. "What were you saying?" he said tightly. Toni sent him a warning glance, but he ignored her. There was only so much of Charlie's bullshit he could take, and he was already very close to the end of his tether.

Aaron's leg pressed against his again, and maybe he was being fanciful, but he was sure the warm pressure was sympathetic.

"I was just asking where you grew up."

Lewis paused. It was the kind of question he'd usually answer right away, no hesitation, but with Charlie, he was wary. Even as he acknowledged that thought, he was conscious of how melodramatic it sounded. Hell, it was a completely ordinary question.

"Stockwell, mostly. In Lambeth."

"Really?" Charlie said. "God, you're lucky. That's a pretty diverse area, right? I went to Bishopton College which"—he rolled his eyes—"not so much."

Mildly, Toni interjected, "Bishopton's a very good school, though. I'm sure I read it's the most expensive private school in Britain, is that right?"

Charlie gave a bark of laughter. "Yeah, well, these days it's practically a *disadvantage* going to private school. I think you'd be surprised how much prejudice I've suffered during my career." He threw back the rest of his drink and set the empty glass down on the table.

"Oh totally," Milly echoed. "Oxford literally discriminates

against privately educated students these days." She trilled a laugh. "I'd never get in if I had to apply now!"

Lewis shared a wry look with Aaron, whose mouth ticked up at one corner before he could drown the smile in his drink.

"I honestly don't get it," Charlie bored on. "For me, people are just... people, you know? I don't care where anyone came from, or what race they are, or Jesus, who they *love*!" He unfolded his legs and stood. "Everyone want another?" His eyes glittered dangerously.

Toni held out her empty glass. "God, yes please. That was scrummy."

Lewis offered his own empty glass but noted that Aaron had barely touched his 'Sidekick'. When he noticed Lewis looking, Aaron just shrugged.

After another bout of ostentatious cocktail shaking, this time with Milly playing the role of glamorous assistant, Charlie handed around fresh drinks.

"I'll help myself to a Scotch," Geoff announced pointedly, prowling around behind the bar.

Charlie ignored him. "You know, Lewis," he said, returning to sit cross-legged on the floor. "I don't know whether I've ever told you how much I admire you." His cheeks were faintly flushed, and Lewis wondered how much he'd had to drink before they arrived.

He gulped down a mouthful of his Negroni and grimaced. Jesus, this one was even stronger than the first. "Admire me for what?" he rasped past the alcohol burn in his throat.

"Well... I mean, look at you. Sitting here, with us, in this amazing place. Considering your background, I'm sure you could never have imagined this in your future when you were a kid."

Lewis lowered his drink, conscious of the effect of the booze on his already volatile temper—and not really giving a shit. "What do you mean?" he said, his voice clipped. "What does my background have to do with anything?"

"Oh, don't play coy," Charlie said, smiling. "I mean the School of Hard Knocks, the University of Life. God, you've no idea—your background is *such* an advantage when it comes to your creative output. And you've certainly exploited it. There's a lot of Lewis Hunter in Skye Jäger, isn't there?" He thumped his heart with his fist. "That's why he feels so real. So street."

Aaron's leg pressed hard against Lewis's again, and Lewis wasn't sure whether that urgent pressure was horror or a desperate attempt not to laugh. Baring his teeth in an approximation of a smile, Lewis said, "I'll tell you this for nothing, Charlie—there are no fucking vampires in Stockwell."

"They stay north of the river," Aaron deadpanned. "Highgate, mostly."

Lewis snorted, and they shared a grin.

But Charlie didn't smile. "I meant," he said tightly, "that your deprived upbringing gives the show a lot of kudos. Marketing *adores* it." To Toni, he added, "I'm *such* an advocate for diversity at Telopix. Anyone will tell you I'm obsessed with creating opportunities for women and other minorities."

Lewis watched in amusement as Toni clenched her jaw, knowing that she wanted to point out that while women might be marginalised, they were not, in fact, a minority.

"Charlie's PA is an African-American," Milly supplied in a confiding whisper. "And a *lesbian*."

Lewis knocked back another mouthful of Negroni, surprised to find his glass empty again. "I don't know what you think you know about my 'upbringing'," he told Charlie, "but it's nobody else's damn—"

"What are we eating tonight?" Toni cut in. "I certainly built up an appetite at the workshop, and the food here is always so…" She struggled for a moment. "Such an adventure!"

Charlie's gaze lingered on Lewis before he turned back to Toni with a mollified smile. "It is special, isn't it? I've recently adopted a probiotic plant-based diet, so your digestive tract is in for a treat tonight."

"Marvellous!" Toni beamed. "Isn't that marvellous, Aaron?"

"Uh, yeah," he said gamely. "I'm mostly veggie myself, actually."

"Good man," Charlie said. "And with only a *little* more effort, you could go totally plant-based. Wouldn't that be great? The planet would love you."

"Your partner probably wouldn't." Geoff chuckled darkly, sloshing his large tumbler of whisky. "All that fermented crap Milly eats makes her fart like a heifer."

"Geoffrey!" Cheeks scarlet, Milly walloped his arm.

"Well, it's true," Geoff objected. "Beans, beans, good for the heart, the more you eat, the more you—"

In a literal example of being saved by the bell, a sonorous bong reverberated around the room.

"Ah, the dinner gong," said Charlie, jumping to his feet. "Giorgio's prepared an outstanding eight-course vegan tasting menu, so we need to start early." With a flourish, he bowed them towards a door that now stood open on the far side of the room. "Please, join me, and let our gastronomic odyssey begin…"

He offered his arm to Milly, and they paraded out together, leaving Toni and Geoff to trail after them with all the enthusiasm of the condemned heading for a picnic at the gallows. With a sigh, Lewis set his glass down. He was about to follow Toni when Aaron touched his arm, stopping him.

"Don't let him get to you," he said quietly.

He may have said more than that, but Lewis could only seem to focus on the comfort of Aaron's hand on his forearm, on the sight of his long fingers resting on Lewis's bare skin. Since when had Aaron touched him like that? Or at all?

"I'll try," Lewis managed eventually, jerking his eyes up to

Aaron's face when he realised he was staring. "But he's *such* a wanker."

"I know." Aaron didn't let go. In fact his grip tightened. "Look, I don't know what was in your drink, but mine was, like, ninety-percent proof."

"Same." He glanced at his empty glass, aware now of a definite fuzziness in his head.

"So maybe slow down?" Aaron suggested gently. "You don't want to end up saying or doing something you might regret."

"You mean, like punching Charlie in the face?"

"Exactly like that."

Lewis smiled; he liked that Aaron was concerned. He liked the softness in his grey eyes when he looked at him. And he liked gazing into them. It made him feel… What *was* that feeling? Sort of warm and cosy and content. Was it…? Was that *happiness*?

Fuck knew.

It was probably just the booze. But still, he enjoyed the sensation. "Don't worry," he said, setting his own hand over Aaron's where it still rested on his arm. "I won't—"

And then he saw the flush rising in Aaron's cheeks and a gleam of something in his eyes. Longing, maybe. Or maybe Lewis was just projecting his own feelings.

He let go abruptly—*Fuck, get a grip, Hunter*—and cleared his throat. "I'll, uh, try not to punch anyone."

"Right." Aaron dropped his gaze, flexing the fingers that had held Lewis's arm. "Good." With a strained smile, he added, "I suppose we'd better get in there."

Lewis grimaced. "And may God have mercy on our stomachs."

CHAPTER FIFTEEN

AARON

By the fifth course, the evening was on a definite downhill trajectory. In fact, it resembled the final stages of a particularly aggressive Olympic bobsleigh run.

It wasn't that the food was unpalatable, Aaron thought, as he gazed down at yet another exquisitely presented morsel—this one was a tiny portion of black rice and fermented white bean puree, arranged on his plate like a yin and yang symbol—it was that Charlie was getting more obnoxious, and Lewis more riled, as the evening wore on.

"And what I love about LA," Charlie was gushing now, "is that they don't give a crap about who your parents were, you know? In America, everyone is self-made. Everyone is equal."

"Bollocks," Lewis said, poking miserably at his rice. He'd hardly eaten a bite all evening and had become increasingly curmudgeonly as the night progressed.

The thing was, Lewis was a simple eater. Aaron wasn't sure why, but he'd noticed years ago that Lewis preferred to eat what Aaron could only describe as kids' food. Ham sandwiches, hot chocolate, crisps. Cheese pizza. He'd graze on the carrot sticks and fruit Aaron left on his desk, but he didn't seek them out himself. Over the years, Aaron had come up with a couple of theories about Lewis's arrested culinary development, but in the end, he'd decided that he didn't want to speculate too much. It really wasn't any of his business. Besides, the why of it didn't matter. Lewis was Lewis, and that was that.

But Aaron could tell that this whole tasting menu business was proving to be an ordeal for him. He looked embarrassed but seemed genuinely unable to do more than pick at the weird and wonderful concoctions set before him.

"What do you mean, it's bollocks?" Charlie said, turning a narrow-eyed gaze on Lewis. Milly sat to Charlie's right at the large round table. Over the last five courses, she'd shuffled her chair close enough that he could drape his arm across its back. As he spoke to Lewis, his fingers toyed blatantly with one of the shoulder straps of her dress.

Opposite them, Geoff stabbed at his phone, apparently having given up on the evening—and possibly on his marriage.

"I mean," Lewis said flatly, "that it's bollocks to say that Americans don't care about your background."

Charlie shook his head as he sloshed more wine into his glass. "I assure you, you're wrong. Have you ever lived in the States? I thought not. I get *so* much less pushback there than I do here. *Nobody* cares what school you went to. For God's sake, they don't even know what a public school is!"

"They understand money and privilege," Lewis growled. "That's the same everywhere."

"Oh no," Milly said. "Charlie's right. Creatively, the States is a much more liberating place to work."

"You know what, Lewis? You'd love it in LA," Charlie carried on. "Lots of your sort there."

Lewis snorted. "Who the fuck are my sort?"

"People who've pulled themselves up by their boot-straps," Charlie said, eyes narrowing. "Why are you so shy about your backstory, Lewis? It's a bloody goldmine."

"My *backstory*?" Lewis rubbed angrily at his shoulder. "What, you mean my fucking *life*?"

Aaron's stomach tensed anxiously. Charlie had a reputation for dropping projects if someone bruised his ego and it was obvious that Lewis was getting near the end of his rope. Aaron set down his fork, his gaze shifting between the two men. The irritated glint in Charlie's gaze worried him.

"Call it what you like." Charlie shrugged negligently. "The point is, you should use it in your work, exploit it. Make it work *for* you, not against you. I'm thinking…" He put his fingertips to his temples, as if channelling signals from outer space. "Ooh… Okay, I'm just spit balling here, but what if we give Faolán a grittier past? He could be an orphan like you. Maybe his parents were murdered by the Leeches? Maybe Faolán even saw them die."

Jesus Christ, how did Charlie know about Lewis being orphaned as a kid?

"That would be literally amazing," Milly gushed. "He could be, like, really dark? Like, maybe he grew up dealing drugs on a violent council estate? Do they have those in America?"

Charlie shot finger guns at her. "Mils, you always get me better than anyone else." To Lewis he said, "Wouldn't that be exciting? To really channel your own background into the new show? You've got so much material you could use."

Lewis didn't answer. He was staring down at his untouched food, nose flaring as he breathed hard. One hand was working at the spot between his neck and shoulder. Aaron had to grip the edge of the table to keep himself from getting up and going to him. He looked over at Toni pleadingly.

Toni's voice was as calm as ever, but there was a betraying

flash of alarm in her gaze when she looked Lewis's way. "You know, Charlie, I think this is probably something to discuss in tomorrow's meeting."

When Charlie met her eyes, his expression was flat, his smile without warmth. "Sure, sure," he agreed, "but it's great to dig into this stuff informally too, yeah? Just turn over the possibilities. There are some things we can get the ball rolling on with Faolán—like reflecting some of Lewis's own life experiences, even if it's not going to work to include his, er, lifestyle." He winked and laughed. "For story reasons, right? Gotta think of the audience!"

Aaron stared at him, his attention briefly diverted from Lewis.

Lewis's *lifestyle?* Was Charlie talking about his sexuality? Surely he didn't believe Lewis would rewrite Faolán as straight, did he? Because that would never happen. Lewis had been clear about that.

Toni said, "Well, I think..."

Aaron tuned out what Toni thought, returning his attention to Lewis, who had gone alarmingly pale and was breathing hard. His gaze was downcast, so Aaron couldn't see his eyes, but he knew—he just *knew*—that Lewis had gone somewhere else again, just like before, at the workshop.

Fuck.

He looked around the table, but nobody else was watching. Charlie and Toni were engaged in a laughing-but-deadly-serious discussion, Geoff was scowling at his phone, and Milly was as smilingly vacant as always.

The table was too large for Aaron to get Lewis's attention subtly, but he wasn't about to sit there and watch him suffer alone, so he pushed back his chair and went over to him. Lewis's shoulders were hunched and tense, the fingers gripping his neck going white at the tips.

"Lewis?" Aaron murmured, covering his hand with his

own. He heard Lewis suck in a wet, shuddery breath and knew he had to get him out of there.

"Sorry, everyone," he announced, keeping his tone easy but uncompromising. "I'm afraid Lewis isn't feeling well. I'm going to take him up to his room."

Toni stared at them, her eyes widening in concern. But she didn't miss a beat. "Oh no," she said. "He mentioned earlier that he thought he had a migraine coming on."

"He did," Aaron agreed, shooting her a grateful look. "I told him he should rest, but you know how he is..."

The fact that Lewis didn't object to the lie only supported Aaron's instincts. Firmly, he took Lewis's arm and encouraged him to his feet. "Come on," he murmured. "Let's go upstairs."

Lewis nodded, swaying as he rose, but keeping his eyes fixed on the floor, for which Aaron was grateful because otherwise he might have noticed Charlie's sharkish smile. A smile that Aaron—who was not a violent man—wanted to punch right off his stupid face.

Keeping a firm hold of Lewis, Aaron guided him away from the table. "Please, carry on," he told the others, with as much politeness as he could muster. "I'll make sure Lewis is okay."

One of the servers obligingly opened the dining room door for them, and Aaron nodded his thanks. Behind him, he heard Charlie say, "Let's open another bottle…"

And then the door shut, and they were alone in the corridor.

"Fuck," Lewis said roughly, sagging against the wall. "Jesus…"

Aaron gave him a few moments to gather himself before he gently touched his elbow. "Let's go upstairs," he said. "You need to eat some proper food."

Lewis only nodded, silent as he trudged along the corridor and up the stairs. Aaron walked at his side, watching him worriedly. He hated seeing Lewis like this; it churned him up inside.

When they finally reached Lewis's room, Aaron hesitated. He didn't want to intrude, but he also didn't want to leave Lewis alone in this state. Luckily, Lewis left his door wide open when he walked inside, and Aaron took that as an invitation to follow.

So he followed.

Unlike his own room, Lewis's was something of a mess. The rumpled bed was strewn with clothes. Papers—an unbound script—lay scattered on the sofa by the window along with his laptop and an empty pot noodle cup, a plastic fork sticking out of it.

Aaron took everything in with one glance, his attention mostly on Lewis who sank onto the end of the bed and dropped his face into his hands. "Fucking hell," he said through his fingers.

Aaron's heart ached to see him so defeated and low. Little Boy Lost, he thought, throat tightening. "You should eat something," Aaron said. "I've got some stuff in my room. Hang on, I'll be back in a mo."

Lewis didn't react, just sat there with his hands over his face, elbows on knees.

If he could have, Aaron would have walked right over there and given him a hug. He knew—it was obvious—that Lewis needed comfort. And it killed him not to be able to offer it. He wondered if there was anyone else Lewis would turn to for that. Owen maybe?

As Aaron hurried back to his room, he considered calling Owen. But although the brothers were close, Aaron had a nagging feeling that Lewis wouldn't want Owen to see him so upset. Aaron certainly couldn't call him without asking Lewis first.

Opening the dresser in his room, he fished out the bag of emergency food he'd bought that afternoon. After Lewis had dismissed him, he'd gone out to walk off the overwhelming feelings the morning had stirred up—to try and reason his way back into the role of efficient PA instead of... Of whatever role he'd been in last night, in Swanage. And then this morning, during the workshop. A far more intimate role than he'd ever bargained for.

The walk hadn't really helped, and he'd returned as unsettled as ever, but he *had* stumbled on a small petrol station in the middle of nowhere, which he'd grimly raided for rations. After the fasting fiasco, he'd wanted to be self-sufficient when it came to food.

He was bloody glad he'd stocked up now.

Carrier bag in hand, he left his room and returned to find Lewis exactly where he'd left him.

Quietly, Aaron closed the door. He wasn't sure how to help, where the boundaries were between them, but looking at the dishevelled mess in the room, he decided that he could at least tidy up. Lewis liked things neat and orderly, despite his personal propensity for chaos. It was one of the man's many idiosyncrasies. So, while Lewis silently struggled with his inner turmoil, Aaron did what he could to bring some external order.

Maybe it worked because, after a few minutes of silent tidying, Lewis got to his feet and disappeared into the bathroom.

Aaron bit his lip, staring at the closed door as he listened to the toilet flush, the tap run, and the sound of water splashing in the sink. His X-Ray vision failing, he tore his eyes away from the door and got on with straightening the bedclothes and laying out his impromptu feast on the covers. It consisted of two giant sausage rolls, a limp cheese-and-tomato sandwich, two grab bags of salt-and-vinegar crisps, and a family-sized bar of milk chocolate.

No doubt Charlie would have regarded such an offering in horror, but when Lewis emerged from the bathroom and saw what Aaron had set out, his lips turned up slightly. While it didn't do much to ease the haunted expression in his eyes, just that small sign of pleasure sent Aaron's heart soaring.

"Where did you get all this?" Lewis said. His voice sounded scratchy, and his hair was damp at the temples and forehead. He must have been splashing water on his face.

It hadn't done much to soothe the redness around his eyes.

"Found a garage when I went out for a walk earlier," Aaron said, fetching two bottles of cold water from the mini-fridge and climbing up to sit cross-legged on the bed. "Come on, let's eat. I'm starving."

Lewis regarded him for a moment, then toed off his shoes and joined Aaron on the bed, sitting opposite him.

Silently, Aaron handed him half the sandwich, watching Lewis pick out the soggy tomato and replace it with a handful of crisps before biting into it and giving a low groan. Eyes closed, Lewis chewed slowly, and Aaron could see some of the tension easing from his face.

He smiled and ate his own sandwich.

Once they'd demolished their sandwiches, the sausage rolls, the crisps, and most of the chocolate, Aaron got up and put the kettle on. "Oh, and guess, what?" he said brightly. "I found *these* too." He held up his prize: a handful of tired-looking hot chocolate sachets, the crappy ones you make up with boiling water. Aaron thought they tasted horrible, all thin and gritty, but they were the only hot drinks Lewis ever helped himself to in the office kitchen.

The smile that broke over Lewis's face then was…hell, it *winded* Aaron. It was part pure happiness and part relief. Aaron felt his own smile falter, and he swallowed hard against a sudden lump in his throat. Quickly, he turned away, busying himself with pouring the sachet contents into mugs.

"Thanks, Aaron," Lewis said behind him. He'd been

uncharacteristically quiet while they ate, but he was sounding more himself now. "You're a fucking magician."

Aaron smiled at that but didn't turn around.

Once he'd made their drinks, trying his best to squish out the lumps and adding an extra sugar into Lewis's, he returned to the bed and handed Lewis his mug.

They sipped their hot chocolate in silence. Night had fallen and Aaron watched their reflections in the dark glass of the window, both sitting sideways on the edge of the bed, like bookends facing each other. It wasn't comfortable; there was too much tension in the room for comfort. But it wasn't awkward either. It was just...quiet.

Unsure what to do next, whether to broach what had happened at dinner or steer clear, Aaron was relieved when Lewis spoke first. "Did you…?" He cleared his throat, set his empty mug on the floor. "Did you hear what he said?"

"Charlie? Yeah."

"All that stuff about making Faolán an orphan. Using my —my mum's…" Lewis shook his head. "He called it my fucking *backstory*. Like it wasn't even real."

"He's an idiot." That didn't come close. "A narcissistic fucking arsehole."

Lewis gave a big sigh and closed his eyes. Brow furrowing slightly, he canted his head to one side and began rubbing at his sore spot again.

Aaron's eyes fixed on his hand, watching the way he kneaded the point where neck and shoulder met. He remembered what it had felt like during the workshop when he'd set his own hand there. How Lewis had subtly relaxed, his tension uncoiling beneath Aaron's touch. How Aaron had felt that same sensation of relief as his own tension, held tightly in his chest, had eased.

He tried to think of something to say that would help Lewis now. But he couldn't think of a single thing. All he could think to offer was what he'd offered before: his touch.

Well, it had seemed to help then, and it would be churlish —*cowardly*—to withhold the one thing he could offer Lewis now.

At least, that was what he told himself.

Carefully, warily, he slipped off the bed and padded to Lewis's side. "Here," he said, coming to stand slightly behind him, "let me..."

CHAPTER SIXTEEN

Aaron

Aaron reached out, brushing his fingers over the curve of Lewis's neck and shoulder.

Lewis's hand stilled, and his eyes sprang open as he glanced up in surprise. Their eyes met, his bruised and weary, and Aaron said gently, quietly, "It's okay. I'm not exactly a pro, but Colin gave me some sports massage tips…"

Lewis made a face. "Fucking Colin," he said, but there was no heat in it. He lowered his hand to join the other in his lap and slightly turned, presenting the sore spot to Aaron.

Aaron swallowed and stepped closer.

Pro or not, he didn't need to be an expert to feel the tension Lewis carried in his shoulders, or the way he relaxed as soon as Aaron began to touch him, carefully exploring the tense muscle with his fingertips before digging in more firmly, eliciting a moan from Lewis that sounded positively pornographic.

If he *had* been an expert, he probably wouldn't have been quite so preoccupied by the pleasing contours of firm muscle and warm flesh beneath Lewis's fine cotton shirt. Or by the way his dark hair curled charmingly behind his ears, or by the warm, arousing scent of his fading aftershave.

And talking of warmth, was it getting hot in here? Because Aaron felt flushed all over, his heart thudding alarmingly as he touched Lewis in ways he'd never dreamed might happen in real life.

When Lewis began unbuttoning his shirt, Aaron froze, hands stilling. His mouth was dry as he watched Lewis shrug out of the shirt, one golden shoulder at a time, before negligently casting it onto the floor and lowering his head to give Aaron better access to his neck and shoulders.

Aaron swallowed, his gaze moving over Lewis's smooth, bare skin. Then slowly, carefully, he lowered his hands and began to stroke and knead again.

"Fucking hell, that feels good," Lewis muttered, taking the words right out of Aaron's mouth. Because yes, this felt good to Aaron too. His cock had plumped up and throbbed insistently as his hands worked. And Christ, that had to be wrong, didn't it? He was supposed to be giving comfort to Lewis, not perving on him.

Lewis seemed oblivious to Aaron's arousal, though. He angled his head to one side, opening up that vulnerable spot to Aaron's touch, and when Aaron leaned in closer to firmly press into the sore muscle—heart beating wildly as he did so—Lewis gave another of those deep, masculine sighs of relief—of *pleasure*—and…

…Aaron snatched his hands away, breathing hard.

Lewis turned to look at him, his brows drawn together in a faint frown.

"What's wrong?" He blinked. "Oh, shit. Is it because I took my shirt off?"

Before Aaron could respond, Lewis bent to retrieve the shirt he'd just cast aside. As he straightened, he rose to his feet, turning on his heel to face Aaron, and quite suddenly, there was no space between them at all.

Aaron froze, and so did Lewis, but neither of them stepped back.

Their gazes locked and as they stared at one another, Aaron felt suddenly stripped bare. Stripped bare and *seen*, right down to his bones.

"Aaron?" Lewis breathed, and still, neither of them moved.

It felt to Aaron as though a moment had arrived that had always been coming, an instant in time he and Lewis had been inexorably, unknowingly, moving towards for years.

He knew he should pull back. That was the sensible thing to do. But Aaron wasn't going to do the sensible thing. Not tonight.

And it seemed Lewis wasn't either. Without taking his eyes off Aaron, he tossed his shirt back onto the floor. "Come here," he murmured, and Aaron stepped closer—just a small step, but enough to eliminate the remaining space between them.

Lewis raised his hand, touching the backs of his fingers to Aaron's cheek. A light, gliding touch. His expression was oddly tender. And Jesus, Lewis *never* looked tender—except that right now he did, and Aaron didn't know what to make of it, not at all. He didn't know what to make of any of this. How to make the move he so desperately wanted to make, or even how to show Lewis that he was desperate to be moved on. So, he just stood there like a rabbit caught in the headlights, waiting and hoping.

Lewis whispered, "It's funny. I'm not even that into kissing, but right now, I really want to kiss you."

Aaron gave a shaky laugh. "Yeah?"

Lewis nodded gravely. "I shouldn't," he went on. "But tonight, I can't seem to remember why."

Breathlessly, Aaron said, "Makes two of us."

"Fuck, Aaron," Lewis groaned. "What am I going to do with you?"

"Just kiss me," Aaron said, his voice breaking on the words. The plea in them was embarrassingly clear, but that didn't matter because Lewis was already lowering his head and taking Aaron's mouth.

His lips were gentler than Aaron would ever have imagined—at least for the first few heart-stopping moments—until Lewis growled deep in his throat and his arms came around Aaron, pulling him in tight as he deepened the kiss.

God, the taste of him, and the scent.

And then Lewis's hands were on Aaron's lean hips, yanking him closer, and they were grinding against one another, moaning as their cocks prodded and pressed through their clothes. And God, but it felt so fucking good to finally, *finally* give in to this. To allow himself this thing that he'd wanted for so long, even if that thing was utterly foolish, utterly destructive.

It might be a mistake, but at least it was one he was choosing to make. He might regret that choice tomorrow—as impossible as that seemed right now—but tomorrow would have to take care of itself.

Aaron gave himself up to Lewis's kiss with a groan, parting his lips and meeting the man's sliding tongue with his own as he clutched at any part of Lewis he could reach, desperate for him.

It was Lewis who pulled back first, gasping for air. Lewis who met his gaze, wild-eyed, and said in a voice thick with lust, "What do you want, Aaron? What do you like best?"

The words were crazy, overwhelming. Aaron had to blink and concentrate to take them in.

His answer came out before he'd formulated the thought properly, "I want you to fuck me. But I'm vers if you prefer… or we can…"

He trailed off as Lewis's gaze heated and his hips bucked

against Aaron's, the blunt press of cock on cock, dulled by the layers of fabric between them, yet still wildly, terrifyingly exciting.

"Yeah?" he whispered. "You want me to fuck you?"

Aaron nodded. "Yeah. Is that okay?"

Lewis's answer was a soft chuckle. "It's very okay." He began undoing the buttons of Aaron's tweed waistcoat, then his shirt. Moments later, he was pushing both garments off, baring Aaron's skin to his avid gaze.

"Wow," he breathed, dropping his head to press a soft kiss to Aaron's shoulder, then another to his neck. And there was that unexpected tenderness again, making Aaron's chest ache.

When Lewis lifted his head, he smiled wickedly, before manoeuvring Aaron around with characteristic bossiness till the back of his knees hit the bed and he tumbled to the mattress with a huff of laughter, Lewis following. For a moment, they just lay there and stared at one another, Lewis's powerful body pressing Aaron into the mattress, his blue gaze excited and wary and lustful all at once. And then Lewis shifted and began moving down Aaron's body, mapping his path with tiny kisses. When he reached Aaron's nipple, he circled the taut nub with his tongue, and Aaron surged up towards his mouth, needing more. With a hum of satisfaction, Lewis gave it to him, tugging at the little berry of flesh with his teeth, sucking it into his mouth.

Each sharp pull made pleasure reverberate through Aaron's body, right down to his balls. When he arched beneath Lewis, groaning his pleasure, Lewis glanced up, his blue gaze glinting with satisfaction as he reached for Aaron's other nipple.

"You're sensitive," he observed as he circled Aaron's right nipple with his fingertip. He pinched it lightly, then slowly twisted, his gaze fixed on Aaron's face, watching his reaction hungrily. Another helpless moan escaped Aaron's throat, and his hips bucked in the air.

Lewis's gaze was hot. "Fuck," he whispered. "Look at you." He twisted Aaron's nipple again, then reached over to soothe it with his mouth, licking and teasing as Aaron panted and writhed beneath him.

Lewis continued his journey down, pressing more kisses as he went. When he reached Aaron's jeans, he undid the buttons, then urged him to lift his hips, drawing off his jeans and boxers, then peeling off his socks, one by one.

"You're gorgeous," he breathed, his greedy gaze moving over Aaron's lean, naked form.

Aaron swallowed, unable to speak. Instead, he watched as Lewis stood and quickly stripped off his own clothes, revealing smooth golden skin and neatly trimmed body hair. A thick, mouth-watering cock that bobbed temptingly.

Once he was naked, Lewis's burning gaze returned to Aaron and Aaron found himself whispering, "Put the light out."

Lewis was silent a moment. But then he turned away and hit the switch, and the forgiving velvet darkness enveloped them, the moonlight shining through the window silvering the edges of Lewis's broad shoulders and strong profile.

Lewis's shadow moved closer, the mattress dipping as he straddled Aaron's hips and bent his head to take Aaron's mouth in another long, drugging kiss, before shifting down to take up where he'd left off.

He trailed his tongue down Aaron's belly, then nuzzled his face into Aaron's groin, before leaning back and taking hold of his aching cock in a loose grip. He paused there, admiring Aaron's dick, the warm huff of his breath making Aaron harden a tiny bit more when he'd have sworn that was impossible.

"Very nice," Lewis murmured at last and lowered his head to swipe his tongue over the leaking head. "*Hmmm.*"

Aaron gasped, and Lewis chuckled, an indulgent, affectionately mocking sound that turned Aaron on in complicated ways, making him want to show Lewis just how desperate his desire was.

He arched up, begging for more. "*Please.*"

Lewis laughed again, but he gave him what wanted, taking Aaron's cock deep into his mouth, letting it spear into his throat as his strong hands held Aaron's hips ruthlessly down.

Aaron cried out, his hands going to Lewis's head, clutching at his hair, his hips fighting Lewis's tight grip even as he revelled in the unrelenting control. Lewis's mouth was warm and clasping, his throat like a glove, his fingers pressing bruises into Aaron's skin that he never wanted to fade.

"Oh fuck, you'd better stop—I'm going to come if you don't," Aaron stuttered out. "And I want to come with you inside me."

Lewis pulled off him with a lusty slurp and looked up. Aaron's eyes had grown used to the dark now. In the moonlight, he saw that Lewis wore that wicked smile that was so goddamned attractive but also so… so endearingly *boyish.* Just for an instant, Aaron had the strangest feeling of being weirdly older and wiser than Lewis, even though he was seven years younger.

Of wanting to protect him.

His heart twisted, and a tiny part of his brain thought, *Oh God, maybe this was a mistake.* But then Lewis was moving up the bed, his gaze intent on Aaron, and all Aaron's doubts fled.

Lewis stretched towards the bedside table and rattled open the drawer, returning with a bottle of expensive-looking lube and a box of condoms. Opening the bottle, he drizzled it over his fingers. As he reached down between Aaron's open thighs, he kissed him again, penetrating his mouth and his hole at the same time, making Aaron gasp into his mouth.

He certainly knew what he was doing. Distracting Aaron

with deep kisses while he gradually, patiently, opened him up, somehow magically replenishing the lube without Aaron even noticing. All Aaron was aware of was the gradual, intensely pleasurable stretch and Lewis kissing him, Lewis's scent all around him.

By the time Lewis was sitting back on his heels to slide on a condom, Aaron was teetering on the edge of orgasm.

Lewis's gaze travelled over Aaron's lean, moonlit body.

"You're so beautiful," he breathed.

Aaron wanted to say, *No, you are,* but he stayed quiet and pliant, watching as Lewis took hold of his right leg and hitched it up, opening him with practiced ease as he shifted forward on his knees, lining his cock up with Aaron's stretched hole.

"Yes," Aaron whispered, arching up. "Fuck me, please."

He saw how much Lewis liked that, the flash of satisfaction in his eyes. And then Lewis was pressing inside him, his gaze on Aaron as he slowly slid deep, and deeper.

Aaron groaned, canting his hips up to ease the way, relishing all of it. The stretching, shoving brutality of it, and the reaching, insidious pleasure, and the other, deeper pleasure of it being Lewis. Lewis inside him.

"You feel amazing," Lewis breathed. He shifted so that he was lying on top of Aaron instead of on his knees. He was still holding up Aaron's right thigh with one big hand as he fucked into him.

Aaron lifted his head, his neck straining, to press a kiss to Lewis's mouth.

He wanted—needed—Lewis's kiss. And he wanted to say things. Stupid things. Things he shouldn't even think, never mind utter aloud.

But he didn't say them. He made himself stay quiet, breathing Lewis in and letting his fingers skim lovingly over the warm, golden skin of Lewis's back as Lewis slowly, deeply, pleasurably fucked him. God, when he came, it was going to be intense. And even though he could barely stand to wait a moment longer, part of him wanted that feeling of *almost, almost* to last forever.

Wanted this moment of belonging to Lewis to last forever.

Belonging to Lewis, body and soul.

In that moment, the simple truth—a truth he'd known but determinedly buried—surfaced, like a buoy in the ocean, bursting free of the water.

He was in love with Lewis.

He'd been in love with him for years.

Suddenly, Aaron's eyes were stinging. He broke the kiss, gasping for air, turning his head to the side to hide his emotional state.

Thankfully, Lewis didn't seem to notice. He lowered his head and passionately kissed the exposed side of Aaron's neck, hitching his thigh a tiny bit higher and sinking an impossible fraction deeper, dragging another desperate groan from Aaron's belly.

The emotional turmoil had no impact on Aaron's building orgasm—maybe it made it even more intense. Aaron had always liked sex, but, yeah, this was different. Abandoned and urgent in an entirely different way.

"I'm close," he managed to stutter out. "Just need your hand. *Please*."

"*Yes*," Lewis breathed, letting go of Aaron's thigh and bracing himself on his left arm as he reached down between them.

Aaron cried out as Lewis's hand enveloped his cock, and after that, it didn't take much at all, just a couple of lazy tugs and he was coming, thrusting into Lewis's hand as the orgasm slammed into him like a wall of water, wiping him out.

He knew he cried out and that he was clinging to Lewis as

the pleasure burst inside him, then rippled outward through his body. He was aware enough to know all of that, but he was also disembodied somehow too.

It was Lewis's voice in his ear, as he too began to climax, that brought him back to himself.

"Aaron. *Fuck.*"

Lewis sounded wrecked, his fingers digging into Aaron's hips as he emptied into him. Aaron pressed a kiss to Lewis's shoulder, squeezing his eyes closed against another impossible wave of emotion.

When it was over, they were silent for a little while, just the sounds of their breathing returning to normal. Then came the ordinary practicality of uncoupling their bodies, disposing of the condom, cleaning up with some fancy wipes that Lewis produced from the bedside drawer in the same expensive-looking packaging as the lube and the condoms.

Lewis quietly took care of all that, wiping away the remains of lube and jizz from Aaron's body as Aaron lay there, grateful for the concealing privacy of the darkness. His throat still felt thick with emotion, his mind teeming with too many thoughts and feelings to parse.

He should get up and leave, he knew that, but it felt as though, if he spoke, or even moved, something might *break.*

Lewis rose and walked across the room to dump the used wipes and condom in the wastepaper bin. His shadowed form in the darkness was familiar and not at the same time. Familiar in shape and attitude, but with the new intimacy of nakedness.

Aaron forced himself up onto one elbow. "Lewis—"

"Please," Lewis whispered. "Can we… not talk?"

Aaron felt relieved more than anything. "Okay," he whispered.

He watched as Lewis picked up the duvet which had long ago fallen to the floor and settled it back over the bed, covering Aaron's body. Then he climbed into bed beside him and tugged Aaron into the shape he wanted, which was, apparently, that of the little spoon. Lewis curled his own body around Aaron, holding him close.

His lips rested against the back of Aaron's neck.

"Go to sleep," he whispered, so Aaron did.

CHAPTER SEVENTEEN

Lewis

It was not the first time in his life that Lewis had woken up in bed with a man only to feel swamped with regret, but it was definitely the worst of all the times it had happened. Because this morning, the man in his bed was Aaron Page, and that made everything different.

Even the regret was different. It wasn't the simple, hard-edged regret of letting someone stay over when he couldn't be arsed dealing with them the next day. No, this regret was far more profound and tainted with a complex mix of other feelings.

At some point in the night, their bodies had separated. Now Lewis lay on his back, staring at the ceiling while Aaron lay on his side, facing away from Lewis.

Lewis turned his head to look at him. At the tousled light brown hair on the pillow, the pale, freckled shoulders. Aaron was still sleeping, his body relaxed, breathing deep and even.

Lewis turned his gaze back to the ceiling. His stomach was knotted with anxiety. All he could think about was Aaron leaving him. He could actually picture Aaron standing in front of him, saying, *"I don't think I can continue working with you any more…"*

Fuck.

He couldn't let that happen. He couldn't lose Aaron.

Why, *why* had he done the one thing guaranteed to fuck everything up?

But Jesus, the sex had been good. Really, really good.

He'd loved that Aaron had let him take charge. Not in a dom-in-a-leather-harness way, just in the way he'd let Lewis touch him however he'd wanted. Let him determine the path and pace of what they'd done. Lewis had loved that. More often than not, he had to compromise on his preference for being in control in bed. Sometimes other guys just weren't into it. Sometimes, even when they said they were—when they used words like 'submissive' about themselves—they turned out to be incredibly bossy about how they wanted to be topped. It was rare to find someone who was truly in tune with him. But Aaron…yeah, Aaron had been perfect. Easily trusting, unbelievably responsive.

Maybe, partly, it had been because they already knew each other so well?

Fuck, now Lewis's dick was hard again. He squeezed his eyes closed and started giving it a silent lecture in an attempt to will the erection down.

There's no point getting all excited. This is not going to be happening again. This was a one-off.

If he could convince Aaron of that, maybe he could actually salvage this? Maybe their working relationship could survive one, isolated mistake?

He had to at least try. He couldn't risk losing Aaron forever.

Just then, Aaron shifted.

"Hmpf." He turned onto his back and yawned, blinking his eyes open sleepily, only to recoil—yes, actually fucking *recoil*—when he saw Lewis lying beside him. He stared at

Lewis wide-eyed for a moment. Lewis could practically see the moment his brain came online and understanding dawned in his grey gaze, his cheeks flushing pink.

"Good morning," Lewis said, amazed at how ordinary he sounded. He might have been walking past Aaron's desk on his way into his office, hot chocolate in hand.

"Morning," Aaron whispered in response. He searched Lewis's face, and Lewis could only hope his attempt at projecting calm ease was working.

"So," Lewis said, when Aaron remained silent. "This situation is… suboptimal."

"Suboptimal," Aaron repeated slowly.

Christ, this was not a conversation to be had lying down. Quickly, Lewis sat up, only to realise that had the effect of baring his chest. *Shit*. There was nothing for it but to bite the bullet and grab some clothes. He jumped out of bed, located his discarded boxers on the floor, and yanked them on in record time, then grabbed a t-shirt out of his case and pulled that on too.

By the time he was done, Aaron was sitting up, the duvet pulled up to his chin. He looked miserable, and a pang of guilt stabbed Lewis.

"This is all very regrettable," he said briskly, "but you need to know that I take full responsibility."

Aaron blinked. "You… do?"

Lewis nodded emphatically. "I don't blame you, Aaron. This is on me."

When Aaron's eyes flashed, Lewis felt a stab of unease.

"And why would that be?" Aaron said with acid sweetness. "Because you're *so* irresistible, I can hardly be blamed for dragging you into bed?"

"What?" Lewis said. "No! I just mean, you know, *I'm* the boss. I should have stopped this before it even started."

Aaron said nothing, but his face was set and unhappy. It was an expression he very rarely wore—there had only been two other times that Lewis could think of, and on both occasions, Aaron had threatened to leave his job. He had only agreed to stay when Lewis had thrown all pride to the wind and begged him to reconsider.

There weren't many people in this world he'd do that for, but yeah, Aaron was up there.

He *couldn't* lose him.

"Look," Lewis pleaded, stepping forward and holding his palms out in a conciliatory gesture. "I'm sure you're wishing this hadn't happened just as much as I am. I really don't want to spoil our working relationship. *No one* gets me like you do, Aaron." His voice cracked on the last few words. He had to clear his throat before he added, "Please. Can we just forget it happened?"

Please, please, please don't leave.

Aaron dropped his head into his hands, rubbing at his temples with his long fingers. Lewis wished he could see his expression. Wished he knew what Aaron was thinking.

"Aaron?"

At last, Aaron raised his head. He still looked unhappy, but it was a resigned sort of unhappiness now—not the I'm-leaving-you kind, and Lewis felt the tightness in his chest ease a fraction.

"Can you pass me my clothes?" Aaron said.

Lewis circled the bed, picking up Aaron's things from the floor, then handing the whole bundle over. He turned away tactfully while Aaron dressed.

"The meeting with Charlie's at ten," Aaron said after a minute.

Lewis turned to find him more or less fully dressed, though his shirt wasn't completely buttoned, and he held his waistcoat in one hand and his shoes in the other.

"Right," Lewis said. "In his office—*collaboration space,* I mean." He gave a weak, crooked smile, but Aaron didn't return it.

"Okay. At least that gives us both a couple of hours to get back into the right headspace." He met Lewis's gaze, and he looked so fucking *sad*—Lewis wanted to go to him and pull him into a rough hug. Whisper in his ear, *It's okay*.

But he didn't. He just stood there in miserable silence, while Aaron said, "You're right. We'll forget this ever happened. No need to mention it again."

Aaron turned and headed for the door.

"Aaron—"

He stopped but he didn't turn around.

"What?" he said, his voice oddly strangled.

Lewis realised he didn't know what he wanted to say then. He couldn't say *thank you,* or *last night was amazing,* or *you're so beautiful,* or any of the things that were going through his mind as he stared at the man he'd taken to bed last night.

So he just said, "I'll give you a knock before we go down."

"Sure," Aaron said, and then he was gone, leaving Lewis staring at the closed door.

At ten to ten, Lewis stood at his window, gazing out at the morning.

Overnight, a soggy blanket of drizzle had crept in, and now it sagged miserably over the countryside. As an example of pathetic fallacy, it was so on the nose that he'd never stoop to using it in a script. Nevertheless, it rather accurately reflected his bleak mood.

After Aaron had left, Lewis had stood for a long time in the intensely silent room, contemplating the detritus of the previous night. The sight of the food wrappers and their empty mugs of hot chocolate had stung in a way he hadn't wanted to think about, but eventually, it had prodded him into action. He'd shoved everything into the bin, straightened the bedclothes, and erased all evidence of last night's...misjudgment.

Then he'd taken a long hot shower, using Charlie's expensive and overly fragranced products to ensure no scent of Aaron lingered on his skin or in his hair.

If only it was as easy to wash away his memories.

Moments from their night together kept coming back in unexpected flashes of feeling or sensation: the warmth of Aaron's pliant body beneath his hands, his trusting responsiveness, the swooping dive in Lewis's belly when their lips first touched.

And the sadness in Aaron's eyes when he'd left, the gnawing fear—the terror—that Lewis had damaged something beyond repair.

What a fucking idiot he'd been to let things go so far.

He glanced at his watch. Five minutes to ten. It was time he headed down for the meeting. Charlie hated lateness, and God knew Lewis needed to stay on his good side after bailing on dinner last night. Yet Lewis found himself delaying, putting off the awful moment when he'd have to knock on Aaron's door and watch him pretend that none of this had happened.

Which made no sense because that was exactly what Lewis wanted him to do, what they both needed to do to get back to normal. The alternative was unthinkable.

"Get a fucking grip," he told the empty room.

Checking himself in the mirror before he left, he was satisfied with what he saw. Despite Charlie's insistence on casual dress, Lewis had put on a suit this morning. He'd brought it because he never knew what to expect at Safehaven, and he was bloody glad he had. The suit put him back in control. It made a statement to Charlie that Lewis wasn't going to play his game, and it made a statement to Aaron too—that the line they'd so carelessly trampled last night was firmly back in place. That there was no expectation of a repeat performance.

Although the prospect of never being able to—

He cut the thought off before it could fully form and tugged at his shirt cuffs. Perhaps the suit made him look a little severe, but so much the better. This meeting, both the imminent one with Aaron, and the dreaded one with Charlie, would be tough. Lewis needed his armour in place.

Even so, his heart was slugging heavily when he left his room and stopped outside Aaron's door. His skin prickled, and he knew, just *knew*, that Aaron stood on the other side of the door waiting for him to knock. He could almost feel him through the flimsy wood.

Lifting his hand, he took a steadying breath and rapped firmly.

Nothing happened. *Shit*. Stomach in freefall, he waited. And waited. Still nothing. Maybe Aaron had already gone down? Maybe he didn't want to open the door, didn't want to see Lewis?

Or maybe he'd left.

His chest tightened in panic. "Aaron?" he called sharply. He'd just lifted his hand to knock again when the door flew open, leaving him with his arm raised as Aaron bustled out, busying himself with his phone, his key, the messenger bag he was flinging over one shoulder.

"Uh," Lewis managed, unexpectedly short of breath and useful words.

Fuck, Aaron looked good. He wore a slim-fitting blue shirt and dark trousers that flattered his slender frame. Like Lewis, he was dressed for business. Unlike Lewis, his expression was perfectly calm, perfectly professional.

And he didn't meet Lewis's eyes once.

"Toni said we should collect her on the way down," Aaron said as he locked his door. "Safety in numbers, apparently." He began to walk toward her room, not waiting for Lewis. "I checked, and there'll be breakfast in the meeting. At least, there'll be coffee. I can't vouch for what Charlie considers acceptable breakfast food."

Aaron was in hyper-efficient professional mode, and it stung like a slap, compounding Lewis's fear that he'd lost something precious last night. Anxiety churned in the pit of his stomach as he hurried to catch up. "I doubt we'll get a decent bacon roll," he said desperately, offering a hopeful smile.

Look at me, he begged silently. *Smile at me.*

But Aaron ignored the comment, reaching into his bag and pulling out a slim folder. He handed it over. "A clean copy of the US pitch," he said. "I thought it might be useful. I put a summary of the main talking points at the front."

Lewis took it miserably. "Thanks," he said. "My copy's covered in red pen."

"Yes," Aaron agreed as they reached Toni's door. Stiffly, he knocked, eyes front and centre, staring at the door as if willing it to open.

It didn't.

Silence grew between them, agonisingly awkward because yesterday—any day in the three years they'd known each other—the silence would have been comfortable. Or, at worst, unremarkable. But this morning it blared loud as a klaxon.

Warning! Warning! Everything's fucked up!

Lewis couldn't bear it. "Aaron, listen," he said, just as Toni flung her door wide open.

"Well, this is it. I hope you—" Her face fell, and she eyed them warily. "What's wrong? What's happened?"

"Nothing," they chorused. It couldn't have sounded more suspicious if they'd scripted it.

Toni frowned as she looked between them both. "Okaaay," she said warily, drawing out the word. "And did I miss the memo about business dress? Because you both look very office-like this morning."

Lewis shook his head. "No memo. This just felt…" Instinctively, he glanced at Aaron for support, only to find him fiddling with his phone. Sighing, he said, "It felt more appropriate today."

If anything, Toni looked more wary. "Meaning what?"

"Meaning we're going into battle, so I'm wearing my best armour."

Toni didn't smile. In fact she pursed her lips as she locked her door and slipped the key into her bag. "It's not a battle, Lewis. That is, it's not a battle we can win. And I'm not planning to die on any creative hills today." She fixed him with a level look. "God knows Charlie's an arse, but you have to compromise; you've got no choice if you want this deal. And you do want this deal, don't you? Not just for RPP, I mean, but for *you*."

She was watching him intently.

He sighed. "Yeah, I do."

She nodded. "Okay then. I still think, if we play our cards right, we'll get some concessions from him."

Lewis didn't answer because he knew she was right. There was more at stake than his personal pride, and he didn't intend to torpedo a deal that could net RPP a pretty penny and launch his own career Stateside. Even so, the thought of giving in to Charlie's demands about Faolán's sexuality rankled in ways he couldn't begin to unpick. "I still don't like it, though," was all he said.

"I know. But we've talked about this. We'll find a way you can live with it."

While they were talking, Aaron had slipped away and was walking ahead of them towards the long gallery. As Lewis and Toni followed, Lewis found his gaze riveted on Aaron's lean figure, on his long legs and shapely arse. An arse he now knew intimately. Christ, had it only been hours ago that they'd been naked in each other's arms? Last night already felt like it belonged to another life, another world. It could have been a dream, except that Aaron couldn't even look at him now, and that was a nightmare. One that left Lewis feeling afraid and alone.

Fuck. He looked away, shocked by the sudden ache in his throat.

Beside him, in a taut voice, Toni said, "Everything all right this morning?"

"Yes, of course," he snapped. "Why wouldn't it be?"

"Well." She gave him an odd look. "Because of the...migraine, yesterday?"

"Oh." He frowned, embarrassed that she'd witnessed his... He wasn't even sure what had happened, only that Aaron had known to get him out of there. Aaron had taken care of him, and in return Lewis had fucked everything up. He set his jaw, pushing the distressing thought aside. "Yeah, I'm sorry about that. Those fucking cocktails..."

Toni seemed content to buy the half-lie. "God, yes. Charlie was—Well, I ended up bailing early, too. He's an ugly drunk." More seriously, she added, "Keep your head in the game today, Lewis. No distractions."

"My head *is* in the fucking game."

Her gaze drifted to Aaron and back, her look weighted. "And what about Aaron?"

"What about Aaron? He's fine."

"Darling, he looks like he's been sucker-punched." She lifted an eyebrow. "And the tension between the pair of you is so thick I could stand a spoon up in it."

"Aaron's *fine,*" Lewis repeated. At least, he would be fine. He had to be. Once they'd left this fucking house of horrors and got back to the office, he'd be fine. *They'd* be fine. Aaron would smile at him again, and roll his eyes, and everything would go back to normal.

Toni gave a sceptical huff. "I hope you're right, Lewis."

When they reached Charlie's office, Aaron was waiting for them at the door. He did look tense, but they were all tense. He looked pale too, and strained. Lewis fought back an inappropriate urge to rub his back or squeeze his shoulder, to hug him.

And since when did he ever *hug* people?

But maybe Aaron felt the same because he turned his head, and for a hot second, their eyes met. *Finally*. Aaron's were turbulent, full of feelings Lewis couldn't parse, but he gave Lewis a curt nod, an *I'm on your side* nod, and the ball of tension in the pit of Lewis's belly unwound a fraction.

He smiled in relief. They *would* be all right; he knew they would.

"Okay," he said, pushing open the door to lead them in. "Let's get this show on the fucking road."

CHAPTER EIGHTEEN

Aaron

Suboptimal.

That was the word Aaron couldn't get out of his head. He kept hearing it in Lewis's stilted, awkward voice. Even now, as they trooped into Charlie's office to discuss the future of the show that had dominated Aaron's life for the past six years, all he could think about was Lewis's summary dismissal that morning.

This situation is… suboptimal.

The single most transformative sexual and emotional encounter of Aaron's life, one that had crystallised years of repressed longing, had been suboptimal. Regrettable.

It was so pathetic it was almost funny.

Only it wasn't funny at all. It was fucking heartbreaking.

"Welcome, welcome," Charlie gushed, ushering them into his huge office. He too was dressed more formally today, in dark trousers and a blousy white shirt reminiscent of *Poldark*.

Floor-to-ceiling windows dominated one end of the room, looking out over a grey and gloomy morning. Platters of pastries and fruit had been laid out for them, and the smell of fresh coffee filled the air.

"I hope you're all well rested and ready to get creative?" Charlie said, rubbing his hands together. "Mils sends her apologies. She and Geoff are, uh, empathy mapping this morning."

Toni smiled, Lewis grunted, and Aaron remained silent.

He had so much feeling knotted up inside, he was afraid it would all come spilling out if he so much as opened his mouth. So, he made a beeline for the coffee and poured himself a generous mugful. Lewis appeared next to him, making himself a tea, stirring in several sugars. Aaron was as aware of him as he would have been the sun, his skin burning every time Lewis cast a look his way. Which was often. Quick, nervous glances that only served to remind Aaron that Lewis regretted what had happened the night before. Deeply.

Aaron ignored those looks, keeping his gaze on his coffee. Lewis's attention was unbearable, and anyway, what did he expect to see?

"How's the head this morning?" Charlie asked, strolling towards them both but addressing only Lewis. His brow furrowed in a reasonably good impersonation of sympathy.

"Hmm?" Lewis said, looking up from stirring his tea. "Oh, uh. Fine."

Toni said, "I was about to ask you the same question, Charlie." Her tone was surprisingly sharp. "We *all* had rather a lot to drink last night."

"Me? I'm fine. Drank a pint of kombucha before bed." Charlie squeezed Lewis's shoulder. "But turmeric tea is what you need for a hangover, my friend. With a little cayenne pepper for a kick."

"Yeah, whatever. I'm not hungover." Lewis manoeuvred his shoulder free of Charlie's grip. Lewis was not a hugger; he really didn't much like being touched at all.

Except last night…

Jesus, Aaron could still feel the silky-smooth skin of Lewis's shoulders beneath his palms, hear his low groan of pleasure and relief. Aaron's heart kicked painfully at the memory. Grabbing a Danish to go with his coffee, he turned away and went to sit at the table.

Truth was, his stupid heart had broken this morning. And, God, every hackneyed word he'd ever written about angst and pining was a fucking lie—there was nothing romantic about this feeling. It just really bloody hurt. Physically and emotionally. All he wanted to do was curl up in the dark and howl out his misery.

Not that he had anybody to blame but himself. He'd known last night how this would play out. He'd known it would be a one-time deal—*all* Lewis's conquests were transitory.

Aaron's mistake was bigger than that, though. It went so much deeper than regretting a casual hook-up. Last night had exposed the truth he'd been hiding from for years—that he'd become a walking cliché, the PA who'd fallen in love with his boss.

A boss who didn't want him.

Well, of course he didn't. Why would he? Lewis was exceptional: talented, charismatic, and gorgeous. He could have anyone he wanted. And Aaron? Even the thought brought a lump to his throat, but it was the truth, and it had to be faced: Aaron had just been convenient.

Lewis had reached for him when he needed comfort, and Aaron had given himself over with pathetic eagerness. Last night, everything had felt so natural and easy, a mutual reaching for one another, but his eyes were clearer this morning, and he could see that he'd only been a convenient fuck. A comfort fuck. One Lewis had immediately regretted.

Suboptimal.

He winced at the memory.

"Okay?" Lewis said, taking the seat next to him. He

looked uncertain and concerned, which pissed Aaron off. He didn't need Lewis's pity.

"Fine," he said shortly, grabbing his Danish. He didn't think he'd be able to force anything down his throat, which was so clogged with emotion he could barely swallow, so he set about shredding it in between sips of his scalding coffee.

After a tense silence, and in a tone of faux jollity Aaron had never heard before, Lewis said, "The pastries are pretty good!" And took a huge bite of his croissant.

Whatever. Aaron didn't have the bandwidth to deal with Lewis's morning-after-the-night-before awkwardness. He just wanted to get this nightmare over with. He was in survival mode now. All he had to do was get through this meeting, this day, the rest of this cursed weekend, so that he could fall apart in the privacy of his own flat.

One step at a time, he told himself. *One minute at a time, one breath at a time.*

Toni joined them at the table. She looked tense, business-like. Which was no wonder, really, given how much rode on this meeting. Aaron had been so caught up in his own drama that he'd almost forgotten the reason they were here in the first place: to strike a deal with Telopix. One that would benefit RPP financially and launch Lewis into a different league.

Across the table, Toni's eyes met his and narrowed in a silent question. Maybe she was trying to ask how Lewis was doing this morning, but since Aaron had no real idea, he just gave a little shrug. Toni's lips tightened, but she didn't say anything, busying herself with pulling out her notes for the meeting instead. Aaron did the same, opening up his laptop, acting the part of efficient, unassuming Aaron Page.

"Ah, fantastic!" He flinched when Charlie's hands landed on his shoulders and began to massage him lightly. "You'll take notes and actions, yeah?"

"I—"

"Awesome!"

"That's not why he's here," Lewis growled.

Surprised, Aaron glanced over and found Lewis's gaze fixed darkly on Charlie's hands, which were still mauling Aaron's shoulders.

"Sure, but he doesn't mind, do you, Andy?" With one final squeeze, Charlie let go. "Good man. Okay!" Finally, he took a seat on the other side of the table and rubbed his palms together. "Let's get started. *Leeches*: USA! I'm excited. Hell, everyone at Telopix is excited about this project. So, before you begin your pitch, let me tell you something about our creative vision for the show..."

At which point, Aaron tuned out, his thoughts returning to the more urgent matter of his personal catastrophe.

It occurred to him that he hadn't felt anything like this level of distress when he and Colin had ended their relationship. In retrospect, that should probably have raised flags at the time. But considering last night's painful realisation about his feelings for Lewis, he now suspected that he hadn't been in love with Colin when they split.

No. Be honest.

He'd never been in love with Colin.

Which was a sobering thought.

And the more he brooded on it, the shittier it made him feel. Colin had been right all along, it seemed. Aaron *had* been in love with someone else throughout their relationship. Only it hadn't been Skye Jäger; it had been Lewis Hunter. Which was a whole lot worse.

And if Colin was right about that, what else was he right about?

Aaron *was* still doing the same job he'd stumbled into three years ago. He *had* turned his back on a teaching career, he *had* refused to pursue other opportunities within RPP, and he'd never even considered applying for more senior roles elsewhere.

Colin had been right about all of that. And as the thoughts unspooled in Aaron's mind, the truth became horribly, humiliatingly clear.

Aaron had been a bloody idiot.

All this time he'd prided himself on his loyalty to Lewis, believing that Lewis needed him too much for Aaron to consider leaving. And, yeah, Lewis *did* need him. He needed him because Aaron put up with him, because Aaron made his life easier, and because replacing him would be a pain in the arse.

In short, because Aaron was convenient.

That would have been a crappy enough reason to stay, yet the real reason was even worse, even more humiliating. And now, after last night, he couldn't hide from it any longer. He'd stayed in his job for three years because he'd fallen in love with Lewis. Because he didn't want to be parted from him. Like one of Lewis's clingy boyfriends, Aaron had hung around long after he should have moved on, hoping for scraps of Lewis's attention, a few breadcrumbs of his time.

Christ, he was no better than Mason. In fact, he was worse than Mason because at least Mason had a successful career. Aaron, on the other hand, had hobbled himself professionally and torpedoed his chance at a healthy relationship with a man who actually gave a shit about him. Worst of all, he hadn't even been honest. Not with Colin, not with Lewis and certainly not with himself.

So what the hell did he do now? How did he get past this?

He had no answer. He couldn't even think straight. Not with Lewis sitting right there, bristling with a tension so palpable Aaron could feel it crackling against his skin. Or maybe that was just the lingering aftershocks from last night, because despite this morning's crushing revelations, his body was still half charged by the intensity of their encounter. He shifted in his seat, the dull ache in his arse another reminder he could do without. And yet, pathetically, one he didn't want to let go of. If nothing else it was tangible proof that he hadn't imagined Lewis's passion, his desire, his—Aaron's throat ached—his unexpected sweetness.

He stared down at his notes, watching the words blur, blinking furiously, terrified of betraying his feelings. Curling his fingers into his palms, he dug his nails into the heels of his hands, concentrating on the sting to distract from the larger swell of emotion he was afraid might overwhelm him.

God, he was pathetic.

Eventually, the flood subsided, and he found himself listening to Charlie again. He'd been talking for some time in an endless, droning monologue.

"...and so essentially our vision is to really push this wide." At least he sounded like he was crawling towards a conclusion. "To engage with the same diverse audience *Leeches* has been building in the European market, but to tailor it for the US consumer. To their cultural touchpoints and moral sensitivities, yeah?"

"That all sounds great," Toni said, cutting in before Charlie could draw another breath. Lewis, meanwhile, had his head down, ferociously doodling on the hardcopy of the pitch Aaron had given him. Toni went on, "And we're totally onboard with a US setting. We'd been thinking New York would be perfect, as one of the oldest cities with a rich supernatural history."

Charlie tapped his temple, then pointed his finger at her. "Great minds, Toni. Great minds. But I was thinking Boston? Because then we could call it '*Brahmins*'—as in Boston Brahmins. What do you think?"

Lewis jerked his head up. "You want to change the name of the show?"

"Everything's on the table." Charlie spread his hands, smiling his shark's smile. "We're throwing it all in the air, Lewis, and seeing where it lands. I mean, don't get me wrong, I love *Leeches*, it's great, but maybe a little obvious? *Brahmins* has that sense of something exclusive and elite, so it makes sense, right?"

"No, it makes no sense at all. What the fuck is a Boston Brahmin?"

Charlie raised an eyebrow. "America's social, political, and cultural elite—the New England aristocracy."

"Never heard of them." Lewis scowled and leaned back in his chair, arms folded across his chest. "Anyway, *Brahmins* doesn't make you think of vampires. You might as well call it '*Toffs*'. The title has to resonate. It has to make a strong, immediate connection with the audience. For a start, they have to know what the fuck it means."

"I think you'll find most educated people know what it means," Charlie said shortly. "But let's table it for now. Although I've got to tell you, the media team *loved* it. They've mocked up some fantastic graphics. I think you're going to adore them."

Aaron felt Lewis stiffen, heard his sharp intake of breath.

"Great!" Toni jumped in quickly. "We'll look at those later. But let's not get distracted from the key point we need to resolve this weekend." Her gaze fixed on Lewis and rested there. "The change of Faolán's sexuality and the introduction of a romantic storyline between him and Amy."

Aaron sat up straighter, his attention snagged. This was the point on which Lewis wouldn't compromise, the rock against which Charlie's ship would break. Despite everything, Aaron was kind of looking forward to watching the wreck. He just hoped it didn't sink the deal.

Beside him, Lewis shifted, sharing a long look with Toni. He didn't speak, and after a moment, she added, "We've been giving the idea some thought."

And we think it's shit, Aaron finished for her.

"And we have a couple of ideas that we'd like to discuss."

Aaron frowned. What ideas? Last thing Aaron knew, Lewis was totally opposed to the changes. He glanced at him, but Lewis was scowling down at his notes again, drawing sharp zigzag shapes all over the paper in blood-red ink.

"Cool, cool, cool," Charlie said. "I'm open. I'm listening. Let me hear where you're going with this."

"Faolán is an important character for lots of reasons," Toni said, her gaze fixed intently on Charlie. "Not least because he's an openly gay man, happy and proud of his sexuality. And Lewis—that is, all of us at RPP—believe it's important to keep that positive representation in the show."

Aaron let out a breath of relief.

"Absolutely," Charlie said seriously, hands pressed together over the centre of his chest. "Abso-fucking-lutely."

Toni's expression hardened. "Good, I'm glad to hear that, Charlie. So our proposal is that we make Faolán bisexual." She held up one hand when Charlie opened his mouth to speak. "That allows him to have a romantic interest in Amy without just, well, turning him straight."

Aaron's heart gave a twist of protest. That wasn't right. Lewis didn't want that. They'd talked about the Skylán romance—okay, 'bromance'—loads of time. Lewis loved it. He wrote it, for Christ's sake. He knew it was central to the show.

"Secondly, Lewis is keen to protect the friendship between Skye and Faolán," Toni continued, "which he feels is threatened by the introduction of a romantic triangle that would focus Faolán's storyline away from Skye. So, we'd like to introduce a new male character to take on the role of Skye's friend and confidante, while allowing Faolán's storyline to develop into the romantic triangle with Amy."

Charlie made some sounds of approval, but Aaron scarcely heard. He couldn't seem to hear anything through the shockwave, as though a concussive blast had left his ears ringing.

This couldn't be Lewis's idea. Toni was talking about ripping Faolán apart. Destroying him entirely. Literally carving out the romantic element of Faolán's relationship with Skye and giving it to Amy, while the vestiges of their intense bond lived on in some nameless new character.

It felt… It felt profoundly personal. It felt like an attack.

And it ignited fury in his belly. Staring at Lewis, Aaron waited for him to object, to tell Toni she'd got it wrong. Waited for him to defend Faolán and Skye's relationship, to tell the truth about what it meant to the show. To Lewis. But he stayed silent, scribbling furiously on his notes, not looking up.

"So, this new character could be, say, another vamp?" Charlie was saying. "Ooh, maybe he's like, fully gay? That way we could keep the LGBT-rep without needing to muddy the waters around Faolán's sexuality. He could still be straight. I'm loving this! What if the gay vamp was a friend from Skye's distant past, one who he once betrayed—"

"No."

To Aaron's surprise, it was his own voice that blurted the word. Perhaps he wouldn't have spoken up normally, but he felt shaky and precarious this morning, like he had nothing left to lose.

And maybe he didn't.

Maybe *Leeches* and Skylán were all he'd ever really had. Maybe they were the only real things in his life. And if that was true, he was going to bloody well fight for them.

"Andy," Charlie said, staring at him, "did you have something to contribute?"

"Yes," he said, heart racing. "I'm sorry, but you can't scrap the Skye and Faolán dynamic. It's the emotional heart of the show. Their bond, their… Well, let's just call it what it is, shall we? Their *romance* is central to *Leeches*. It's what fuels the fandom."

Charlie looked at Toni with the expression of a man surprised that his toaster had offered an opinion. "Well," he said, "there are more complex things to consider than the 'fandom'." The air quotes around the word dripped with sarcasm.

"Really?" Aaron snapped back. "Because I'm pretty sure that without us, you don't have a hit show."

Charlie lifted an eyebrow. "Us?"

"Yeah, I'm a fan. So what? I'm a fan, and I can tell you that the Skylán romance is what fans want—"

"There's no romance," Lewis growled beside him.

Aaron flinched, not expecting an attack from that direction. "What do you mean?" he said faintly, turning to Lewis. "You know there is. You've written it."

"I bloody well haven't," Lewis said, still scribbling on his notes, still not looking up. "A romance between them would screw everything up. It would undermine their whole relationship. I won't go there."

"It wouldn't screw anything up," Aaron said. "And anyway, you've already gone there—there's already a romance between them."

"It's not *romance*," Lewis said scathingly. "It's far more important than that, more enduring, more profound." Finally, he threw down his pen and looked at Aaron, his blue gaze piercing. "Sex would just cheapen it."

Aaron's face heated, but he pushed aside all thoughts of last night. This wasn't about that. "Sex and romance aren't the same thing," he said tightly. "It doesn't matter whether or not they're shagging—they're still in love. Everyone can see it. Why do you think there's so much *Leeches* fanfic out there?"

"Just because a few fans imagine—"

"Loads of fans!" Aaron protested. "There are thousands of Skylán fanfics, Lewis. Stories about their relationship, their friendship… God, their love for each other. It's so important. Seeing that kind of romantic connection between two men in a mainstream show like *Leeches*? Come on, you know how empowering that kind of representation is for people like…"

He hesitated over the word 'us'. "For people like me. It's what makes me—"

Lewis grabbed his wrist. "Aaron," he said repressively.

It was very clearly a warning between a boss and his underling, but Aaron had no patience for that crap this morning. He shook his arm free. "No, this has to be said. Faolán is *gay*. He's always been gay. You can't make him conveniently bisexual just to suit the storyline. Faolán is gay, and there *is* a romantic relationship between him and Skye. Fans aren't imagining it. And it's there because you put it there, Lewis. Deliberate or not, you wrote it into the show. And it's *important*. It's meaningful for people. God, I've written tens of thousands of words about it! And if you try to erase it now, try to pretend it was a totally platonic relationship all along, then you're just as—"

"*You* wrote about it?" Lewis said, staring at him. "What do you mean, *you* wrote about it?"

Fuck.

Fuck.

Nobody else said anything, but Aaron felt Toni's eyes on him. And Charlie's, avid and eager. Aaron flushed, his face burning. But he'd said it now, so why not tell them everything? He was proud of his fanfiction and was seized again by the conviction that he had nothing left to lose. "What I mean is that, in my spare time, I write Skylán fanfiction."

It was half terrifying, half electrifying to finally reveal this vital, creative side of himself to Lewis. Blushing, he added, "I'm quite good at it, actually. I've even won a few awards."

But Lewis did not look impressed. In fact, he looked astonished. Aghast. "You write fanfiction? About *Leeches*?"

"I do, yes."

"Oh, this is wonderful," Charlie crowed. "Fanfic's all porn, isn't it?"

"*No.*" Heart pounding, Aaron kept his gaze locked on

Lewis, imploring him to understand. "It's nothing like that. It's romantic. It's *romance*."

But there was no understanding in Lewis's expression. His mouth twisted in scorn, and he pushed away from the table, getting up. "I can't believe this," he growled, stalking to the window, shoving his hands through his hair. "I can't believe you'd do this. Those are *my* characters. You have no right to twist my show into *Fifty* fucking *Shades*!" He spun back around. "Tell me you don't post this crap online."

His contempt struck with the force of a physical blow, and Aaron couldn't draw enough breath around the sharpness of his pain to answer.

But he didn't need to.

"Jesus Christ," Lewis snarled, whirling back to the window. "You work for the fucking show!"

Aaron's heart laboured. "It doesn't hurt the show. Most fans—"

"You need to leave," Lewis said, keeping his back turned. "We'll discuss this later, but you can't be in this meeting."

Toni said, "Lewis, I don't think that's necessary—"

"We're making confidential creative decisions," Lewis said through gritted teeth. "The last thing we need is it ending up all over the fucking internet."

Aaron sucked in a shocked breath. "I would never—"

"Just go," Lewis said coldly. "I'll talk to you later."

"Fine." Tears pricking, tears of rage and hurt and humiliation, Aaron snatched up his laptop. "You're the fucking boss."

He had a brief impression of Lewis flinching, of Toni's distress and Charlie's crowing delight before he swept out of the room.

The door slamming behind him echoed the final cracking of his heart.

CHAPTER NINETEEN

Lewis

The rest of the meeting was a blur.

As they resumed their seats, Toni met Lewis's gaze and frowned slightly, signalling concern—perhaps asking if he was okay to go on.

He just looked away, out of the window at the steadily falling rain.

After that, he was aware of Toni and Charlie talking, animatedly at one point, but not what they were saying. He knew he should pay attention. Charlie was probably making the most of Lewis's distraction to bring all his firepower to bear on Toni. But still, he couldn't pull himself together. His mind couldn't let go of those last minutes before Aaron had left.

"I've written tens of thousands of words…"

How could he not have known? The fanfic thing was bad enough, but to not know that Aaron dabbled in writing at all? How could he not have known something so *fundamental* about him?

Years Aaron had worked for him. Every day, the two of

them spent hours together. Aaron knew Lewis better than anyone else, and Lewis had, perhaps foolishly, imagined it went the other way too. No lover had ever come close to that level of intimacy with Lewis. The only other person was his brother Owen, and even Owen didn't really understand Lewis's writing, which was hands down the most important thing in his life.

But Aaron knew everything. His knowledge of *Leeches* was better than anyone else's, maybe even Lewis's, and his instincts about the characters and storylines were pitch perfect. Somehow, over the years they had worked together, Lewis had come to think of Aaron as… well, that was the question, wasn't it? How *was* it Lewis thought of him?

It was always Aaron who Lewis turned to when he wanted to know how the show's fans would react to something. During their script discussions, Aaron always spoke passionately about what different groups of fans wanted and expected and loved. That wasn't all Aaron did, though—he was also the most intuitive person on the show's editorial team. His eye for detail was incredible, and his memory was astonishing. It was always Aaron who reminded the team about those tiny connections between characters and past episodes that they could layer in for those sneaky inside jokes that the fans loved so much. His input was so valuable that, at some point, it had got that Lewis didn't really consider a potential storyline good to go until Aaron had given it the nod in his quiet, unassuming way.

When it came to *Leeches*, Lewis's own precious baby, he'd shared everything with Aaron.

And all this time, he hadn't even *known* that Aaron wrote fanfic.

Lewis stared at the large puddle that was forming on the surface of the helipad outside while Charlie droned on about speeding up story delivery to maximise audience engagement.

Fanfic.

He was still boggling over it. Aaron *knew* how he felt about fanfic. They talked about it regularly during their script discussions—Lewis had reluctantly agreed that it was a decent barometer for how the fans felt about all sorts of stuff, but he'd never imagined that Aaron was so intimately acquainted with it because he was part of the fanfic community himself. He'd assumed Aaron skimmed that stuff because of his job. Because he was details-orientated and curious and thought the information would be useful.

Lewis was pretty sure there wasn't one single time they'd had a conversation about fanfic when Lewis had failed to express disbelief that anyone would want to read or write that sort of hyper-sexed, romanticised drivel. He grimaced a bit at the thought of those many past cutting comments, but his simmering anger soon rallied. After all, wasn't that observation justified? He might not have read any fanfic, but he knew the vast majority of it was sexual fantasies about characters who would never actually end up together in the official versions of whatever work was being bastardised.

Where was the artistic merit in taking someone else's fully fledged characters and shoving them into a series of gratuitous sex scenes? That wasn't just unimaginative, it was fucking *tragic.* Everyone with a laptop thought they were a fucking writer these days.

And yet, he found himself wondering whether he'd recognise Aaron's writing if he searched for it online. The thought of reading it was...uncomfortable. Sex scenes written by Aaron about Skye and Faolán? Way too personal. Yet he couldn't help wondering whether he'd recognise how Aaron's versions of Skye and Faolán interacted. How they flirted and kissed and fucked and did all the things that Aaron so wanted them to do in the real show.

"You know how empowering that kind of representation is for people like me."

Aaron's gaze when he said those words to Lewis had been bright with hope. And why did that make Lewis feel so fucking *angry*? Like Aaron was putting something on him, something he didn't want and hadn't asked for?

Abruptly, without thinking, Lewis stood up. His chair rocked back on its rear legs but didn't topple. Toni startled, and Charlie broke off what he'd been saying to glare at him.

Charlie opened his mouth—probably to rebuke him—but before he could get out a word, Lewis said shortly, "Let's reconvene another time."

He turned away from the conference table and headed for the door without waiting for a response.

"You want to stop *now*?" Charlie squawked behind him. "Ten more minutes and we can put this whole thing to bed."

"Sorry," Lewis clipped out unapologetically. "There's a lot to think about, and I need time to do that."

He yanked open the door and strode out. Behind him, he could already hear Toni using her soothing reasonable voice.

Crossing the big hall quickly, he made for the stairs, taking them two at a time, a restless urgency fuelling him as he made his way to Aaron's room. As soon as he got there, he pounded on the door.

Aaron opened it more quickly than he expected, as though he was spoiling for this. He didn't look the least bit cowed. In fact he looked as pissed off as Lewis felt, his usually easy, smiling mouth compressed into an uncompromising line, his jaw set.

"If you're here to apologise—" Aaron began, his voice tight and angry.

"Apologise?" Lewis exclaimed. "For *what?*"

Aaron's gaze narrowed, and he folded his arms over his chest. "Okay, in that case, I have no idea why you're here."

"You have no idea? Really?" Lewis fisted his hands by his sides. "You lied to me."

"I did not!" Aaron raked back at him, equally furious. "Just because I didn't tell you that I wrote—"

"It was a lie of omission," Lewis ground out. "You knew how I'd feel about it. Why else wouldn't you tell me? Fucking hell, I told you everything about *Leeches*. You know every goddamned thing that's happening in the show for the next season and a half. And you honestly didn't see fit to tell me that you're part of a fucking fanfic community that obsessively rewrites the show online?" He threw up his hands. "You can't see that that's a potential conflict of interest here?"

Aaron looked away, but his jaw was still obstinately set.

"And you decide to spill this, when?" Lewis went on relentlessly. "In a fucking meeting with Charlie Alexander? The one guy we need to keep sweet. Fucking hell, Aaron!" He rubbed at his shoulder, which was aching again, a gesture that only served to remind him of the night before and Aaron's hands on him.

His stomach twisted, and he dropped his hand to his side.

"You're making way too big of a deal about this," Aaron said wearily. "It's just...for fun. We don't even talk about the sort of stuff I learn about through work. Hell, most of what I write is AU."

"What the—?" Lewis broke off, shaking his head.

"AU—alternate universe. You know, a different reality than the one in the show."

Lewis scowled. "I know what AU means. I just don't see what that's got to do with anything."

Aaron sighed. "I know you don't. You're angry, and you want to have an argument. What's more, you want to *win* the argument—you always do when you're in this mood. So, you're not going to listen to anything I have to say right now. The best thing for both of us would be to end this conversation and go and cool off—"

"Don't do that," Lewis fumed. "This isn't like that."

"Fine," Aaron said mildly. "It's not like that. I'm imagining that you're having one of your tantrums."

"One of my *tantrums*?"

Aaron gave a humourless laugh. "Yeah, you know those mood swings you have? The ones that I'm expected to manage as part of my highly rewarding career? Along with replacing your iPhone charger every couple of weeks, talking your ex-lovers off ledges, and making sure you eat a couple of portions of fucking fruit and veg each week, so you don't die of scurvy." He shook his head. "Christ, I'm a mug."

"I—What?" Lewis blinked, unsure where that conclusion had come from.

Aaron knotted his hands behind his head and brought his elbows together, letting out a noisy rush of air before turning away and walking back into his room. Lewis followed him, letting the door close behind him.

Aaron was now staring out of the window, frustration in every lean line of his body.

"I've been such a fucking idiot," he muttered without turning around.

"*You* have?" Lewis shot back. "How do you think I feel? My personal assistant just announced that he's a fucking security risk—"

Aaron whirled around at that, his arms dropping back to his sides, his expression furious. "No, I didn't," he bit out. "Jesus, will you just be honest about what's happening here? *Nobody* thinks I'm a security risk. Charlie apparently thinks fanfic is hilarious, and Toni obviously thought you were being a dick throwing me out of the meeting. Despite all this ridiculous posturing, not even *you* think I'm a risk—that's just something you've come up with between chucking me out of the meeting and knocking on my door to justify your weird reaction!"

Fury and outrage fired through Lewis. "My *reaction* is weird? You're the one writing fucking *Leeches* porn."

Aaron paled at that, though a slash of red still stained his cheekbones. As mortified as he plainly was, though, he still insisted through gritted teeth, "It's not porn. And you need to calm down, Lewis. What I do in my own time is none of your—"

"It is when you're fucking around with my characters."

"They're not just your characters anymore. And it's called transformative work—Google it."

"I don't give a shit what you call it, but it needs to stop. Right now."

Silence. Aaron stood by the window, watching Lewis across the wide expanse of the bed, scrubbing a hand anxiously through his hair. "You can't tell me what to do in my own time."

Christ, did he really not get it?

"You can't work for me and write fanfiction about my show, Aaron."

"Oh, bullshit. What the hell do you think I'm doing? Nicking your brilliant ideas and using them in my own stuff?" He frowned suddenly, rubbing his mouth. "Okay, I did use the Highgate Vampire myth in a fic, but that was years ago. Way before I started working for you—and way before Ryan used it. Hell, he might have got the inspiration from my fic."

"*Before you worked for me*?" Lewis reeled as a new and sickening thought struck him. "Wait, is that why you took the job? Oh my God, of course it fucking is! Jesus. You thought you could slip one of your fanfics into my hands, didn't you? Or was it a spec script?" His anger sharpened as a worse realisation dawned. "Fuck, is that why you *stayed*? Because I assume there's a reason you've put up with all my fucking 'tantrums' for so long."

With a noise of frustration, Aaron turned away and stared out of the window. "Jesus Christ, you're obtuse. I stayed because…" His voice faded, and he rubbed a hand through his hair again. "Look, I swear, my position here has never had any effect on my writing. I've never used anything in a story that wasn't in an aired episode."

An *aired* episode.

So, he had thought about it, then—how it would look to use confidential information in his stories. Somehow, the calculatedness of that just made it worse.

Staring at Aaron's back, Lewis was struck by the miserable thought that he didn't know him at all. How could he when, for all these years, Aaron had been keeping secrets from him —and then springing them on him like this, at the worst possible moment, making him look like an idiot who didn't even know what his own PA was up to?

"I should fucking fire you for this," he muttered.

Aaron stiffened, and when he turned around, his grey eyes were blazing. "Well, that would be convenient, wouldn't it?"

"No, it would actually be very fucking *inconvenient*."

"Ha!" There was no humour in Aaron's bark of laughter. "Come on, Lewis, we both know what this is really about."

"Yes, it's about you embarrassing me in front of Toni and Charlie. It's about you lying to me for *years*."

"Like you give a shit how I spend my time at home. No, this is about me waking up in your bed this morning!"

Lewis jolted back, appalled. "This has nothing to do with...with…that."

Aaron's grey gaze flared with anger. "Oh, come on," he bit out. "Ever since we stepped into that meeting—before that, even—you've been freaking out about last night. I doubt you were even paying attention to what was going on before I spoke up. And then what I said gave you all the excuse you needed to start venting at me and chuck me out."

Lewis stared at him in silence for several moments, and Aaron met his gaze.

"Yeah," he said wearily. "You know what I'm saying."

"No," Lewis said stubbornly, shaking his head. "I don't. I'm not quiet because I'm agreeing with you. I'm just trying to get my head around this fucking madness."

"Seriously?" Aaron said, his expression unimpressed. "Are you forgetting that I'm not one of your model-turned-actors who thinks you might hang around for longer than five minutes? I *know* you, Lewis—you fuck them and leave them. Or in my case, I suppose, fuck them and fire them."

"I don't—I'm not—" He felt airless all of a sudden. "That's not what this is."

Aaron said nothing, but his gaze was cold and angry.

Lewis said desperately, "I don't *want* to fire you, for fuck's sake. Look, if you take all your fanfictions off the internet and stop writing more, we'll forget—"

"No."

Lewis stared. "What do you mean, no?"

"I mean I won't take them down. And I won't stop writing."

"Aaron, listen—"

"No, *you* listen. Are you seriously telling me this *isn't* about you freaking out because we had sex last night?"

The sudden rush of heat to Lewis's face honestly surprised him. He couldn't remember the last time he'd blushed. "If you're asking whether I regret what we did last night, then yes, of course. It was a mistake, and I've already apologised for that." The flash of hurt in Aaron's eyes at those words made Lewis's stomach twist, but he forced himself to go on. "But that doesn't mean I *blame* you for what happened—I thought I was really clear about that. Was I freaked out this morning? Yes, okay. I *was* freaked out. Was I worried about our future working relationship? Yes, of course! But then, on top of all that, we go into a meeting—*this* meeting of all the meetings it could have been—and you choose that moment to land this on me." He shook his head, genuinely bewildered.

"Are *you* seriously telling me you can't see why this would be an issue?"

Aaron met his gaze, and for several long beats, the silence between them stretched.

Then Aaron said, "I can see why it's an issue for *you*. You hate fanfic. Hell, sometimes I think you hate the *fans*. But an issue for the show? For Telopix? No, I don't see that at all."

"I don't hate the fans!" Lewis protested.

"No? But you don't like it when they get too possessive, do you? You don't like *anyone* messing with your perfect, singular vision of *Leeches* that no one can ever argue with."

The unfairness of that took Lewis's breath away. He didn't tolerate much dissent, that was true, but he had tolerated it—hell, welcomed it—from Aaron.

"You've argued with my scripts plenty of times, and you *know* I've made changes based on your comments. For fuck's sake, Faolán's whole character is—" He broke off, staring at Aaron, his chest heaving.

You. Faolán is you.

It felt like the words were physically there, reverberating in the silence between them, even though he hadn't said them aloud. Could Aaron feel it too?

In the end, it was Aaron who broke the heavy silence, saying, almost irritably, "I'm sorry, okay? That was unfair. You do listen to me."

He walked over to the bed and sank down with a weary sigh, resting his elbows on his knees. After a moment, he said in a lifeless voice, "So, who came up with the third character idea? Was it Toni?"

"Yeah," Lewis admitted. After a pause he added, "We can make it work, Aaron. The third character will just be Faolán with a new name—that relationship will still be the heart of the show. The new Faolán-love-interest will be the *actual* new character. But we'll make sure he's awesome too. It'll be another layer."

Shit, why did he suddenly feel like he was pleading?

"Don't you think Charlie might notice?" Aaron asked flatly.

"Nah. He talks a good game, but Toni and I reckon all his knowledge comes from audience research. I doubt he's watched more than one or two episodes, if that. So long as he thinks he's got his way, he'll be happy."

Aaron, who was staring at the ground, nodded, though Lewis had the feeling it wasn't in response to what he'd just said, but perhaps to some other unspoken question. At last, he looked up and said simply. "You're right. You're a great writer, and you can make it work. You *will* make it work."

"Hey, it's not all down to me," Lewis said, smiling weakly. "We're a team. We'll all play a part in making it work, right?"

Aaron didn't smile back. Instead, he levered himself to his feet and met Lewis's gaze. "Not this time, Lewis."

"Not this—What? What do you mean?"

"I mean that I'm not going to be part of the team anymore," Aaron said. "I think it's time I moved on."

What the fuck?

A bolt of pure panic went through Lewis, and it was all he could do not to grab hold of Aaron and tell him that if he thought he was moving anywhere, he was very much mistaken. Instead, he held his hands up in a conciliatory gesture. Distantly, he noticed they were shaking.

"Okay, wait, just… just listen, okay?" His voice sounded amazingly calm, but inside he was in pieces, emergency lights flashing and sirens wailing as he realised that, just as he'd feared this morning, Aaron was going to leave over this.

And Lewis couldn't have that. He just *couldn't*.

"I shouldn't have said that about firing you," he said quickly, meeting Aaron's calm, grey gaze. "I was just—angry. A lot of shit has happened in the last couple of days, and I get that it's been a mindfuck for you—it has for me too—but let's not be hasty and throw away something amazing because we're freaking out here. We're a *team,* Aaron. Like I said this morning, I've never worked with someone who gets me better than you do, who gets the show, the characters, hell, *everything.*" He took a step towards Aaron and had to check his own instinct to reach for him. "You make everything work so much better, you know? You sharpen every line you edit and improve every scene you cast your eye over. I don't trust anyone else's gut the way I trust yours."

It was the kind of thing that usually had Aaron flushing with pleased embarrassment, but not today. Today, he gave a bark of unamused laughter. "So, what you're saying is that I've basically been acting as an uncredited development editor on the show, is that right?"

Lewis blinked at that unexpected comment. "Um—I suppose so." Then, belatedly, understanding dawned. "Wait, are you—Is that what you want? It's just that when those roles have come up, you've never gone for any of them, so I assumed…" He trailed off. The truth was, he hadn't assumed anything. He'd been too busy being relieved that Aaron seemed to be happy to stay as his PA.

"You assumed what?" Aaron said, looking up. "That I wouldn't be able to land a job that I apparently already do for you—while simultaneously acting as your PA? Because I definitely don't recall you encouraging me to apply." His expression was deceptively neutral, his voice calm, but the words sliced into Lewis like barbs.

Heat flooded his face. He swallowed. "I think you can do anything you put your mind to," he said honestly. "Like you say, you're already doing that job, and I'm sorry if I didn't make it clear how much I appreciate your work. The fact is, I don't care what your job title is. It's not about that for me. I just want the best people working on *Leeches*. If you want me to get your role formally reassessed, I'll do that, no question. I can tell you now that you're already paid more than some of the junior editors because Toni and I insisted to the board that your salary should reflect the work you do, but I can ask RPP to look at your package again and—"

"I wasn't asking for—" Aaron began, then broke off with another frustrated sigh. "It's not about that."

"Then what is it about?" Lewis begged. "Just tell me what to do, and I'll do it. You know I will." He searched Aaron's face, hoping to find some sign that Aaron could be persuaded, but there was nothing. He just looked tired and sad. Defeated, somehow, even though he should surely feel like the victor here because Lewis was the one pleading for a second chance.

Aaron rubbed at the back of his neck. "It's about everything I said in that meeting. Skye and Faolán. Their relationship. The show. Those things *mean* something to me. I don't want to be part of destroying the thing I love."

Lewis stared at him. Of all the things Aaron had said, that one *hurt* because no one loved the show more than Lewis did. And he resented the accusation that he was about to destroy it. Angry now, he closed the distance between them in two short strides and grabbed Aaron's arm, yanking him closer. "Why are you being so goddamned dramatic about this? This isn't you. You don't do shit like this."

Aaron glared and shook him off. "This *is* me. You've always known how much I love the show. Well, newsflash: I love it way more than I ever let on. I love *Skylán*"—his eyes flashed when he used the ship name—"and I write whole fucking *novels* about them falling gloriously in love and having sex with each other in a million different ways and getting all sorts of happy-ever-afters together. And you know what? That's *important* to me. I can't even imagine my life without it."

"Well, that's all fine and dandy," Lewis snapped, "but fanfic won't pay the rent, no matter how many 'awards' you win. I don't get why you'd throw your career away over a fucking hobby."

The flash of pain in Aaron's eyes at that dig made him feel like a shit.

"I'm not throwing my career away," Aaron said. "I'm going to apply for the script development role for Toni's new pilot. Apparently, she thinks I can do it."

"Of course you can do it," Lewis repeated contemptuously. "You could do it with one hand tied behind your back. But it's a few months' work at most. Then what?"

Aaron shrugged. "It'll be good experience and tide me over while I apply for something more permanent."

Lewis's heart was hammering now with mingled fear and anger. Aaron was serious about this.

"So that's really what you want?" Lewis said in disbelief. "To leave a successful show you've worked on for three years —a show *you* love—to work on a pilot that might never get greenlit?"

Aaron nodded tightly. "Whatever you think of my contribution, to everyone else I'm just Lewis's PA. I'm the guy who can get them a meeting, or a call, or a response to an email. You saw how Charlie treated me this weekend. If I want to take my career in this direction, I need to start building up my CV with credible experience."

Lewis took a deep breath, willing himself to be calm, even as the panic built. "Okay, I get that, and like I said, I can have your role reassessed and—"

"Lewis," Aaron interrupted. He paused, blinking hard, and now his grey eyes had a betraying shine to them. "I'm saying it's time I moved on. Don't get me wrong. It's been a pretty great three years. I've enjoyed working with you a lot. And I've learned loads, but—"

"Don't do this," Lewis whispered. "Please. Aaron."

But Aaron kept going, as though he hadn't spoken. "—but I can't work for you anymore. I've not been focusing enough on my own career goals, and it's past time I did."

For several long moments, they just stood there, looking at

each other. Lewis felt weirdly numb. Gradually though, the knowledge settled into his bones.

He'd been left. And even though nothing had changed yet, it was over. He could see that Aaron had made the break in his own mind, and there was nothing Lewis could do to change his decision.

All the fears that had risen in him this morning when he'd first woken up had come to pass. Last night, he'd finally and irrevocably crossed the invisible line, and now, just as he'd always feared, he'd lost Aaron.

His chest ached with a pain he couldn't name. Slowly, he nodded. "Okay," he said. "If that's what you want."

"It is," Aaron said, not meeting his eyes.

"Do you want me to speak to Toni? About the pilot role?"

Aaron shook his head. "I can deal with it. Thanks."

The note of dismissal in that last word was clear, so Lewis took the hint.

Turning abruptly, he yanked open the door and stalked out. No looking back. What would have been the point? Aaron had been crystal clear: their partnership was finished.

And Lewis had no intention of hanging about to watch it die.

CHAPTER TWENTY

Aaron

Four weeks later

"Bloody *hell.*"

Aaron swore as he wrangled himself, his coffee, and his recalcitrant umbrella through the doors of RPP in the teeth of a howling gale.

"Lovely weather for ducks," Dymek observed from behind the reception desk where he was sipping a mug of tea and looking smugly cosy.

Aaron made a face as he shook rain out of his hair and off the sleeves of his coat. "I think the ducks have given up and gone home."

"Yes, because it is raining cats and dogs." Dymek held up his phone. "Four hundred useful English Idioms."

"Four hundred?" Aaron smiled. "Piece of cake."

"That is number thirty-six." Dymek nudged a stack of post on the desk, looking hopeful. "You will take this up?"

Aaron's heart gave a silly stutter at the sight of the envelopes addressed to Mr. Lewis Hunter. "Nope," he said, lifting a hand to fend them off. "Still not my job."

"Yes, but he has a new temp today—"

"*Another* one?"

Dymek gave him an old-fashioned look. "Nobody is surprised but you."

That was probably true.

In the weeks since he'd left Lewis—left his *job,* he corrected—Aaron had found himself looking back on their time together with growing nostalgia. Time and again, memories of the good moments surfaced—those long nights eating pizza and brainstorming ideas in Lewis's office, the heart-stopping thrill of being swept up in Lewis's creative process, the shared looks and jokes, and most of all, those quiet moments of connection when they both seemed to understand each other without words.

All of which made Aaron watch the endless procession of temps with a mixture of envy and impatience. So what if Lewis could be demanding? So what if he had a strong personality? Didn't they get what a privilege it was to work for him, to be around all that fierce creative energy?

Aaron had figured that out five minutes after first meeting him.

And part of him, a not-inconsiderable part of him, missed it. As much as he knew that leaving had been the right decision, as much as he was enjoying the challenge of his new role, and as much as Toni was a supportive and conscientious mentor, Aaron missed Lewis.

He missed him a lot, right down deep in his bones. In his heart.

No point in denying the reason, either; that cat was out of the bag, and there was no shoving it back inside. Aaron was in love with Lewis, was likely to be for some time to come, and being estranged from him like this hurt.

What Lewis might be feeling, Aaron didn't know because Lewis had been avoiding him like the plague since their agonisingly silent car ride back from Safehaven almost a month ago. No emails, no messages. Nothing. As if he'd simply cut Aaron out of his life entirely.

Aaron knew better, though. The office was full of gossip about Lewis's short temper and impossible behaviour, and Aaron knew him well enough to understand that he felt hurt by what he must consider to be Aaron's defection.

It wasn't the same sort of pain Aaron was going through, but it was pain, and he was sorry for it.

The whole situation was a bloody mess so, no, Aaron was not taking Lewis his post. Slipping back into that role would only churn up the already-stormy waters. That job would fall to the unlucky soul destined to be this week's temp, or, God forbid, Lewis could fetch his own bloody post.

By the time Aaron reached his desk, daylight was filtering through the heavy autumn clouds. As usual, he was the first one in. Toni was a night owl, and most of her teams mirrored her hours, which meant Aaron got to enjoy a quiet and productive start to his day because he still preferred to come in early. Not that he didn't stay late, too. But he had a lot to learn and was determined to make the most of this opportunity.

God knew, it had come at a price.

He set his coffee on his desk and booted up his laptop, deliberately not thinking about the hot chocolate he hadn't bought from Grinder. Having given up his large PA desk, he now sat at one of the much smaller desks in a pod with the rest of the team developing *Bow Street,* a new historical drama about the early days of policing in Georgian London. The pod was in the far corner of the open-plan space around the corner from the kitchen and Toni and Lewis's offices. The *Bow Street* team hotdesked, hooking up their laptops to whichever screen they wanted. Since Aaron was usually first in, he almost always got the best spot, next to the window with his screen out of view of nosy passers-by—just in case he had time over lunch to work on his fanfic.

Not that he had much time for it these days. Or much inclination.

Ever since the weekend at Safehaven, he'd found his fanfic well dry. Desiccated. Completely arid. And he hated it. When he didn't have a fic on the go, it felt like some vital part of him was missing.

At first, he'd blamed Lewis and their mortifying meeting with Charlie. But that wasn't fair, and more importantly it wasn't true. No, the real problem was that whenever he sat down to write about Skye Jäger, the face he saw in his mind's eye belonged to Lewis Hunter.

And maybe that was no surprise at all.

Aaron was still considering this as he hung his wet jacket on the coat stand, but he lost track of the thought when he spotted Sophie hurtling around the corner from the direction of Lewis's office. Her face lit when she saw him.

"Thank God," she said, reaching his desk. "Tell me you know his LAN password?"

Aaron sighed and sat down. "Morning, Aaron, how are you? Did you have a good evening? Terrible weather—"

She waved his sarcasm away. "Yes, yes, I'm sorry. But he's managed to log himself out of the server, and the new temp will be here in half an hour. If he's still raging—"

"It's his date of birth," Aaron said. "One, seven, N, O, V—all caps—with two exclamation marks."

"*Thank* you." She pressed her hands to her chest. "You're a lifesaver."

Taking a sip of coffee, not looking at her, he said, "Is he really on his fourth temp?"

"Fifth," she said bleakly. "Yesterday's quit at lunchtime."

Aaron winced. "I heard he's unhappy with some of the decisions being taken about the US version of *Leeches*?"

"So rumour has it," Sophie said. She cocked her head. "You know, I'm sure I could convince the powers that be to give you a rise if you wanted your old job—"

"No." He said it firmly because it was at least the third time she'd asked. "I like my new job, thanks. And Lewis will —He'll be all right. It's just this US deal that's got him all worked up."

She lifted a knowing eyebrow. "If you say so," she said before turning on her heel and hurrying back towards Lewis's office.

Aaron let that go and got down to work. *Bow Street* wasn't *Leeches,* but Aaron was enjoying working on the scripts, bringing everything he'd learned from Lewis, as well as his own considerable fic-writing experience, to the table as he polished and tightened every line.

So absorbed was he in his work that he didn't notice Chika come in, an hour later, until she said, "Morning, Page, how's it going?"

Chika Nnadi was fresh from uni, working for a pittance as a runner. Aaron liked her. She was smart, enthusiastic, and fun, with seemingly boundless energy. She loved vintage clothes and wore astonishingly complicated eye makeup that looked amazing even first thing in the morning.

"Good," he said, looking up from his laptop. "I was just —" He laughed. "Uh-oh. Have you been for a swim?"

Chika was in the process of peeling off a pair of sopping wet knee-high socks. "I know, right? This bloody rain."

"You need some wellies."

The look she gave him was the kind of pitying expression kids give their embarrassing parents.

"Vintage wellies?" he suggested.

Ignoring that, she wiggled her toes and said, "Is it okay if I sit in on your meeting with the storyliners today?"

"Sure."

"Only I was meant to be sitting in on the *Brahmins* development meeting, but Toni said..." She lowered her voice. "She said it was liable to get heated. Charlie Alexander is calling in from Barcelona, and apparently, he and Lewis

Hunter..." She made an explosive gesture with her fingers. "Boom."

"They're really calling it *Brahmins*?" He hadn't thought Lewis would cave on that as well. "It's such a shit name."

"I know, right? It sounds like a historical."

"They should go with something like *Boston Bloodsuckers*. Or maybe just *Bloodsuckers*."

"Ha!" She laughed, delighted. "That's *way* better. It's got a double meaning and everything. You should suggest it."

Aaron shook his head, his throat suddenly tight because a month ago, that's exactly what he'd have done. He and Lewis would have brainstormed better ideas, bounced them off each other until they came up with something they both loved. "Not my job anymore," he said. "I'm sure Lewis can handle it."

"You think?" From her tone, she doubted it. "I could hear him shouting halfway down the corridor on my way in. Jason says he's lost the plot."

"Jason should know better than to gossip," Aaron said and regretted the snap in his voice the instant he saw Chika's face fall.

"Sorry," she said, lashes lowering. "I didn't mean to—"

"No, it's fine. You're fine." He forced a smile. "Lewis can be...difficult. But he's a good man. Really. He's just..." *In pain* was what sprang to mind. Not the superficial hurt of Aaron's leaving, that's not what he meant, but the deep-down pain that had grown into Lewis's bones. Old pain. Aaron wished Lewis had someone to help him heal those old wounds; he wished that someone could have been himself.

"*Leeches* means a lot to him," he went on. "It's his baby. He hates Telopix messing around with it, and he hates having to let them."

"So why doesn't he just say no deal? He owns *Leeches*, right? It's not RPP's call."

"Yeah, but like I said, Lewis is one of the good guys. He

might rant and rave, but he wouldn't scupper the deal and let RPP lose out on that revenue. Not unless there was something he really couldn't live with."

And if he could live with tearing Faolán in half, he could probably live with anything.

The office was starting to fill up by then, Libby and Marc coming in and bitching about the weather as they dried off. Toni, when she appeared, looked as immaculate as ever. But that was because she always took a cab to work. Perks of being the Head of Drama.

Aaron found himself thinking about how Lewis had come in today. He'd probably walked, never mind the weather, because his flat was only half a mile away and he hated public transport. And cabs. Aaron always made sure there were a couple of changes of clothes in his office, for the days when the weather was crap. Or for when Lewis pulled an all-nighter.

That was, Aaron *had* always made sure there were a couple of changes of clothes in his office. If Lewis spent the day in damp socks today, it wouldn't be Aaron's fault. And, for God's sake, he shouldn't even be thinking about it!

Irritated with himself, he checked his email. Unlike in his old job, he didn't have to keep an eye on his inbox all the time, and so didn't bother opening it up during the quiet, early hours of the day. That helped him focus on his editing, and what a joy it was to have real time for that rather than squeezing it in around his PA work.

This morning, there was nothing urgent waiting for him. He scrolled through idly, deleting as he went. There were a couple of flirty messages from Tag O'Rourke, who'd recently landed a role in the *Bow Street* pilot. Aaron was delighted for him, but still hadn't agreed to go out for drinks despite Tag's continued charm offensive. And he *was* charming. Young and eager, objectively gorgeous. Just not really Aaron's type.

Aaron's type was tall, dark, and Lewis.

Plus, Tag did *not* need to be dating a guy with Aaron's kind of baggage.

Still, it wasn't like Tag was suggesting they move in together. Maybe a light, flirty fling was just what Aaron needed to wash Lewis out of his hair?

And, ugh, hadn't he given Mason that exact same advice?

He continued scrolling and then stopped, his heart giving a ridiculous jolt at the sight of Lewis's name in his inbox. It was the first time Lewis had contacted him since Safehaven, the first time he'd done anything but awkwardly grunt in Aaron's direction when they'd both mistimed things badly enough to end up in the kitchen together or were forced to pass each other in the corridor.

Despite all that, Aaron couldn't suppress a spike of excitement. Or a smile, because he'd always been amused by the way Lewis approached email as a form of messaging and wrote most of the email in the subject line.

From: *Lewis Hunter*
To: *Aaron Page*
Subject: *I need the latest Leeches series bible for Telopix because they don't fucking understand what the show is about*

I can't find it

Kind regards,
Lewis
Lewis Hunter
Creative Director
Reclined Pigeon Productions
Charecroft Way
London

The 'Kind regards' were part of the automatic signature Aaron had appended to his emails, so he was under no illusion that Lewis was sending him his regards, kind or otherwise. He sighed, mostly at the way his stomach was still leaping about like a landed fish. Really, he should tell Lewis to find his own damned file, but—

"Aaron?"

Toni was heading his way, her large—empty—coffee mug dangling from the fingers of one hand.

"Morning," she said. "Listen, I know it's not your job, and I hate to ask..." She did look rather uncomfortable. "But we've got a Zoom call with Charlie this morning..."

"Do you need me in the meeting?"

Fuck, he hated the hope that sang through him, the treacherous, homesick craving to return to the familiar. To Lewis.

But Toni was shaking her head. "No, no, no. I don't think that would be a good—No, it's just that we need the series bible, and Lewis can't find the latest version."

Fighting a flash of disappointment, Aaron said, "Oh, right. Yeah, he emailed me." He glanced back at his screen and realised that the email had come in hours ago—at 04:13 in fact. It didn't bode well for Toni's meeting that Lewis had been emailing at that time of morning, er, night. Lewis occasionally suffered from insomnia, especially when he was stressed about something and wasn't eating right.

Aaron's stomach twisted at the thought, and he was struck by a sudden, powerful memory of sleeping in Lewis's bed. Of the heavy weight of Lewis's arm around his waist, holding him tight against his bare chest, of the comforting sound of Lewis's peaceful breathing as he slept.

And of how much Aaron had loved him in that moment.

The feeling left him airless.

"Any chance you could ping the file over to us both?" Toni was saying, checking her watch. "The meeting starts in fifteen, and the last thing we need is Charlie thinking we can't find our arses with both hands."

Shaking off the memory, Aaron nodded. "Of course. It's in

the shared drive. I'll send you both a link. Should I send Charlie a copy, so you don't have to share your screen?"

"You're a star," she said. "*Thank* you. Oh, and I read your script notes on episode two. Spot on. Could you liaise with Marc about the impact of the changes?"

"Yeah, we've got a storylining session this afternoon," Aaron assured her. "We'll work the notes in if you're happy with them."

"Ecstatic, as always." She beamed. "You're doing great work, Aaron. Which comes as no surprise whatsoever. Now, I need a coffee before this hell-fest begins. Can I get you anything?"

"No, thanks. And good luck with the meeting. I hope..." *What? I hope Lewis is okay? For God's sake, Page, get a grip.* "I hope you get what you need out of it."

"I'll settle for avoiding an all-out slanging match. But you know Lewis..."

"Yeah, I know Lewis."

After he'd sent the file, he started going over his script notes to prepare for the meeting with Marc. But a few moments later, he became aware of...a presence. Of eyes on him. He glanced up, and his heart slammed into his ribs at the sight of Lewis standing a few yards away with Toni and Dave Peterson, the Development Producer for *Leeches*: USA—or, rather, *Brahmins*. They were hovering outside the meeting room. Toni was talking, Dave was nodding, and Lewis was watching Aaron.

He looked gorgeous in a tailored white shirt, sleeves rolled up to reveal strong forearms, his hair tousled and curling a little, the way it did after he'd been out in the rain.

Their eyes met, glanced off each other, and came back again as if magnetised. God, it was ridiculously good to see him. How stupid was that? But it was true. Aaron had missed him, missed even the sight of him. Tentatively, he offered a smile. A smile that wavered when Lewis frowned and looked away, those divots deepening between his brows as he glared down at the floor. When he glanced up again, his blue eyes were wary. And then, to Aaron's mingled delight and dismay, he began walking towards his desk.

Aaron scrambled to his feet, wanting to meet Lewis on equal terms. Then, feeling like he was standing to attention before a superior officer, quickly turned his stance into an awkward perch on the edge of his desk that looked anything but relaxed. "Hey," he said, utterly failing to sound casual.

Lewis nodded, his gaze averted. Up close, Aaron noticed that he looked pale and drawn, purple smudges beneath his eyes. No wonder if he'd been emailing at four in the morning.

"Uh, thanks for sending the link to that file," Lewis said. "Don't know why I couldn't find it."

A thank you? That was unexpected, and disarming. "You're welcome." Aaron said carefully, "Is everything—? I mean, how's it all going?"

Lewis gave a sharp, unamused laugh and didn't respond. Or maybe that *was* his response.

Aaron expected him to leave then, but he didn't, and an awkward silence descended. Desperately searching for something to say, Aaron was aware of Marc and Chika watching them avidly, yet all he could think about was the scent of Lewis's Neroli Sun aftershave and the memories it triggered of touching his bare skin. Of tasting his mouth. Of Lewis fucking him.

And shit, *why* had he allowed those thoughts to surface?

Panic rising, Aaron was about to blurt something inane about the upcoming meeting, when Lewis said, "So how's...?" He flapped a hand towards Aaron's new team. "Are you enjoying it?"

"Yes!" Relief made him gush. "It's good. It's great! *Bow Street* will be a fun show, I think. You know, if you like historical crime stuff. I'm doing a lot of script notes and storylining, which is cool."

Cool? He winced.

But Lewis only nodded. "Yeah, you're great at that. I miss —" He cut himself off abruptly, colour rising in his cheeks. "Have you thought about, uh, opportunities with *Brahmins*? Charlie will need a storyliner who knows what the fuck they're doing."

"Shit. Charlie won't be the showrunner, will he?"

"Fuck, no. He's got someone lined up in Vancouver. That's where they're filming it. Cheaper than LA. If Charlie's interested, his PA, Paula, could put you in touch, though." He looked uncomfortable, frowning. "I could mention it to him, if you'd like?"

Aaron stared. Was Lewis…? What *was* this?

"That would be… Er, thanks. I'll think about it."

Lewis looked at him intently, in the way Aaron imagined an artist might study their subject. Or a scientist their specimen? Then he opened his mouth to speak, but before he could say anything, another voice carolled across the office.

"Aaron! Hoped you'd be in."

Turning, Aaron saw Tag O'Rourke striding towards them carrying a bag from Grinder and wearing a bright white smile. "Got you something," he said, setting the bag on Aaron's desk with a flirtatious grin. "I'm not above buying your affections."

An odd kind of rumbling sound came from Lewis's direction. Thunder, possibly, judging by the stormy expression on his face.

Tag, blithe spirit that he was, didn't notice.

"I'm here for a meeting with Sandra," he told Aaron. Sandra was the *Bow Street* casting director. "Aaaand I wanted to know if you're going to the Monster Mash-Up on Friday. Tell me you are. Everyone is." He glanced at Lewis, his smile dimming. "How about you, Mr. Hunter?"

The Monster Mash-Up was RPP's Halloween costume party, one they hosted every October for staff and freelancers and pretty much anyone involved with the company. It was always brash and riotous, and Aaron went most years. Colin had always loved it. Well, he'd loved the free bar and flirting with all the cute actors.

Lewis, in the three years Aaron had worked for him, had never gone.

"If I wanted to wear fancy-fucking-dress," he said now, "I'd be a fucking actor."

Speaking over him, Aaron said, "I'm thinking about it, yeah." Although he hadn't really given it any thought at all. His mind had been too full of other things lately.

"I'll look out for you, then." Tag wiggled his eyebrows suggestively. "I'll be the cute zombie with a craving for man-flesh."

From the other side of their pod of desks, Chika snorted. "Subtle!" she called. "Very subtle."

"Who's trying to be subtle?" Tag reached out and brushed Aaron's wrist with his fingers. "See you there? And enjoy your treats. I stuck in a couple of those Cookies and Cream brownies you're always after."

"You didn't need to..." Aaron said, but Tag was already heading off towards Sandra's office. "Catch you later!"

In fact, the Cookies and Cream brownies were Lewis's favourite treat. He glanced back towards Lewis, about to offer them to him, but he was already gone. Aaron just glimpsed him following Toni and Dave into the meeting room before the door closed behind them.

"Nom de dieu," Marc whispered in his lovely French accent. "Lewis Hunter needs to get laid."

Chika raised her eyebrows. "Are you offering?"

Marc made a very gallic sound in the back of his throat. "There has been nobody since... Aaron, what was his name? That one who was all..." He sucked in his cheeks and pushed his mouth into a ridiculous moue.

Despite the weight in his chest, Aaron was amused. "Mason? The model?"

"Yes, Mason the model. And that was weeks ago. Perhaps Lewis is pining for those pouting lips?" Marc cast a dark look at the closed meeting room door. "He is like a big thundercloud floating around the office, no? And we have enough of them today."

Yes, Aaron thought, returning his attention to the closed door. Quite enough, and yet not nearly as much as he wanted.

CHAPTER TWENTY-ONE

Lewis

Lewis was cyber-snooping on Aaron when Toni walked into his office on Friday morning.

A couple of weeks ago, one of his now-departed temps had mentioned that everyone at RPP could see everyone else's online calendar. Normally, he'd have ignored that sort of comment, but for once, his ears had pricked up, and he'd demanded to be shown how to access them.

Now he was contemplating Aaron's upcoming day.

A morning full of meetings was followed by *"lunch Tag"* at Grinder at one p.m. The afternoon looked quieter and then he seemed to be planning to go along to the Monster Mash-up. His calendar was blocked out from seven p.m. till midnight for the party but he also had a six p.m. to seven p.m. slot marked out as "tentative" with the comment *"Tag pre-drinks?"* Which made Lewis scowl—two Tag meetups in one day? Clearly, unlike Lewis, Aaron recorded his private appointments in his office calendar as well as his work ones. In fact, Lewis could see that he'd even included his weekend plans.

He had the whole of Saturday blocked out with the description *"Leeches Ff meet up - Castlegate Hotel 10am reg - panel 2pm."*

Leeches Ff... Leeches fanfic?

And was Aaron talking on a panel?

"What are you glaring at?" Toni demanded.

He looked up to find her watching him with an amused expression. "Do I need a reason for glaring now?"

Laughing, she settled into Aaron's chair on the other side of his desk. Except it wasn't Aaron's chair anymore, was it? His scowl deepened.

"Do sit down," he said sarcastically. "Make yourself at home."

She ignored that. "I have good news."

"Go on." His flat tone indicated that he thought this doubtful, but Toni continued, unperturbed.

"Charlie's happy with the latest outlines we sent through. He doesn't seem to have noticed that Michael is actually a thinly disguised version of Faolán." She grinned. "And everyone over there loves 'straight Faolán'. They're getting really excited about casting him."

"Well, excuse me if I don't jump up and down for joy," Lewis said drily. "Seeing as how it's a huge, unwanted compromise that I'm still struggling with."

"I know it's a bit shit," Toni said, sighing, "and I do appreciate you making these compromises to land the deal. But you're going to have to get on board, Lewis. This is the reality if we want to proceed."

"Have you raised the title thing again?" Lewis replied. "I thought we agreed we were going to dig our heels in on that."

Toni winced. "Yeah, about that. It's on the agenda for our call on Monday, but now Charlie's gone ahead and had his art team work on all those mock-ups..." She trailed off.

Lewis ground his teeth. "Toni, I can't live with fucking *Brahmins*!"

"Then come up with something better," she shot back. "We can't just say no to everything! We have to have an alternative suggestion—"

"We do have an alternative suggestion! Fucking *Leeches*!" Lewis rolled his chair back and stood abruptly, clutching his hair.

"Christ, you're tetchy these days," Toni said, eyeing him disapprovingly.

He gave an inarticulate growl and turned away, pacing to the window.

"I gather you're not having much luck with your temps," Toni said in a deceptively smooth tone. "Still missing Aaron?"

Lewis just grunted. The latest temp, Clare, wasn't too bad—she'd lasted three days so far, which was better than any of the others. Maybe he was mellowing. Or maybe it was just that she was a bit older than the usual ones he was sent and had worked in TV before. Plus, she didn't take any shit from him. He quite liked her, actually. She would never get involved in script stuff, like Aaron, but he could see her working out purely on the PA side.

But yeah, he missed Aaron, though perhaps not for the reasons Toni thought. At least, not *mainly* for those reasons. He missed talking to Aaron about the show. Missed his insights, the way they sparked off one another. But most of all, he just missed *seeing* him. Talking to him about everyday stuff. Coming out of his office to find Aaron frowning at his screen or poring over a script. The way he'd look up at Lewis with that open, easy smile that Lewis would give his fucking left arm to see again.

Now when Aaron looked his way, his expression was wary. Guarded.

"How's he getting on?" he said at last. It was the first time he'd asked about Aaron.

"Really good," Toni replied. "He's great at the structural

stuff, isn't he? And I love the way he gets into the bones of every character, even the minor ones."

Lewis nodded without looking her way. "Yeah, he's got a real thing about making sure every line a character says makes sense in their internal world." He snorted. "It can get kind of annoying actually. He's a real nit-picker."

Toni chuckled. "He certainly stands his ground on stuff he feels strongly about."

Lewis turned back to face her. "I told him I'd speak to Charlie about whether there might be a role on the US show for him, a storyliner maybe. Seeing as how this pilot's a temp role."

To his surprise, she frowned at that. "I really don't want to lose him, Lewis. Yeah, the *Bow Street* role is temporary, but there'll be something else soon enough. We can keep him bouncing between projects till something longer-term comes up. Jenny's on maternity leave from the start of December, and there are a couple of new projects in the pipeline for next year." She met Lewis's gaze. "If he goes to work on the US show, he'll end up moving over there."

Lewis felt suddenly very odd. Almost shaky, like his blood sugar had abruptly dropped. He set his hand on the back of his chair to steady himself. "Yeah," he said, trying to sound calm. "You're probably right."

Thankfully, Toni didn't seem to notice his odd little turn. She gave an airy wave of her hand. "Let's just see how things go for the next couple of weeks," she said as Lewis settled back in his chair. "Then I'll sit Aaron down and have a proper chat with him about his future. Oh, and by the way"—she leaned forward and tapped her nails on his desk, her eyes gleaming with sudden amusement—"guess what gossip I heard last night that is completely and utterly unsurprising?"

"Astound me."

"I seriously doubt you'll be astounded. The lovely Milly

has officially left Poor Geoff and is now shacked up with Charlie."

"*Quelle surprise.*"

"It's not exactly scoop of the year," Toni admitted. "God knows why she and Charlie dragged it out so long. Poor Geoff. It was painfully obvious what was going on when we were at Safehaven."

"I bet he didn't give Geoff a second thought. Charlie's a careless bastard. He screws people over—screws projects over—then buggers off back to his mansion and leaves everyone else to clear up his fucking mess."

"Yup," Toni said. "So let's try to keep him sweet till we nail the deal."

Lewis grunted.

Toni got to her feet. "I'd better be off. I've got a nine-thirty call. Do I take it you'll be giving this evening's festivities a miss?"

Lewis glanced at his screen again, where Aaron's calendar was displayed.

"Actually, I thought I might come along for once."

Toni gaped at him. "*You?* Coming to a fancy dress party? You *hate* fancy dress."

Lewis shrugged. "It's been a while since we had an office party, and you always say I should make the effort."

"I do," Toni agreed. "So, what are you going as?"

"I haven't decided," he said. "I'll have a look online. I'm sure I can get something sorted out."

"For tonight? At this notice?" Toni replied. "Er—think again. You might want to come up with a plan B."

Aggravatingly, Toni was right. Lewis spent half the morning trawling the internet for a fancy dress outfit he could bear to put on, but everything half-decent was either unavailable or couldn't be delivered in time. He was considering getting on the phone to RPP's off-site wardrobe department and begging them to lend him something when he had a flash of inspiration. At the wrap party for the first season of *Leeches,* he'd been given one of Skye Jäger's signature leather trenchcoats. Since Lewis, like Jay Warren who played Skye, was dark-haired, all he needed was black trousers, shirt and boots, a pair of sunglasses, and maybe some fake vampire teeth. It would be a decent workplace joke for him to go to the party as Skye. Plus, once he'd got rid of the teeth, he'd feel like he was dressed pretty normally.

Content with his new strategy, he spent the rest of the morning powering through his emails. At quarter to one, his phone alarm went off, and he stared at it for a moment.

He'd set the alarm up earlier when he'd been looking at Aaron's diary.

"Lunch Tag"

Grinder at one p.m.

It would be ridiculous to go just because he knew Aaron would be there. But a small masochistic part of him wanted to see Aaron with Tag. Wanted to see for himself whether there was something going on between them. It was obvious Tag wanted there to be something going on, but when he'd seen them the other day in the office, Aaron had seemed... almost embarrassed by the attention Tag was giving him. Though perhaps that was just because Lewis had been watching. Aaron wasn't the sort of guy who showed off like that. It was funny, really. Lewis had had a lot of boyfriends who'd set out to make him jealous by flirting with other guys, and he'd never given a damn. Had always found that sort of behaviour kind of absurd and off-putting.

But when he'd seen Aaron with Tag...

Fuck.

Yeah, he had been jealous, even though Aaron hadn't even been playing along with the flirtation. And even though Lewis had no claim on him.

Lewis closed his eyes and pinched the bridge of his nose. This was getting ridiculous. He thought about Aaron all the fucking time. Couldn't stop remembering what it had been like in bed with him. His kisses, his hands on Lewis's body. Lewis's hands on him. The feeling that they were sharing themselves in a way Lewis had never experienced before.

It turned out that Lewis's great fear of losing Aaron as his assistant at work had been... well, missing the fucking point really. He didn't actually miss the fact that Aaron was no longer organising his diary or sorting out his laptop cables or making sure he had everything he needed for his calls, even though he was obviously way better at all those things than anyone else. But right now, Lewis didn't even care about any of those things.

He just missed Aaron.

The trouble was, he didn't have a fucking clue what to do about it. Aaron's only tie to him had been the job, and now he'd moved on. What could Lewis do now? Ask him out? He didn't exactly have a good track record with relationships. As one of Lewis's exes had once memorably said, *"I think asking me out was your way of saying goodbye."*

He simply wasn't relationship material. There were plenty of men who could testify to his many, many flaws in that department: fear of intimacy, obsession with work, inability to trust, self-centredness, unwillingness to commit. The list went on and on.

The truth was, Lewis wasn't sure he even knew what a functional relationship looked like. His dad had walked out when he was two and Owen was seven. And then he'd lost his mum...

In the years that had followed, Lewis had come to accept

that love, affection, and commitment weren't his to give. As much as he loved his loyal and fiercely protective brother, who'd grafted and fought for them to stay together, Lewis just didn't have that emotional depth himself. Not when it came to romantic relationships. He was too egocentric, too impatient. Too *cowardly* to give enough of himself. And so, when he'd discovered sex, he'd never been able to put it in the same category as those softer feelings. Or any emotion really.

Not until that night. With Aaron.

He closed his eyes, remembering. Remembering his lips tracing a delicate route down Aaron's body.

Why had it been so different with him? He'd slept with loads of other blokes, and it had just felt... *normal.* Carnal, yes. Pleasurable, of course. But only in a physical, transitory way. When he pressed his lips to other men's skin, it had been with the intention of arousing and persuading. With the aim of bringing his partner pleasure, and in hopes of being given pleasure in return.

A means to a predictable end.

Not with Aaron, though. With Aaron, when he'd laid his lips on that smooth skin, it had been with something that felt worryingly like adoration. As he'd traced that path of kisses down Aaron's body, his chest had been full and aching with some unnameable yearning. Not just to fuck Aaron but to share the feelings swirling inside him.

Even now, remembering that was terrifying.

His phone beeped again.

It was ten to one.

He paused for a moment, then swore softly and rose from his chair, reaching for his jacket.

It would be good for him to see Aaron with Tag. He may as well force himself to face reality sooner or later.

~

There was no sign of Aaron in Grinder when Lewis got there, so he joined the queue and ordered a mint hot chocolate with extra whipped cream and sprinkles and a ham sandwich with white bread and no salad. The server tried to talk him out of the ham sandwich, pointing to the list of more complicated options on the blackboard behind him.

"We do a great Croque Monsieur," he said earnestly. "Or how about the Serrano ham, tapenade, and Manchego cheese piadina?"

Lewis tried to keep hold of the fraying strands of his temper. "If you can do a Croque Monsieur, you can do a plain ham sandwich," he pointed out tightly. "Charge me the same for it if you like. Hell, charge me more! But can I just have what I asked for?"

"Okay, dude," the server said, in a tone that suggested he thought Lewis was unhinged. "If that's what you want. Eat in or takeaway?"

Lewis cast one last look around the place—there was still no sign of Aaron.

"Takeaway."

A few minutes later, he was handed his sandwich and hot chocolate and headed for the door. But just before he got there, he finally spotted Aaron, sitting at a table near the window on his own, scrolling on his phone.

Aaron was wearing jeans and Converse and a burnt-orange hoodie that brought out the warm, autumnal notes in his light brown hair. He looked good.

Really good.

Lewis didn't know what name to put to the weird hollow feeling in his stomach. Maybe regret. And a sort of achy longing.

Standing in the middle of the café, he waited for Aaron to notice him, but when Aaron didn't even look up from his phone, he squared his shoulders and made his way over.

"Hi," he said as he drew closer. "Are you in for lunch?"

Aaron glanced up, his expression startled.

"Oh, hi!" he said, looking anything but thrilled. "Yeah, I'm having lunch with a friend." He waved vaguely in the direction of the now-long queue of customers at the counter. "He's just getting our food."

"Right." Lewis didn't look round.

"You're taking yours back to the office, I see," Aaron said. Did he sound relieved? Tense, certainly. Uncomfortable.

Lewis said, "I am, yes."

Brilliant.

An awkward pause. Aaron bit lightly at his lower lip, then nodded at the cup in Lewis's hand. "Hot chocolate, extra cream?"

Lewis glanced down. There was chocolate-flecked whipped cream oozing out of the little hole in the lid. "How did you guess?" he said drily.

"Elementary, my dear Watson." With a tentative smile, Aaron said, "Has it been a bad day then? If you're going for the hard stuff, I have to wonder."

"I've had better ones." He held up the paper bag. "In fact, I've brought in the big guns: ham sandwich. White bread, no salad."

Aaron made a face. "Must be serious."

"Nothing I can't handle." He said it too sharply, not wanting to sound needy, and Aaron stared at him for a moment. Then he shrugged.

"Sure."

Another silence. Lewis ploughed on through it, waving his sandwich bag at Aaron's chest, "So is this your Hallowe'en party outfit for tonight?"

"Huh?" Aaron looked puzzled, lowering his eyes to his chest as though to remind himself what he was wearing.

"I thought maybe you were channelling a pumpkin?"

Aaron spluttered a laugh at that. "Are you casting aspersions on my weight?"

"What? No," Lewis protested and tried hard not to remember the feel of Aaron's lean, bare body beneath his own, in his arms... He cleared his throat. "I'm going by colour alone. You're more of a parsnip, shape-wise." He grimaced as soon as the words were out. Christ, could he sound any more inane?

Luckily, Aaron seemed to find it amusing. He grinned and said, "I'm not sure that's a compliment, but I'll let it go. And no, this is not my outfit. We're not all allergic to fancy dress, you know."

"What are you going as, then?"

"Some demony, warlocky sort of thing."

"A demony warlock," Lewis repeated slowly. "What's that?"

Aaron shrugged. "I won't know till later. I have a bunch of stuff I'll throw on and see how it turns out. Robes. Cloaks. Wands."

"*Cloaks*?"

Aaron shrugged, but his light grey eyes twinkled with humour. "Yeah. That kind of thing."

Lewis shook his head. "For a demon, you need *wings*, my friend. And wands? For a warlock? No, no, no."

"No?"

"At the very least a staff! Wands are for little kiddy wizards!"

Aaron laughed, a throaty chuckle that reminded Lewis of old times and did something fierce to his dick.

He was almost glad that Tag chose that moment to arrive.

"Oh, hi again," Tag said in that insufferably friendly tone he always used. He smiled at Lewis as though they were best friends and set his tray on the table. It held two bowls of disgustingly healthy-looking green-sludge soup and two big glasses of freshly squeezed juice. No doubt all five of Tag's five-a-day were catered for on that tray.

"Hi," Lewis said with a tight smile. Probably a rictus. "I was just"—he lifted his sandwich bag again and shrugged.

"Right," Tag said. "Back to the grindstone, is it?" He pulled back the other chair at the table and sat down, passing a set of napkin-wrapped cutlery to Aaron.

"Yeah," Lewis said weakly. "Busy day."

He glanced back at Aaron, who was watching him with a strange expression.

"See you back at the office," Lewis said, toasting Aaron with the cup of hot chocolate that he didn't even want anymore.

"Yeah, see you," Aaron echoed. And for a moment, Lewis just wanted to… stop the world. Hit some giant pause button that would make everything grind to a halt, except him and Aaron.

Say, *"I made a big mistake. Can we…*

… go back?"

But no. The world was still turning. Now Tag was setting the empty tray down on the only other seat at the table and unwrapping his own cutlery, and Lewis had no reason to linger another moment. He glanced at Aaron again, who still wore that odd expression, nodded, and made for the door without another word.

When he got outside, his mind was in a whirl. Or more like a tornado.

The thought of returning to the office was impossible. Instead, he consulted his phone, located the nearest green space—a small park—and headed that way.

By the time he got there and found an empty bench, his hot chocolate was cold. He set it down on the wooden seat beside him. A blob of whipped cream flew out of the little drinking hole, as though in temper at being ignored, and landed on the wood. Lewis sighed, then set the sandwich down beside it, any appetite he'd once had entirely gone.

For a while, he just sat there as his mind stormed incoherently, replaying images of Aaron in the café: the startled expression he wore when he first saw Lewis, his wry chuckle as they joked together, shifting his chair to make room for Tag.

Tag.

Tag liked Aaron, and he didn't mind showing it. He was an uncomplicated guy. Uncomplicatedly good-looking, friendly, inoffensive. He was probably really together about relationships too. He could probably make Aaron feel special and taken care of.

Loved.

The sudden stab of pain that thought produced was astonishing.

Lewis determinedly shoved all thoughts of Aaron and Tag aside and made himself look around the park. A handy distraction trick, that, the same one Aaron had used on him in Safehaven. Grounding himself in the here and now, logging all the sights and sounds and smells around him.

It was a very ordinary little park, made nicer by the unseasonal warmth of the day. The sun shone valiantly, despite a bank of grey cloud that threatened to overtake it, and probably would in little while. It seemed to be a well-used park. There were joggers, dog-walkers, a few women doing what looked like some serious exercise in the middle of the grass, and a constant stream of little kids scooting and biking and skipping past with their carers on their way to the crowded play area.

Absorbed as he was in his job, it was easy for Lewis to forget about this sort of stuff. Ordinary life. No vampires, no great story arcs or triumphant character redemptions. Just the day-to-day stuff, with the ordinary dramas: love, romance, family arguments, health problems, money problems.

The boring stuff, as he had always thought of it.

The stuff he mostly ignored in his own life.

A weird, bewildering lump appeared in Lewis's throat and would not be swallowed away. Shit, was he going to *cry*? What the hell was up with him? Hurriedly, he got to his feet, turning to gather up his abandoned lunch.

For some reason, his gaze snagged on the little brass plaque on the bench. *"For John Spencer Craig (1954-2015), partner, best friend, and co-parent to our corgis, who loved this park."*

It was a stupidly ordinary message, so why did it bring unfamiliar tears to Lewis's eyes?

Why did it make him feel like such a fucking *loser*?

Why was he, right now, eaten up with envy that a cheerful-but-penniless barista-slash-actor was currently sitting with Aaron Page eating the most utterly dismal soup Lewis had ever seen?

Blinking, he dashed away incipient tears with an angry swipe of his hand, gathered up his rubbish, and stalked away to dump it all in a nearby bin.

He didn't feel remotely calm enough to return to the office yet, so he did a circuit of the park, then took the long way back to the office.

By the time he entered the building, he felt oddly wrung out. He lifted a hand in acknowledgement of Dymek's greeting and carried on to the lift lobby, stabbing the call button, before pulling out his phone to see what he'd missed. Damn. The monthly budget call. Toni wouldn't be happy about that.

The lift rose sluggishly, spitting him out on the fourth floor, and he trudged to his office. His stomach was hollow with physical hunger, but his appetite was non-existent. He should eat something, he knew—a chocolate bar from the vending machine would have to do.

But when he reached his desk, he found something waiting for him there: a clear plastic bowl of pineapple, blueberries, and cantaloupe, with a Post-it note on top in Aaron's handwriting.

"Man cannot live by ham sandwich alone. A."

Lewis's heart twisted.

He dropped into his chair, stared at the fruit bowl, and wondered how to get the food past the lump in his throat.

CHAPTER TWENTY-TWO

AARON

By nine o'clock, the Monster Mash-up was in full flow, and Aaron was contemplating how soon he could head home. The music was loud, the laughter louder, and the hotel ballroom was awash with witches, ghouls, zombies, ghosts, and several iterations of vampire. None of whom held a candle to Skye Jäger.

Aaron stood with the *Bow Street* team, nursing the crimson concoction Tag had fetched him from the bar—his third of the evening. It was called a Bloody Vampire and consisted of vodka, cherry vodka, gin, grenadine, and soda water. It was...lethal. Tasty, but lethal.

Much like Tag tonight, whose costume consisted of a tiny pair of silver shorts, a blood-smeared barista apron that he'd discarded shortly after they arrived, a lot of body paint, and his customary bright white smile.

"I'm a zombie barista, of course!" he'd announced, grinning, when Aaron had asked what he was supposed to be.

Tag was easy company, cheerful and uncomplicated. Gorgeous, too, if you liked beautiful young men with washboard abs and perfect teeth. Which yes, Aaron did, he supposed. Just not as much as he liked glowering Heathcliff types with secretly gorgeous smiles that could only be coaxed out by someone in the know.

Right now, Tag and Marc and Chika were talking animatedly, laughing about something that Aaron had missed.

In truth, he wasn't really listening, too busy mulling over his lunchtime encounter with Lewis.

Although it had started out awkwardly, it had ended up being the easiest conversation they'd had in a month. Almost like old times. He hadn't wanted Lewis to leave and had watched the speed of Tag's progress through the queue and back to their table with an ungenerous feeling of regret. Had he been there alone, he'd have been able to invite Lewis to sit down. Would he have done it, he wondered, given the chance?

He knew he'd done the right thing by taking the *Bow Street* role. Knew too that the best thing for him was to stay away from Lewis. But the truth was, he missed Lewis desperately.

So, in fact, it was lucky he'd been there with Tag. Tag's presence had saved him from temptation.

Not that Aaron had escaped from their encounter unscathed. Even now, he found himself dwelling on every word they'd exchanged. Not to mention that look in Lewis's eyes that Aaron felt sure he hadn't seen before. An awkward intensity, a vulnerability that had squeezed all the air out of Aaron's lungs and made him want to do stupid things.

Like leaving a pot of fruit and a jokey note on Lewis's desk. *Why* had he done that?

Suboptimal, he reminded himself. *Sub. Optimal.*

"Wow, look at you!"

He was yanked out of his brooding by Toni, who sailed towards him in scarlet heels, a slinky red dress, and a towering Bride of Frankenstein wig. She bussed his cheeks, French style.

"You look glorious, Aaron. Those *eyes*!"

Dutifully, he fluttered his lashes. "Chika went to work on me. They're meant to look smoky and wicked." He lifted one berobed arm. "Suitable for a warlocky-wizard, apparently."

"They're smoking all right." Toni flashed a grin, looking rather wicked herself. And rather tipsy. "If I were ten years younger. And a man…"

Aaron laughed. "I should be so lucky."

"You *would* be lucky," Toni agreed and took a long swallow from her glass of champagne. "God, I needed that. I've just escaped from schmoozing the talent." She waved her glass towards the bar where several actors from RPP's shows had gathered. Jay Warren was among them, the actor who played Skye. He was unmissable—a head taller than the others, with clean-cut features, perfectly coiffed hair, and his face all lit up with laughter at something Alyssa Bursill was saying. She was the pretty blonde actress who played Amy.

A different breed, actors, made of starlight and ego. Aaron suspected it was something of an ordeal for them to mix with the hoi polloi like this. Not that they really mixed, usually sticking together to avoid the starstruck minions gazing from afar. Safety in numbers, he supposed.

Personally, he wasn't interested in mixing with them either. He preferred to keep his distance, not wanting his vision of the characters to be influenced by the personalities of the actors. He spotted Mason among them, though, looking as stunning as always—but if Mason was hoping to run into Lewis, he was in for a disappointing night. Still, judging by the sidelong look Jay was sending him, Mason might not be going home alone tonight. And Jay wasn't the only one. Aaron had noticed Tag staring at Mason earlier too.

Aaron found it dispiriting to discover how little that bothered him. He'd made it clear to Tag over the last couple of days that he didn't want to progress beyond flirty, platonic friendship, and Tag had taken the rejection with typical good humour. But really, how sad was it that Aaron felt only relief? Tag was objectively gorgeous and fun and—

"Now *that's* a heavy sigh," Toni said, interrupting his thoughts. "Not in the party mood?"

There was something bright and enquiring in her expression that made Aaron avoid her eyes. "No, it's just… It's been a long few weeks, I suppose. You know, leaving—Starting a new job and everything? I'm a little frazzled."

"There's a lot of that about."

"Yeah?"

She knocked back the rest of her champagne. "I was talking to Lewis—"

"Hey, gorgeous." Tag, who had broken away from Chika and Marc, sidled up and slipped his arm through Aaron's. He smiled, running friendly fingers up and down his arm. "Need a refill?"

Aaron looked down to find he'd already drained his Bloody Vampire. He was pleasantly tipsy but wasn't intending to get drunk tonight, hoping for some writing time later. Desperate for it, in fact. He needed to get back into the zone. It had been weeks since he'd written anything outside of work.

"I'll have a beer," he said. "But let me get it. You don't have to wait on me."

"Hey, zombie barista, remember?" Tag pulled a gruesome face and leaned in to jokingly nuzzle Aaron's neck. "Do you want brains with that, sir?"

Ticklish, Aaron was laughing and pulling away when Toni grabbed his arm and said, "Oh. My. God."

"What?" Aaron and Tag said together.

Toni just nodded towards the door, her eyes very wide. When Aaron turned around to see what she was staring at, he jolted so hard he just about hit the ceiling.

Skye Jäger stood in the doorway, glowering at everyone as if he'd walked straight out of Aaron's daydreams, trademark leather trenchcoat flaring out behind him, dark glasses reflecting the shimmering party lights.

Only it wasn't Skye Jäger.

"That's Lewis," Aaron said faintly, his heart doing strange wobbly things in his chest.

Just as he said it, Lewis's gaze snagged on their little group. For a moment, he just stared, his expression impassive. Then he gave a curt nod and turned away to stalk towards the bar. The crowd parted before him. And who could blame them, faced with a man who looked like that?

Dressed as Skye, Lewis was breathtaking.

"Oh my God, is that Mr. Hunter?" Chika asked, pushing in to see what the fuss was all about. "It is! He's come as Skye Jäger. That's awesome!"

The corner of Toni's mouth ticked up in amusement. "Are you sure?" she said, raising a brow in Aaron's direction. "He looks more like the Green-eyed Monster to me."

Aaron pretended not to hear that. He wasn't sure what Toni thought she knew, but whatever it was, he knew better. Lewis had made his feelings painfully clear at Safehaven—if he was jealous, it would only be because seeing Aaron hanging out with the *Bow Street* team reminded him that he'd lost him on *Leeches*. And there was no point in Aaron wishing otherwise.

"Come on," he said, grabbing Tag's hand and turning away. "Let's dance."

Aaron had never been into clubbing, and fortunately, the hotel ballroom was nothing like a real club, but the music was loud, the crowd was mostly young, and the bar was free—and since Aaron was already a bit boozed up, it wasn't too hard to let go. Chika and Marc followed them onto the small dance floor, while Toni tottered over to join Jason and his heavily pregnant wife at one of the tables. Behind them,

Aaron noticed Lewis drawing attention at the bar. Jay Warren was with him, and they were laughing together, taking selfies.

Determinedly, Aaron turned his back and focused on the music, on Chika and Marc larking about next to him. On Tag, who was dancing very close, displaying his delicious, nearly naked body to anyone who was watching. Life was good, Aaron told himself. Life was great!

And he had absolutely no business pining for things he couldn't have.

Between the music and the Bloody Vampires, Aaron was able to lose himself in the moment. In several moments, in fact. About an hour of them. It was fun, letting go, pushing everything out of his head except the rhythm and the movement of his body.

Dancing like no one was watching.

Except that wasn't quite true. Because every time Aaron happened to catch a glimpse of Lewis—which was often, given that Lewis was prowling around the ballroom—it seemed that Lewis's gaze was on him, or just sliding away from him. Even when he was with other people, his attention seemed to be on Aaron. One time, Aaron looked up to see Mason leaning in close to Lewis, his expression very intent as he spoke quickly, gesticulating with his hands. But it was obvious Lewis wasn't listening. He was nodding absently, his gaze repeatedly flicking towards Aaron and away again.

Lewis's attention was messing with Aaron's head—but it was undeniably thrilling. It provoked him to show off, to dance a little more sexily and rather closer to Tag than he otherwise might have done...

Eventually, though, the buzz waned, and Aaron began to feel hot, tired, and thirsty. Turned out that wizard robes were bloody annoying on a dance floor. No wonder you never saw Gandalf or Dumbledore strutting their funky stuff.

He signalled to Tag that he was going to get a drink and

Tag leaned in, one arm looping around his neck to whisper-yell into his ear. "I'll come too!"

Chika and Marc followed, Marc heading to the bar to fetch them more drinks while the rest of them collapsed into an array of chairs and loveseats clustered around a low table near the bar.

"What's his deal?" Tag said a little later, once they had their drinks and had cooled down a bit.

He was cosied up next to Aaron, his toned body glistening beneath the zombie body paint, one arm stretched invitingly along the back of the loveseat.

Aaron took a pull of his beer. "Whose deal?"

"Lewis Hunter's." Tag gestured towards the far end of the bar. "He can't take his eyes off of you."

Aaron's cheeks warmed as he glanced in the direction Tag indicated. Sure enough, Lewis was standing with Jason and a couple of the *Leeches* crew. Jason and the other guys were joking and laughing, but Lewis was watching Aaron, frowning, and this time his gaze didn't slide away.

"Looks to me like he's into you," Tag said, raising curious eyebrows.

"He's really not."

"Come on." Tag sipped his bright orange cocktail. "Did you guys have a thing? I thought I picked up an odd vibe earlier."

Alarmed, Aaron glanced at Chika and Marc, but they hadn't heard. They had their heads together and were deep in conversation—scandalous conversation judging by the expression on Marc's face. Good. Aaron did not need *that* rumour floating around the office.

"Nah, it's just work stuff," he told Tag breezily. "Lewis was pissed off when I took this other job—he wants me back as his PA, and it's not going to happen."

"No?"

"Nope. I've moved onwards and upwards. There's no going back."

Tag grinned, clinking his glass against Aaron's beer bottle. "Onwards and upwards, then." Draining his glass, he set it down. "Another?"

"Sure."

Tag rose from the loveseat, then smiled widely. "Oh, hi, Toni. Come and join us."

Aaron glanced up to see Toni approaching, looking rather more dishevelled than last time they'd met. "This bloody wig," she complained, dropping with relief into an empty chair. "It's roasting."

"Take it off, then," Aaron said. He'd discarded his wizardly robes as soon as he'd sat down and was left in black jeans and a skinny t-shirt bearing the legend *What's up Witches?* in silver sequins.

She looked at him, aghast. "My hair's been under a hairnet for hours!"

Aaron laughed, but stopped when Tag nudged his knee, nodding at something over Aaron's shoulder. "Watch out," he said quietly. "Incoming."

Turning, Aaron was startled to see Lewis striding towards them, a determined, if pained, look on his face. Aaron rose to his feet to greet him, and Tag rose too.

"Don't worry," Tag whispered in his ear, slipping his arm around Aaron's waist. "I'll protect you."

"Lewis!" Toni exclaimed, beaming as he joined them. "You look a-may-*zing*. Are you after Jay Warren's job?"

"No," Lewis said flatly—in lieu of *hello,* presumably.

Even as he answered Toni's question, his gaze was on Aaron, who found himself acutely aware of Tag plastered to his side with his obscenely short-shorts, acres of bare skin on show, and all those gleaming, toned muscles.

Aaron didn't know where to put his free hand.

Lewis gave a curt nod, unspeaking. But his gaze didn't

move away.

From beside him, Tag said, "Mr. Hunter—we really must stop meeting like this."

Lewis turned to him. "Tag, isn't it?" he said after a pause. "What happened? Did you forget your costume?"

"Don't be an arse." Toni prodded his leg with her foot. "Sit down. Where's your drink?"

Lewis just shrugged.

"I'm going to the bar," Tag said, levelling a cool gaze at Lewis. "Another beer, Aary?"

"*Aary?*" Lewis snorted, just as Chika broke away from her laughing conversation with Marc.

"Hey, Aaron," she said. "Is it true you write *Leeches* fanfic?"

Shit.

Even at the best of times, Aaron hated having this conversation. Most people didn't really get fanfic, and God knew Lewis actively despised it—as would no doubt become clear to everyone else in the next three minutes. But he wasn't about to deny it; he wasn't ashamed of his fanfic. Still, he couldn't keep from casting a defiant glance at Lewis before he said, "I do, yeah."

"That's so *awesome*!" Chika beamed at Marc. "See? I told you."

Marc gave him an odd look. Tag said, "Wait, wait. What's fanfic?"

Chika stared, mouth agape. Aaron felt like staring too.

"You've never heard of fanfiction?" Chika said in disbelief. "Really?"

"No," Tag said slowly. "Should I have?"

Aaron laughed. "Probably. All the kids are doing it these days."

"Oh, totally." Chika grimaced. "I used to write terrible One Direction fic at school." She looked at Aaron curiously. "I didn't know people still wrote it at your age, though."

"*My* age?" He tried not to splutter like a maiden aunt. "I'm twenty-seven!"

Chika giggled. "No, it's cool. I'd love to read some. Do you post on AO3?"

"I do," Aaron said cautiously. Did he want people at RPP reading his fic? No, he bloody well did not. It was personal, intimate. Only to be shared with those in the secret club. The idea of it being passed around, goggled at—mocked—by his colleagues was intolerable. "I'm not telling you my pseud, though. Sorry."

Chika looked warily at Lewis. "He wouldn't get in trouble, would he?"

Lewis glared, the divots between his brows deepening.

"Of course not," Toni cut in, although she sounded less than enthusiastic. Aaron raised an eyebrow in her direction, and she shrugged. "I don't have a problem with fanfic, Aaron, but I do wonder why you spend so much time working on material you can never use."

"Never use?" he said. "What do you mean?"

"Well, obviously, you can't sell it. I suppose you could change the names and repurpose—"

"It's not about selling it."

"Come on," she said, smiling. "It's an apprenticeship. A good one, I grant you, but beyond a certain point, writing fanfiction won't help you become a professional writer."

"Who says I want to be a professional writer?"

Toni gave him a baffled look. "Why wouldn't you?"

"Never give anything away for free," Marc warned him bleakly. "It's your talent, yes? Your time. You deserve to be paid for it. And if *you* give it away for free, it cheapens the value of the product for the rest of us."

Aaron looked between them both. "Wow," he said. "You really don't get it. Fanfic isn't about any of that. It's not an apprenticeship or a ladder up to something 'better'. It's valuable in its own right. It's about the joy of writing for your own pleasure. And about sharing your work with a community of like-minded people. It's about..." He didn't want to sound sanctimonious, but it was the truth, so what the hell? "It's about creativity for creativity's sake."

"Very noble," Lewis said. In the low light of the ballroom, his eyes had darkened to shades of midnight. He was studying Aaron intently.

"It *is* noble," Tag said loyally.

Lewis ignored him, his hot gaze prickling across Aaron's skin.

Tag turned to look at Aaron. "I love how passionate you are," he went on. "And I totally get it. I mean, obviously I want to make my living as an actor one day."

Lewis grunted. Aaron glared at him.

Tag was oblivious. "But if I don't, I'd probably still act—even if it was only in am-dram, you know? For the love of it."

Only in am-dram.

"But that's just it," Aaron said. "What's wrong with am-dram? What's wrong with amateur musicians playing in the pub on the weekend? What's wrong with people painting by numbers because painting gives them joy? Why is art only considered worthwhile if it brings in money? Why do you only get to call yourself an artist if you do it as your job?"

There was a beat of silence amid the noise of the party. Aaron was aware he'd climbed onto a soapbox and was about to awkwardly climb off again when Lewis said, "You're talking about the democratisation of creativity. Getting rid of the gatekeepers."

Surprised, Aaron looked at him. Lewis had that little stitch between his brows that he got when he was figuring something out. "Yes," Aaron said. "Yes, exactly. We all have creative souls that need feeding. Why tell people it's not worth writing, or painting, or singing unless they're going to make a living at it?"

"Nobody's stopping people from doing any of that,"

Lewis pointed out. "But why not create your own, original stuff?"

"Because…" How to explain? "Because when you respond to a story through fanfiction, or fan art, or whatever floats your boat, you become part of a community. Part of a conversation with other fans, with other fic writers—sometimes even with its original creators."

Lewis cocked his head. "So you'd call fanfiction a...response to the original work?" he said slowly. "A reply?"

"Call and response, exactly." Spiralling excitement surged through him as he realised that Lewis was starting to understand. "Fanfic writers build on the original work and then on each other's work. It's a… an ongoing transformation of the original. And if the creators are engaged with their fans, they'll transform the original work in response. There's a feedback loop."

Lewis's eyes hadn't left his, their gazes locked. "You mean like with Skye and Faolán. Their relationship."

Aaron shrugged, blushing as he remembered the last time they'd discussed that particular topic. "There are lots of examples."

"But that's what *you're* talking about. You think I should...respond to the fans' interpretation of their relationship—*your* interpretation of it."

"I think all shows benefit when their creators engage with fandoms, but I'm not saying you have to—"

"But I have been engaging, haven't I?" Lewis was staring at him now, an odd look on his face. "That's *exactly* what I've been doing for the past three years, with you. Call and response."

Aaron's heart kicked wildly. Call and response indeed. The call of Lewis, and Aaron's response—his fanfic, his professional devotion, his physical obsession. Each element tidily compartmentalised to enable him to avoid the truth that had burst free at Safehaven.

A truth Aaron wished he could still avoid. Could still chop up into manageable pieces.

Lewis ran a hand through his hair, then looked up, eyes wide, as though a thought had just struck him. "Fuck, it started the day I met you," he said. "I was going to kill Faolán off after the season three cliff-hanger, but then you said, 'don't bury your gays' and I..."

Aaron could only stare, transfixed by the bright look of epiphany in Lewis's eyes. It was painful to see, agonising to hear Lewis acknowledge the significance of their creative relationship now that Aaron knew it would never be anything more.

That a professional partnership was all Lewis had ever wanted.

Aaron tore his gaze away, eyes prickling. He swallowed, or tried to, his throat thick with emotion. "I'm going to get a beer," he said abruptly. "Tag, you want anything?"

"Another Zombie?" Tag lifted his empty glass. "But I'll come with you."

Aaron could hardly tell him no, despite his urgent need for a moment alone to unscramble his thoughts. Feeling Lewis's gaze on his back, Aaron ploughed into the crowd, Tag weaving ahead of him, getting a lot of attention in those silver shorts. And clearly loving it. He was a very friendly guy, Tag. Very tactile.

Aaron moved more slowly, dropping back when Tag reached the bar and wiggled in next to Mason. And suddenly, Aaron couldn't face the crowds. Or the bar.

Or Tag.

He took a sharp left turn and headed towards the loos in search of solitude. But there were too many people coming in and out, so he diverted towards a green emergency exit sign at the end of the hotel corridor, pushed on the bar across the door—prayed he wasn't about to set off an alarm—and stepped out into the night.

It had been a bright day, warm for the time of year, but the evening was fresh, crisp with the scent of autumn. Even here, in the centre of London, there was a slight woodsmoke tang in the air.

He found himself in what looked like a delivery bay at the side of the building, the constant swish of traffic on the Uxbridge Road muted by the bulk of the hotel. Someone was singing off-key in the distance, horns tooted, and laughter and music drifted out from the party.

Aaron leaned his back against the wall and closed his eyes, allowing the air to chill his heated skin as his thoughts circled back to Lewis. For a moment, it had felt like Lewis had seen and accepted a part of Aaron that nobody outside fandom had ever understood before. Or valued.

Colin certainly hadn't.

And if Lewis had, if he'd really understood…?

God, but somehow that just made everything worse. Made Aaron's longing for him worse, made the hopeless certainty that part of him had been ripped out—that he'd ripped it out himself—even harder to bear. Christ, would he never get over Lewis Hunter?

He stared up at the small patch of night sky visible between the buildings, mortified by the hot prickle of tears in his eyes.

Suboptimal. Remember that? *This is suboptimal.*

Ugh, he was *not* going to cry over Lewis bloody Hunter. He'd done enough of that in the days after Safehaven. It was time to—

The emergency exit opened again, and Aaron's heart sank. He didn't want to be rude, but he couldn't face Tag. Not right now. Not feeling like this. He opened his mouth to ask to be left alone when a voice said,

"Aaron?"

Not Tag.

He turned on his heel.

Lewis stood a couple of feet away, eyes gleaming in the darkness. "Are you…?" He frowned. "Is everything okay?"

"Yes, fine," Aaron said weakly. "I just needed some air."

Lewis glanced back towards the half-open door, his brow furrowed. "Did you, uh, lose your boyfriend?"

Aaron blinked at him. "My what?"

"*Tag*," Lewis said with withering emphasis, as if that couldn't possibly be his real name.

Aaron sighed. "Tag's not my boyfriend."

"Your date, then."

"Not my date, either."

"No?" Lewis shuffled, uncharacteristically ill at ease. "You certainly looked friendly in there."

Aaron gave an awkward huff of laughter. "Tag's a friendly guy. But we're not… It's not like that."

"Thank fuck," Lewis said on an explosive breath. "Because he's at the bar right now, chatting up fucking Mason Nash."

Aaron laughed, properly this time. "Yeah, I saw that coming. Mason's quite, um, alluring."

"He's a fucking idiot," Lewis said and started walking towards Aaron, taking slow but purposeful steps.

Heart kicking against his ribs, Aaron stood a little straighter, bracing for… He didn't know what. "Don't be unkind," he said. "Mason's all right. A bit self-absorbed, maybe, but he can be quite sweet—"

"I wasn't talking about Mason."

Lewis was close enough now that Aaron could feel the riptide tug of his presence, his own body's physical yearning to close the gap between them. Instead, he backed up until his shoulders brushed the wall behind him.

But Lewis kept coming, not stopping until they were toe to toe. For the longest time they just stared at each other. Lewis was breathing hard now, as if he'd been running, his chest rising and falling beneath his dark shirt. And his eyes…

God, they were almost black, but fervent, gleaming with intent.

Aaron's gaze dropped to Lewis's mouth. It was a beautiful mouth. As expressive when he was amused as when he was irritated. Not that he was either of those things right now.

Aaron wasn't sure what Lewis was right now.

Shakily, Aaron sucked in a breath. "What are we doing?" he whispered.

Lewis didn't answer with words, just set his hands on the wall either side of Aaron's body. Caging him. Aaron's pulse rocketed, his lips falling open as an unexplored part of himself yielded to Lewis's subtle—okay, not so subtle—assertion of control.

"Call and response," Lewis growled, all gravel and smoke. And with that, he leaned in to capture Aaron's mouth with his own.

His kiss was electrifying, a jolt of joyful relief.

Aaron didn't move—couldn't move—just closed his eyes and leaned back against the wall, parting his lips, and giving himself up to the urgency of Lewis's kiss. To the press of Lewis's hard body against his own and the soaring release of ceding control, of stopping fighting, of just...letting it happen.

Mistake or not, he wanted this.

Lewis growled, soft and low in his throat, and his hands lifted to cup Aaron's face. It was an odd gesture, tender and possessive at once, and it lit something fierce in Aaron, sending him arching up and away from the wall, pressing himself greedily against Lewis's body, unable to get enough of him, to get close enough to him. And it seemed that Lewis felt the same, because now they were clinging to one another, kissing desperately, their hard cocks straining as they stumbled back against the wall together.

Christ, were they going to do it right here? Aaron felt frantic enough, overtaken by a desire so blinding he could hardly see straight.

I would, he thought wildly. *If you asked, I would. Right here.*

"Fuck," Lewis groaned. Instruction or curse, Aaron couldn't tell. "Fuck, *Aaron.*"

He was biting at the tender skin below Aaron's ear, making his legs tremble. Literally *tremble.* Aaron slid his hands inside the leather trenchcoat, yanking at Lewis's shirt, desperate to touch his bare skin, unable to think of anything other than getting closer. Getting fucked.

Right. Fucking. Now.

Abruptly, Lewis let him go, pulling back with a shuddering breath and holding Aaron at bay with one hand on his chest. "Wait," he said, panting hard. "*Fuck.*"

Aaron gave an embarrassing little mewl of frustration, knowing he must seem unhinged. Fortunately, Lewis didn't look much saner, his dark hair sticking up in wild spikes, his chest heaving. Eventually, he managed to articulate, "Bed." He cleared his throat and added, "We need one."

It was so blunt and so Lewis that Aaron laughed. And like a miracle, Lewis laughed too, low and throaty, coaxing out those dimples that always made Aaron melt.

With anyone else, that laughter might have killed the mood, but not with Lewis. With Lewis, it just made everything even better somehow, Aaron's desperation not waning but shifting into something less fierce, and more profound. Carefully, he lifted an unsteady hand to Lewis's face and stroked the stubble on his jaw, his heart swelling with affection and confusion and unbridled yearning.

Nothing had changed between them, not really. It would all end in flames, he knew, but right now, he wanted it too much to care. His eyes filled. He blinked them clear and gave a ragged laugh.

"My flat's three stops on the tube. It has a bed."

"Forget the fucking tube," Lewis said, "We're getting a fucking Uber."

CHAPTER TWENTY-THREE

LEWIS

Lewis couldn't face going back to the party, but Aaron's stuff was still inside, and, apparently, he had to tell Tag he was leaving—though Lewis had to wonder whether the guy would even notice given how he'd been drooling over Mason.

While Aaron went back into the hotel, Lewis stalked around the outside of the building to the front door to wait for the Uber Aaron had ordered.

He paced the pavement, antsy and thrumming with the same nervous energy that had been riding him all evening. God, it had been a weird night. Even now, as he waited for Aaron with his dick hard and his stomach twisting with nervous excitement, there was a voice inside him warning that this was a mistake.

He hadn't come for this. He'd come for the same reason he'd gone to Grinder at lunch time—to see Aaron and Tag together, to confront the reality of Aaron *with* Tag.

Like an arachnophobe forcing himself to handle spiders. Exposure therapy.

Or maybe that had just been an excuse because his first

glimpse of Aaron had driven any such noble thoughts out of his head.

Aaron should have looked ridiculous in his cheap fancy dress shop wizard robes, but he'd looked sexy as hell with his eyes made up, all dark and smoky. And when their gazes had met…

Despite that fucking himbo, Tag, plastered to his side, Lewis had seen the longing in Aaron's gaze, and it had set his heart hammering and his stomach tightening. And after that, there was no thought of fucking exposure therapy, just a driving need to get Aaron alone.

Except Aaron never *was* alone. All evening he'd been stuck to Tag's side, and to the *Bow Street* team he was so tight with these days, drinking and dancing and laughing. Until eventually, Lewis had had no choice but to man up and face them all. Try to talk to Aaron while that baby hunk with his stupid gleaming muscles pawed Aaron possessively.

He'd wanted to shove Tag off of Aaron and take his place. Like he was staking a claim or some idiotic thing like that. Which was fucking insane because Lewis *never* got jealous. He wasn't the sort of man who cared enough to feel that way about anyone.

Until Aaron.

But it seemed that seeing Aaron with Tag had finally fired up his latent capacity for jealousy. Then again, maybe this wasn't the first time. Looking back, it was pathetically obvious that the antipathy Lewis had always felt towards Colin—who was objectively a fairly inoffensive guy—had also been jealousy.

Lewis scrubbed his hands over his face. This was crazy. He'd come here tonight determined to dowse the flames of his infatuation with Aaron, and instead he was stoking the fire.

Shit.

Was this a mistake? It probably was, wasn't it? He was

leading Aaron on, giving him the wrong idea. But what the fuck was the *right* idea?

"You okay?"

Lewis whirled around to find Aaron watching him warily. He had his robes bundled up under his arm, a dark bomber jacket zipped up over his sparkly t-shirt. If it wasn't for those smoky eyes, he'd look like an ordinary guy walking down the street.

Except that Aaron would never be ordinary to Lewis.

"I'm fine," Lewis said, and it was, weirdly, true. All the questions swirling around in his head dissipated when he gazed at Aaron, and Aaron gazed back, those grey eyes careful and assessing. Knowing.

A car swooped up to the kerb, and they turned. It was their Uber.

They got inside. The driver nodded a greeting, but didn't say anything, and since he didn't have the radio on, the whole journey was accomplished in an oppressive silence that seemed to ramp up the tension that had been building in Lewis all night.

It was a relief when they finally arrived. Climbing out of the car, Lewis followed Aaron to his front door, watching as he took out his keys and opened up to reveal a flight of stairs leading up to his top-floor maisonette.

"Straight ahead," Aaron said, holding the door open for Lewis to precede him.

There was only one door at the top of the stairs, so Lewis went through, stepping into the dark interior, followed by Aaron, who switched on the light.

At which point Lewis nearly jumped out of his skin. *"Fuck!"*

There was a man standing in the corner, tall and dark and threatening and…

… it wasn't a man. It was a life-size cut-out of… *Skye Jäger*?

"Jesus Christ," Lewis gasped, pressing a hand to his chest. He felt like a gigantic idiot. "I thought that was a real person."

Aaron gave a helpless laugh. "I'm sorry," he said. "I'm so used to it, I forget it's there."

Finally, Lewis laughed too, a strange, relieved sound. "Where the fuck did you get it?"

"In an auction at a convention," Aaron said, his smile a bit embarrassed. "It was before I started working for you. Jay was there, but I'd actually gone hoping to meet you."

"Me?"

Aaron rubbed the back of his neck. "Yeah," he said softly. "You were supposed to be there, but you called off."

Lewis cleared his throat. "I'm sure Jay made a pretty decent consolation prize." He turned back to the cut-out and noticed there was writing on it in silver sharpie. Moving closer, he bent down to read the words aloud. *"Congrats, JägerMeister, you definitely deserve this! Jay Warren (aka Skye) xoxo."*

"JägerMeister?" Lewis said, looking over his shoulder.

Aaron flushed deeply, his expression suddenly agonised.

"Oh," Lewis said, understanding dawning. "That's your pseudonym?"

Aaron closed his eyes. "Lewis—"

Shit. This was really killing the mood.

"Forget I said that," Lewis said quickly, walking back to Aaron and smoothing his hands over his shoulders. Aaron met his gaze, an uncertain look in his eyes.

Christ, he was… really lovely.

Lewis wasn't even sure what it was he found so appealing. Aaron had a very nice face with regular, handsome features and a slim, strong body that Lewis appreciated. But those were not the things that made his chest ache. It was the little expressions that flickered over Aaron's face as they talked, the warmth in his eyes, those moments of silent understanding. The sense Lewis had of *knowing* Aaron and being known in return.

Liking him and being liked.

Maybe even… maybe more than that.

"Aaron," he said, and in that instant, he felt an unfamiliar bolt of happiness, even as a lump rose in his throat and his chest tightened almost unbearably.

Aaron's expression softened, the wariness chased away by something wondering. He raised his hand to touch Lewis's face, his thumb smoothing over Lewis's cheekbone.

"Like I said earlier," Aaron said softly. "I have this bed."

Lewis swallowed. "Can we go there now?"

Aaron's smile was sweet. "Yeah."

The bed was smaller than Lewis's, as was the bedroom itself, but Lewis barely noticed. He was too busy kissing Aaron, yanking off his t-shirt, then reaching for the button on his fly. Soon the narrow strip of carpet next to the just-about-double bed was strewn with their discarded clothes and they were tumbling, naked, onto the mattress together.

Aaron landed on his back, Lewis above him. For a long moment, they gazed at one another, and Lewis had that sense, just like last time, that this—being with Aaron—was different from anything he'd ever experienced with anyone else. That it was more than the easy physical pleasure of two bodies coming together for satisfying sex. Overwhelmed suddenly, he tore his gaze away, ducking his head to press his lips to Aaron's throat, one hand skimming down the warm skin of Aaron's side.

Jesus. How could he feel so turned on and so emotionally twisted up at the same time? He felt like he couldn't get enough of Aaron, inhaling his scent in greedy great lungfuls as he nuzzled the man's throat. His dick was as hard as it had ever been, and at the same time, his chest was aching with a yearning he couldn't put a name to.

"Do you want to fuck me again?" Aaron gasped, and Lewis's cock jerked against his thigh, making him laugh breathlessly. "I'll take that as a yes."

It *was* a yes. It was, because Lewis didn't just prefer to top —he *only* topped. And yet when he leaned up on his elbow and met Aaron's silver gaze again, he found himself saying, "Last time, you said you were vers."

Aaron blinked. "I am. I just didn't think..." He trailed off, then started again. "I kind of had you down as the sort of guy who only tops? Which, I know, is—"

"I am," Lewis said, half-wondering where these words were coming from. Who had taken over his fucking brain? "I've never bottomed. Well, yet."

Aaron's gaze was very intent. He looked as though he was *reading* Lewis, and it made Lewis feel stripped bare somehow. *Seen*. Weirdly, he didn't hate it. In fact, it felt like...like he'd recaptured something he'd lost when Aaron had left, all those weeks ago. Something he'd really fucking missed.

"I'd bottom for you," he said hoarsely. And he meant it. Not because he was so desperate to have Aaron's dick inside him, but because he wanted to give him something he'd never given anyone else.

And what else did he have to give?

Aaron's gaze didn't waver. He reached up and touched Lewis's face, his thumb brushing over his cheekbone again in that tender gesture that made Lewis swallow hard. Then he urged Lewis closer, bringing their mouths together in an achingly sweet, whisper-soft kiss.

Lewis closed his eyes, letting Aaron take what he wanted. When the kiss ended, Aaron didn't move away, and their lips were still touching as he murmured, "I'd love to do that with you. But not tonight, okay? I don't think this is the right time for that."

The wave of relief that washed over Lewis surprised him. Relief and gratitude. Aaron *had* read him. Of course he had because Aaron could always read him.

Sudden memories of the weekend at Safehaven swamped him—memories of Aaron caring for him in ways no one else ever had or could.

In ways Lewis didn't deserve and would never be able to reciprocate.

"Aaron," he whispered, and it was almost a plea, because there was something profoundly painful about that realisation. Something that he was petrified even to look at.

He closed his eyes again and pressed his mouth against Aaron's, grateful when Aaron parted his lips and the kiss deepened and became carnal. He stroked Aaron's body with his hands and canted his hips, relishing the way Aaron moaned when their cocks rubbed together.

Yes, this was better. Easier by far.

Beneath him, Aaron opened his legs and wrapped them round Lewis's hips. The movement brought their cocks in closer contact, and they both moaned.

And suddenly it didn't matter, who was fucking or being fucked, or sucking and being sucked. All that mattered was that Aaron was with him, their mouths moving together, Aaron arching up, stroking Lewis's back, tightening his thighs on Lewis's hips.

Lewis thrust his hand down between them, taking both of their shafts in a clumsy grip, and began to tug, and it was fucking amazing. They needed lube, it wasn't slick enough, and he wanted to be inside Aaron and have Aaron inside him—he wanted everything, but none of it mattered, because right now he had Aaron beneath him, wrapped around him, pressed to his lips and in his hand. He was breathing Aaron in, and tasting him, and touching him, and it was so fucking *perfect*.

"Lewis, God, please," Aaron babbled. "Please, I'm going to come, *Lewis*."

"Yes, fuck. Do it."

They came together, semen spilling stickily between them over Lewis's hand, and that was perfect too. Messily, gracelessly perfect.

Lewis rested his forehead on the pillow as his breath returned to normal, loving the warm gust of Aaron's breath in his ear. Aaron's rueful, "That was *very* fast."

The kiss that followed, to the side of Lewis's neck.

Lewis turned his head. Met that soft, silver gaze. "If you give me a little while, we can go again."

Aaron smiled. "How long do you need?"

CHAPTER TWENTY-FOUR

Aaron

The second time was slower.

Aaron wanted to be fucked. He was pretty forthright about that, and he genuinely did want it—had been craving Lewis's cock inside him for weeks—but he also wanted to put Lewis's hasty offer to bottom on a back-burner. Somehow, he knew that no matter what Lewis thought, it was not something he would find easy to give. Lewis would need some time to work up to that with his partner. And while Aaron was only too happy to do that for him, it was not something he was about to embark upon without knowing whether this was just another one night hook-up.

Instead, he lay back and gave Lewis free rein over his own body.

For him, it wasn't difficult in the way he instinctively knew it would be for Lewis. He trusted Lewis. Trusted Lewis to take care of him and make it good. And sure enough, Lewis spent ages preparing him, using his mouth and tongue and fingers, and a stupid amount of lube, until Aaron was a sobbing, begging mess.

Lewis guided him up onto his knees, sliding into him from behind, his hands firm and sure on Aaron's body. He gave him the hard, dominant fuck that Aaron was desperate for, angling his thrusts so perfectly that Aaron was practically drooling into the pillow, his cock leaking as Lewis pounded into him, over and over.

When Lewis finally, *finally* touched Aaron's cock, he came like a geyser. Just from Lewis's fingers gently circling his desperate shaft and stroking once. And God, but Lewis seemed to love that, growling curse words against Aaron's ear as his come coated Lewis's hand for the second time that night. Lewis's own orgasm came seconds later, and as he climaxed, his teeth fastened on Aaron's shoulder in a possessive bite that stopped short of pain.

Afterwards, Lewis was very quiet. Aaron half expected him to get up and leave, but he didn't. He cleaned up in silence and when Aaron got back into bed, tugged Aaron close in that little spoon position again, one arm snug about Aaron's waist, his lips resting on the nape of Aaron's neck.

It was surprisingly easy to fall asleep like that, but in the morning, when Aaron awoke, it was to find that, like last time, they had drifted apart in the night.

Lewis was still sleeping when Aaron turned to face him. Aaron allowed himself the luxury of watching him for long minutes as he breathed soft, slow, sleeping breaths, and occasionally frowned or twitched.

Every expression, every movement fascinated Aaron.

Hell.

He had it bad. Really fucking bad. And he already suspected that, when Lewis woke up, things probably wouldn't go the way Aaron hoped. For whatever reason, Lewis hadn't been able to stay away from him last night. But Aaron could tell he'd *wanted* to stay away. The sad fact was, Aaron wanted the whole forever deal with Lewis, while Lewis was reluctant even to have a one-night stand with him.

Which wasn't exactly a recipe for success.

It was all too easy to envision a future of serial one-night stands between them, ultimately leading nowhere and causing untold misery and work stress.

As Aaron lay there, gazing at the man he'd fallen in love with, he realised that he wasn't prepared to put himself through that. He deserved better, and honestly, so did Lewis. Lewis deserved the truth. So Aaron was going to man up. Own his own feelings. Set out his own stall.

And that wasn't something he wanted to do naked.

With a final look at Lewis asleep in his bed, Aaron slipped out from under the covers, grabbed some clean clothes, and left the bedroom, shutting the door softly behind him.

It was still dark outside as he padded into the bathroom and flicked on the light, blinking in the sudden glare. After he'd locked the door, he stood for a moment regarding himself in the mirror. Last night's smoky eyes were this morning's sooty smudges, his hair was a wreck, and his face was pale, washed out by the harsh light.

Aaron's gaze came to rest on the purple mark at the juncture of his shoulder and neck. He lifted a hand to touch it, remembering the feel of Lewis's teeth there. Remembering the heat, the hunger, the urgency of his desire.

He blinked at his reflection, vision blurring, and turned away from the mirror. "Get a grip," he said softly. "Get a bloody grip."

He took a quick shower, scrubbing at the remains of Chika's eye makeup, towelled off, and dressed in a t-shirt and jeans. The mark Lewis had left was still visible, peeking out above the neck of his t-shirt when he wiped a hole in the steamy mirror to check. He'd need to wear something with a collar to MTWCon later; the last thing he needed was Janvi asking questions.

When he left the bathroom, the bedroom door was still closed, so Aaron headed into the kitchen and put the kettle on. And the radio, volume low; he was too jittery for silence this morning. He'd forgotten to grab socks, and the laminate floor was chilly beneath his bare feet as he padded about, emptying the dishwasher and opening the curtains to the gradually brightening morning.

The kettle had just boiled when he heard the click of the bedroom door opening. Heart skipping, Aaron turned around to find Lewis lurking in the kitchen doorway wearing last night's black jeans and his dark shirt, still unbuttoned. He looked bed-rumpled, sleepy, and sexy as hell.

"Uh, hi," Lewis said, blinking in the daylight. "What time is it?"

Keeping his tone light, Aaron said, "About half-eight." He held up a mug. "Tea?"

Lewis hesitated, brow furrowing. "I, um…"

"It's not a trick question."

Lewis gave a strained smile. "Right. Thanks. I'll just…" He nodded towards the bathroom, edging away as if Aaron might bite.

With a sigh, Aaron busied himself in the kitchen, fetching teabags, sugar, and milk. He dropped four pieces of bread into the toaster as he listened to the toilet flush and water run and splash in the sink. And then silence.

A long silence.

The toast popped up, making him jump, filling the flat with its comforting aroma.

Still no Lewis.

Aaron had just started to wonder whether Lewis had escaped through the bathroom window and was even now scaling the building, Spiderman-style, when the bathroom door unlocked, and he emerged. His dark hair curled damply where he'd tried to tame it, and, disappointingly, he'd buttoned his shirt. But his feet were still bare, and that, combined with his grim expression, lent him a vulnerable air that plucked at something powerful in Aaron's chest.

He gritted his teeth against the feeling. "Come and sit down," he said, gesturing to the stools at the little breakfast bar that separated his kitchen and living room.

Surprisingly, Lewis did as he was asked and sat across from where Aaron was stirring sugar into a mug of tea.

"Here," Aaron said, pushing the mug towards him.

"Thanks." Lewis spoke quietly, wrapping both hands around the mug and gazing into its steamy depths. "But you don't have to feed me breakfa—"

"It's just a cup of tea," Aaron said with rather more snap than he'd intended. "It doesn't mean we're married."

Lewis gave a huff, not exactly of laughter. "Right," he said. Then, "Look, last night was…" He cleared his throat, and Aaron braced himself not to react; he knew what was coming. No need to make a scene. "Last night was fucking fantastic, actually. But I need to level with you. I don't want you to get the wrong impression."

Smiling through his teeth, Aaron said, "What impression do you think I got?"

A shrug, fingers tightening around the mug. "I wouldn't want you to think that this"—he gestured between them—"is going anywhere beyond sex. Because it's not. It can't."

"I see." That stung, even though Aaron had been expecting it. Stung? Jesus, it hurt like a fucking gut punch.

Lewis glanced up through his gorgeous dark lashes. "But maybe we could, you know, do this from time to time?"

"Do *this*?" Aaron shook his head, blinking hard as he stirred milk into his tea. His voice rose as he said, "You mean fuck? Like…'friends with benefits'? Fuck-buddies?"

Silence. On the radio, the presenter was talking excitedly about the weather. *Cold, with an autumnal nip in the air this morning. And don't forget to put the clocks back tonight!*

"Look," Lewis said grimly, "I know this isn't exactly what you want. And I apologise if I led you to believe otherwise, but sex is all I can offer."

"Is it?" Aaron said, with more feeling than he'd have liked. "Why? Because I don't believe for a second that's all you want."

Lewis's frown deepened into a scowl. "That's just how it is. It's how I am. I don't—I'm not the kind of man who gets his name on a bench."

"His name on a bench?"

Lewis waved off that piece of whimsy. "What I mean is, if you're looking for a committed relationship with dates and corgis and... and a fucking *future,* then you're looking in the wrong place." He rubbed at his jaw, fingers rasping over his dark stubble. "I can't give you that. I'm sorry, but I'll never be able to give anyone that."

It was the bitter resignation in Lewis's expression that punctured Aaron's frustration, that set his heart twisting with compassion instead of anger. More gently, he said, "Why do you say that? Why do you think you can't give someone a future?"

A bark of disbelieving laughter. "Come on. When have I ever had a relationship that lasted more than a couple of months? And when have I ever given a fuck about it ending? I'm not made for...for..." He trailed off with a shrug.

"For intimacy?" Aaron suggested, remembering the brush of Lewis's lips against the nape of his neck as they'd settled down to sleep. "For feelings?"

"Right." Lewis looked away, blinking. His eyes were suddenly very bright in the morning light, stark against his wan face. "You know I'm a selfish arse. I'm impatient, and rude, and I can't give enough of myself to anyone. I never could. Not even to—" His voice cracked; he cleared his throat. "Not even to my mum. Or Owen."

Aaron stilled, unsure how to react. Lewis *never* talked about his family. So he let the radio fill the silence between them while he gathered his thoughts, watching the muscles jump in Lewis's jaw. Eventually, Aaron said, "I think that's bollocks, actually."

Lewis stared across the breakfast bar, his expression bleak. "That's because you don't know me," he said. "You don't know me at all."

"Oh, I think I do. I think I know you very well, Lewis. And you know me." Aaron braced himself against the counter, refusing to back down from the truth. The truth he'd been hiding from for too long, the truth Lewis needed to hear. "Friends or colleagues, or whatever you want to call it, you and I are very close. We already have an intimate relationship, Lewis; we've had one for the last three years."

"No." Lewis rubbed at his shoulder. "No, that's different. That's just work. That's… It's not the fucking same."

Gently, Aaron said, "I know it's scary to get close to people, to depend on them, but you *can* do it. I think, deep down, you want to do it."

"Yeah? Well, you're totally fucking wrong about that. I don't—" He glared, still rubbing at his sore shoulder. "That's the last fucking thing I want, believe me. As soon as you start depending on people, boom, they're gone."

"That's not true."

"Isn't it? *You* fucking left—" He cut himself off, scrubbing a hand angrily across his eyes. "Fuck," he said, with feeling, staring down into his tea.

Aaron's heart was slugging away, anxious and guilty, but he knew this was about more than him leaving his job. Even if he hadn't already suspected that Lewis's childhood trauma still dogged him, his reactions during the workshop at Safehaven would have given it away. Treading carefully, he said, "And so did your mum?"

Lewis's head shot up. "What? My mum didn't leave. She *died.*"

"That's still leaving, isn't it? So of course it's going to hurt when someone else you… you depend on leaves."

"It's not—" Lewis swallowed, stopped speaking.

"Look," Aaron said. "I promised myself I'd be honest today. And I know you appreciate honesty, Lewis. I know you don't like to be bullshitted. So here it is, the truth: I didn't leave my job because I didn't want to work with you. The opposite, really. I left because I had—I *have*—feelings for you." He winced at the euphemism, tried again. "Because I'm in love with you and have been for a few years."

Lewis stared, rigid as a rabbit in headlights.

Into the silence, Aaron said, "I only admitted it to myself at Safehaven, after we…" He stumbled, eyes fixed on Lewis's pale, panicking face, and plunged on. "I think I half knew, but after we slept together, I couldn't ignore it anymore. I realised I'd been putting my career, my whole life, on hold." He gave an awkward laugh. "We both know I should have moved into another role by now, but I just couldn't. Because I didn't want to leave you."

Still, Lewis didn't speak. In fact, he looked like he wanted to run.

"It's okay," Aaron assured him. "I don't expect anything from you—this is for me to handle. I just want you to know that when I left the job, I wasn't leaving you. I wasn't abandoning you. I'll always be here for you, as a friend." He gritted his teeth against the next part, but made himself say it, "And as something more, if you want that. For my part, I think we could have something special. I think we already have something pretty special."

After a silence, Lewis said, "If you knew me, you wouldn't say that."

"But I do know you, and I am saying it."

Lewis looked bleaker than Aaron had ever seen him. He sucked in a breath, paused, and through gritted teeth said, "When my mum was dying, do you know what I did?"

Oh God. "Lewis…"

"I fucking left her."

The grief in his face was too much to bear. Aaron felt it in his chest as if it were his own. He reached over, gripping Lewis's hand, but Lewis snatched his arm back.

"The nurse brought us into the room to say goodbye, and I —I couldn't fucking do it. So I ran. I ran and left Owen to deal with her alone. I couldn't even give them that much of myself. So don't you—" He sucked in a shuddering breath, pushed himself to his feet, toppling the stool over in his haste. "Fuck. I have to go."

"Lewis, wait." Aaron darted out from behind the breakfast bar.

"Where are my shoes?" He was looking around blindly. "I can't find my fucking—"

"Lewis." Aaron gripped his shoulders, turning him. "You were a *child*. For Christ's sake, of course you couldn't cope, but that doesn't mean you—"

"That's what I do!" Lewis spat, pulling away. His face was ravaged, eyes like bruises. "I leave people, Aaron. I leave people who need me, and I don't give a fuck about it afterwards. So you… You should just…"

Aaron couldn't help himself. He surged forward and put his arms around Lewis, pulling him close. "It's okay," he said fiercely, holding him tight. "It's okay. Come on."

At first, Lewis resisted, staying stiff as a board in Aaron's arms, but gradually, his shuddering breaths calmed, and he began to unbend, letting his forehead sink down onto Aaron's shoulder.

They stayed like that for a while, Aaron gently stroking his back.

"I can't give you what you need," Lewis said eventually, brokenly. "I'm sorry, but I can't."

Aaron's throat ached, his eyes hot with tears. He tried to blink them away before Lewis noticed. "All right," he said. "It's okay."

"I can't be the man you want."

Aaron didn't answer. Lewis was already the man he wanted, for all the good that did.

"Listen," he said, pulling away but keeping his hands on Lewis's shoulders. "Sit down, okay? Have some tea before you go. I'll get you some toast."

Lewis shook his head, swiped at his eyes with the back of one hand. "Jesus," he said, looking anywhere but at Aaron. "Sorry."

"Stop apologising."

He huffed but didn't resist as Aaron guided him to the sofa and urged him to sit. Lewis sat, legs giving way abruptly, his head dropping into his hands. It took some willpower on Aaron's part not to reach out and stroke his hair, but Lewis was fragile, and Aaron didn't want to overstep.

Instead, he retreated to the kitchen. Their tea had cooled, so Aaron popped it into the microwave for a few seconds. Keeping one eye on Lewis, he warmed up the toast and spread it with butter and Nutella, piling it all onto a plate.

Returning to the living room, Aaron set the tea and toast down on the coffee table and took a seat in the chair opposite Lewis. Not a good idea to sit next to him right now, no matter how much Aaron longed to put an arm around those tense, unhappy shoulders.

After a couple of silent moments, Aaron said, "There's Nutella," and Lewis lifted his head.

His expression was harrowed, but there was a glint of something in his eyes that pierced Aaron with hope.

Lewis muttered, "I love fucking Nutella."

"Who'd have thought?" Aaron tried not to let his smile wobble.

Still keeping his gaze averted, Lewis reached out for a slice of toast. It went down pretty fast. So did the second slice, and then Lewis picked up his tea and took a sip. Amazing, the power of a little tea and TLC—Aaron could actually see

Lewis's shoulders relaxing as he sat back on the sofa, finally looking up to meet Aaron's gaze.

They weren't easy eyes to meet, troubled and unhappy.

"Sorry," Lewis said again. "I've fucked everything up."

"No, you haven't."

"I'm not usually this fucking dramatic."

Aaron offered a slight smile. "In fairness, neither am I."

Lewis sipped his tea, then frowned suspiciously. "Is there sugar—?"

"There's two!"

A flicker of a smile briefly touched Lewis's lips, before his expression clouded again. "I should get out of your hair. You have a thing today, right? A convention."

"I do…" Aaron didn't ask how Lewis knew. "It's MTWCon—Meet the Writers."

"Fanfic writers?"

"Yup, writers," Aaron said lightly. "I'm on a panel, so… Yeah, I should probably get my head together."

To put it mildly. How the hell was he supposed to discuss the intricacies of Skye and Faolán's relationship in front of a room full of people when his heart felt like it had been through a cheese grater?

"You're braver than me," Lewis said, setting his tea on the table and standing up. "I hate those fucking panels."

"I know." Aaron rose too. "But I usually enjoy them. They're fun."

"Well, that's because you're…" Lewis trailed off, and they watched each other across the coffee table. Lewis said, "Look, I really am sorry. I didn't mean to hurt—"

"Don't." Aaron held up a hand to stop him. "I've said what I wanted to say, and so have you. We both know where we stand, so let's just...move past this, okay?"

Lewis swallowed, his throat bobbing. "Right. Yeah."

And that was that. The End. Fade Out.

All at once, a wave of grief washed over Aaron, grief for

himself and for Lewis. For the hurt and damaged little boy who'd lost his mother, for the grown man who didn't believe he could care. And for the relationship between them that might have been something, but now never would.

Turning away, Aaron said gruffly, "Why don't you find your stuff? I'll get you an Uber."

It only took them five minutes—Lewis hadn't had much with him—and then they were standing awkwardly at the door to Aaron's flat.

Lewis held Skye's trenchcoat over one arm, fiddling with it as he said, "I guess I'll, uh, see you at the office?"

"Sure."

"Maybe we could…?" He trailed off, apparently at a loss.

"Yeah," Aaron said thickly. "Maybe."

Lewis nodded. "Well, I should…" He gestured towards the door.

"Yep." Aaron checked his phone. "Your ride's almost here."

Neither of them moved. And because this was the end, the last time they'd share this awkward intimacy, Aaron leaned forward and brushed his lips against Lewis's stubbled cheek, lingering just for a moment to feel the warmth of his skin for the final time.

"One day, I hope you realise that you can have everything you want," he said roughly. "And that you deserve it."

Lewis had no response to that.

After he'd left, Aaron went to the window to watch him climb into the Uber. At the last moment, Lewis glanced back, and Aaron lifted his hand in farewell.

He waited until the car had driven away before he let the tears fall.

CHAPTER TWENTY-FIVE

Lewis

London streamed past, but Lewis saw nothing. Felt nothing.

Or, rather, he felt *everything*.

Raw, emotionally flayed, he didn't even know how to start processing the last twelve hours. His night with Aaron, how he'd felt as they'd fucked… No, not *fucked*.

What, though? *Made love*? He made a face—it was a phrase that made him want to retch—but yeah. That was more like what they'd done.

He leaned his head back, closing his eyes, remembering how it had felt to have Aaron open and pliant beneath him, looking up at him with those beautiful, trusting eyes. Giving himself, laying himself bare, letting Lewis see how much he wanted him.

The same way Lewis had wanted Aaron.

The same way he'd always fucking want Aaron.

Although Aaron had probably been glad to see the back of him after the pathetic scene he'd made this morning.

Lewis groaned, pressing the heel of one hand against his

forehead as if he could erase the memory of his stupid fucking drama-queen confession.

Why the fuck had he told Aaron about that? He'd never told *anyone* about that night at the hospital. Nobody knew his shame except Owen.

And now Aaron, whose first instinct had been to hug him and offer tea and toast.

Lewis's throat tightened, eyes filling. Shit. In the back of a fucking *Uber*?

He breathed deeply through his nostrils, caught the driver flicking a wary glance at him in the rear-view mirror, and turned to stare out of the side window at the buildings whipping past.

His phone rang.

Stupidly, his heart lurched in a spasm of hope that it was Aaron. Fumbling his phone out of his pocket, he almost threw it out the window when he saw Charlie Alexander's name flash up on the screen.

Over the last few weeks, Charlie had started calling him *all the fucking time* to 'thought-shower' his hackneyed ideas for *Brahmins*. And Lewis had to humour him, had to pretend to take his crap ideas seriously, because otherwise Charlie would throw his toys out of the pram.

Even so, he declined the call.

He couldn't deal with Charlie today. Or any day, really, but especially not today.

Eventually, the car pulled up outside Warrington House. Lewis muttered his thanks and climbed out. The door was barely shut before the driver pulled away from the curb. Lewis trudged up the steps into the foyer of his mansion block, nodded to the porter on duty, and climbed the staircase to his third-floor flat.

Halfway up, his phone pinged. Charlie again. Lewis ignored the message.

Inside his flat, it was very quiet, and he hesitated in the

entryway after the front door closed behind him, not quite sure what to do next. His ears were ringing, mind still racing, and in the heavy silence, he could hear the thumping of his own heartbeat.

He felt distinctly, painfully alone.

Forcing himself to move, he dumped the leather trench-coat in the hall cupboard and headed through the living room into his bedroom. On the way, his eyes snagged on the white rug that Aaron had helped him clean the day they went to Safehaven.

Lewis hadn't known then that the world was about to collapse around his ears.

On autopilot, he stripped off his clothes, dumped them in the laundry basket, and padded into the bathroom. He avoided his reflection in the mirror, had no desire to look himself in the eye.

Turning the water up to full power, making it as hot as he could bear, he set about washing away the traces of sweat and come from the night before.

Unfortunately, his mind was harder to clear.

I do know you… We already have an intimate relationship, Lewis; we've had one for the last three years.

That was bollocks. Work relationships weren't the same as personal relationships, whatever Aaron might think. And anyway, Aaron *didn't* know him. How could he? Lewis was very careful about what he shared with the world.

Until this morning.

Fuck knows why he'd confessed his darkest secret to Aaron, the one person whose good opinion mattered to him. But he seemed to be making a lot of bad decisions around Aaron these days...

Still feeling raw, he dressed in his softest jeans and his favourite cashmere sweater. Unhelpfully, his mind reminded him that it was the same sweater he'd worn that evening in

Swanage, when he'd almost kissed Aaron on the beach beneath the stars…

Mooching into the kitchen, he put the kettle on and grabbed a jar of instant hot chocolate, spooning twice as much powder into the mug as the instructions suggested. As the water heated, Lewis gazed out over the street, unseeing.

Usually, after a satisfying sexual adventure like last night, he'd feel energised. Up for anything. But today he just felt...empty. Blank.

On the counter, his phone buzzed again. His heart gave another pathetic lurch, and he glanced down to see a message from Charlie fucking Alexander.

Need to speak to you, Lew. Brain's popping! Call me?

Lew? Fuck no.

He turned his phone over, screen down.

Once the kettle had boiled, he poured the water over the powder, stirred the mug lackadaisically, and carried it into the living room. His laptop sat on the coffee table, and he switched it on automatically. There were three emails from Charlie at the top of his in-box, all called *Diversity Baby!*

After being warned by the Telopix communications team that changing Faolán's sexuality might not go down well on social media, Charlie had been bombarding Lewis with his ideas to make the change more palatable. As far as Lewis was concerned, each idea was more ridiculous than the last, which was no surprise because *Brahmins* was shaping up to be an irredeemable shitshow. A shitshow that he had to live with for the sake of the deal, but that he refused to think about today. Charlie could wait until Monday.

Closing his email, he took a swig of the hot chocolate, grimacing at the lump of powder that disintegrated on his tongue as he opened Facebook. He scrolled through some posts, then checked Twitter and Instagram. There was the usual social media fan chatter about the show, plenty of speculation about the US version. Most Brits thought it would be worse than the original, but some were excited about longer seasons and more content. And there was some hilarious dream casting, as if Telopix had the budget for Hollywood megastars.

He also spotted a couple of links to fanart and fanfiction. Out of curiosity, he followed one link that took him to a couple of genuinely impressive digital renderings of Skye and Faolán in a clinch. Over-romanticised, perhaps, but professionally done. And striking.

Lewis felt an odd lurch in the pit of his stomach as he studied the image of Faolán in Skye's arms, gazing up adoringly into his dark eyes. It was...touching.

The other link was to a fanfic recommendation, and he hovered his cursor over it for a long time. He'd never read any fanfiction, for obvious reasons. Why would he want to read the amateur butchering of his own creation? But since he'd found out about Aaron's fanfic habit, and after last night's conversation about creativity and gatekeepers, Lewis was starting to see things in a new light.

Just like the fanart, fanfiction was simply an interpretation of his work, right? And anyway, *did* he own Skye and Faolán? He may have invented them, but that didn't mean others couldn't bring them to life too. Couldn't enjoy their own creative interpretation of the story and characters.

Maybe he'd been a precious arse about it all these years.

Taking a deep breath, he clicked the link and found himself on a site called Archive of Our Own. Its banner read: *A fan-created, fan-run, nonprofit, noncommercial archive for transformative fanworks, like fanfiction, fanart, fan videos, and podfic.*

He had no idea what podfic was, but okay. What astonished him, though, was that the site had almost four million members, and over eight million works.

Eight *million* works.

Turned out there were millions of people creating art for

free, sharing their talent with others for fun. No fame, no glory, no money. That was… That was fucking astonishing.

Curious, he started reading the fanfic he'd clicked on and… Okay, technically the writing wasn't great. But it had heart; he could see it in every line. It had passion. The author really fucking *loved* the characters they were writing about, which stood in stark contrast to Charlie and his Faolán-bro, who only existed to appeal to a notional audience demographic.

Clicking back to the home page, Lewis realised that he could search by fandom. To his astonishment, *Leeches* had racked up over 41,000 fanworks.

And some of those would be Aaron's.

His heart gave a flustered kick. He bit his lip, considering. Reading Aaron's fanfiction felt intimate, like peeking into his mind. Should he do it? His fingers tingled, stomach tensing with anticipation.

Yes, the weird nervy feeling knotting in the pit of his stomach was anticipation. He was excited to read Aaron's work; he wanted to feel that connection to him.

And it wasn't like reading someone's secret diary, was it? This was work Aaron had sent out into the world for anyone to read. So why not Lewis?

Before he could change his mind, he clicked into the search bar and typed 'Jägermeister'.

And there he was: JägerMeister — 112 works.

Pulse racing, Lewis started to scroll. The stories were arranged in descending chronological order, each one tagged with episodes it related to, as well as other things like 'angst' or 'pining'.

That made Lewis smile because Aaron had always been a fan of the angsty episodes.

His fic titles were cool too. Lewis recognised quotes from Stoker and other classic vampire texts. But then, Aaron had always had a knack for coming up with clever titles.

Charlie should ask him to improve on *Brahmins*, for fuck's sake.

Not sure which story to start with, Lewis checked out the stats. Each one had a number next to 'hits', 'kudos', and 'comments', so he chose a story that had a lot of all those things: 32 chapters, 76,323 words, 39,000 hits and 2500 kudos.

Fanfic? It was a fucking novel.

Settling back in the corner of his sofa, he balanced his laptop on his thighs, sipped his hot chocolate, and began to read.

The first thing he noticed, clear as a clarion, was Aaron's voice. Maybe because Lewis knew it so well from the countless notes Aaron had provided on his own work, but he heard Aaron's concise language in every line. No purple prose here, thank God.

The dialogue, of course, was spot on. It would be, with Aaron writing. But it wasn't the same as the show's dialogue. Less pacy, giving the characters more time to explore their thoughts and feelings. One of the advantages of prose over screenwriting.

What struck Lewis most as he read was the power of the internal point of view. Hearing Faolán's thoughts was… Well, it was no surprise that he sounded a lot like Aaron. Faolán was, as Lewis had only recently come to understand, somewhat based on Aaron: Skye's cute and faithful sidekick with an undertone of forbidden sexual tension. Not that Faolán had started out precisely that way. It was only after Aaron had started working at RPP that Lewis had recognised Faolán's long-term potential.

Shoving that thought aside, Lewis started scrolling through the story titles again. His eye caught on one called, innocently enough, *Pizza Night*. It made him think of all those late-night pizzas he and Aaron had shared, as they worked. Clicking through, he began to read.

Pizza Night by *JägerMeister*
Leeches
After Amy storms out, Skye and Faolán are left alone...(Coda: S05e10 "Bushido")

Bushido. That had been a tricky episode, and an important one. It had picked up multiple seemingly unconnected threads from previous episodes which had then needed to be woven together into the end of season five storyline. Lewis distinctly remembered working through a whole weekend with Aaron on that episode, and Aaron's infectious enthusiasm, even when faced with the knottiest of plot problems.

Curious, he read on.

When everyone else has left, they end up sitting on the floor with the pizza box open between them.

Margherita, extra-large.

Skye prefers simple food, and Faolán is happy to indulge him. They've never discussed it, but Faolán suspects Skye's undeveloped palate is a result of having been turned so young.

He never had a chance to develop adult tastes.

Now, Skye's sitting with his back against the wall, long, lean legs stretched out before him. They're still clad in the black jeans he was wearing during the fight, and there's a rip near the top of one thigh—courtesy of Merrick's vicious wooden stake.

Through the tear, Faolán glimpses a flash of ivory skin. He looks away hurriedly.

"I adore pizza," Skye says. He's already working on his fourth slice. "But you really need to go to Naples for the good stuff. Specifically, Naples circa 1898. Glorious."

Faolán huffs as he reaches for another slice. "Given that I don't own a time machine, I'll have to make do with Domino's. And can you slow down? I'm starving, and this is actually a meal for me instead of a..." What had Skye called it? "...a gastronomic indulgence?"

Skye slides him a smiling look. "True. But too much pizza will make you fat, my friend, whereas I..." He takes an enormous bite. "Will never change."

"Sure," Faolán says darkly. "Until someone sticks a stake between your ribs." He's looking at the slash in Skye's jeans again; it had been too close. And even though Amy's already delivered the lecture, Faolán can't help but say, "You should never have gone there alone tonight. Amy's right. It was rash."

Skye doesn't answer until he's finished his mouthful—impeccable manners, vampires. "Well," he says, "since we're talking about imprudence, you should not have been there at all. I specifically told you I could handle it."

"Handle it?" Faolán almost chokes on his pizza. "You weren't handling it. Merrick had that stake to your—"

"All right." Anger flashes in Skye's eyes.

Or at least that's what Faolán would have called it a year ago. Now he knows better. Now he recognises that stormy expression as fear.

"It was dangerous tonight," Skye says shortly. "You and Amy could have been killed. Or worse."

"Worse?"

Skye gives him a speaking look and doesn't elaborate. He doesn't need to.

"Okay, fine. But you could have been killed too. And I couldn't—" Faolán shakes his head, feeling his throat tighten. "I know this might shock you, but I'd actually miss you. If you were, you know, dead."

Skye eyes him. Faolán concedes, "Dead-er."

After a pause, Skye says, "As it happens, I'd miss you too. You make my life—my existence—tolerable."

"Tolerable?" Faolán smiles. "Now, don't go getting all mushy on me."

Skye lets out a put-upon sigh, but when his eyes meet

Faolán's, there's a glint in their depths, one Faolán hasn't seen before. A hint of the boy he'd once been, perhaps?

"This is very tolerable." Skye gestures between them with his slice of pizza, encompassing the food, the dimly lit room. Perhaps even the night itself. "Very tolerable indeed. I should have been sorry to miss it." Then his expression grows more complex, and he adds, "Thank you, Faolán, for... For coming to my aid."

"Any time," Faolán says softly, hiding his pleased smile.

Lewis swallowed against the sudden lump in his throat.

Skye was him. Aaron was writing *him*.

He clicked into the next story without even registering the title. This was a longer one that started in Skye's point of view.

As he read, his stomach knotted, heart thudding hard.

Skye kept to the shadows because shadows were all he deserved—the bright lights of fame and fortune were for others, for those who had lived unstained lives. For the blameless.

Then, later:

"What's wrong with hot chocolate? It reminds me of happier times."

In truth, it reminded him of home, of the summer heat of Rosenhelm in the years before his turning. And of his mother, who had died defending him. Not that he'd ever confess as much to a human like Faolán...

And finally:

Skye had become a man before his time, on that dark night when his world had been torn apart and he'd woken to a crimson dawn with his family slain and the blood of monsters running through his veins. The night that had changed him forever, and that haunted him still.

It was as if Aaron had looked through Skye and seen

Lewis, seen the parts of him he hid from the world but that bled onto the pages of his scripts and into Skye Jäger.

Seen him more clearly than he'd ever been seen before.

I think I know you very well, Lewis. And you know me...

He was jolted from the story and his thoughts by the shrill ringing of his phone from the kitchen.

Charlie, again. Fuck.

Lewis stumbled into the kitchen and snatched the phone off the counter. "Isn't it the middle of the fucking night over there?"

"Lewis, there you are." Charlie's tinny voice buzzed down the line like a wasp, his displeasure clear. "Didn't you get my messages?"

"It's Saturday morning," Lewis said, by way of an answer.

"And that's why we pay you the big bucks!"

Telling himself to stay calm, not to react, Lewis prowled back into the living room. "What do you need, Charlie? I'm busy."

A chilly silence. Then, "I've had some fantastic ideas about tackling really serious LGBTQIA+ issues. Well, credit where credit's due, it was Mils who came up with this idea. I adore the way women think. So empathetic. And don't you just *love* cracking open the glass ceiling for them? Anyway, Mils was thinking that with the gay vamp character, what if he'd literally been hanged for being gay? Like two hundred years ago, he'd been caught in the act, and—"

"Nope," Lewis said, cutting him off.

A disgruntled pause. "Excuse me?"

"I'm not creating a gay character who's been executed because of his sexuality. That still happens in the world in case you weren't aware. It's not fucking entertainment."

Stiffly, Charlie said, "Well, what Mils was thinking—and obviously, it's *her* idea, not mine—was that this would be a way to use our platform to highlight—"

"I said no, I'm not doing it. You want to tackle that issue, make a documentary. Was there anything else?"

After a silence, Charlie said, "Yes, actually. I commissioned some audience insight work, which has been *amazingly* useful, and as a result, we're going to change Faolán's name to Harker. It got a much stronger response for 'masculinity' and 'capability' among the 25-35 male demographic."

Lewis closed his eyes, locking his jaw against a curse. "Let me guess, because it sounds less *gay*?"

"What? God, no. Jesus, Lewis, the idea hadn't even occurred to me." And now he sounded smug. "Harker is actually a reference to Jonathan Harker from—"

"Stoker's *Dracula*. Yes, I know."

"Right, well. It's a clever little nod, right?"

"Nope, it's obvious. But that should suit his character just fine."

Another silence came down the line, this one louder. "I might be way off base here," Charlie said tersely, "but I'm sensing some resistance. Some blocking energy. Frankly, I'm starting to question your commitment to *Brahmins*."

Lewis felt a beat of panic. *Shit, he'd gone too far*. He needed to roll back, say something placating to smooth things over. Apologise.

Only he couldn't do it. He couldn't make himself say the right words. When he opened his mouth, nothing came out. Because Charlie was right. He hated everything about *Brahmins,* from Faolán turning into a straight dude-bro called Harker, to the new gay character being pre-fucking-buried. His eyes drifted back to his laptop, to Aaron's extraordinary, heartfelt story. Not the sort of thing you'd ever see on TV, and yet somehow a story that captured the heart of what *Leeches* was all about. Captured it, built on it, and expanded it.

The anaemic pastiche Charlie Alexander was creating couldn't hold a candle to Aaron's work. And suddenly, Lewis knew that he couldn't do it. Could not be part of this clusterfuck.

"Lewis?" Charlie's mosquito voice whined in his ear. "Did we get cut off?"

"No."

"Great, so what we'll do now is—"

"I mean *no*. I'm not doing it."

Charlie went quiet, then said, "Not doing what?"

"Any of this bullshit. I won't let you screw over my show."

"What the fuck does that mean? If you're trying to up the price—"

"It's not about money." His eyes strayed back to his laptop, but in his mind's eye he saw Aaron in the kitchen at RPP, outraged that Charlie wanted to change Faolán's sexuality. "*Leeches* means too much to me, and to people I care about, to fuck it up like this."

A harsh bark of laughter. "Ah, now I get it. This is about Andy, isn't it?"

"Who?"

"Your fanboy assistant—the one you're shagging."

Lewis felt a jolt of fury. "What the fuck are you talking about?"

"Oh, come on," Charlie said nastily. "It was obvious at Safehaven that you were panting after him. What's the deal? If you fly the rainbow flag for the homo-agenda, he'll bend over and let—?"

"Fuck you," Lewis said and hung up.

In the silence of his flat, his words echoed with frightening finality.

Shit.

Shit.

Had he just…pulled the plug on the whole deal? Probably. And probably Toni would kill him. No, there was no probably about it. Toni *would* kill him, and Charlie would make sure

Lewis was *persona non grata* at Telopix for the next decade or more.

But, Lewis didn't care. He felt too good to care, too elated. *Finally*, he was out from under that fucking awful deal. No *Brahmins*, no dude-bro Harker. No Charlie fucking Alexander.

Unexpectedly, he laughed. A rusty sound, too loud in his quiet flat.

Then he shouted, "Fuck yes!"

And, God, but he wished Aaron was there. No one else would appreciate this moment like Aaron. No one else would share his ecstatic relief.

He wanted Aaron like he'd never wanted him before…

Or maybe like he'd always wanted him: at his side, sharing the lows and the highs. As his friend, his ally, his constant companion.

His lover.

The man, Lewis realised with sudden, shocking clarity, that he loved. The man he couldn't live without for another fucking day.

Snatching up his phone, Lewis grabbed his keys and bolted for the door.

"It's a ticket-only event," insisted the vampire manning the table next to the hotel entrance.

Lewis growled, repeating silently: *don't punch the fans, do not punch the fans.*

"Fine," he said, "I'll buy a ticket. I'll buy ten fucking tickets. I just need to find Aaron Page. He's—"

"We're not selling tickets on the door."

He was a hair's breadth away from *Do you know who I am?* when a young woman in a *Leeches* t-shirt saved him the trouble.

"Oh my God, Greg," she said, flushing scarlet as she rushed up behind the Nazi-vampire. "That's *Lewis Hunter*!"

Greg's eyes widened comically. "No way."

To the girl, Lewis said, "Hi. Can you take me to Aaron Page?"

"Uh, yeah!" She looked delighted. "Like, *now*?"

"Exactly like now, yes."

With an air of self-conscious pride, the girl—Lauren, he found out—led him through the nondescript lobby of the nondescript hotel. Lewis kept his eyes peeled but saw no sign of Aaron. There were, however, numerous versions of Skye, Amy, and Faolán. And as he walked through the milling crowd, he heard a slow rise in whispers and felt the growing heat of attention.

Unlike Jay Warren, and every other actor he'd ever met, Lewis hated attention. He was uncomfortably aware of the eyes on him as he followed Lauren through a small conference room lined with stalls selling fan merchandise—t-shirts, mugs, posters, autographed photos of the actors. "This is the dealers' room," Lauren explained as they walked past the stalls.

At the far end, they reached a closed set of double doors, and Lauren stopped, peering through a glass panel before looking back at Lewis and smiling brightly. Her colour was high in her cheeks, her eyes shining. She looked happy, excited to be there. "Everyone's going to freak out. They'll be *so* excited you're here. We all love your writing."

"Is Aaron in there?" Lewis said as she hauled open the door.

"Of course!" she said and ushered him in.

And she was right, Aaron was there.

He was right there, under a spotlight on the small platform that had been set up at the front of the room, sitting with two other people: a pretty Asian woman, about Aaron's age, with short hair dyed pink at the tips, and an older woman sporting glasses and a teacherish expression.

The older woman held the mic and was in full flow. The audience—maybe forty or fifty people—listened with rapt attention. That included Aaron, who perched on a barstool on the far end of the stage, nodding as the woman spoke.

He looked… God, he looked good. He looked fucking perfect. Of course, he always looked perfect because he was Aaron: the most perfect thing in Lewis's life.

His heart gave a soft thump of relief. Relief and joy and…happiness.

Fuck, how had he ever thought he could survive a day without Aaron at his side?

Leaning back against the wall, Lewis settled in to listen. Now that he was here, he was prepared to wait. And eager to hear whatever Aaron had to say.

"...and so that's where I get my ideas from," the woman on stage concluded. Smiling, she said, "Who has the next question?"

A microphone was being passed around the audience, and several hands shot up. But to Lewis's horror, Lauren got hold of it first. "Everyone," she said, feedback squealing as she held the mic too close. She laughed. "Sorry! But this is amazing—we have a surprise guest!"

Lewis bolted upright, away from the wall. "Wait, no, I'm not—"

Too late. Everyone had turned to stare, the room filling with surprised gasps and excited whispers. Not that Lewis was really listening; he only had eyes for Aaron, who was staring at him over the heads of the crowd.

Their gazes locked, Aaron rising slowly to his feet in utter bewilderment.

"This is such an honour," said the woman on stage. "Ladies and gentlemen, please welcome the creator of *Leeches* —Mr. Lewis Hunter!"

CHAPTER TWENTY-SIX

Aaron

Lewis paled, eyes widening with horror as the audience stared at him, waiting for him to say something. Aaron half expected him to turn on his heel and stalk out the door, but instead, he pressed his lips together in a determined expression and walked forward, down the narrow aisle between the two sets of chairs to the temporary stage where Aaron and the other panellists sat.

Aaron watched his approach with concern. When Lewis had left his place, a few hours earlier, he'd still been in a bit of a state, but he seemed calmer now, as though he'd pieced himself back together. Now, he looked composed and handsome in butter-soft jeans and a fitted sweater that hugged his broad shoulders and showed off his lean torso. And the audience was noticing too, one woman mimicking fanning herself to her companion while others took pictures with their phones.

Luckily, Lewis seemed oblivious to all the attention. In fact, he seemed oblivious to pretty much everything and everyone apart from Aaron. His gaze was laser-focused on

Aaron, making Aaron's skin prickle and his heart thump in wary anticipation—of what, he didn't know, but he braced himself when Lewis stepped up onto the stage and headed straight for him.

"I'm sorry," Lewis murmured when he reached him, leaning in close. "I didn't mean to crash your panel."

He smelled really good.

Aaron beat back the urge to bury his face in Lewis's neck and just *inhale*. Instead, he murmured, "It's fine—honestly, everyone's going to be stoked you're here." He paused, then added, "But why *are* you here?"

Lewis opened his mouth to answer but was interrupted by Michelle, who was determined to take control of the situation. She was a Big Name Fan among the Skylán Community, and the panel had been her idea. Prior to Lewis's arrival, she'd been hogging the stage unashamedly. Now that Lewis had turned up, there was no way she'd be handing the mic over.

"Mr. Hunter," she gushed, hurrying towards him. "This is such a huge honour! Let me just say that I'm delighted to welcome you on behalf of the MTWCon committee. Everyone here today is a huge *Leeches* fan." By now, she was standing next to him, and she shoved the microphone under his nose.

Lewis cleared his throat. "Um—thanks. I didn't plan to come up on stage or anything, I just came to"—he jerked his thumb at Aaron—"see, um, JägerMeister here."

A ripple of laughter went through the audience, and Michelle said, "Really? I thought—that is, I'd *read*—that you don't like fanfic?"

Aaron winced at the question, along with half the audience. Oblivious to her own gaucheness, Michelle thrust the microphone back in Lewis's direction, right under his nose. It was exactly the sort of personal-space-infringing move that Lewis detested, and Aaron waited for him to push the mic away irritably, or perhaps to make a sarcastic comment. But amazingly, he did neither.

Instead, he glanced at Aaron for a moment before saying, "Let's just say I've only recently discovered its merits."

The audience cheered spontaneously, a few people whooping and whistling. Aaron stared in astonishment, and Lewis gave him an uncertain smile and a little shrug.

Since when had Lewis been reading fanfic? And *whose*? Only last night he'd been arguing—

And then Aaron remembered.

"That's your pseudonym?"

Shit. Had Lewis been reading *his* work? The thought sent sudden heat rushing into his face, and now Lewis's uncertain expression was morphing into one of amusement as he noticed Aaron's reaction.

Someone in the audience jumped up. "Do you read *Jäger-Meister's* fics?" she asked, echoing Aaron's thoughts. "Isn't he amazing? He's totally my favourite—he's why I'm here today!" Her gaze shifted from Lewis to Aaron, and she clasped her hands over her heart and said in a rush, "I love your work!"

She sat down again, and everyone stared at Lewis expectantly, waiting for his response. When he said nothing, Michelle prodded the mic in his direction. He looked down at it briefly, then up again at the audience and said, "I have read some of JägerMeister's work, and"—he nodded at the girl in the audience who had just spoken—"yeah, it's fucking amazing."

More whooping.

Aaron realised he had a huge lump in his throat. He tried to swallow against it discreetly and felt his eyes sting. He could hardly believe what he'd heard. Lewis had read his work. And he'd *liked* it. He'd thought it was *"fucking amazing"*.

Aaron didn't bother wondering whether Lewis meant it—Lewis wouldn't say something like that if he didn't. He could never bring himself to tell the easy, complimentary lies that oiled the wheels of the entertainment industry. Painfully honest, that was Lewis.

Which made his praise now all the more precious.

Overwhelmed, it took Aaron a long few moments to focus on anything beyond keeping his emotions in check, but eventually, he noticed that this weird situation was turning into a Q&A. There were at least ten people in the audience with their hands up, waiting to ask Lewis something, and Michelle was loving her moment of glory.

"Chap in the green t-shirt," she said briskly, pointing at someone in the third row. "What's your question?"

The guy stood up, clearing his throat nervously. "Hi! We're all pretty excited about the new US version of the show." A muttering in the room suggested that might not be *entirely* the case. "My question is: what's the timeline on that? And have you done any casting?"

A strange expression flickered over Lewis's face. It was probably too quick for anyone else to have noticed—already he'd dragged a polite mask over it—but Aaron saw it, and he eyed Lewis carefully as he gave his answer.

"It's not a done deal yet. We're still in talks with Telopix. It might happen, but only if I'm happy that it won't compromise my vision for the show."

What?

Lewis glanced Aaron's way briefly, and their gazes met and held while the audience buzzed over that unexpected answer.

"Paula," Michelle said. "You look like you've got a question."

Aaron looked up at that, alarmed. Michelle was pointing at a woman with dyed black hair and distinctly vampirish make-up in the front row, who was straining her arm up towards the ceiling like a schoolkid desperate to give an answer. And yes, that was Paula Lester, aka The Skylándalorian, the biggest of Big Name Fans. She was an influential writer and reader in the Skylán community, a massive shipper, and an even bigger shit-stirrer who had started more wars in her time than Genghis Khan.

Breathlessly, she said, "I've been a Skylán shipper since 'Only Blue Skies From Now On'? The episode where they first met? In season three?" At this point, Aaron remembered that Paula was also one of those people who ended every sentence with a questioning intonation—a verbal tic that was one of Lewis's pet peeves. It was pretty much guaranteed to provoke a cutting remark from him. Or worse.

"I reckon most of us in this room are Skylán shippers?" Paula went on. "And we've all seen the clues you've buried in the show? That Skye and Faolán are actually in love?"

God, this was getting worse—it always pissed Lewis off when people accused him of intentionally writing implicit Skylán romance into the show. Aaron waited anxiously, sure he'd see Lewis's jaw tightening or his lips pressing into a hard, irritated line. But weirdly, it didn't happen. For once, Lewis seemed to be listening.

"So, my question?" Paula said, "Is will you ever take their love story out of the subtext? Like, will you actually put it on screen?" She gave a stagey pause. "Or is it just queerbaiting?"

This time Lewis actually reached for the mic, tugging it out of Michelle's hand and pacing forward, to the front of the stage.

Oh fuck.

Aaron braced himself. Lewis was about to start ranting about how people only saw what they wanted to see and how they shouldn't assume that what they took from the show was what the writer intended. How it was his show, his characters, and entitled fans had no fucking right making demands.

If he did, Paula would slate him across every social media platform and *Leeches* forum in the free world and—

"That's a really good question, Paula."

Aaron glanced at Lewis sharply.

"The thing is," Lewis went on, his attention still on Paula, "*you* might've seen that Skye and Faolán are in love, and maybe a lot of other people have seen it too. But"—he paused, his gaze darting back to Aaron—"but Skye hasn't seen it. Not yet."

Aaron's heart lurched in his chest, and the audience was so quiet you could have heard a pin drop.

"Skye doesn't understand why he keeps rescuing Faolán," Lewis went on, his focus still on Aaron. "Or why he gets so pissed off when Faolán goes off on one of his solo investigations. He doesn't even see how close he's let Faolán get to him. Skye thinks he's a lone wolf... when he's actually part of a mated pair."

And right then, Aaron knew that Lewis wasn't just talking about Skye. Slowly, pulse lumbering, he stood up, his gaze locked with Lewis's.

"Skye's a stupid bastard," Lewis went on, voice cracking. "He doesn't deserve someone like Faolán, but—"

Abruptly, he shoved the mic at Michelle without even looking at her and crossed the stage to Aaron. For an instant, they eyed each other, and then Lewis took Aaron's shoulders and turned him until they were angled away from the crowd.

"I'm so sorry," he said urgently, his words pitched too low for anyone else to hear. "I've been a fucking idiot."

"Have you?" Aaron managed through numb lips.

Lewis nodded. "I couldn't see it, even though it was staring me in the face. Even though I wrote about it every fucking week in the show."

"See what?"

Lewis's expression softened, caught somewhere between alarm and hope. "That I love you."

His words rang between them, as startling and resonant as a struck bell. Into the silence Aaron gave a choked sob, helpless against an overwhelming rush of relief and joy, and

Lewis wrapped his arms around him, drawing him into a fierce embrace.

"I do, I do," he crooned in Aaron's ear. "God, I do. I love you. I'm sorry. Forgive me."

Unable to speak, Aaron turned his head and caught Lewis's lips with his own in a desperate kiss, his heart slamming in his chest. When they finally tore their mouths apart, they were both panting and grinning stupidly at one another.

"You do realise that there will be pictures of this on the internet already?" Aaron murmured, flushed and laughing softly at the pained expression that appeared on Lewis's face.

But when they finally turned around to face the music, Lewis said drily, "Erm, are you sure about that?"

No one was paying them the slightest bit of attention. Every single head was bent over a phone, looking at… something. Some people were wearing headphones, while others were listening to tinny voices playing out over their phone speakers.

"What are they all watching?" Aaron asked, puzzled.

"Uh, Aaron?" He turned to find Janvi holding out her phone to him, eyes wide. "You and, um, Lewis, should probably take a look at this."

He took the phone from her and glanced down at the video waiting to play on the screen. It was a still of a man. His mouth was open—the video seemed to be starting when he was already mid-speech—and the glass of wine he held looked about to spill.

It was Charlie Alexander.

"What the hell?" Lewis said beside him. Aaron started the video.

The still image stayed as it was, but now acid-yellow text rolled onto the screen.

"Charles Alexander is Head of Global TV at Telopix Entertainment. He is currently working on adapting cult British TV show, 'Leeches', for the US audience."

The text faded out, and new text appeared.

"Mr. Alexander's profile on the Telopix website says he is 'passionate about improving diversity and representation in the entertainment industry'."

The text faded again.

"Now hear what he really thinks."

Then the still image came to life. It wavered for a moment as the camera was moved, clumsily adjusted, and settled in place. When the picture resolved, a woman could be seen at the far edge of the frame. She was wearing a purple halter-top dress.

Toni.

This was Safehaven. This was the night of that disastrous dinner.

"Jesus, Mils," Charlie said. *"Lewis won't be interested in Tristan—he's obviously banging his twinky assistant."*

Beside him, Toni stiffened with affront and began to say something—Charlie chose that moment to reach across and snag the bottle of wine on the table in front of her and refill his glass. The sound of his movements obscured her words.

"Don't be so bloody bourgeois, Toni," he said next. He rolled his eyes in her direction to underline his point but only succeeded in looking utterly wankered. Which, yeah, he probably had been by then, after all those cocktails and the wine that had been flowing all night. *"Lewis isn't even here. And if he was, he wouldn't be offended. From what I hear, he's a very open-minded guy."* He winked at whoever was on the other side of the table. *"Well, gays are, aren't they? All that masculine energy's bound to make you horny as fuck, am I right, Geoff?"*

Geoff. It was Geoff on the other side of the camera.

Poor Geoff.

Poor Geoff watching his wife practically climbing into Charlie's lap all night.

Poor Geoff fiddling with his phone while everyone else

talked. Aaron bit his lip against a smile, torn between amusement and horror.

"Oh yes, bound to," Geoff said mildly. *"The main character in his show's gay, isn't he?"*

"Skye?" Charlie shrugged. *"Who the fuck knows? Officially, Skye's straight, but all the chemistry's with the male sidekick."* He sighed. *"Maybe Lewis just can't write a straight love story."* He achieved a slow, drunken wink. *"But we're fixing that in the new version."*

"Fixing it?" Geoff said. *"Why do you need to fix it? You're into diverse representation, aren't you? Milly's always banging on about it."*

On-screen-Charlie drained his nearly full wine glass, then leaned across the table.

"You have to say shit like that these days," he said. *"But you know what, Geoff? The truth is, in this industry, you gotta work within the limits of the possible. We're going to sink tens of millions into this project, and if Lewis fucking Hunter thinks I'm going to jeopardise a cent of that money by letting him shove his homo-agenda down everyone's throat, he's insane. US audiences won't put up with that shit. They don't want a pair of arse bandits as the leads. They want boy meets fucking girl, okay? And anyone who tells you different is a fucking liar."*

At the edge of the screen, Toni stood up jerkily. *"I'm pretty tired,"* she said in a stony voice. *"I'm going to—"*

The audio cut off, the picture seizing on a still of Charlie wearing a drunken expression and Toni's standing figure from the neck down. More text rolled up.

"'I guess I'm a dreamer, but you know what? Maybe if we spend less time looking at spreadsheets and more time trying to achieve our dreams, we'll actually get those diverse, authentic voices we all need so badly.' From 'The Diversity Dream,' a TED talk by Charles Alexander, Head of Global TV at Telopix Entertainment."

"Oh my God," Aaron muttered. He scrolled down and

saw there were already hundreds of comments, with more piling up.

He glanced at Lewis, who was still staring at the screen, his lips pressed together. Then Lewis looked his way, and his eyes were dancing with amusement.

"You don't seem… *very* upset?" Aaron said carefully.

"I spoke to Charlie this morning," Lewis said. "Before I came here. We had words, and I…" He lowered his voice. "Well, I pulled the plug on the US show."

"You *what?*"

Lewis shrugged. "It wasn't worth it. He was destroying everything I loved about it." He smiled, squeezed Aaron's arm. "Everything we've built together."

"But… the money? Your career?"

Lewis gave a half-smile. "The RPP board isn't going to be happy, but ultimately, *Leeches* is my baby. If they're so pissed off they want to fire me, I'll take it elsewhere. But I don't think it'll come to that." He grinned. "And actually, this video is going to help. A *lot*."

Aaron laughed. "God, yes. No one's going to take Charlie's bullshit seriously now." He elbowed Lewis. "So. Good old Geoff in the end. He must have uploaded this."

"Hell hath no fury, I guess…" Lewis cupped Aaron's cheek then, smiling into his eyes. "That was a crazy weekend, but I'll always look back on it fondly as the weekend when we finally—" he paused.

"—fucked?" Aaron guessed.

"—kissed," Lewis confirmed at the same moment.

They both laughed.

Aaron said, "Now you think I'm a shallow, sex-obsessed nympho."

"That's where you're wrong," Lewis said. "I think you're *my* shallow sex-obsessed nympho. And I love you."

Happiness fizzed through him, fierce and dizzying. Aaron couldn't stop grinning. "I love you too."

CHAPTER TWENTY-SEVEN

Lewis

"You're going to love this," Lewis said gleefully as he climbed back into bed, iPad in hand.

"Mmpf, what?" Aaron muttered, stirring. He'd been drowsing for the last hour.

They'd come back to Lewis's place after leaving the convention, and more than twenty-four hours later, they still hadn't got up. Not properly anyway. Lewis had raided the fridge a couple of times, and then there had been that long, steamy shower… But mostly, they'd spent the whole time in bed.

Aaron yawned and raised himself up on his elbows. The sheet fell away, revealing his lean, tightly muscled chest. Lewis's mouth watered.

Jesus, how could he *still* want sex? He grinned at the thought, then looked up, catching Aaron's eye, and grinned wider.

"What?" he said.

Aaron raised a brow. "I know what you're thinking." His voice, husky with promise, went straight to Lewis's cock.

"Yeah," Lewis said, leaning over to kiss him. "You're right. But before we go again, you have to watch this. It's fucking awesome."

He leaned back against the headboard and handed the iPad to Aaron, watching as Aaron absorbed the image on screen. It was Charlie again, except this time, the video wasn't a covertly filmed one. It was much slicker-looking and entitled, *"My apology"*. Lewis had already watched it, after speaking with Kushal, his lawyer.

The video showed Charlie Alexander sitting at a wooden kitchen table. He wore a plain white shirt, and his hair was tied neatly at the nape of his neck. His eyes were red-rimmed, making him look as though he'd been crying.

"Oh my God, he's put this out *already*?" Aaron squawked.

Lewis snorted a laugh and leaned over to start the video.

"Okay," Charlie began. *"So, if you've seen the leaked video of me when I was drunk, talking about the show I've been working my ass off on, then this is for you."* He closed his eyes, inhaling, then exhaling hard before continuing. *"I'm here to apologise. I want to apologise to everyone out there who I may have unintentionally hurt with my words. And I want to apologise to my many,* many *LGBTQIA+ friends, who know this is* not *who I am."* He swallowed and wiped at his eyes. *"And there's one particular person I need to make amends to."*

Aaron glanced at Lewis. "You?" he said, amazed.

Lewis chuckled, and on screen, Charlie said, *"Myself."*

For a moment, Aaron just stared at Lewis, open-mouthed. Then he burst out laughing. "No way!"

"Oh, but *yes way*," Lewis said through his own laughter. "Keep watching. It gets better."

Charlie gave a brave smile, then continued. *"The truth is, I've been struggling with alcohol for a long, long time, and that night was a wake-up call. Literally."*

"Literally?" Aaron echoed, his eyes twinkling with amusement. "Milly's rubbing off on him, I see."

"The morning after that night, when I woke up, I couldn't remember anything. Nothing. Eight hours just—gone. Which I guess makes sense, since I was, in essence, a completely different person during that time. So much so that I had literally no memory of it."

"Oh my God," Aaron said, his eyes wide. "He's actually trying to suggest that he's not responsible for saying those things, isn't he?"

"Yup."

The on-screen Charlie ploughed relentlessly on. *"All I could think, over and over, was, 'Charlie, you're an alcoholic. When you're drunk, you turn into someone else. Someone you don't even recognise, like Jekyll and Hyde. The things you say—that's not you. That's not who* Charlie Alexander *is.'"* He sighed. *"So I guess I'm going to take some time out now. To work on myself. To make amends to myself."*

"Jesus, he's a *monster*," Aaron whispered, but he was laughing too, and so was Lewis.

"What about the show you were working on?" A disembodied female voice—Milly—came from behind the camera. *"Will Telopix be parking that now?"*

"No, of course not," Charlie said, plastering the brave smile back on. *"Telopix is committed to bringing Leeches to the US—and we're not going to make any changes to the characters. If there's one thing this whole nightmare has taught me, it's… well, I need to trust people more."* He paused, bending his head to his chest, as though to collect himself. Then he looked up again and said, *"The truth is, it's not easy for me to be real with people. I'm not making excuses. I should have been more open about who I am and what I believe. I should have trusted people to understand that. And you know what? That's on me. I get that. So, I'm gonna work on trusting my gut a little more and worrying a little less about what the money guys say we need to do to please audiences."* Another sigh. *"I'm going to take the time I need to go and do that work. But in the meantime, the show must go on, so I'm going to be*

handing over my creative vision to an amazing team of people. The original writer, Lewis Hunter—who's a very dear friend of mine and has been incredibly supportive through this whole thing—is going to take the lead on the project, and everyone at Telopix is right behind him."

"What?" Aaron said. "You're his *very dear friend?*"

"I am now," Lewis said. "Apparently."

"Did he call you while I was sleeping or something?"

"Nope. But Kushal did. Apparently, Charlie's being sent on an enforced sabbatical for the next six months, and I've been assured that he won't have any further involvement in the show. Ever. I'm getting total creative control."

"That's amazing!" Aaron said, smiling. He tossed the iPad aside and straddled Lewis's thighs, setting his hands on his shoulders. "I did wonder when you were supposed to have found time to be supportive to Charlie, given that we've been shagging nonstop since yesterday afternoon."

"I'm being supportive by allowing Kushal to look over the amended contract Telopix sent over to ensure there's no possibility of Charlie ever having any involvement in the show again," Lewis replied, stroking his hands up Aaron's sides and enjoying his shiver of pleasure.

"So you're... putting the plug back in, as it were?" Aaron asked, shifting his hips.

Lewis gave a moan at the pleasurable friction on his cock and leaned forward to kiss Aaron lightly. "If the contract looks okay, I think I'll go ahead. But I'm a cynical bastard, so I'll let Kushal review everything and advise me before I make any final decisions. I'm definitely not rushing into anything while I have the upper hand."

"The upper hand?"

Lewis grinned. "Turns out Telopix are desperate to mend the reputational damage this whole incident has caused—and I won't let the opportunity to capitalise on that pass me by. Speaking of which..." He trailed off, unsure how to raise the subject that had been niggling at him since his brief talk with Kushal.

"What?" Aaron asked, leaning back on his heels.

God, he was lovely.

Lewis gave his head a little shake to dislodge his brain from the direction it was heading in and returned to the subject he'd just been thinking about. "How would you feel about working on the show again? With me?"

Aaron went very still.

"It's nothing to do with us, or *this,*" Lewis said hurriedly. "It's to do with the show. No one else has ever got what I'm reaching for, the way you do. You know the characters inside out—I see that even more clearly now that I've read some of your own writing. You'd be a huge asset to the team."

Aaron took a deep breath. Opened his mouth, closed it again. Eventually, almost reluctantly, he said, "I'm sorry, but… no."

The stab of disappointment Lewis felt at that response was painful, but he managed a nod. "Okay. Can I ask why? You love the show more than anything."

Aaron's mouth quirked up on one side. "Not *anything,*" he said. "I love you more."

Warmth spread through Lewis's chest at that declaration. "Well, you can have us both," he said lightly. "We kind of come as a package deal."

Aaron's half-smile grew. Sweetened. "I'll always love the show, and I'll always want to talk about it with you. But right now… right now I want to finish the job I'm doing on *Bow Street*. Who knows? It might even get greenlit. It's shaping up really well. I like the way the characters are developing and"—he shrugged, blushing a little—"a lot of my ideas are making it through."

"Yeah?" Lewis said, and the little thrill of pride that went through him helped to assuage his sadness over Aaron's refusal. "I can't wait to hear all about it."

"And I'll tell you," Aaron promised, shuffling closer again. "After."

Lewis grinned, "After what?"

Aaron brought his delicious body right up against Lewis's till their chests were pressed together and their lips were brushing. "I think you know," he murmured.

Lewis made a rueful face. "The truth is," he said wryly. "I don't think I actually *can* go again, not quite yet. You've exhausted me, my love."

He expected Aaron to laugh, to tease him—he wouldn't even have minded—but Aaron's eyes went soft. "Your love?"

"Yeah," Lewis whispered hoarsely, his heart aching in the best way.

Aaron sat back a little, smiling sweetly. "If I'm honest," he said, "I could murder a pizza right now." He waggled his eyebrows suggestively. "We both need to refuel."

Lewis laughed. Amused, happy, joyous.

"But can I still stay the night?" Aaron asked, "Even if I don't put out?"

"Oh, you can stay," Lewis said, kissing the corner of his mouth. "Tonight, tomorrow night, and every other night of our lives."

"Okay," Aaron murmured between kisses. "Well, let's start with tonight."

EPILOGUE

Aaron

Eighteen months later

"Uh, Aaron?" Marc said. "Don't you have that Telopix call now?"

Aaron jerked his head up. "What?" he said, then glanced at the clock on the wall and yelped—it was five to eight. The call was in five minutes—twelve o'clock LA time.

Shit.

"Damn, I forgot," he said, jumping to his feet. He saved and closed the file he'd been working on, then unhooked his laptop and stuck it under his arm.

"I'll be in early tomorrow," he promised and, when Marc nodded tiredly, added, "We're nearly there. We'll have these revisions wrapped up tomorrow."

"Then we're going out and getting drunk," Marc said, pointing at him. "You promised."

"Scout's honour," Aaron said, touching his forehead with the tips of his fingers before rushing off towards the lifts.

Since they'd got the news that *Bow Street* had been picked up, the team had expanded to twice the size and been relocated to the first floor. Filming on season one was wrapping up soon, but a last-minute change of plan on the season finale had had Aaron and Marc working flat out for the last few nights creating new pages for the final days of filming.

Even so, Aaron had other commitments that had to be met, no matter how busy he was in his main job, and this call was one of them.

Aaron held his finger on the call button, as though he could physically drag the lift to his floor with how hard he was pressing it. Finally, the painfully slow doors shuddered open, and he hopped inside, stabbing at the button for the fourth floor.

His phone buzzed in his pocket, and he pulled it out, grinning at the text notification from *My-Incredibly-Well-endowed-Lover*—the contact name that Lewis had insisted Aaron use for him.

"Where r u?? Call starting NOW! I need u!"

Aaron texted back, *"ETA 45 secs"*

The horribly slow lift finally juddered to a halt. The doors opened half an inch, stalled for several tense seconds, and then finally, reluctantly, opened the rest of the way.

Aaron jumped out as soon as there was enough space to squeeze through and jogged to Lewis's office.

The rest of the floor was empty, the lights all muted, just that one room blazing. Aaron let himself in, winking at Lewis, who had already dialled in to the call.

"It's all right," Lewis told the others, palpably relieved. "He's here now. He'll, uh..." He waved frantically at the screen. "...get the video sorted."

Amused, Aaron took the chair Lewis had already set next to his, behind the desk. "What's wrong with the—?"

"I don't know!" Lewis's hair had the spiky look it got when he'd been pulling at it. "They can't see me. The camera's on, but it's just not working."

After a quick glance at Lewis's laptop, Aaron reached out

to smooth down Lewis's hair, then slid the camera cover off the lens.

Lewis just looked at him. "You've got to be fucking kidding me."

Grinning, Aaron squeezed into view on the webcam. "Hi," he said, lifting a hand in greeting. "Sorry about that, and sorry I was running late."

Brad and Ava, from the Telopix media team, smiled back at him through the computer screen. "Hey," Ava said. "Awesome to talk to you again, Aaron. We really appreciate you guys doing this so late in the day for you."

"No problem," Aaron said, before Lewis could gripe about the time. "I was still here anyway. And it's always a pleasure to talk about *Leeches*—uh, that is, *Bloodsuckers*."

"Awesome!" she trilled. "We just wanted to touch base on a couple of details about the panel before our call with the Comic-Con people this afternoon."

Telopix were launching their version of *Leeches*—now called *Bloodsuckers*—in September, and the first episode was premiering in July at Comic-Con International in San Diego. Getting a panel at the event was a massive coup, something Aaron still wasn't sure Lewis fully appreciated. Since starting his role as Director of Fan Relations, Aaron had focused on opening up a two-way channel of communication between existing *Leeches* fans and both the RPP and Telopix teams. After more than a year of official fan events, both online and in person, the buzz around both shows had started to gather serious mainstream attention—helped by Skye and Faolán's first, and frankly scorching, on-screen kiss in *Leeches*—and when Aaron had approached Comic-Con, he'd found himself pushing at an open door.

"So," Brad said, straight white American teeth gleaming, "the awesome news is that the *Bloodsuckers* panel is already sold out!"

"Awesome," Lewis repeated drily. "I'm awestruck."

Beneath the desk, Aaron squeezed his knee, half in amusement and half in warning. "It *is* awesome," he said, raising a brow at Lewis.

It really was, and the most exciting thing for a fanboy like Aaron was that he and Lewis got to go to San Diego Comic-Con—the Mecca for pop culture fans the world over. Assuming, that was, Lewis didn't bolt in horror at the thought of appearing on a panel in front of thousands of fans...

Turning back to the screen, Aaron said, "So what did you guys want to discuss?"

And just like that, Brad and Ava snapped into work mode in that unsettling way corporate types had of switching from best friends to ruthless bastards in the blink of an eye. After about an hour of dotting i's and crossing t's, and agreeing to a list of actions as long as Aaron's arm, the meeting wound up.

Brad and Ava wished them an 'awesome day', and Aaron ended the call.

The office was suddenly very silent, still, and quiet, and they sat for a moment without speaking, absorbing the peace. Aaron was reminded of those nights back when he'd worked for Lewis and they'd stayed late to tinker with script revisions, eating pizza, and polishing lines.

Good times, those.

"What are you thinking about?" Lewis sounded fond, amused, his eyes as warm as his voice in the way they so often were these days. "You're smiling."

"Am I?" Aaron felt his smile broaden. "I was just remembering eating pizza with you in here, back in the day, going over *Leeches* scripts after everyone else had gone home for the night."

Lewis huffed out a soft breath. "I remember."

"It's, uh..." Aaron shook his head. "It's hard to believe that neither of us realised they were basically dates."

That made Lewis laugh. "Yeah, we were idiots."

"Well, one of us was..." Aaron turned in his chair, knees

bumping Lewis's. Even now, after sharing a bed every night for a year and a half, that accidental touch set a frisson of excitement fizzing in his belly. He smiled. "I spent a lot of time imagining what would happen if I just reached over and kissed you."

Lewis's eyes darkened. "Yeah?"

"Yeah. Can you imagine?"

"I can," Lewis said huskily. "I can imagine *exactly*."

"But that would have broken rule number three, of course."

Lewis's eyebrow lifted. "Rule number three?"

"No sex," Aaron said, smiling. "Remember? The first day we met, you laid down the law: confidentiality, honesty, and no sex."

"Hmm," Lewis hummed. "I guess two out of three isn't bad."

Reaching forward, he brushed his lips over Aaron's—warm, familiar, electric. For a moment—okay a couple of moments—Aaron allowed the kiss to deepen, the heat to build, the air between them to thin as they reached for each other, urgent and awkward in the cramped space. Then Aaron pulled back, laughing.

"Okay, Casanova," he said, catching his breath, "as much as a shag on the office carpet has its appeal, I think I'd rather take you home to our bed."

Lewis grinned, his hungry expression transforming unexpectedly into something warm and sweet. "I still love it when you call it home."

They'd officially started living together about a year ago, Aaron giving up his place and moving into Lewis's gorgeous mansion flat. They'd tussled over who paid what until Aaron had put his foot down and insisted on paying his fair share. So now it was home to them both, and Aaron loved it.

"Of course it's home," he said, leaning in and kissing

Lewis again. "It's where you are, and that will always be home for me."

Blinking rapidly, Lewis nodded. Then he took Aaron's hand and stood, tugging him to his feet. "Come on then," he said softly, brushing their lips together one more time. "Take me home."

The End

THANK YOU, DEAR READER

Thank you for reading this book!
We hope you enjoyed grumpy Lewis and sunshine Aaron's story.
We had an amazing time writing this angsty-rom-com together—so much so, that we're now planning #2 and #3...

We love hearing from our readers. You can find all the different ways to connect with each (or both!) of us below.

If you have time, we'd be very grateful if you'd consider leaving a review on an online review site.
Reviews are so helpful for book visibility and we appreciate every one.

Joanna & Sally

CONNECT WITH JOANNA

Email: authorjoannachambers@gmail.com

Website: www.joannachambers.com

Newsletter: visit my website to subscribe for up to date information about my books, freebies and special deals.

Connect with me: click the cute little icons below!

Joanna

facebook.com/joanna.chambers.58
twitter.com/ChambersJoanna
instagram.com/joannachambers_auth
bookbub.com/profile/joanna-chambers

CONNECT WITH SALLY

Email: sally@stargatenovels.com

Website: www.sallymalcolm.com

Newsletter: visit my website for news, book recs, and giveaways. All new subscribers get a free copy of *Rebel: An Outlawed Story..*

Connect with me: click the cute little icons below!

Sally

facebook.com/ /sally.malcolm.3
twitter.com/Sally_Malcom
instagram.com/sally.malcolm
bookbub.com/authors/sally-malcolm

ALSO BY SALLY MALCOLM

CONTEMPORARY ROMANCE

Perfect Day

Between the Lines

Love Around the Corner

Twice Shy

HISTORICAL ROMANCE

* *Rebel: An Outlawed story*

King's Man

The Last Kiss

* free for newsletter subscribers

Read on for an excerpt of ***Perfect Day***

PERFECT DAY (EXCERPT)

Perfect Day

"The sort of book you finish with a heartfelt sigh of satisfaction and a dreamy smile" — All About Romance

When Joshua Newton, son of Long Island's elite, fell in love with ambitious young actor Finn Callaghan, his world finally made sense. With every stolen moment, soft touch, and breathless kiss, they fell deeper in love.

Finn was his future, until Joshua made the worst mistake of his life…

Eight years later, Finn has returned to the seaside town where it all began. He's on the brink of stardom, a far cry from the poor mechanic who spent one gorgeous summer falling in love on the beach.

And the last thing he wants is a second chance with the man who broke his heart eight years ago. Finn has spent a long time forgetting Joshua Newton—he certainly doesn't plan to forgive him.

Drawn together by circumstance, yet kept apart by their history, old feelings soon begin to stir. Back in the place where their romance began, Joshua and Finn finally come to realize the truth: love lasts.

Even when you don't want it to, even when you try to deny it, love lasts...

~

READ ON FOR AN EXCERPT OF PERFECT DAY…

~

The next morning Joshua got up early, as usual, and headed down to the coffee shop. He flung open all the doors and windows to air out the lingering damp and set the tables down onto the almost-dry floor.

Lexa and Ali showed up later, hungover and brimful of talk about Finn Callaghan.

"Oh my God, Newt, he's so *beautiful,*" Ali sighed as she half-heartedly wiped down the counter.

"And funny," Lexa added, almost grudgingly. "I mean, mostly you think actors are pretty dumb in real life, right? But he's actually really sharp."

"And he can sing."

"Hell, yeah," Lexa said, although her brow twitched into a frown. "Kylee got her claws into him real fast."

Ali huffed in agreement and Joshua said, "Kylee Adams?" She owned the Rock House and probably had a good decade on Finn.

"Who else?" Lexa grumbled. "She was all over him like a rash."

Glancing between them, Joshua sensed the ebb and flow of jealousy and tried not to add his own to the mix. He may have had no one significant in his life since Finn, but he knew full well that Finn had earned a reputation with women. It didn't come as a surprise that he'd spent the evening flirting.

Besides, Joshua had had years to get used to the idea of Finn dating women. Not long after he'd landed his role as a vampire hunter in *High Stakes,* Joshua had stumbled across a picture of him online: Finn with a blonde and beautiful girl on his arm, looking every inch the poster boy for the all-American guy.

He had no right to be upset. He'd been the one to end things between them. Finn owed him nothing. Still. Kylee Adams...?

"Anyway," Lexa said, straightening up from the table. "The barbecue is definitely on and Sean said to invite you, too, Newt."

He blinked at her. "Really?"

"Yeah, he said—Oh my God!" Her hand flew to her mouth, and then she ran it hurriedly through her hair. "It's them," she hissed to Ali. "They're coming in!"

Joshua had all of three seconds to brace himself before the door opened and Sean strode in, all long limbs and easy strides, and behind him—

God, but it was *nothing* like looking at pictures online. Joshua wasn't even slightly prepared.

Finn filled the room, sucked all the air from Joshua's lungs. Maybe he took a step back, or maybe he froze in place, he didn't know. And he didn't know where Finn was looking, whether he even saw him, because Joshua's eyes were fixed on the floor, his head pounding with a thousand thoughts that all echoed to the same rhythm: *it's him, he's here, it's Finn.*

It's Finn.

"Hey," Sean said from a million miles away. "You got a couple coffees for two hungover dudes?"

Lexa and Ali rushed to serve them, darting behind the counter and leaving Joshua adrift in the middle of the coffee shop. He couldn't move, didn't know what to do, just stood there clutching the rag he'd been using to wipe down the tables. All he could think about was the last time they'd been in the same room together, that terrible last day at his house when Finn had stormed and raged with tears spilling down his face.

This is bullshit, Josh! None of it matters. Just—please, okay? Don't do this. I'm begging you, man.

Don't. Please...

"Hey, Joshua," Sean said, relentlessly friendly. "Sorry you couldn't make it last night." He glanced around the coffee shop. "How's the dishwasher?"

Joshua made himself look at Sean and not the man standing rigidly behind him, although he could feel Finn's tension pulsing towards him. "It's fine," he managed to say. "All cleaned up."

"Oh, hey," Sean said, like he'd forgotten. "This is my brother, Finn." He turned and gestured. "Finn, Joshua Newton. Joshua, Finn Callaghan."

A number of things happened all at once: Finn's eyes touched his for half a heartbeat, Joshua jerked his head in something like a nod, his mouth sandpaper dry, and Finn said, "Sean, I'll see you in the car."

And then he left, disappeared out the door, leaving Sean looking awkward. "Ah," he said, scratching a cheek. "Sorry about that, he's not normally such a jerk. But I guess he's hungover *and* jet-lagged..."

Joshua tried to smile, afraid it looked more like a rictus, and edged his way behind the counter. His legs felt weak. He needed to sit down.

Meanwhile, Lexa and Ali were taking customer service to the next level and heading out after Finn, carrying both coffees to the car. Sean seemed resigned, rather than surprised, and didn't stop them. But as he followed he glanced over his shoulder at Joshua. "Hope we'll see you on Saturday? Barbecue at the house—if that's okay with you?"

He muttered, "Of course," and Sean smiled and then the door closed and Joshua sank boneless against the counter.

It was over. He'd done it. He'd seen Finn again, heard him speak, looked him in the eye. And that had to be the worst of it, right?

Only maybe not, because one thing had been crystal clear: Finn Callaghan hadn't forgotten and he most certainly hadn't forgiven.

~

ALSO BY JOANNA CHAMBERS

Enlightenment series

Provoked

Beguiled

Enlightened

Seasons Pass *

The Bequest *

Unnatural

Restored

* exclusive bonus stories for newsletter subscribers

Winterbourne series

Introducing Mr Winterbourne

Mr Winterbourne's Christmas

The First Snow of Winter

The Labours of Lord Perry Cavendish

Capital Wolves duet

Gentleman Wolf

Master Wolf

With Annika Martin

Enemies Like You

Porthkennack series (Riptide)

A Gathering Storm

Tribute Act

Other novels

The Dream Alchemist

Unforgivable

Novellas

Merry & Bright (festive anthology)

Humbug

Rest and Be Thankful

Read on for more information about how you can start the ***Winterbourne series*** for **free** today

THE WINTERBOURNE SERIES

Introducing Mr. Winterbourne (#1)

~ Start this series for free when you subscribe to my newsletter ~ sign up from the homepage of my website www.joannachambers.com ~

Lysander Winterbourne appears to lead a charmed life. Handsome, amiable, and a renowned sportsman, he is the darling of London society. As far as Adam Freeman is concerned though, Lysander is just another spoiled aristocrat.

A wealthy mill owner, Adam has no time for the frivolous world of the ton, but when his younger brother becomes engaged to Althea Winterbourne, he reluctantly agrees to be introduced to society–with the Winterbourne clan's golden boy as his guide.

Resigning himself to a few days of boredom, Adam is surprised to learn that there is much more to Lysander than his perfect surface. But will Adam have the courage to introduce Lysander Winterbourne to his own secret self?

~

Mr. Winterbourne's Christmas (#2)

Lysander Winterbourne and Adam Freeman have been living happily at Edgeley Park for the last eighteen months. By day Lysander is Adam's estate manager, by night, his lover, but neither man has spoken of their deeper feelings. Is this a happy-ever-after or just a convenient arrangement?

When the two men are invited to Winterbourne Abbey for a family Christmas, matters quickly come to a head. Snowed in at the Abbey with a house full of guests, they have to face up to shocking revelations, long-held secrets and a choice Lysander never expected to have to make…

~

The First Snow of Winter (#3)

~ A Winterbourne prequel story ~

1814: Captain Sam Alderton returns to England from the continent with his life in tatters. Maimed and directionless, the last thing he wants to do is spend Christmas with his family and their close friends, the Huxleys—especially Jasper Huxley, who he almost kissed five years before.

Sam plans to avoid the festivities, but when the first snow of winter arrives, and he and Jasper are trapped alone together at Alderton Hall, they find themselves revisiting old traditions and painful memories together—and discovering that things may not have been quite as either of them thought five years earlier.

~

The Labours of Lord Perry Cavendish (#4)

Lord Perry Cavendish knows that he's seen as a not-too-bright, amiable, sporting sort of chap. The type who can hold his own in the boxing ring, drink most men under the table, and offer a useful opinion on a piece of horseflesh—but not much else.

When Perry visits his friend, Lysander Winterbourne, he is introduced to the Honourable Jonny Mainwaring, a free-thinking artist who is everything Perry is not: unconventional, emotional… and very talkative.

At first, Perry is overwhelmed by the vibrant, witty Jonny Mainwairing, but when he agrees to sit for him, he discovers the real man beneath the dramatic flourishes, and the undeniable physical attraction he feels for Jonny begins to develop into something more.

But Jonny is not to be easily won over. While he has a long-standing weakness for brawny men like Perry, he's still smarting from his latest heartbreak and determined to change his habit of throwing himself into each new affair without pausing to recover from the last.

Can Perry convince Jonny that he is more than just an empty-headed young buck, and that they could have a real future together?

CPSIA information can be obtained
at www.ICGtesting.com
Printed in the USA
FSHW022238281121
86533FS